"Budz writes poetically, with grand descriptive power. His characters are worriedly and necessarily in one kind or another of trouble. You'll itch and fret for them, moms and brothers and lost kids and all. The very advanced tech surround, though, immerses the reader, and I want another dose." —*San Diego Union-Tribune*

"*Clade* is a very accomplished first novel—indeed, it's a very accomplished novei full stop. Budz's characters are well drawn, the California setting is vivid, and, without preaching, he makes some strong points about the fragility of our environment.... A striking debut."
—*Sci Fi Weekly* (A- pick)

"Budz has imagined a world with sufficient texture and resonance to make it not only a rewarding place to explore, but one worth thinking about, and one worth revisiting." —*Locus*

"A fast-paced read animated by an engrossing, nervous energy." —*Booklist*

"Smart, well written, and highly imaginative, *Clade* does for cutting-edge biology what *Neuromancer* did for a cyberfuture. Budz may well have created a new genre: biopunk." —Kevin J. Anderson, *New York Times* bestselling coauthor of *Dune: House Atreides*

"A remarkable book. Scientific, tense, gritty and thoughtful, *Clade* pulls you into a bioengineered tomorrow that may come startlingly true." —David Brin, bestselling author of the Uplift series

ALSO BY MARK BUDZ

Clade

Crache

I D O L O N

MARK BUDZ

BANTAM SPECTRA

IDOLON
A Bantam Spectra Book / August 2006

Published by Bantam Dell
A Division of Random House, Inc.
New York, New York

This is a work of fiction. Names, characters, places, and incidents either are the product of the author's imagination or are used fictitiously. Any resemblance to actual persons, living or dead, events, or locales is entirely coincidental.

Bantam Books, the rooster colophon, Spectra, and the portrayal of a boxed "s" are trademarks of Random House, Inc.

ISBN-13: 978-0-553-58850-7
ISBN-10: 0-553-58850-8

Printed in the United States of America
Published simultaneously in Canada

www.bantamdell.com

OPM 10 9 8 7 6 5 4 3 2 1

FOR MARINA

The human body is the best picture of the human soul.
—LUDWIG WITTGENSTEIN
PHILOSOPHICAL INVESTIGATIONS: IV (178E)

We have become so accustomed to our illusions that
we mistake them for reality.
—DANIEL J. BOORSTIN
THE IMAGE: A GUIDE TO PSEUDO-EVENTS IN AMERICA

IDOLON

1

White-hot fog. It boiled over the halogen-lighted streets—scalding to look at but cool against the skin.

Kasuo van Dijk pulled his overcoat tighter against the dank mist, shut the door to his unmarked car, and stepped onto gritty concrete.

This part of North Beach was philmed in classic noir. Most of the storefronts and apartment building façades were a mélange of grays and blacks lifted from *The Maltese Falcon, Raw Deal,* and half a dozen other celluloids from the 1930s and '40s. In places, some of the architectural and decorative elements had been colorized. Vivid greens, reds, and blues bled from the shadows, saturating the landscape with flamboyant contusions of color borrowed from Romare Bearden and Warhol.

Nothing was ever what it seemed, he reminded himself. Nor was it otherwise.

A few blocks east of Hyde, toward Telegraph Hill, the décor changed abruptly to the delirious exuberance of Gaudi and Hundertwasser. Organic transmogrifications not unlike the Peter Max–, Bob Masse–, and Roger Dean–fueled psychedelia of Haight-Ashbury. To the southwest, van Dijk could just make out the staid browns and clean, if somewhat stark, Edward Hopper lines of Pacific Heights.

Van Dijk took a moment to philm himself in a composite image of Toshirô Mifune, from Kurosawa's *Yojimbo,* and Hiroyuki Sanada from Yôji Yamada's *The Twilight Samurai.* The pseudoself—humble demeanor hiding implacable, barely restrained violence—was what people not only expected from him, given his first name, but respected. It was part of the job, like wearing a tie and an HK 9mm minicentrifuge.

He started toward the small brick-and-corrugated-sheet-plastic warehouse that had been converted into low-income apartments. A uniformed officer stood guard outside the first-floor entrance, the tip of a cigarette flaring from time to time like the beacon in a lighthouse.

The uniform's name appeared in front of him: Kohl, Peter. Van Dijk cleared the eyefeed with a quick mental *Delete* and turned his gaze on the street cop.

"Detective." Kohl pulled himself out of his slouch.

"Who else is here?" van Dijk asked.

"My partner. Janakowski. He's inside, waiting for you and the crime-scene boyz to show." Kohl took a final calming pull on his Hongtasan, then flicked it nervously away. The butt hissed as it arced to the ground, sputtering out before it struck the damp concrete. Oily steam snaked up from a half-empty cup of black coffee at his feet.

"Who found the body?"

"One of the residents." Kohl blinked as he accessed an online police log. "Girl named Lisette," he said, reading from the plog. "Age eleven. Lives in the apartment just down the hall, supposedly with her mother. But Mom ain't around. Hasn't been for a while, by the look of it."

The victim's apartment was on the second floor. Van Dijk checked the elevator for obvious evidence. It was out of order. That left the stairs. Stairwells tended to collect all kinds of DNA-marinated detritus. Cigarette butts, half-empty plastic bottles, crushed cups, pinched bubble caps, shattered eye droppers, and dermadots for those who couldn't afford or didn't want direct deposit via mechemical assembly. As he mounted the concrete steps, a number of crumpled candy wrappers chirped to life, regaling him with cheerful play lists and animated nanoFX.

In the hall, van Dijk made his way past Teflon-white doors set in gray cinder block. Janakowski waited on the left, at the far end. As van Dijk passed the next-to-the-last door on the right, it opened a fraction, revealing a pair of luminous blue eyes. The eyes met his for a beat, then retreated. The door snicked shut.

Lisette.

Van Dijk moved past the door, dropping the thin smile from his face. He greeted Janakowski with a curt nod.

"You need me for anything, Detective?" The officer stepped away from the sealed door and hitched up his belt, anxious to get going.

Van Dijk tipped his head back down the hall. "That the girl?"

"Yeah." The officer nodded, his jowls ruddy under the strident LED ceiling lights. Someone had taped red paper, printed with white flowers, to the panels. The black desiccated shadows of dead bugs speckled the underside of the paper and the dim lantern glow.

"Keep the kid company till I'm finished in here."

"I gotta take a leak."

"In that case, you better get Kohl to relieve you."

"Very funny, Detective." The officer ambled down the hall, his brow furrowed in concentration as he messaged his partner.

Van Dijk logged into SFPD central data, allocated a new library for the case, then pushed open the door to the victim's apartment.

———

The body was philmed in vintage Hollywood. It had that silver-screen patina, glam even in death. Angelic hair, sassy red lips, gold-sequined gown, a cheap diamond necklace and earrings. Except for the costume jewelry, it was all high-end ware, all programmable.

Van Dijk mentally queried the SFPD datician assigned to him. *Image ID?*

"The philm appears to be a composite of Barbara Stanwyck and Gene Tierney," the sageware said after a moment.

The woman lay on a tempergel futon against one wall. Glossy satin sheets covered the mattress. A fluffy down comforter, white as snow, spilled off the end of the bed like a glacier.

Record, van Dijk thought, activating the nanocams embedded in his retinas. *Visual. Audio. Ambients. Auto upload. Save.*

There was a brief delay as the microvilli array of nanoelectrodes in his skull picked up the neural firing pattern for each command and relayed it to a brain-computer interface interpreter, which in turn routed it to a datician for implementation.

He panned the room slowly. Intermittent temperature, humidity, and time readings blinked along the bottom of his field of view. Other than the futon, there wasn't much. A table and chair. A graphene d-splay screen, tuned to some ambient meditation channel soft-focused on lotus leaves. A collapsible plastic shelf, bare except for several pairs of shoes, loose jeans, large hats, and a cheap canvas jacket big enough to lose herself in.

Lose herself from who? van Dijk wondered. All that nice philmware. Why would she want to hide it, even if it was ripped?

Through the window opposite the futon he had a clear view of Telegraph Hill, all blue-striped trees and green-scaled buildings.

Where she was headed—or what she was running from? Either possibility seemed likely.

Nothing in the bathroom. The usual assortment of toiletries, hair- and toothbrushes, patchouli-scented soap. No makeup, but then she wouldn't need it with the philm she was waring. Nothing in the tiny kitchenette, either. There was no stove, only a hot plate on the countertop. The refrigerator was small, barely large enough for the six-pack of bottled water and jar of Cajun simmer sauce. It wasn't the kitchen of a chef. Which meant she'd eaten out a lot, probably at the fast-food franchises along the Marina and the Embarcadero.

Van Dijk turned his attention to the body. It looked as if the woman had been dead for several hours. Exactly how long was hard to tell at this point. Her skin was cool, but electronic skin skewed

all of the normal postmortem signs of death, everything from body temp to lividity and rigor. E-skin
typically slowed the rate at which a body cooled, but
not always. He wasn't even sure of her age at this
point. 'Skin had a way of overwriting not just the
physical but the perceived. The mind filled in blanks
it shouldn't, the way it did a missing word, supply-
ing implicit meaning rather than explicit.

"ID," he said out loud, scanning the victim's
DiNA code. There was a brief pause as the datician
searched for the information.

"Unknown," it replied over his earfeed. "Not On
File."

NOF meant one of two things: either the bar-
code-encrypted concatenation of her DNA had been
tweaked, or she was an unchipped and undocumented immigrant.

The cause of death wasn't immediately obvious.
There were no external injuries—strangle marks,
suspicious discolorations, blunt trauma contusions,
knife or bullet wounds. No blood or other fluids.

That left the less obvious. Drug overdose, or viral
or bacterial infection from dirty e-skin were the
most common. Internal injuries were possible, as
were natural causes, but not likely under the circum-
stances.

Which were...? Van Dijk had no idea.

Footsteps echoed in the hallway. Van Dijk stood.
End, he thought, terminating the superimposed
readout just as the crime scene unit, led by Leslie
Apodaca, appeared in the doorway.

"All yours," he said.

"What have you got?" Apodaca said. She was a
petite woman, short in both height and temper.

Even her hair, as close-cropped as that of a soldier or Buddhist monk, sent a clear don't-mess-with-me.

"What you see." Van Dijk nodded at the body. "I just got here a few minutes ago."

"Who is she?"

"NOF."

"Figures." Apodaca messaged her team to scan for finger- and blood-prints, residual heat. They sprayed every bare millimeter of the room with chemical tweezers in the hunt for soft DNA, fibers, hazmat, and biomat.

Van Dijk headed for the door. "Don't forget to copy me on the report."

"You're not gonna stick around?" Apodaca didn't bother to look up from the body.

"I'm saving myself for the autopsy."

The door to the kid's apartment stood open a crack. As he stepped inside, a toilet flushed. The small studio apartment was sparsely furnished— none of the furniture matched, he noted—and empty. The door to the bathroom opened and Janakowski came out, zipping up. "I was gonna bust a pipe," he said.

"Where's the girl?" van Dijk said. "Kohl looking after her?"

Janakowski shot a panicked glance in the direction of the kitchen, where a Vurtronic d-splay pasted to one of the cupboards flickered with Chinamation ghosts. "She was right there."

2

The Transcendental Vibrationists were downloading a new philm. Or getting ready to, Pelayo Tiutoj thought.

Instead of the familiar collection of rose-stem bones and clockwork joints the TVs had been screening for months, there was nothing but static.

Background radiation from the universe.

A small group of worshippers had gathered in the War Memorial park across the street from Iosepa Biognost Tek's downtown Santa Cruz office. Pelayo counted five in the gathering. The TVs huddled in a tight cluster at the foot of a squat palm, rocking in unison and chanting benignly to themselves. Their loose, resham-style robes had coin-sized pieces of glass sewn onto the fabric, which spat thorny flashes of light at him.

The other loiterers in the park were doing their best to avoid or ignore the meditation session. They sipped cappuccinos. Window-shopped the d-splays pasted to the bricks of the central clock tower. Watched the graphene leaves on the War Memorial tree flicker with the faces of the dead.

One of the TVs looked up, caught Pelayo's gaze, and held it with vacant black eyes. A whiff of lilac skincense drifted in the air, sticky with perspiration. The man's lips moved.

"What?" Pelayo asked before he could catch himself.

The man's lips moved again, a barely audible hiss of burn-in-hell vitriol. "Slavation is near."

Pelayo flipped off the TV. Knee-jerk response. Most TVs didn't hemorrhage goodwill. They couldn't give a rat's ass what people thought of them. They knew, deep down in their sanctimonious hearts, that they were ascending to the Omega point while everyone else rotted in this pisshole of a life.

A sly Mona Lisa sfumato darkened the corners of the TV's mouth before he bent his head in prayer.

Santa Cruz. The town had always been schizophrenic. Place couldn't decide if it was a retirement community or a Mecca for hippie nostalgia and political radicals. Social activism on one hand and conservative fundamentalists on the other. Self-styled liberals came to steep in the tireless counterculture aura and convince themselves they really were open-minded. Others came to be part of *The Endless Summer* surf scene, to connect with the vampires in *The Lost Boys,* or walk in the footsteps of the Tick Talk Man in *Cryptaphica.*

Pelayo shifted his attention to the off the shelf philms the street crowd was waring. He liked to stay current. Fashion changed quickly. There was no predicting a smart mob. No forecasting when a spontaneous commercial consensuality would precipitate out of the cinesphere.

Nagel was popular, with his noir, razor-edged beauty. So was Beardsley—erotic, sensual. Still in

demand after a month, along with the usual Jung at
Heart variations, Giger cyborganics, and Picasso-
inspired cubism that always seemed to be in vogue.
There were even a few F8 cameos. The band had recently uploaded a new cast. The song, titled "As F8
Would Have It," had spiked at number one at least
once a day for ten consecutive days. A megahit. So
now all of the pop cult philmheads and vidIOs
wanted to look like they'd just stepped out of the
cast and onto the sidewalk.

The majority of the e-skin out there was grainy,
relatively low-res. Most philmheads could only
afford secondhand, street cheap, or black-market
celluloid. Thin membranes of programmable
graphene—fabricated out of nanoscopic semicon-
ductor threads—that were capable of displaying not
only graphics but texture. As a result, Pelayo saw
a lot of monochromatics cruising the streets—
stripped down black-and-white pseudoselves that
people hoped to colorize later.

Pelayo was lucky; his 'skin was fully chromatic.
One of the perks he received as a test subject for
Iosepa Biognost Tek. IBT provided him with the latest experimental ware. The only downside was, he
never knew what he was going to look like until it
was too late. Last time around, he'd ended up with
Aubrey Beardsley breasts, Jackson Pollock hair, and
Tiffany-esque stained-glass lips. Mix-and-match shit
he wouldn't normally be caught dead in.

This time, he hoped, would be different.

He returned his attention to the TVs. They liked
to think they were different. But they were just the
same as everyone else, philming themselves to
change the way they looked and who they were on

the outside. Do it long enough, and in theory that was who they would become. Hyperreal and ultimately hyperstantial. That was the plan—the hope.

He logged into the public datician and checked the time: 9:46. Fourteen minutes until his appointment. He'd gotten the message yesterday. Short notice, and a couple of weeks sooner than expected. Usually, he went twelve weeks between reconfigures. This time it had only been ten. Something had come up.

Which meant there might be bonus pay, if the philm required more than the normal amount of debugging.

He hurried through the morning crowd, jostled by Rhett Butler and a three-hundred-pound Dorothy with bulging red slippers. Last thing he wanted to do was arrive late, piss Uri off. Motherfucker could crimp wire with his asshole.

Crossing the street, he passed a kiosk newscreen that was airing an advertisement for Atherton Resort Hotels. It showcased a massive building that had been philmed as a Tibetan monestary. The hotel had been built into a mountainside. It had featureless stone walls with tiny windows, and looked more like a fortress than a resort.

"The perfect retreat," a voice crooned over his earfeed. "There is no other place like it in the world."

There were Atherton resorts all around the world, rephilming reality for those willing to pay. In Third-World countries they took on the ambiance of theme parks, philmed in old Hollywood movies that sensationalized or glamorized these places. In Africa, it was *Casablanca*. In Baghdad, it was *Lawrence of*

Arabia. Mexico looked like *The Night of the Iguana* or any number of other films with quaint stucco villages, contented donkeys, and cheerful mariachis clamoring about love.

"Leave the world behind," the voice-over said. A walled garden blossomed on the screen. "Cast yourself in the world of an Atherton resort today."

That's what Atherton sold: e-scape. People were desperate for something, anything, to change their lives. Pelayo could feel that same urge tugging at him. Deep, umbilical, the need to find a way out, to change either himself or the world. Grasping at whatever shadows he could to make that happen.

Pelayo turned from the kiosk and found himself face-to-face with a disembodied ad mask.

Local businesses used the helium-buoyed masks to target potential customers, based on their DiNA code and philm download history. This one resembled a Japanese theater mask from the Noh Show, a costume shop near the Boardwalk. According to the adcast, the mask represented Sisiguti, a frowning gold-faced demon with a red tongue and bloodshot eyes.

"Morning," the mask said. Instead of launching into a sales flash or catalog listing, it switched from external audio to his earfeed. "I was hoping I'd catch you."

"Atossa?" Pelayo stopped. "I thought you weren't scheduled to go online until this afternoon." He could never keep her schedule straight.

"I was supposed to. But Vij isn't feeling well. She threw up or something. So I'm filling in for her."

"I'd swing by," he said—she worked five blocks

away, at Model Behavior, remote opping the ad agency's masks—"but I'm running late."

"That's okay, I just wanted to say hi." The mask tilted sideways and smiled. "See you later?"

He cut a quick glance past her to the main entrance to the IBT building. "What time you off?" he said.

"Four."

He nodded. "I should be done by then."

"How about I come by your place after?" Atossa said. "Bring some Asian Rose or Beau Thai?"

"You don't have class tonight?" She was taking an adult ed in philmography, and usually knee-deep in homework.

"We're doing independent study projects. I'd like to tell you what I have in mind. See what you think."

"Sounds good."

The mask drifted forward, pecked him on the lips, then drifted aside, allowing him to pass.

"Love you," she said.

"You, too."

Three meters from the main entrance, the Che Guevara philm he'd downloaded at the end of his last clinical trial faded as a datician in the building registered his DiNA cast and placed his current test 'skin into sleep mode in preparation for a new skinjob.

The IBT building had rethemed since his last visit. It was now Victorian, with redbrick masonry walls, arched windows, and a barrel vault of glassine panes suspended in a Gothic wrought-iron frame.

Like an Atherton resort hotel, IBT was one of those places that existed mainly as an idea. There was a building, but it could be any building, real or unreal, from any place, any time.

On either side of him, lofty palm trees in marble planters formed a leafy colonnade that shaded the center atrium from the industrial-strength glare pouring in through the tall factory windows.

"You're late," Uri said over his earfeed. The words, pinched thin with annoyance, stripped the kiss from his lips.

3

The customer, a tall woman in her late teens or early twenties, stepped tentatively into the Get Reel cinematique. The glass door—etched with sleek Egyptian Deco—swung shut behind her with a stiletto-sharp click.

The woman looked not only scared but desperate. She wore inexpensive disposable 'skin, the kind of business ware that companies issued to low-wage employees to project a uniform corporate image. It was already starting to cloud up as it biodegraded. She didn't have any appliqués that Marta could see. No obvious nanomation, pierces, logos, or tats—just cheap diamond earrings and a shapeless Third-World dress woven from coarse yellow cotton.

Poor. New to town. Probably a refugee. Probably illegal.

The woman blinked toffee-brown eyes, then ran one hand over close-cropped hair the texture of coffee grounds. Her gaze darted around the narrow store, taking in the floor-to-ceiling collages of old celluloid movie and vidIO snippets, the plastic display cases filled with 'skin grafts, the shelves of lip collagen and spray dispensers of bacterial makeup, the dolls outfitted with a variety of prosthetic nipples, lips, and labia.

Marta glanced at the Japanese partition that screened the back room of the shop, making sure her boss was still occupied, and hurried from behind the display counter. "Can I help you?"

The woman started at the sound of Marta's voice. "I don't know."

Marta couldn't place her accent. West Africa, maybe. Mali. "Is there anything in particular you're interested in?"

The woman's gaze returned to Marta, grazed her like a rock skipping across water, then skittered away, alighting on a rack of skincense phials. "I was told..." Her voice snagged. "I need your help."

"Hold still, for fuck sake!" Jhon's voice bellowed from the edit room in the back of the store.

The woman froze. Her pupils dilated, brimming with adrenaline-fueled fear.

"You keeping moving," Jhon went on, "and I'm not responsible if the graft doesn't take. Understand?"

"The owner," Marta explained, hoping to quell the woman's anxiety. "He's editing the philm on a customer. We have a few minutes."

The woman bit her lower lip. She looked unconvinced, ready to flee. An argument erupted on the sidewalk just outside the store, a thunderclap of shouts that made the young woman hesitate.

Marta touched her lightly on the wrist. "What exactly are you looking for?" she asked.

A place to stay for a couple of days. A warm meal. That was what Marta typically saw in the store.

The woman hollowed her cheeks. "I was told to come here."

"By who?"

The woman glanced at the partition. "Sister Giselle."

Sister Giselle ran a number of local homeless shelters. Marta was one of the people the nun referred at-risk illegals to for "counseling."

"All right." Marta let out a breath. More than just a place to lie low for a few days. "I'll see what I can do."

Some of the panic receded from the woman's eyes. She swallowed, forced a smile as thin as a pressed flower.

Marta felt an echo of the smile play across her own lips. She led the woman to a changing booth and sat her down on a stool. "I need to get some information from you. It's important you tell me the truth. Understand?"

A nod. "You want to know how long I've been here and where I'm coming from."

"Yes," Marta said. "For starters."

The woman was from Nigeria. Nadice. She had arrived two days ago as part of an internal workforce reorganization by Atherton Resort Hotels. Atherton owned and operated a worldwide network of philm resorts for vacationers and business travelers who wanted a safe place to stay. Nadice had worked for Atherton Lagos as a maid. Upon her arrival in Atherton San Jose, she'd run.

"I don't want to have an abortion," the woman explained.

"You're pregnant?"

The woman nodded. "I found out just before the transfer."

"Is that part of your contract with Atherton? No children?"

"Yes."

So the child was an accident, Marta thought, or an excuse. A convenient way out.

"I want my baby to have a chance," the woman went on. "I want her to be free. I don't want her to get caught in the same situation I did."

Assuming the child made it to term. In all likelihood a security marker authorizing her xfer to the Bay Area had been spliced into the wetronics of her corporate 'skin. Normally security markers expired on a specific date, or after a set amount of time. But they could also be keyed to the life of the 'skin or the duration of employment. When the degradation reached a certain point, nonlethal neurotoxins would be released into her system.

"Have you been to a doctor?" Marta asked.

The woman ducked her head and touched a hand to her abdomen. "I'll go as soon as I can."

"What about diseases?" Marta asked. "Are you sick? Carrying anything?"

The woman looked up, indignant. "No. Nothing I know of."

"Good. If you're right, that will make things easier." Marta gave her an unmarked squeeze ampoule.

The woman took the white plastic capsid and turned it over in her hand, careful not to touch the nozzle. "What's this?"

"Something to counteract the release of toxins from your 'skin. You need to dose yourself once a day. There are seven doses. That means you have a week to find someone who can reconfigure whatever you're waring."

The woman frowned. "I thought that's what you...the reason Sister Giselle sent me here."

"No, I'm not set up for that. You need to make other arrangements." The support network for refugees and illegal aliens was ad hoc. Marta had a contact who supplied her. She didn't know who supplied him and didn't want to.

"I want to get rid of the 'skin completely," the woman stated. "No more philm. No more images. I just want to be me."

Marta pressed her lips into a thin line. The woman wasn't just looking for a place to stay. She was looking for a new life. "That will be harder. More expensive. Do you have a job lined up? Experience?"

The woman shook her head. "Just cleaning. That's all I've ever done." The woman lowered her gaze. Embarrassed, apologetic, she brushed raw fingertips across the Atherton watermark staining her right cheek. Marta hadn't noticed the stylized A before, with its central cross, ghosting her 'skin. Otherwise, she didn't appear to be a member of any particular philm cast.

"Not a problem," Marta said. "You should be able to find something as a waitress, or in retail."

"Like you."

For some reason people always assumed that if she was helping refugees she must be one herself. They assumed she had suffered, too. How else could she understand their plight? Why else would she want to help, if she wasn't one of them?

"What about family or friends?" Marta said. "Is there anyone in the area who can help?"

"No. I'm alone."

"Where's the father?"

The woman jerked one shoulder in sharp dismissal. "There isn't—he's not here."

But not gone, either. The real reason she was running, Marta decided. "You still at the shelter?"

The woman nodded and white-knuckled the ampoule, resolute. "Who do I see to get rid of the 'skin? Do you know anyone?"

"Maybe," Marta allowed. Why? Why was she going out of her way to help this woman? "I'll make some inquires. It might take a couple of days. Don't come here. I'll find you."

"Thanks."

"Don't." The gratitude chafed. Marta didn't want the responsibility that came with it. "I'm not doing you any favors."

The woman blinked but held her gaze.

"My advice," Marta said. "Go to domestic security, apply for asylum. There's still time. You're in no condition to do this. Not now. It would be different if it was only your life you were risking."

The woman scraped her lip with her teeth. It wasn't what she wanted to hear. All the more reason it needed to be said.

"Why are you doing this?" Her fingers tightened around the dispenser.

"Because you need to know what you're getting into."

"What I mean is, why are you helping me if you think it's such a bad idea?"

The question always came up. It wasn't only curiosity. They wanted reassurance, an explanation ... a reason to trust her. "Because someone helped me once." What she told everyone, even herself from time to time.

"So you were like me. Once."

"No." Marta had never been like her. "We're different," she said. "For one thing, I wasn't responsible for another life."

The woman moistened her dry, chapped lips. "But you know what it's like to want to get away. To start over."

"I know you can't run forever. I know you can't ever get away. Not the way you want or think. Soon as you put one thing behind you, another takes its place."

The woman started at the scrape of chair legs in the back room.

"That's what I'm talking about," Marta said. "Always looking over your shoulder. That never ends. The fear is always there."

The woman took a breath, hardening her resolve. "Would you have done anything different, if you'd been pregnant?"

Marta hesitated. Too long. All the answer either of them needed.

"Image will take a couple hours to set," Jhon said, his voice louder, closer. In the main shop now. "Don't scratch it. You do, it could smear."

"You got any anti-itch stuff?" the kid asked. He couldn't be more than eleven or twelve.

"All out." Jhon paused. "Sorry."

"Bullshit."

Hard to tell if the kid was referring to the apology or store inventory. Marta turned to the woman. "You better go now." She nudged the curtain aside to look out.

Jhon stood next to the partition with the kid, who was fumbling through the bins of skin cream on the back wall. Their backs were turned.

"Now," Marta said. She stood and made her way out of the booth, accompanying the woman to the front door.

The aroma of grilled tempeh and steamed rice drifted in from the Wok This Way two doors down.

"Be careful," Marta said. "You aren't..."

"I'll be fine," the woman said. "What you already said—I'm not like you."

A moment later she was gone, carried away by the roiling current of Pacific Avenue, philmed in the luminous watercolor foliage and quaint seaside architecture that recalled saltwater taffy, merry-go-rounds, red-striped towels, and beach umbrellas.

Marta turned back to the store.

"Fuck outta my way," the kid said, giving her a shove.

As he scooted past, she caught a glimpse of the images that Jhon had snipped from dusty electrons. The kid had cast himself as a member of the Lost Boys. Bloodless white 'skin, red lips, bat-black jackets with upturned collars. The Lost Boys weren't an exclusive philm cast. All it took to become a member was image grafts from the original movie or the later Chinamation adaptation.

It must be nice, Marta thought, to know where you belonged in the world; who you wanted to be.

"Who the hell was that?" Jhon said, his breath heavy, his eyes pallid, jittery despite the graphene philm covering his corneas. He'd supposedly clipped his eyes from Bruce Lee in *Enter the Dragon*. But Marta could swear that a little of Peter Lorre's Hans Becker, the pasty pedophile from the 1931 film classic *M*, had crept in.

"Window-shopper," she said.

He moistened his keloid-smooth lips, leaving a snail trail of saliva. "She buy anything?"

"No."

He frowned. "Spent a lot of time with her for nothing."

"She couldn't make up her mind."

"You seem to get a lot of those."

Marta shrugged. "She wasn't ready to buy. I pressure her, and she doesn't come back. Next time, she goes someplace else."

"Been happening a lot lately." His tone as sour and puckered as his sweat-yellow shirt.

"I don't want to sell them something they don't want."

"Right." He blinked. "Well, keep up the good work."

Before she could retort, he turned and trundled back to his office, where she knew he would spend the rest of the afternoon mining digitally preserved celluloid and archived vidIO for usable images.

What he did in his free time. All the time. Holed up behind his grapheme, not just letting the past wash over him, but through him.

Marta shivered and hugged herself against the chill aura of the philm samples and the toxic flicker of old video.

Her muscles ached under the virtual radiation. Tired. She needed to sit down, rest for a few minutes.

Six months she'd worked at the Get Reel. Too long. She could feel the skeleton of her life showing through her philm, radiograph-white bones etched on black microfiche. It was time to move on, before she became fully exposed.

Tonight, she'd call Sister Giselle and warn her not to refer anybody else to the Get Reel. Tomorrow, Friday, she would look for another job, someplace new where she could start over. Again.

4

Music swelled the chest of Giles Atherton, filling him to the point of bursting. He felt himself rising up with the rest of the Right to Light congregation, all of them straining as one to be with God.

They were all drawn to that center, like iron to a magnet. The force was there, always pulling. There was no escaping it. The only release was to give oneself over to it.

And yet Atherton remained trapped within his body. God wasn't ready for him to cast off his flesh. Not yet. He had work to do. The lightness he felt was a promise of the joy that awaited him after he carried out his earthly duties.

For the service, he had chosen a patrician suit and philmed himself in a pseudoself based on Martin Luther and John Brown, in order that the spirit of those men, long dead, might enter him. By casting himself in their image he became something other, greater, than himself. He not only resurrected them in mind, but in body. In that way he was born fully into the body of Christ. Perhaps the same was true for all men of faith. They embodied those who had gone before, an extension not only of their faith but of their lives. That way their work on earth continued, unbroken, as if they had never died. The torch passed from one hand to the next, from one generation to the next, down through the ages.

Atherton combed precise fingers through his cloud-white hair, a delicate puff that contrasted sharply with the graphite-hard eyes and charcoal-gray suit. He turned to his wife, seated next to him. Lisbeth's face was uplifted, turned to the light from the chrome-and-glass ceiling, her eyes folded shut in prayer. The sharp-edged lines of her Tamara de Lempicka-inspired philm fractured the light around him as her lips moved in prayer, silently reciting the words she was thoughtcasting to the Church's datician. Like a lot of people, she needed to subvocalize a mental command for it to be clearly annunciated and accurately translated by the nanoelectrodes in her brain-computer interface.

It was the same petition she had offered up every week for the last three months, since the disappearance of their daughter. Atherton looked for the words on the d-splay screens mounted on the three steel-frame crucifixes, lined up in a row from tallest to shortest, that supported the tent-like canopy of the church. The d-splays flickered with vidIO images taken from classic Billy Graham revivals, *700 Club* episodes, and Promise Keeper rallies.

Sometimes it seemed as if the images of luminous rapture from those programs pierced his flesh to take up residence in his soul. The upraised hands, the tears of joy, and the bowed heads, respectful, reverent, and at peace. They lived in him, like flames feeding on wood, consuming him. Some nights the intensity of their burning left him feverish, his mouth dry, his thoughts addled by a parched, throbbing ache.

Fuel for the fire, he thought. In the end that was what everyone was. Burn with the holy spirit or burn in hell. Those were the options.

Atherton refused to believe that Apphia had run away of her own free will. She had been tempted, misguided.

He had seen it coming. He hadn't been blind. He had done what he could, his only regret was that it hadn't been enough. He should have been stronger.

"What's wrong with F8?" Apphia fumed.

"You tell me." Atherton wanted her to think for herself. He wanted her to see the truth on her own, without having it pointed out to her all the time.

"Nothing!" Apphia stamped her foot. "Everything is a sin to you. Just because I ware something doesn't mean I'm going to act in a certain way or be exactly like whoever I'm waring."

"We had an agreement." By allowing her to get 'skinned, he had hoped she would choose images that would bring her closer to God.

"Other parents let their kids screen stuff. It doesn't mean anything. It doesn't turn them into bad people."

He had caught her philmed in one of the proscribed downloads she had agreed not to ware in exchange for his permission, "Moment of F8." A passage from Romans condensed on the surface of his thoughts. " 'For

*they exchanged the truth of God for a lie and wor-
shipped and served the creature and not the Creator.' "*

Apphia fisted her hands at her sides. "She's no different than the people you philm yourself in."

"She's a false idol," he said. "A graven image."

"And the people you ware aren't? Do you actually
think they're going to make you a better person? Most
of them were assholes."

His face flushed. He sensed Lisbeth eavesdropping
on the conversation from the living room, and her presence tempered his response. "The subject is closed," he
stated.

Apphia spat out a laugh. "It was never open."

"That's enough, young lady." He pointed up the
stairs to her room. "We'll discuss this when you've had
a chance to calm down." In the meantime he'd activate
the parental controls in the 'skin to prevent any further
downloads.

"You're the one having the stroke," she said,
"not me."

———

Finally, he saw Lisbeth's plea appear near the apex
of the cross on a panel reserved for individual en-
treaties.

*Apphia. Fifteen years old. Missing for three months.
Please pray for her safety and return home. Soon!*

The prayer rose and dissipated. A few moments
later another prayer, entered by someone else in
the congregation, replaced it.

Atherton found Lisbeth's hand, bundled her fingers in his, and squeezed. "Are you okay?"

She nodded, then swallowed, her throat muscles

working. The tendons in her neck stood out, as taut as steel wires.

"Everything will be fine," he said.

"I know." She sighed, but remained tense. Her trust in God wasn't absolute. Not like his.

It helped that he had a plan. God helped those who helped themselves.

5

"You want to tell me what's going on?" Pelayo said.

Uri glanced up from the immersion tank he was calibrating, a look of irritation on his face. "The usual."

In other words, don't ask, don't tell. Pelayo had signed a comprehensive liability waiver and nondisclosure agreement that was as binding as a straightjacket.

"Any restrictions I need to know about?" Pelayo said. "Philms I should avoid, any contraindicated ware?"

"Only one," Uri said. The skintech grinned, revealing rows of shark teeth. As far as Pelayo could tell, the implants were real. Pelayo imagined the asswipe polishing them every day. "You have to abstain."

"From what?"

The grin sharpened. "What do you think?"

Pelayo frowned in disbelief. "You're kidding."

Uri's smile slackened, going limp. "We don't want you dirty-dicking yourself."

"You serious? No intimate contact?"

Uri shrugged. "If you don't like it, no problem. I can always find someone else to take your place. Plenty of test subjects out there wanting to screen the latest philm."

Pelayo sniffed. "How long are we talkin'?"

"Six weeks, maybe longer. Depends on the results we get."

Pelayo shook his head. Unfuckingbelievable.

Uri spread his hands. "Those are the terms and conditions. Your choice. Take it or leave it."

———

The test philm required new e-skin, not simply an upgrade to his existing ware. The old 'skin needed to be stripped off.

"Nothing you haven't gone through before," Uri said with calculated indifference.

Knowing what to expect didn't make the process any easier to face.

Pelayo floated in the tank, splayed on a bed of surgical gel. Despite anesthetics, the viral aspic burned. Uri was taking his time. The air in the tank reeked of honeysuckle mixed with formaldehyde.

"Can we get on with this?"

"Patience," Uri cooed. He blinked, parsing a new internal readout. "We don't want any mistakes."

Pelayo shivered as the burn grew cold. Son of a bitch...

"Okay." Uri straightened.

At the same time, Pelayo felt himself sink. Gel oozed up around his mouth, nose, and eyes—swallowing him whole. Like amber encasing an insect, it cut off his breath, sealing it in the moist coffin of his body...

———

He came awake suddenly, flat on his back on the sponge pad at the bottom of the tank. The surgical

gel was draining away like bathtub water, taking
with it flakes of peeled yellow dopant and the crimson threads of severed synthapse connections.
Leaving behind the cellophane-smooth gray of virgin e-skin. Under the translucent membrane he
could see his own naked skin, pallid and puckered,
bleached of all color to provide as plain a background as possible for the philm images that would
eventually pixilate and texture the 'skin.

He gagged in air. Choked on raw oxygen, then
jackknifed into a sitting position, veils of gel clinging to his arms and legs like tattered cloth. An acid
bead of saliva dribbled down his chin as cinegraphic
images appeared on the membrane, blurry at first,
then slowly sharpening.

"...fuck outta here," he said, the words sputtering out, frothy and bilious.

"Take it easy," Uri said, bending over the tank, his
gaze drilling down like the lenses of a microscope.
"Everything's fine. All we got to do now is download
the philm and you'll be good to go."

The grin was back, mocking, carnivorous.

———————

The 'skin came with a soot-gray suit, the creases in
the pant legs origami-sharp, a white silk shirt, and
red silk tie. While he slipped on graphene-covered
dress shoes, Uri brought him the jacket and overcoat.

"They part of the ware?" he asked.

Uri nodded. "No different from the 'skin. You got
menu options for fabric type, color, and pattern.
Same for the shirt, shoes, and tie."

"Simage capability?" Pelayo asked. In addition to philm, most new 'skin—even street jobs—included a tightly woven mesh of nanotrodes that mapped the topology and kinetic movement of the 'skin to generate a simulated image for use online.

"Fully integrated," Uri said. "You can even pick and choose which 'skin options you want to cast. That it?"

"All I can think of, for now."

"There may be a couple of updates," Uri said, "last-minute wrinkles we're in the process of ironing out. If that happens, you need to come in as soon as you get the call. Same day. Is that clear?"

Pelayo gave a pro forma nod. "I hear ya." Same old Uri, keeping him on a tight leash so he could yank his chain.

———

On the surface, the philm was conservative, an uninspired adaptation of 1940s or 1950s film noir. A bleak grayscale pseudoself sporting a knife-edged mustache and black, slicked-back hair. The face of an analog wristwatch was stenciled on his left wrist, mechanically resolute gears grinding out seconds, minutes, hours.

Inside was different. He couldn't put his finger on it, the feeling. Some odd acid-etched pattern of raw tics and urges. Too new yet to make their wishes known. That would come in time, a sense of direction, of place, in the world...the main reason people wore philm in the first place. Belonging. It made them part of a cast, a global cinematic tribe with shared interests and values.

It was always a little disconcerting at first. The jagged uncertainty and wrenched dislocation that came with new philm and undebugged 'skin.

Pelayo stepped from IBT's front lobby onto the sidewalk and accessed the public datalib with a quick mental command. Half a second later the spectral voice of a datician tickled his earfeed. "How may I assist you?"

"What can you tell me about the source material for the philm I'm currently waring?" he said. In the past, source images had been a good indicator of the market IBT was aiming for and what he could expect from the philm.

"One moment, please." A nearby mask, an Italianate muse, drifted down to look at him. "It's a composite," the datician said. "The persona doesn't appear to be drawn from one single film, but several."

"Such as?"

"Spencer Tracy in *Fury*. Orson Welles in *The Lady from Shanghai*. Burt Lancaster in *Elmer Gantry*. There may be others."

Pelayo had never heard of any of them. He squinted at the downloaded images projected on his retinas. "I don't get it."

"Explain, please?"

"The purpose of the philm. Why come out with an obscure composite?" Normally, philms had a distinct, readily identifiable character or brand name, like Scandalicious, F8, or Marilyn Monroe.

"Most composite images try to integrate a number of thematically or symbolically related tropes," the datician said.

"Maybe," Pelayo allowed. Something was going

on. Whatever it was, it didn't fit into the normal prerelease pattern. Who would download the philm if there was no recognizable lifestyle, pseudoself, or ideology people could identify with and plug into?

Lagrante, Pelayo thought. He might have some ideas. If not, he'd know someone who did or could find out.

A face in front of him morphed into the newest downloadable image of F8. At the same time, the philm manifested on half a dozen other faces in the surrounding crowd as the autoupdate kicked in, instantiating in every cast member who'd preordered the latest release.

"Slavation is near."

Pelayo's head snapped around. The TV stood a few meters away, under the pink awning of a flower kiosk philmed in yellow polka dots and blue daisies.

"Great," he muttered. Just what he needed. He loosened the razor wire on the inside of his belt in case things got nasty. It wouldn't be the first time a philmhead had come after him, hoping to rip a copy of whatever new ware he was testing.

Pelayo started across the street, saw that the cluster of TVs hadn't moved, and veered onto Pacific Avenue, hoping to lose himself in the crowd.

He walked quickly, passing art galleries, clothing stores, cafés, and gift shops philmed in cheerful watercolors. Two blocks later, reflected in the oblique window of a fajizza bar and grill, he spotted the TV doggedly trailing after him, a featureless shadow only partly dissolved by the sunlight.

6

The homeless shelter in Santa Cruz had once been an elementary school, back when kids attended class in person. Even though those days were long past, the wide halls of the three-story building still reverberated with the sporadic outbursts of children . . . loud, violent squalls that ended as quickly as they began. The elderly residents were worse; their moans drooled endlessly into the night.

Because Nadice was pregnant, she had been assigned a semiprivate cubicle in a second-floor classroom. The cubicle contained a futon that folded into a couch, a collapsible cardboard table, and stackable white plastic trays in which to store her belongings. She shared the classroom with an aged woman who snored when asleep and wheezed when awake. A sun-faded alphabet clung to the walls near the ceiling, Cheshire As, Bs, and Cs stenciled on the ancient plaster. Instead of whiteboards and chalkboards, several Vurtronic screens hung from the earthquake-cracked walls. One was tuned to time-lapse cloud formations. Another followed flocks of migrating birds under the hygienic white glare of the LED track lights. The room's only nonvirtual window faced east and overlooked the ruined tarmac of a fenced playground.

"You can stay a week," one of the social workers who volunteered at the shelter had said when she first arrived. "I'm afraid that's the best I can do. After that..." Her voice trailed off, vaguely apologetic.

The woman's face was pinched, but resolute. Nadice wondered what government regulation lay behind the one-week limit, but didn't argue. "I should be able to find a new place by then," she said. A week was better than nothing.

They sat in a cubicle in a first-floor classroom that had been subdivided into work spaces using recycled sound-absorbent partitions. The tatty fabric on the privacy screens was programmable, and appeared to be networked. All of the screens displayed the same Chinese restaurant motif of golden dragons, verdant, mist-shrouded mountains, and generic pink blossoms.

"Do you have a job?" the social worker asked.

Nadice peeled her gaze from a white crane balanced on one leg in concentric rings of pond water. "I worked for Atherton, Lagos. But I quit after they transferred me here."

"They wanted you to give up the baby for adoption?"

Nadice shook her head. "Abortion."

The social worker grimaced in sympathy, then nodded. It was an all-too-familiar story. The woman rephilmed the palm of her hand, activating a compact d-splay. "You were employed by them in what capacity?"

"Housekeeping."

Information populated the d-splay. "Contract work?"

Nadice nodded. "Five-year indentured." More text scrolled.

"How much time left?"

Nadice forced her gaze from the d-splay. "One year, seven months."

Give or take. She had stopped counting the days and hours. It made the time slow to an agonizing crawl.

The social worker frowned. The red and white horizontal bands on her face twisted as she focused on Nadice's cataract-dull 'skin. The alternating red and white lines were a classic Rudi Gernreich, popular in Africa. "Have you been"—the woman pursed her mouth—"naturalized?"

A tactful way of inquiring if Nadice had been issued a work authorization permit or officially applied for asylum.

"Not yet." Nadice picked at a dry burr of skin on her lower lip. "My manager said that they couldn't file the application until the baby was..." Her lip stung. Nadice tasted blood and pressed the burr back into place.

"I see." The social worker moistened her own lips. "What about the father? Where is he?"

"Lagos."

"Is he going to come after you? Cause trouble?"

"No."

The social worker's eyes narrowed, skeptical. "You're sure?"

"Yes."

Because there was no father. But she couldn't say that, no one would believe her. Sometimes she didn't believe it herself.

"Is anyone else going to come looking for you?"

the social worker said. "Besides domestic security, I mean."

"I don't think so."

"No family? Friends?"

"No," she lied. If Atherton Resorts ever found out about her grandmother, the company would use the old woman to get to Nadice or garnish her for what Nadice still owed on her contract.

The social worker checked the d-splay on her palm, glanced up. "Anything else I should know about? Medical problems. Drug use. Like that."

Nadice shook her head. No way the social worker would take her in if she knew Nadice was working as a mule, smuggling illegal ware. Ditto the salesperson at the cinematique. She would never have given Nadice the antitoxin: too high-risk—at least until the ware was delivered and she was clean. And maybe not even then. Nadice couldn't take the chance. It was a gamble, waiting to take the antitoxin, but it was better than not having it at all. Or a safe place to stay.

"All right." The social worker stood and the d-splay went blank, replaced by her Rudi Gernreich philm. "Try to get some rest. I'll make some calls, see what we can do."

The crumbling blacktop outside of the window was guarded by netless, doddering basketball hoops. The skeletal remains of a jungle gym, swing set, and slide haunted a sandbox off to the side, the salt-bitten metal little more than cobwebby threads of rust. When she closed her eyes, she could picture the kids that had once played there, laughing and yelling, boiling over with excitement. She could almost imagine herself with them, plugged into a different past, a different life.

A few hours after the social worker talked to her, she was visited by Sister Giselle. The nun, philmed after a character in an old television program, wore a habit with a goofy cornette. Nadice couldn't recall which program, only that it had been revived a few years back. There were times Nadice wished she could fly like the nun in the sitcom. Have the wind pick her up and never put her down.

"I don't want to be deported," Nadice told Sister Giselle. "I can't go back." That much, at least, was true.

The nun sucked on uneven, tea-stained teeth. "I know someone who might be able to help."

Nadice gripped one of the nun's hands. "Thank you." The bones felt thin and frail under her smooth, unwrinkled 'skin.

It had been a mistake to let Mateus talk her into smuggling for him. But she had been desperate, willing to do anything. Or almost anything.

She checked the time. Not quite three. Plenty of time until her six o'clock parley with him.

───────────

She'd met Mateus in Lagos, a month after he'd been hired by the resort. He seemed nice enough at the time. Polite, respectful. He didn't try to feel her up. Not like some of her shift managers.

He worked security. She wasn't sure if the philm he wore—something he called H-town crunk, whatever that meant—was part of the job or not. He looked like he'd done time in a supermax, philmed

head to toe in badass prison tattoos. The black line
art didn't sing or dance or do anything except radi-
ate attitude. His muscles bulged with crucifixes, rose
petals that dripped blood, twisted strands of barbed
wire and fiery skulls that laughed with predictable
scorn.

"I can get you out," he whispered to her one
night, a week when she was working graveyard.
"Treal."

His word for true and real.

"Anyplace you wanna go," he promised. Then, as
if in answer to her unspoken question, "All I got to
do is arrange for a transfer. Knowmsayin?"

They stood in a laundry room, where she was recycling used linen, the hum of a big commercial UV
sterilizer muffling their words.

"In return, I give you some luggage to take with
you. Simple as that."

She met his gaze. Was he trying to bait her?
Trap her? His eyes, flat as tarnished brass, revealed
nothing.

"What kind of luggage?"

He winked at her. Grinned.

"No." Her jaw tightened.

"Think about it," he said.

When he was gone she'd swallowed, out of fear
and relief; felt the votive flicker of possibility warm
her waxy breath.

And quickly snuffed it out.

Two weeks later, one of the bellboys didn't show
up for work. He'd taken a job in Moscow, a coworker
told her.

A few days later, another boy took his place.
A new hire. It went on like that, once every few

months. Quietly, unobtrusively, employees transferred to another world, and to a new life. Nadice
sensed Mateus watching her, the fishhook snag of
his gaze tugging at her, wearing her down.

It was only a matter of time. He seemed to know
this, even if she didn't. He could see things she
couldn't. Signs written on her face that were invisible, or unrecognizable, when reflected in a mirror.

Then the baby came.

It was as if his eyes had...not put the child there,
but watched it take shape inside of her.

Somehow he'd known that she would find herself
in this position. He'd known that at some point she
would need a way out. He wanted to help her, he
said. But in return he expected to be helped.

Nadice hadn't even known she was pregnant until a routine biomed scan brought it to the attention
of the Atherton on-site physician.

"Conception occurred four days ago," the doctor
informed her.

Nadice sat in a sterile white examination room,
the pink crepe gown pulled tight across her thighs.
Chill air caressed her spine. "That's impossible."

The doctor nodded at the wall-mounted d-splay
in front of her, where an image of a womb appeared.
Her womb. A magnified inset showed a globular
clump of cells.

"Fertilization occurred earlier this week. This is
the resulting blastocyst, following implantation in
the endometrium, the lining of the uterus."

"That's the baby?"

"Yes."

"I don't understand." Shaking her head. It didn't

seem real. Not the baby, not what he was saying. None of it.

"You should have been more careful," the doctor said. His tone, as stringent as the walls, stripped away all pretense.

"But I didn't—"

"Any unauthorized pregnancy is grounds for termination," he went on. "Those are the terms of your contract."

Nadice bit her lip, diffident. Despite his benign exterior—he had philmed himself as Albert Schweitzer, wrinkled with compassion—she found him intimidating. Rumor among the staff was that Atherton hired inexperienced interns, fresh from medical school, because it was cheap. The philm concealed incompetence or insecurity, which he tried to hide by being stern.

Feeling exposed, she smoothed the crepe gown across her lap. "What are you going to do?"

"That depends."

"On what?" The thin paper dimpled under the clammy pressure of her fingers.

"What you decide to do. It's your choice."

So she had gone to Mateus. What choice did she have? Without him, she would lose either the baby or her job. With him, she might keep both.

"When one door closes, another opens." She mouthed the Spanish proverb, heard her grandmother's voice in the words. The old woman's parting gift, whispered in her ear just before Nadice boarded the magtrain from Tangiers to Lagos, where she expected to spend the next five years and maybe the rest of her life.

Now she was carrying not only the baby, but something else. What that might be, she wasn't entirely sure.

"It's better if you don't know," Mateus had said, just before he dosed her. They sat in a room in a cheap modular hotel, halfway up a tower of stacked hexagons. He'd philmed the room in blue, pink, and yellow stucco. Mediterranean or Mexican, she thought. Beyond the flimsy graphene-coated walls, Lagos sweated, the breath of the city congested, thickly phlegmatic.

Her chest tightened. "Is it dangerous?"

"Don't worry. Everything will be fine. Trust me, gurl. I've done this before. Lots of times."

He handed her the dustware. She stared at the purple bubble cap, uncertain what to do. Was she supposed to carry it by hand? Swallow it?

"You have to breathe it in." He sniffed, his nostrils flaring.

Fingers trembling, she inserted the capsule into one nostril, hesitated, her gaze fixed on Mateus, then pinched and inhaled.

Acrid vapor coiled into her, a damp oily smoke that smelled of dead geraniums and hot metal filings.

Mateus caught her by the wrist, lowered her hand, and took the spent capsule from her. "How you feelin'?"

She clenched her empty hand into a fist, forced a deep breath, waited for her pulse to slow. "Customs won't know about it?"

"Naw. 'Cause it's there, but it ain't there. Like

that. Soon as they go to look at it, it changes. Mutates into something else."

She could feel the ware now. An erratic, insect-fast fluttering somewhere inside her. She wasn't sure where. Everywhere and nowhere. The fibrillation was hard to nail down. It flitted around, banging against bones, tendons, and nerves, like a moth trying to free itself from a cocoon, struggling reflexively toward light.

Nadice folded her arms beneath her breasts, barricading herself against the uneasy feeling. She squeezed herself, applying pressure to her ribs and abdomen until the bile in her stomach settled.

She was not going to fall apart, she told herself. She was not going to panic. She was going to hold on, to the baby and herself.

7

The basement morgue reeked of n-zyme disinfectants, centuries-old formaldehyde, and refrigerated sweat.

Van Dijk wrapped his coat tighter against the stainless-steel chill and hard parabolic glare from the pendant surgical lights. He hated this room. He felt naked in it, stripped of whatever it was that made him human. Life broken down in the acid of cold, hard analysis, distilled into its most basic chemical elements.

"Well?" he said. "You got anything yet?" His voice ricocheted off the white ceramic floor tile.

The coroner, Onjali Kostroff, looked up from the autopsy table where the body lay under a white sheet. "She just came out of the tank."

The "tank" was a liquid bath of dissemblers that detached the electronic skin from a body without destroying the matrix of artificial atoms and nanomechanical components in the graphene substrate.

"And?" He moved closer to her, drawn by the need for physical warmth as much as information.

"Trace levels of nRG_4U and bam/B. Not enough to kill her."

"She a user?" Van Dijk didn't really care, one way or another. The only value the information had was that it might point him to a regular dealer or supplier he could question. Motive didn't show up in test results.

"No." Kostroff shook her head. She wore her honey-blond hair in a ponytail, pulled back from Garbo features rendered in soft-focus repixilation above her blue nanopore face mask. "I don't think so. The drug levels were almost undetectable. Offhand, I'd say they were sexually transmitted or the result of incidental contact."

One of the local clubs, he thought, where the beat of the music practically pounded the drugs into you.

"You got an ID?" he said.

Kostroff removed the shroud. Gone were Barbara Stanwyck, Gene Tierney, and anyone else the victim had ever been or wanted to be. All that remained was a nameless young woman, naked except for the dull cloudy 'skin that had separated from the underlying flesh. The programmable graphene reminded van Dijk of the dead skin shed by a snake—brush up against it and the substrate would slough off in a shriveled, micron-thin sheet. In addition to the gold-sequined dress, Kostroff had removed the azure-tinted necklace and earrings. They were with the dress in a sealed plastine evidence bag on the counter.

"DiNA bar code came up negative," Kostroff said. "Ditto her soft DNA fingerprint. Nothing on file."

"Masked," he said, "or undocumented?"

Kostroff shrugged under her loose-fitting scrubs. "There seem to be a lot of junk nucleotide sequences. It will take some time to filter those out, see if we get a match."

"What else?"

Kostroff blinked as she parsed an online d-splay. "The 'skin is from an unknown manufacturer."

"Import?"

"Or a modified bootleg." Kostroff began a careful visual examination of the body, paying close attention to the eyes and the inside of the mouth.

"You find a serial number or manufacturer ID?" van Dijk asked.

"Nope. It's clean."

"Anything identifiably foreign? Materials? Electronics?"

"Not yet."

Which didn't necessarily prove the 'skin was homegrown. It could simply be a fresh import, too new to be in the datalib.

With a surgical laser, Kostroff shaved the cornea from one eye, exposing the translucent gray disk of an eyefeed d-splay. She snipped the CNT input wire, tweezed the disk off, and flagged it for latent-image analysis of the flash memory buffer.

"Any information on the philm?" Van Dijk asked.

"It's definitely not off the shelf. I ran the usual faceprint scan, and it came up negative."

"Custom job?"

"Yeah. It looks high-end. Designer."

Van Dijk ran a hand through his hair. If it was a one-off OEM, that put a different spin on things. Original equipment manufacturers weren't cheap. "What about a cause of death?"

"Nothing conclusive on the preliminary scans." Kostroff straightened. "I'm going to open her up as soon as I finish the preliminary. You want to stick around?"

"Not really."

But want had nothing to do with it. He watched as she inspected the vaginal cavity for anything obvious the dissemblers might have overlooked, followed by the anus and the rectum.

"Any sign of forced entry?" he asked.

Kostroff shook her head. "There're no indications of trauma. No minor tearing or bruising."

"Unforced?" he said.

"Not recently." Kostroff straightened.

"What about the mouth?" he asked.

"Clean."

With a ceramic scalpel, she made the Y-cut, starting at the shoulders and ending at the pubis.

"What's going on there?" He pointed out a puffy, spongy-looking section of tissue along the edge of the cut.

"I don't know." She ran a CNT-tipped probe over the area. "Looks like the e-skin has grafted onto, or replaced, some of the underlying tissue and nerves."

"I didn't know that was possible."

"Neither did I."

She biopsied the region, then removed the internal organs, weighed them, and set them aside. "You got a hard-on yet?" she said.

It took him a moment to realize the question wasn't part of the official autopsy log she had been dictating. "Should I?"

"Half the cops who come down here do."

Van Dijk frowned. He couldn't tell if she was joking or not. He'd never been able to get a read on her. Most people in the department hadn't. "Yeah?"

"You'd be surprised. Men and women. Personally I don't see the attraction. Stiff, yeah. Cold, no."

"Maybe some guys just want to find out if there really is a light at the end of the tunnel."

Kostroff frowned. Whether it was his halfhearted attempt at humor or something else, he couldn't be sure. She inspected the shaved scalp, then retrieved a cranial saw from the instrument tray next to her in preparation for resecting the top of the skull. "You sure you're up for this?"

Van Dijk made a face as she positioned the blade over the forehead. "I'm not that hard-core."

She snorted. "Maybe you should be."

"I'll work on it. In the meantime—"

"Yeah. I'll send you the report as soon as it's done." Kostroff thumbed the I/O on the saw. With a whine, the diamond-tipped teeth on the blade chewed through bloodless tissue into cold, gritty bone.

8

Pelayo lost the TV on the magtube from Santa Cruz to Palo Alto.

The guy had either given up or lost interest. It didn't seem likely he had rephilmed himself—that wasn't how TVs operated. They rescreened en masse and in sync. There was little individual variation. The overall theme was unified, consistent. It went against their core faith to deviate from the big picture.

Stepping off the train, into the raw unfiltered glare on the station platform, Pelayo opened an online message, mentally keying in the address for Lagrante Broussard. There was no answer, a sure sign the rip artist was in.

———

Lagrante worked out of an apartment on the second floor of a four-level parking garage. A quarter of a century ago, in the aftermath of the Point Pinole quake, the structure had been converted into emergency housing for refugees. Over the years, ad hoc businesses had moved in, gradually displacing the hapless apartments. Actual residential space was now confined to the outer walls, where windows of aging photoelectric plastic strained the light to piss yellow.

The exterior architectural philm was a hodge-podge of styles: sleek Le Corbusier strip windows, aluminum Art Deco trellises, and colorful glass tesserae set in decorative arabesque patterns on the walls, support pillars, and outer circumference of the Moorish horseshoe-shaped arches that framed the entrances.

Pelayo cut a quick glance up-down the street—nothing but the usual assortment of waterfront workers, street vendors, couriers, and delivery truck drivers—then ducked past the tinder-dry fronds of a squat palm tree next to the open security gate.

Inside, the smell of brine gave way to espresso, grilled vegetables, chicken kebabs, and falafel in warm pita bread. He hurried through the street-level food court, the tables, partitions, and planters that subdivided the space. It was noon and the place was jammed, the din deafening despite the suspended ceiling panels.

The elevator was just as loud, a cacophony of newzine segments, nanoFX commercials, vidIO game clips, and ad masks as watchful as gargoyles. Most of it hadn't changed since his last visit, four months ago. New look, same worthless content.

Hopefully, Lagrante would have something more to offer.

———

The rip artist was screening Archibald J. Motley, Jr. with a touch of Romare Bearden that added a jagged, almost demented edge to the otherwise suave exterior. Raw jazz seeped out of his pores, as unfiltered and unhurried as the Hongtasan hanging from his lips.

"What's playin'?" Pelayo said. He could see himself reflected in the black lenses of the sunglasses Lagrante wore as an extension of his anatomy.

" 'Kind of Blue.' " The cigarette bobbed, scattering volcanic gray ash. "You know?"

Pelayo shook his head.

"Miles Davis. It's a classic." Lagrante let out a breath and creaked back in his leather chair. He ran a hand over the triangle of stubble on the right side of scalp. "That's some crunk 'skin you're waring. Treal retro."

Lagrante fancied himself an artiste, an adherent of the true and real when it came to philm, clothing, and music. It wasn't about being genuine, in a radiocarbon sense. It was about being true to the spirit of authenticity. Pop wasn't treal unless it was a riff on Andy Warhol. Otherwise it was simply derivative, no different from a Chinese knockoff. According to Lagrante, treal was all about taking something old and making it new, spinning it in a different direction without losing the gestalt, the existential integrity, of the original.

"Well?" Pelayo asked.

Lagrante tilted forward in the chair. "Looks first run. I haven't seen anything else like it."

"Influences?"

"Hard to say for sure." He tapped his chin thoughtfully with one finger. "Offhand, I'd say Bible-thumping minister with a little Wall Street mixed in. You've got Pastor Lud and Pat Robertson mixing it up with Peter Douglas from *Stalk Market*. Conservative and clean-cut on one hand, gritty and cutthroat on the other. Kind of sends a mixed message."

"To who?"

"Corporate executives. Politicos. Lawyers. That's the target audience. If I had to venture a guess."

"Not exactly your demographic. That what I'm hearing?"

Lagrante shrugged. "There's no shortage of business types who want to come off as straitlaced, but not rigid. Competent and self-assured but not immoral." He pursed thin lips. "How long you been out of the tank?"

"Couple of hours."

Lagrante stood. He stubbed out his Hongtasan in a dissembler-shiny ashtray, then walked around Pelayo in a slow orbit, as if checking out the lines on a hooker. "How was the install?" he said. "Clean?"

"As far as I know." If there were any problems, he wasn't sure Uri would have told him.

"Awright." Lagrante cracked his knuckles. "Let's pop trunk on this motherfucker. See what we got."

———————

"Well?" Pelayo asked. He stared at Lagrante's brow, knotted in concentration over his glasses.

Lagrante didn't answer. Pelayo wasn't sure if Lagrante was listening, if he was too deep in to hear anything, or just ignoring him. In the ashtray, all that remained of the Hongtasan was a minute curl of paper.

"I'll be damned," Lagrante finally whispered. He let out a low whistle infused with frustration and admiration.

"What's that supposed to mean?"

Lagrante sucked on his front teeth. "The platform

is new. Hardware. Firmware. Software. We're talking from the ground up."

"You saying you can't rip it?"

Lagrante pinched the bridge of his nose, then let the glasses slide back into place. "I need to do some research, make some inquiries. Check if there's a crack out there. Know what I'm sayin'?"

"Yeah. I'm fucked."

"Relax. IBT wouldn't hull one of its guinea pigs. Not on purpose, leastways. They need the test data."

"Thing is, they don't care if I get hulled or not. If you screw up and something goes wrong, that counts as data, the same as anything else."

"It won't come to that," Lagrante assured him.

Pelayo sniffed, uncomfortable with the rip artist's laissez-faire attitude. "Easy for you to say."

"Everything will be fine. Don't worry, you'll get your percentage. It might take a little longer this time around, that's all, but it'll be worth it. Trust me. That's some bomb-ass shit you're waring."

Pelayo's gaze drifted past Lagrante to the artwork on the walls. Reproductions of several Archibald J. Motley, Jr. paintings and grainy photos of jazz musicians wreathed in cumulus smoke. "How long?"

Lagrante tipped back in his chair. "Couple of days. I should have something definite by then."

Pelayo nodded. "Any word on Concetta?"

"Nothing yet."

"You been saying that for three months." Part of the latest deal he'd cut with Lagrante involved information. In exchange for giving him access to IBT's test 'skin, Lagrante would put out feelers for Pelayo's missing cousin. So far, it had been a bust, and he'd begun to wonder if Lagrante was using Concetta to string him along.

Lagrante's hand fluttered to his chest, all wounded—like an injured bird alighting on his green silk tie. "These things take time. Especially if the gurl don't want to be found."

Or if someone didn't want her to be found. Pelayo exhaled through his nose.

"It might not happen," Lagrante said. "You knew that going in. It was a long shot—no guarantees."

"Yeah, yeah. Doing everything you can."

"What's up with that other cousin of yours?" Lagrante drummed fingertips on the mahogany veneer of his desk. "Marta. She into something these days?"

Pelayo shrugged. "I haven't talked to her."

"You don't keep in touch?"

"Not lately."

Lagrante arched one brow over the square dash cut by his glasses. "You two playin' some kind of spit game?"

"Been busy. That's all." He shifted his attention to a Miles Davis poster, preserved behind thin glassine.

"I always liked that gurl." Lagrante grinned. "Nice hips. She gave me a call. You believe that?"

Pelayo's gaze resettled on Lagrante. "When?"

"This morning. Wanted to know if I could strip some corporate-secured 'skin. Or point her to someone who could."

"Strip? Why?"

"She wouldn't tell me. I was wondering if you knew what was going on."

"What did you say?"

"I asked if she wanted to go clubbin' with me. Maybe check out my embouchure in return for my services."

━━━━━━━

Stepping from the food court onto the street, Pelayo hunched his shoulders against the afternoon tumult of delivery trucks, stevedores, and desalination workers. His nerves flickered. He couldn't head home. Not yet. He couldn't sit still. He needed to move, to go someplace, anywhere, even if it was in circles.

He needed to think.

He caught a bus that slotted into the Nimitz magrail. The articulated train took him past the South Bay desalination plants and hydroelectric wave turbines, Sausalito windmills, and finally the loose archipelago of Bodego Bay oil platforms that had been converted to aqua farms and hydrogen extraction plants.

Pelayo leaned his head against the bubble window next to him. Combed unsteady fingers through the uncomfortably long hair of his new pseudoself. Listened to the muted sigh of wind through the tinted diamond.

Lagrante couldn't be trusted. Pelayo knew that. The rip artist would do and say whatever it took to keep him from going to another black-market philmhead or bootlegger. They'd been doing business for two years. So far the arrangement had worked out well. Pelayo provided Lagrante with direct source-code access to the 'skin and the philm he beta tested. In return, Lagrante gave him a cut of whatever he got for the pirated ware.

But if Lagrante couldn't rip a copy of the philm,
all bets were off. He had a feeling something had
changed. Pelayo could no longer count on Lagrante
to keep his best interests at heart.

Or Marta's.

9

Marta stepped from the magrail onto a platform jammed with agricultural workers from the hydroponics farms, greenhouses, warehouses, packaging plants, and distribution centers around the Pajaro Beach Flats.

Her nostrils flared, taking in the smell of sweat, brine, leaky hydrogen fuel cells, rotten vegetables, uncollected garbage, newly baked bread, resignation, hope, and despair. She had grown up here; she hated this place and loved it. Like everyone else, she vowed to leave, yet always returned. Every path out seemed to lead back, each step part of a convoluted series of Möbius-strip events.

Marked by the crumbling smokestack of an old, coal-fueled power plant, the Flats extended from Moss Landing in the south to Watsonville in the north. A hundred years ago, crop irrigation wells along the coast had leached the soil dry and saltwater incursion from the Monterey Bay had poisoned the once-fertile farmland.

As Marta walked home, a cool breeze off the Bay carried a whiff of raw sewage across the daily bustle of beggars, fast-food vendors, warewolves, and pimps. The stink seemed to be coming from the big landfill on the northernmost edge of the Flats. In the course of excavating the sedimentary layers of old tires, scrap metal, and nonbiodegradable plastic, someone must have broken a waste treatment line.

Through the haze, Marta could just make out the canyon-walled streets cut into the landfill-like trenches in some huge archaeological dig. The dwellings there were subterranean—a warren of tunnels and rooms excavated from garbage and buttressed with sheet metal, rusted box springs, discarded refrigerators, washing machines, stoves, and other kitchen appliances.

South of the Trenches the residences moved above ground, a hodgepodge of motor homes, semi-trailers, Quonset huts, and shipping containers anchored to reinforced concrete pads that had been set on the level, bulldozed sand.

Narrow streets and footpaths—jammed with scooters, motorcycles, and bicycles—connected a dozen or more distinctly philmed neighborhoods. New Malecon followed the beach seawall for three kilometers, its stacked multilevel boxcars philmed to look like the famous boulevard in Havana, Cuba. The Red Lantern district of Little Shanghai butted up against Putingrad, Zona Sagrada, Al Mansur, and Carib. All philmed as places that the community's legal and illegal immigrants had either lived or wanted to live.

Her sister Concetta hated philm. After seeing what it had done to the neighborhood and the people, she stopped waring 'skin. In neighborhood association meetings, she'd argued against the use of architectural philm to renovate the Flats.

Marta sighed and wondered if she'd ever understood where her sister was coming from...

"It's not the same as redevelopment," Concetta told
Marta after a meeting at which the planning commis-
sion had decided to move forward. "It's not an improvement."

"It makes people feel better," Marta said, "about
themselves and where they live. What's wrong with
that?"

They sat in a secluded New Malecon café, sipping coffee, the crumbs of a shared blueberry scone scattered on
the table between them. Soul Inheritance, a Cuban R&B
band, percolated through slow-churning fans. Outside,
moonlight foamed against the seawall on restless waves.

"It's not helping." Concetta glanced at a group of TV
missionaries bunched at a corner table and leaned forward, keeping her voice low in the metal-walled room.
"It's making life worse, not better."

"I know." Marta sighed. It was a familiar argument.
"People don't want to see things the way they really are.
They want to cover up their problems. Hide from them."

"It's more than that." Concetta sipped coffee, holding
the mug with both hands. "People don't know what's
real anymore, and what's not."

Marta blew on her coffee. "And you do."

Concetta nodded at the TVs. "All I'm saying is that it
makes people easy targets. Easy to program them."

"People are always looking for something better,"
Marta said. "There's nothing new about that."

Concetta stared into her cup. "Philm just makes the
sell job easier. Lot more innocent victims now than there
used to be. All I'm saying."

Marta didn't like the tone of her sister's voice. "What
have you gotten yourself into?"

Concetta shook her head but not in denial; whatever she was doing she couldn't, or wouldn't, talk about it.

A week later her sister was gone, vanished. A week after that, Marta discovered the refurbished shortwave hidden in their bedroom closet.

———

That had been three months ago. And still there had been no word from Concetta. Had she left in disgust, fed up with the refurbished motor home that their stepmother had philmed to resemble a Hollywood bungalow?

Or was her disappearance a symptom of some deeper malaise?

Each day Marta thought back to the period leading up to Concetta's disappearance. Had her sister said something—on purpose or accidentally—to hint she might be leaving? She culled her memory for a stray phrase, a seemingly innocuous comment, and came up empty. There was nothing. Only the radio, which might or might not have been there all along. Looking for a missing blouse one day, she had found the top with the radio in a corner of the closet reserved for storage. No telling how long ago Concetta had put it there. Or why the blouse had been with it.

———

To Marta's surprise, Nguyet was home, rattling around in the little kitchenette. She'd forgotten it was Nguyet's early day. One day a week she worked an early shift at the vegetable-processing plant, going in at 3:00 A.M. and coming home by three in the afternoon. When Marta left for the Get Reel that morning, she hadn't noticed Nguyet was already gone.

Marta poked her head into the kitchen, where Nguyet was preparing dinner. Fish patties and fried cactus.

"How's he doing?" Marta asked.

Nguyet looked up from the hissing skillet and shook her head, somber.

Yesterday her father hadn't been able to stand on his own. Marta had to help him to the dinner table.

"He refuses to get out of bed," Nguyet said, her mood sour. "Except to go to the bathroom."

"Again?" It was the third time that week.

"I called Don Angelo, the chiromancer. But Rocío refused to see him. Your father spat on the poor old man, and then tried to choke him."

The chiromancer was in his nineties. Hardly a match for a warehouse worker, even a bedridden one.

"What about you?" Nguyet peppered the fish. "Are you okay? You don't look so good."

"Headache." She hadn't told either of them she wasn't feeling well, hadn't wanted them to worry.

An uneasy truce existed between them. When her father had first started seeing Nguyet, Marta resented the woman, refused to accept her. She didn't want, or need, another mother. She'd gotten along fine for years. Even when Nguyet officially moved in with them, Marta had treated her as a guest, a temporary housemate. To accept her fully, as a permanent addition to the family, would hammer the final nail in the coffin that held the remains of her real mother.

To her credit, Nguyet didn't try to become Marta's

stepmother, surrogate sister, or best friend. Quietly, yet inextricably, she slipped into the role of care-taker, an arrangement Marta could live with now that her father was on disability and antidepressants. Without Nguyet, it would be impossible to take care of him. Concetta's disappearance had hit him hard. He blamed himself. Marta's meager income wasn't enough to live on and pay for the drugs to treat his damaged spine and melancholy. Even the black-market generics in the Flats were high-priced.

"I have a neighborhood planning meeting to-night," Nguyet said. "From eight until ten. I can't be here to babysit him."

"Okay. I'll see what I can do. Maybe I can talk some sense into him."

"Shit." Nguyet returned her attention to the skil-let, where the cactus had started to smoke.

Typical. Marta couldn't tell if the remark was di-rected at her or the burning cactus. Let it go, she told herself. It wasn't worth it.

She made her way down the narrow hallway that led to the closet-sized bedrooms in back. Her father wallowed in bed. His back was uncomfortably straight, held rigid by the brace his workman's comp had paid for. He was watching a newscast on a cheap Vurtronic display he'd pasted to the ceiling so he didn't need to sit up. The d-splay was low-res graphene with equally flimsy bandwidth. Light from the d-splay peeled the color from his face and the rattan veneer on the drawn window shade next to him.

He didn't look at her when she entered the room and took a seat on the chair next to the bed. He kept his attention fixed on the news story, a preview of an upcoming Paris fashion show where the latest philm and cosmetique offerings from fashioneers like IBT and Skincense would be unveiled.

She searched his face, trying to read the thoughts behind the ferrous-hard eyes and gritty, scar-nicked stubble. "You look like shit," she said, breaking the standoff.

He rolled his head sideways on the pillow. "You don't look so great yourself," he said.

Marta knotted her hands into fists. "You can't just lie there."

"What a joke." Her father scoffed and returned his attention to the d-splay. "Your sister saw it coming."

Marta's throat tightened. "Saw what?" Her voice husky, barely a whisper.

"Philm."

She swallowed at the ache, trying to force it down. "What about it?"

"Everybody wants to be somebody else. They can't be satisfied with who they are anymore."

She stared at him. "What does that have to do with Concetta?"

"People think they can change from the outside in," he said. "Instead of the inside out."

"Why are you telling me this?"

"You should turn that radio down," he said. "It woke me up this afternoon. Came on a couple of times. Annoying as hell."

Marta's stomach tensed. "What"—she moistened her lips—"what are you talking about?"

He frowned, concentrating. "Someone, a woman or a kid maybe, reading a bunch of numbers."

"What kind of numbers?"

"Beats the hell out of me. Didn't make no sense. It went on for a couple minutes each time, then stopped."

"That's it? Just numbers?"

He grunted. "Worthless piece of shit. I tried to change the station but couldn't. Had to turn the damn thing off."

A shadow leaned into the room, spread across the floor in a stain. Marta turned. Instead of Nguyet, a man stood in the doorway. He leaned casually against the jamb, all suited up under a beige overcoat, his hair slicked back, a gray felted Lancaster fedora in one hand. Nguyet appeared behind him, flustered, her face a bright sheen.

"Marta." The man tipped his head, first at her and then her father. "Uncle Rocío. How you been?"

Recognition kicked in. "Pelayo," she said.

He stepped into the room, out of context in the retro philm he was waring. "It's been a while."

How long had he been standing there? she wondered. How much had he heard?

"I tried to stop him," Nguyet said. "But he barged right in."

Pelayo fixed Marta with a hard, flat gaze. "We need to talk," he said. "Now."

10

At six, Nadice caught a Bay Area magrail and headed northeast to Dockton.

She stared out the bubble window next to her, watching cars cross the Golden Gate Bridge in bright mercurial threads of light.

Fifteen minutes later the train passed Suisun Bay on her left, sped through Pittsburg and Antioch into the capillary network of waterways and sloughs formed by the Sacramento and San Joaquin Rivers. According to a tourist information feed, the water had been fresh a century ago. But the rivers shriveled as the oceans rose, turning the delta of the Central Valley into an inland sea populated with pontoon-supported bridges, walkways, and buildings that spread like melanomas along the brackish slow-moving currents.

Dockton. It spread out before her, a tumorous growth of creaking, brine-encrusted epoxy board, sheets of brittle photoelectric plastic, heat-cracked tires, rust-scabbed metal, and peeling architectural philm.

Earlier, Nadice gave the train the address Mateus had made her memorize. Now, the bus section she was seated in detached from the train, shunted onto a paved loop, and dropped her off at a stop next to one of the road-accessible tributaries.

Inhaling the stench of a nearby waste-reclamation plant, Nadice climbed wooden stairs to the top of the levee. On the other side was a small marina. She couldn't see any water between the pontoon docks. But the buildings bobbed sluggishly, rising and falling to an unseen rhythm. The latest F8 hit, "The Vivisexionist," drifted from the flea-market booths set up a short distance away. Nadice squinted against the early-evening glare, shading her eyes with one hand. Most of the makeshift structures—motels, bars, stores, and cafés—were held in place by gangplanks and frayed Kevlex line. Many appeared to have been boats at one time. Other buildings had been constructed directly on the dock, where they clung like barnacles or limpets. The town was a hodgepodge of architectural styles—everything from French Quarter Bourbon Street to Pacific Tiki bar and Aegean stucco. In a few places, programmable philm appliqués decorated the epoxy board and sheet-metal siding. The letters on one decal, a sign for a travel agency called Gone Fission, pulsed in toxic radioactive green. Below them, a flying fish sporting four dragonfly wings leaped up out of a pond. At the peak of its arc the scales sloughed off and the fish turned to look at her.

"Hello," it said, the voice a flat monochrome over her earfeed. With a quick flick of its tail, the fish detached from the sign and swam into the air.

Startled, Nadice stepped back.

Gossamer wings fluttered, holding the fish at eye level in front of her. It seemed to be made out of half-burned paper, something between smoke and ash.

"Would you like to book a sample-collection trip?" the fish asked.

Nadice relaxed. The fish was an advertising gimmick, no different from an ad mask. Through the dust-filmed window next to the sign, she could make out a display case filled with the preserved skeletons and husks of various mutated animals and plants, presumably from the delta. Digital vidIOs and still-lifes papered the walls. Otherwise the place looked empty.

"Perhaps a sightseeing tour?"

Nadice shook her head. The fish sounded more like rote adware than a human-operated telepresence. But maybe it would be able to help. "I'm trying to find this place. Delta Blu's."

"It's not part of the regular package."

She shrugged—forget it—and walked away. Behind her, the whisper of the wings dimmed.

"Wait." The fish appeared next to her, its tail thrashing to match her pace. "I can help."

Right. "I don't have any money." She turned her attention to the flea-market stalls. Most of the tables were littered with junk. Secondhand clothing. Shoes. Dented, half-empty canisters of glues, sealants, lubricants. Old earbuds and goggles. Spare boat parts. She looked for someone who might be willing to give her directions. The faces she met were hard, the sidelong gazes they cast suspicious but opportunistic, searching for any opening or sign of weakness. She set her mouth in a tight line, jaw muscles bunching.

"I can take you there," the fish said.

She pried her gaze from the crowd and brushed at a loose strand of hair dislodged by the backwash from its tail and wings. "I already told you. I can't afford it."

"No problem," the fish said.

She shook her head. There had to be a reason, something the fish wanted from her in return.

"This way." The fish glided ahead of her, weaving its way through the open stalls the way it might a shipwreck.

A teenage boy grinned at her over a pile of electronic hardware, jade teeth flashing in the setting sun. A short, grizzled woman sized her up from behind racks of glass beads and handmade jewelry.

Nadice quickened her pace. "How far is it?"

"Not far."

The planks were uneven, made even more treacherous by an occasional undulation or sideways pitch that sent her stumbling. The aroma of pickled seaweed and cumin-spiced stir-fry drifted on competing strains of music. LED lights glowed to life in boat cabins, shacks, cafés, and nightclubs, growing brighter as the sky darkened from pale blue to periwinkle. The fish glimmered. Its white skeleton winked in and out under scales that alternated between opaque and clear, depending on how they caught the light.

As the heat of the day retreated, local residents emerged from the ramshackle woodwork to smoke, drink beer, play cribbage. Most wore caps, loose-fitting shirts, and pants, the cotton or bamboo fabric stained yellow by perspiration. A few were philmed in off the shelf downloads. Of those she recognized, F8, Forever Jung, and XXXodus were popular. Not much animé. Some Russian graffitika in hard-boiled grays and black.

"How much farther?" she asked.

"Almost there."

The fish veered right, onto a narrow footbridge. The bridge arched over a dank estuary. Two meters down, water stirred thick tangles of reeds, releasing the rank, turgid stench of garbage and organic decay. A sucking sound tugged at her, threatening to drag her into muddy depths. She quickened her pace and the bridge deposited her on an island crisscrossed with raised epoxy-board walkways— meandering paths that staggered from one stilt-supported hut to another.

The huts were dark, lit only by the stagnant light of the moon.

The fish took another right, onto warped planks that had been set directly on wet ground. Mud squished under her weight, releasing methane and thick, swirling clouds of mosquitoes.

Nadice stopped. Something didn't feel right. She didn't see a sign for Delta Blu's, no indication of any activity at all. The place was completely deserted. "Are you sure this is right?" she asked.

"It's just down here." The fish flipped in midair to face her.

Despite the muggy greenhouse heat, a sharp chill pricked Nadice's arms. "I don't think so." Throat tight, she backed away from the reed-constricted path.

A board creaked behind her. She swiveled, caught a toe on the upraised corner of one board, and stumbled.

Fingers wrapped tightly around her upper arm. She gasped just as a hand clamped over her mouth, stifling a scream.

"Easy, gurl." The voice like honey in her ear. "Don't flip on me."

Mateus.

She steadied in his grip, calmed by the familiar voice, and felt her chest relax. "You scared me."

"No reason to get throwed."

He was in full crunk mode, wired to the philm he was 'skinning. Back in Lagos she had noticed that whenever he was tight the slang got heavier, thicker, as he slipped deeper into the pseudoself he was screening.

"I wasn't sure where to go," she explained. "I thought I'd gotten lost."

"I feel ya."

"You could have told me about the fish," she said.

"Fish?" He shook his head. "No fish here. Maybe farther into the delta, where it ain't so polluted."

She looked around, but the fish was gone.

"Come on." He cut a quick glance around. "Let's get inside fo things get crucial."

————

A hand-scrawled sign on one boarded-up window advised visitors that Delta Blu's was closed. A thin man with nervous eyes and a bony Adam's apple let them into a windowless room filled with a maze of dark, soundproofed cubicles. The place reeked of mildew, sweat, and listless sex.

Something shifted in the cube closest to Nadice.

She flinched as a pair of blood-red circles swiveled to look at her.

The thin man snickered. As her eyes adjusted, the rings resolved into faint coronas of light leaking from around the edges of a pair of corneal inserts.

"Snippers," Mateus explained. "Cut images from digitized celluloid and vidIO for splicing and rephilming."

There was one snipper to a cubicle. Some lounged in chairs, others sprawled on gelfoam mattresses. Their expressions were slack, their faces spectral, as if they existed between worlds... neither substantial nor insubstantial, but ensnared in some hyperstantial netherworld.

Like the fish, she thought. Detached. Somehow it had gone from a flat picture to solid 3-D.

"You're pirates," she said. "Bootleggers."

The snicker degenerated into a snort. "What we are is none of your business," the man hissed. He stared at her chest and masturbated the stubble on his chin.

"In here," Mateus said. He guided her into a room filled with d-splays. A few of the screens depicted artistically rendered nudes and genitalia. Others were more hardcore. Across the dimly lighted hallway, through a partly open door, a naked woman lay on a futon. Japanese kanji crawled along the insides of her thighs, trickled down her abdomen like rainwater on neon-tinted glass. Instead of nipples, pink roses flowered from ceramic-smooth breasts.

Mateus appeared not to notice. She expected

some lewd comment, but suddenly he was all business. He closed the door, locking it.

"Sit down." He indicated a chair in the center of the room. "We need to check the status of the ware. See if it's ready." He went to a chrome equipment rack against one wall.

The chair looked clean, no obvious stains. There was even a little depression in which to rest her head. The padded armrests adjusted to her height. The chair tilted back, and she found herself staring up at a ruby-red mouth on a ceiling-mounted d-splay. She wet her lips and saw the tip of a tongue, her tongue.

"Relax," Mateus said, walking up to her. "You're tense."

He sounded different. He'd dropped the slang for some reason, the attitude. She lowered her gaze from the ceiling d-splay and saw he'd rephilmed himself. Gone were the crunk gang tattoos. The color of his 'skin had changed, too, lightened from burned coffee to pale pink.

She tightened her fingers on the armrest. "Who are you? Where's Mateus?" She hadn't heard the door open.

"Mateus is taking a short break. He'll be back as soon as we're done here."

She tried to sit up and found she couldn't. Invisible threads cobwebbed her nerves. He leaned close and his gaze pinned her, tugged on something embedded deep inside her, as if trying to pull it out.

Nadice drew a sharp breath.

"Don't worry." The man grinned, revealing rows of triangular teeth. "This won't hurt a bit."

She woke to a dull, bone-deep ache. Her mouth felt parched, her tongue swollen. It hurt to swallow, all the way to the base of her spine.

"What it do, gurl? How ya feelin'?"

Mateus bent over her. Nadice swallowed, forced a spike of air deep into her lungs. "What happened?"

"Ware ain't ready yet. Needs another day or two, I guess, before it's okay to rip it out. Too early, and it gets hulled."

"To you, I mean. Who was that guy?"

Mateus worked his jaw from side to side. "He works for the man."

"What man?"

"The one ballin' for this shit."

Her gaze drifted past him to the d-splays. "So what does that mean? What happens now?"

"Means we got to do this again in a couple days, gurl. Whenever we get the call. Feel me?"

"Then that's it, right? After that, we're done." She could put all this behind her.

"Not exactly."

Nadice stiffened. "You said this was it. All I'd have to do."

"I got another delivery to make." Mateus wet his lips. "In Singapore. You're the only mule I got available."

"We had an agreement."

"Shit happens, gurl." A resigned shrug in his voice. "You know how it is."

"No." Nadice went to push herself out of the chair. "You can find someone else."

Mateus gripped her arm. Hard. "You give me any

trouble on this, gurl, and I turn you in to Atherton. That what you want?"

She bit her lower lip against the pain. His grip tightened, squeezing tears from her eyes, until she finally shook her head.

His grip eased. "Good." He patted her. "That's what I like to hear."

11

"Nice philm," Marta said. "How long have you been waring it?"

Pelayo watched her twirl a partially empty water glass on the glossy green surface of the table between them. "Not long."

"Who's it supposed to be? Or is that some deep, dark secret you're not allowed to talk about?"

Pelayo spread his hands, *nolo contendre.*

They sat at a table in the Jade Dragon, a fast-food franchise where Little Shanghai rubbed shoulders with the Zona Sagrada. As expected, there were a lot of people philmed in Hip Sing and Fuk Ching gangware, along with the standard Bruce Lee, Jet Li, and Fu Manchu aficionados. Speakers from the ceiling blared music from an alt prog band called Bali Lama. The aroma of soy sauce seasoned with habañero peppers spiced the courtyard outside the main restaurant.

"New clothes, too," she observed. "They part of the 'skin? Or is that proprietary, too?"

Pelayo leaned forward and picked up the menu in front of him. The subwoof bass from the speakers kicked at his eardrums, heavy as steel-toed boots. "I saw Lagrante this morning," he said.

Ice rattled in the glass. "He rip the new ware?"

"He said you talked to him."

She shrugged, and he knew he'd touched a nerve. She watched him from behind a veil of indifference. He said nothing, content to wait her out, and after a moment she ran one finger along the curve of one ear, tucking back long black hair and exposing the lithe outline of her neck.

"You could have come to me," he said.

"No."

"Why not?"

She looked up from the glass. "None of your business."

Pelayo weighed her gaze, but couldn't tell if she was trying to protect him or avoid him. "I might be able to help," he said.

"What makes you think I need help? Your help?"

Good question. "What kind of trouble we talkin' about?"

She shook her head. "There's nothing you can do."

"How do you know?"

"Don't," she said.

"What?"

"Just leave me alone." The hair behind her ear slipped free, fell in a thick cascade across her face.

"If that's what you want." He set the menu down and slid the chair back, scraping loudly on the floor tile.

She jerked her head, tossing the hair back. "You don't know a goddamned thing," she said.

He eased back into the chair. "About what?"

"Anything."

Meaning her. Things had never gone the way he wanted between them. For some reason, they always ended up at odds. It had been that way for as long as he could remember, cousins that had almost, but never quite, kissed. "Lagrante didn't say shit. You wanna keep it that way, no problem."

"You're just jealous."

"Maybe," he conceded. Except that there was no maybe about it.

She let out a breath and, deflated, looked suddenly drawn and pale, perhaps even a little sick.

"You seem tired," he said, his voice softening.

"I'm fine," she snapped. But some of the rancor had bled from her. "I've been busy, that's all." She rested her head in her hands.

He fought the urge to reach out and touch her on one slender wrist. He might have been able to at one time, years ago. Not anymore. They'd settled into different orbits, any attraction between them more a perturbation of memory than anything else.

"Any word on Concetta?" She was peering at him from between her long, delicate fingers.

Pelayo shook his head, glad that she'd been the one to bring it up. "Not yet. Still waiting."

Marta made a face but seemed resigned. Not only had she expected this, Pelayo realized, she'd come to accept it.

Was that why Marta hadn't come to him? Because her sister had...and had never come back? How much did Marta know?

"I'm not the one who's in trouble," Marta said. "I'm just trying to help somebody out, is all."

"That sounds like Concetta. Not you."

"I don't think so."

"I do."

"It's not like that." She pulled her hair back from

her face and held it tight against the top of her head with both hands. "This is different."

We're different, she seemed to be saying...distancing herself from her sister.

"Help out how?" he asked. "New ware? Philm? DiNA?"

Marta smoothed her hands back, down to the base of her neck, and clasped them together. "Removal."

"Full strip?"

"Yeah. The 'skin's degrading. I don't know how long. A few days, week at the most before the neurotoxins kick in."

Pelayo shook his head. "That's not what Lagrante does."

"I know. But I thought he might be able to hook me up."

"And?"

She lowered her hands to the glass on the table. "He said he'd get back to me."

"Sounds familiar. How much is he charging?"

"He didn't say."

"In other words, expensive. I hope your friend's rich."

Marta stiffened. "She's not my friend."

A woman, then, not a man. "If she doesn't have any money, what do you or she have that a rip artist might be interested in as payment?"

Marta blinked. "What the hell's that supposed to mean?"

"You don't think Lagrante's above asking for payment in trade?" It was unfair, a low blow, but he wanted to shock her, help her understand exactly what she was getting into and what kind of people she was dealing with.

Marta's cheeks flushed. "Not everyone's a—" She bit her lip.

"Go ahead"—His fingers curled inward, digging into moist palms—"say it."

He knew what she was thinking. Slut. Whore.

Instead, she said, "You're pathetic," and got up, shoving the chair back so hard it toppled over, clattering against the table behind her.

The thudding beat covered most of the ruckus. But a few people turned, drawn to the commotion.

"At least I know who I am," she said. "What I want, who I want to be. Which is more than you can say."

Pelayo could feel eyes on them, curious to see how the telenovela would play out.

It didn't. He wouldn't let it. He remained in his seat, *omerta*, until she turned and stomped out.

So much for trying to scare some sense into her, prevent her from following in her sister's footsteps.

Pelayo stared down at his fists, clenched white-knuckle tight on the table, emptied of everything, including his anger.

12

From her executive office on the top floor of the Iosepa Biognost Tek building, Ilse Svatba could see beyond the seawall and the dervish lights of the Boardwalk to the far side of the Monterey Bay. A dagger of moonlight glinted on the water. It pierced the clear diamond window in front of her, slicing through the nanometer-thin film of graphene coating the surface.

Turn her back and the sterling dagger would still be there, aimed at a point directly between her shoulder blades.

Her neck prickled at the thought. It was a good reminder of the threats that lurked, waiting to strike, if she let down her guard.

A virtual d-splay appeared toward the bottom of her field of view, announcing the arrival of Giles Atherton.

She mirrored a section of the window, reflecting the office around her. Framed in Art Nouveau curlicues dolloped with pewter leaves, she considered her attire.

How to present herself for the meeting? That was the question.

She mentally opened a selection menu and canceled her current philm, a découpage of knitted bamboo fiber, copper foil, glass beads, and peacock feathers.

Should she go soft and voluptuous, lipstick smeared? Elegant waif? Or something more ostentatious?

She selected an outfit from IBT's upcoming Gil Elgren line of pinups. Black lace brassiere, fishnet stockings, garters.

She pirouetted, critical, gauging the effect.

No. Atherton was a sesquicentenarian—practically posthuman. The Betty Paige look would have little or no effect on him. Besides, she didn't want to taunt him, merely tantalize. And intimidate, it was true. Even if they were business partners, there was no sense giving him the upper hand.

She tried Alphonse Mucha next, replacing the black lace and fishnet with a diaphanous lavender gown. Ankle-length, sleeveless, her hair a thick flowering cascade of honeysuckle pink that caressed her neck and bare shoulders.

Too faery, she decided. It put *her* in the wrong mood.

In the end, she settled on Art Deco, circa 1928. A shift-style dress, mustard yellow, with a straight bodice and collar. Waistline near the hip. Hem pleated, falling to just below the knees. A matching bell cloche hat and lustrous pearl necklace completed the ensemble.

A perfect combination of sophisticated but sensual professionalism. She rephilmed the office next, replacing the Scandinavian wood floor with black-and-white checkerboard tiles. She papered the walls with a Poiret print of repeated parrots, rendered in flamboyant green and pink. Seashells scalloped the ceiling. For the light fixtures and door, she selected a stylized papyrus motif, articulated in classic Metyl-Wood veneer. Lastly she downloaded a new voice, something dusky, less puerile than her own nasal alto.

"All right," she announced, testing the voice. It curled around her, as sensuous as a midnight clarinet. "I'm ready."

Atherton was dressed in a tweed jacket with brown suede patches on both elbows, a paisley bow tie, flannel Oxford baggies, and loafers. His collar-length hair—parted marginally on one side—was tan, silver-streaked, and slightly unkempt. A pair of round wire-frame spectacles rode low on his tapered nose.

The style was professorial, she thought, intended to put her at ease by projecting an air of polite if effete intelligentsia. Instead, it came off as self-conscious, or self-indulgent. He didn't ware the look well, and seemed uncomfortable.

She took a small measure of satisfaction that his attire was out-of-date. Expensive, hand-tailored, but unlike hers his electronic skin didn't support programmable fabric.

For the moment, she had something he didn't. IBT was the only philm studio that could provide the technology and services he needed. That gave her the advantage in any confrontation.

Ilse smiled warmly and extended her hand.

"My dear." He bent to peck her hand. "A pleasure, as always."

"Likewise."

He straightened and stepped back. She withdrew

her hand, conscious of the saliva cooling on her skin. She should have worn gloves.

He appraised her, arching one brow inquisitively. "A beta version of the new ware, I presume."

She ran a hand down the front of the dress... relishing her role as model even as she mocked it. "Do you like it?"

He applauded her with a smile. "My compliments to the fashioneer. Does it meet spec?"

"Can I get you anything? Coffee. Tea?" She refused to let him dictate the pace of the conversation.

"Is that a no?"

She moved toward the safe haven of her desk. "It's a courtesy, Giles."

Atherton trailed impatiently after her. "I didn't come all the way up here to stand on ceremony, Ilse."

She sighed, as if indulging a child, then ran a fingertip along one Sphinx-bordered edge of the desk. "It's early in the test cycle."

"What does that mean?"

"Patience."

"By now you should have some preliminary data from the clinical trial."

Ilse turned to face him from behind her desk, fingers pausing delicately on polished ebony. "We're still in the process of 'skinning the first group of test subjects and acquiring feedback."

Atherton leveled his round wire-frames at her, sighting down the barrel of his nose. "But so far the interface is functional? Stable?"

"Uri's keeping a close eye on the situation. Rest assured, if there's any indication of a problem, I'll let you know."

Three years ago, Atherton Resort Hotels had contracted with IBT for an OEM 'skin, an original equipment manufacture that would support peer-to-peer shareware. Not only would users be able to philm themselves via standard download, they would be able to xfer images between one another. Combined with a rootkit neural interface, the result would be a shared sensory environment.

It had been a challenge. Atherton had provided the third-party wetronics for the new electronic skin. Adapting and integrating them into the existing graphene substrate of embedded nanofibers and quantum dots had been a nightmare. It had also, almost certainly, been illicit. Ilse felt certain the tronics were of foreign manufacture, probably black-market, and had been illegally imported.

Smuggled. There was no sense sugarcoating her involvement or the queasy legal ramifications.

That was one area where Atherton held the upper hand. From the beginning, she had made a conscious decision to assume that the project involved military or government interests and that a blind eye would be turned to any trade restrictions or national security violations. But she hadn't asked. Officially, she didn't know the third-party ware wasn't legal. She didn't want to know. Her only interest was in the financial and technological benefits IBT would realize from the project. Beyond that, she didn't care. It was none of her business.

"You'll keep me apprised," Atherton said.

"Of course."

"I'd like to review the preliminary data as soon as it becomes available," he said, brushing aside her reassurance.

"Certainly."

"By the way"—he tipped his head at her dress—"how's the new line progressing?"

The question took her by surprise. "Fine. On schedule."

"Do you have a release date?"

She flapped a vague hand. "General availability is in a few weeks. Why?"

He shrugged. "Just curious." He seemed almost embarrassed.

Her gaze sharpened. "You wouldn't be trying to wheedle a pre-GA copy? Would you?"

"Of course not." He held up both hands and beat a hasty retreat. "Nothing of the sort."

She let a sly smile, bordering on conspiratorial, creep into place. "I may be able to arrange it."

He shook his head, then quickly made his way to the door, as if he had overstayed his welcome. "I'll be in touch."

She nodded and watched him leave, wondering what had he neglected to tell her.

———

Giles Atherton emerged from the IBT building... and found himself caught in a smart mob on Pacific Avenue. One of those crowds that suddenly formed, for no apparent reason, around an event.

Typically they were the result of advertising—some biochemically or electronically mediated urge that people spontaneously, thoughtlessly, responded to. No different from a simple micro-organism.

He hated smobs, it was like stepping into a seething

colony of bacteria. Information exchange. Quorum sensing. Kin selection. Group swarming.

His cheeks flushed, then prickled. Sweat broke out, and festered in his armpits and on the nape of his neck. His scalp began to itch.

He cupped a hand over his nose and mouth to ward off a plume of incense from an aromatherapy vendor.

Where the hell was Uri? He coughed, a real lung scraper, and searched the cars on the street. The skintech had insisted on seeing him immediately after the meeting with Ilse. They needed to talk, Uri had said, presumably about something that could only be discussed in person.

A crowd of Lost Boys and Gashlycrumb Tinies formed around him, seemingly out of nowhere.

Eyes watering, Atherton bulled his way through the smob. He loosened his tie and collar, and hunched his shoulders against the suffocating press.

He passed a clot of Transcendental Vibrationists. The TVs sat in the middle of the sidewalk, shaking tambourines, beating drums and chanting. An accordionist, philmed as a Day of the Dead skeleton wearing a leather vest, sombrero, and cowboy boots, regaled him from the recessed entrance to an office building. Several steps farther on, the haunting notes of a harmonica unfurled from a breezeway between two buildings. Peals of childish laughter echoed off the barrel vault overhead, where a clown was twisting balloons into animals.

The cacophony washed over him, followed by a wave of dizziness. Nausea boiled up from his bowels. He choked on a lungful of air and felt his gorge rise against the smell of pickled seaweed being sold at a nearby Sue-Shē kiosk.

"Relax," he told himself through gritted teeth. "Breathe."

Three Barbies approached, long-legged, with unnaturally large breasts, and coiffed hair. One of the young women cut a passing glance at him.

"Apphia?" he said.

The Barbie quickened her pace, heels sharp. Atherton, tasting bile, stumbled after her. "Apphia. Wait."

The girl spun, defiant. "Leave me alone, you fucking perv. Before I call the police on your ass."

It wasn't his daughter. It couldn't be. Apphia would never speak that way. Not to him, or anyone else. He'd raised her better than that.

"My mistake," he muttered, apologetic.

"No shit," the girl said, spitting the words. Full of spite for him, or whatever she thought he represented.

Bent over the dagger of pain in his stomach, Atherton watched her hurry to catch up to her friends. When she was gone, disappeared into the crowd, he glanced around, disoriented, uncertain where he was. He didn't recognize any of the storefronts. The street names were unfamiliar. Suddenly it felt like he was the one who was lost, not Apphia. His faith was being tested, not hers.

He had to believe that his daughter would find her way back. Her repudiation of him wasn't a repudiation of God. It was the messenger she hated, not the message. Jesus would shepherd her back, return her to the fold. To doubt this was to doubt God, a failure on his part.

Still, a lost sheep should be searched for. It was an act not only of duty, but of love. Without that there could be no forgiveness. No reconciliation.

A low-slung Mitsubishi sedan eased up to the curb next to him and glided to a stop. The passenger door slid open. Inside, Uri, dressed as a Russian Mafioso in black denim, gestured for him impatiently.

Breathing heavily, Atherton slumped into black contoured leather and leaned his head back against the cushioned rest. The ceiling and dash were brushed stainless steel, inlaid with green tourmaline, the diamond windows and adjustable frame fully programmable and stealth-enabled.

"What are you doing all the way down here?" the skintech asked.

Atherton dismissed the question with a brusque wave of one hand. "You're late," he said.

"Traffic was heavy."

"Just get us out of here," Atherton said. He shut his eyes, feeling suddenly weary.

The sedan slid away from the curb and commotion.

"How did the meeting go?" Uri said.

"Fine." At last, Atherton could breathe again. The ache in his stomach and the pressure in his chest were easing. He opened his eyes. "I asked when the new fashion ware was due out."

"And?"

"She didn't connect it to the beta test. She thought I was interested in obtaining a prerelease of the philm."

Uri's lip twisted in a smirk. "That sounds like

her. Self-centered bitch. Thinks the world revolves around her."

"She was philmed in one of the new dresses. That made things a lot easier. Less suspicious." Atherton fixed him with a pointed gaze. "Right now, I'm far more worried about you."

The sneer slipped from Uri's face. From his shirt pocket he produced a small vial containing a barely visible biopsy chip.

Atherton took the vial for closer inspection. "Is this it?"

"The quantum-coupled switches aren't completely in phase yet," Uri said. "They're in the final stages of becoming coherent." He had been enthusiastic all along—something about a stable electron tunnel in the quantum circuitry—convinced from the beginning that the quantronics he'd obtained from a fly-by-night research lab would prove viable in vivo. "As soon as the resonance state is stable we can integrate the circuitry into the production release of the 'skin."

"How long are we talking?"

"A day or two."

"So"—Atherton shifted his attention from the vial to Uri—"what's the problem?"

A muscle in the side of Uri's face twitched. Once. Twice. "One of the initial test subjects died. Earlier today. I don't have the exact time of death."

Atherton closed his eyes, stared into the darkness for a moment. "How?"

"I'm not sure. I just found out about it a couple of hours ago. The cause of death hasn't been determined."

The burning sensation in Atherton's stomach

rekindled, along with the pressure in his chest. He squeezed the vial, then reopened his eyes.

Uri wet his lips. "It might not have been the ware."

"But it could have been."

Uri nodded. "That's what I need to find out."

Atherton relaxed his grip on the vial. "What about the mule? Is she going to be a problem, too?"

Uri shook his head cautiously. "I don't think so. She should be easy to keep quiet. Her handler might be more difficult."

"Why? What happened?"

They were cruising through a quiet neighborhood known as the Jewel Box, because the streets were named after gems: Garnet, Emerald, Agate. The houses were midtwentieth-century modern. Frank Lloyd Wright, Walter Gropius, Le Corbusier.

"Nothing," Uri said. "I just don't trust him."

A lie. Atherton could smell it on the skin-tech's breath, sour and clammy. Uri had done something—or knew something—he was keeping to himself. That might be for the best. Then again, maybe not.

"Don't worry," Uri said, "nothing will get out of hand."

Atherton decided to back off. For the time being. He returned the vial. "Tell me about this phemeticist you've contacted."

"Zhenyu al-Fayoumi." Uri pocketed the vial. "I'm meeting him tonight."

Once the quantum component was in place and bootleg copies of IBT's new 'skin became widely available on the street, they needed to know what was likely to happen as the shareware spread—what patterns and modalities of behavior would emerge. For that, they needed a whole new set of mathematical tools and evolutionary models.

"You're sure about him?" Atherton said. "He knows what he's doing? He can be trusted?"

Uri chafed. "The Lamarckian inheritance of acquired traits was disproved over a hundred years ago. As a theory, it's considered a joke—synonymous with quack science."

"I fail to see how that proves he can keep his mouth shut and do what he's told."

"He can't talk about he's working on. No one in the scientific community would take him seriously. He'd be a laughingstock."

"You're saying he has a chip on his shoulder—something to prove."

"If he says anything, he'll be risking his job and his reputation. He's not going to take that chance. This is an opportunity to pursue a line of inquiry that would otherwise get him discredited."

Atherton pressed his lips into a tight line. "I don't like being used as a means to someone else's end."

"You're worried he'll try to take advantage of the situation?"

"I refuse to be held hostage."

"That's not going to happen. If he's our best option, we're also his. Outside of us, there's no one he can turn to."

"All right." Atherton worked his jaw from side to side. "Just make sure you keep a tight leash on him."

Uri touched the tip of his tongue to his teeth. "You aren't the only one who doesn't want to get bit."

"And find out what happened to that test subject." That, more than anything, had him on edge.

"Is that it?" Uri said after a short pause.

"For now."

The Mitsubishi slowed to a stop next to a deserted sidewalk near the yacht harbor. They were still a long way from the Boardwalk. But even from this distance, music flayed the damp air, brash as the neon/LED glare that detonated off the bellies of low-hanging clouds.

"I'll let you know how it goes in the morning," Uri said. He eased out of the car and dissolved into the night like venom in dark, oily water.

13

Judy's Garlands was back in business. A month ago, the salon had been closed by the San Francisco health inspector for running an illegal bathhouse and 'skin parlor out of the basement. To van Dijk, it looked like the salon was on the up-and-up, back to hairstyling, nails, nanimatronics, and minor cosmetic surgery.

For the moment. It wouldn't be long before the 'skin parlor was back in operation. The owner didn't have much choice. Not if he wanted to stay in business. There were thousands of unlicensed 'skintubs in back rooms, frequented by philmheads who couldn't afford to go to a regulated parlor or wanted cracked ware and bootleg philm they couldn't get legally.

Dirty 'skin was becoming more common, resulting in a rash of medical problems—everything from eczema and cyte infections to neurological disorders.

The cosmeticians were all philmed as Judy Garland, each from a different film. *A Star Is Born. Meet Me in St. Louis. Till the Clouds Roll By. Ziegfeld Follies, Ziegfeld Girl.*

The receptionist at the front desk wore a white blouse and a blue skirt, hair parted and pulled back.

His complexion was soft, his eyes luminous. Van Dijk didn't recognize the musical.

"*Babes on Broadway?*" he ventured.

"*In Arms,*" the man said in a suggestive, if somewhat scratchy, singsong. Evidently, he took pleasure in the vaguely sexual hiss, or didn't want a digitally remastered version of her voice that wasn't absolutely authentic and true to the real Judy.

Van Dijk nodded. "Harvey around?"

The receptionist cocked his head and introduced a flirtatious sashay into the voice. "Who shall I say is calling?"

"Andy Hardy."

The receptionist gave him a florid eye roll. "Don't tell me. *Meets Debutante.*"

Van Dijk smiled. "*Love Finds.*" The only other movie in the long-running Andy Hardy series that starred Judy Garland.

The receptionist spread his hands, *c'est la vie,* like the wings of a flamingo. "Do you have an appointment?"

"Walk-in." Van Dijk flashed his badge. At the same time he transmitted a DiNA verification code to the building security.

The receptionist pouted as he was autonotified of the verification. "In that case, do you have a warrant?"

"It's not that kind of visit." Van Dijk made his way past the desk and the Harvey Girls, as they liked to call themselves, busy with customers at their styling stations. Six Judys turned to eye him with petulant disapproval. They glared, but said nothing as he mounted the narrow stairs to the second floor.

"You could have at least philmed yourself for the part," Harvey said from behind an old wooden desk. Reproductions of Judy Garland movie posters papered the walls of the office. *The Harvey Girls*, wholesome and sumptuous, were the focus of the room, center stage behind the desk and larger than life.

Van Dijk shrugged. "You know me. I hate to give the wrong impression."

Harvey scowled. As usual, he'd philmed himself as John Hodiak, the male lead in the poster, with black hair and a thin, swallowtail mustache. He wore a black jacket, a white starched shirt, and a shiny red silk tie. "Is that what this is about?" he asked. "False pretenses?"

Van Dijk eased into a low-slung chair, chrome-framed with leopard-spot fabrique that stiffened under his weight. Through the big window next to him, the only one in the room, he caught swirling fog-obscured glimpses of the Tenderloin's cabaret and bordello cinescape. The district was heating up for the evening, glowing with sultry reds and hot pinks. "You tell me."

"I've got nothing to hide. I'm clean."

"I can see that." Van Dijk crossed an ankle over one knee, then tented his fingers under his chin.

After a beat, Harvey sighed in resignation and grudgingly slipped into his uncomfortable role as police informant. "I suppose you want to know if I know anything about that girl who died."

"Well?"

"What do you think?"

"I didn't figure her for one of yours." Judy's Garlands was strictly Y-chromo. "But if you think that means you're off the hook, think again."

Harvey shook his head. "I don't know where she got 'skinned. Or what she was waring."

"But you'd know if there was bad 'skin going around."

"Business has been pretty clean of late."

"What about bad blood?"

Harvey smoothed his mustache with deft strokes of one index finger, first the left side, then the right. "Always bad blood. You know that."

"Bad enough to kill?"

"Word I'm getting from some of the cinematiques is that she was new to the club scene."

"How new?"

"Hard to say. Couple of months, maybe. Give or take."

"So she was trying to break into the trade as a dancer, sex worker, whatever, and no one knows who she was or where she was from."

"You know how it is in this business. Everyone is someone else—and no one is who they say they are."

"I also know that if you don't put out," Van Dijk said, "you're shut out."

Harvey squirmed. "All I've heard are the usual rumors, that's all. Nothing out of the ordinary."

"Such as?"

"You know." Harvey waved a vague hand. "The 'skin she was waring was totally new. High-end. All of the rip artists wanted to get into her pants. But she wasn't putting out. That might have pissed some people off."

"New ware from who?" There were hundreds of philm studios releasing updated 'skin and downloads. For every legit shop, there were thousands of illegal ones.

Harvey shrugged. "Good question. That would imply intimate information about something I'm no longer involved in."

"You've always been a very intimate girl."

Harvey flounced dark lashes. "But very circumspect." He dimpled his left cheek with a fingertip. "Or is it 'cised? I can never remember."

Van Dijk leaned forward. "This is not the time to play hard to get. I'm not in the mood."

"You never are." Harvey sniffed. "Party pooper."

"I'm serious."

"Uptight, darling. But who's splitting hairs?"

Very slowly, van Dijk puckered his lips and kissed the air between them.

Harvey affected an air of exasperation. "Why do I always have to be the one to tell? What's in it for me?"

"Depends."

"That's what you said last time, and look what happened. I get raided and closed down."

"I know. I feel bad about what happened. But sometimes there's only so much a guy can do to protect a girl."

"Oh, all right." Harvey sighed. "IBT. They're on everybody's lips these days. I don't know why. If you ask me their stuff is crap, hopelessly derivative. But I suppose there's no accounting for bad taste."

———

In his car, van Dijk got a call from Kostroff. He routed her to a d-splay on the inside of his windshield.

"You're not going to like this," the medical examiner said.

"Tell me something I don't know."

Kostroff blew at a strand of hair that had curled around one corner of her mouth. "Cause of death in your stiff was acute neuroleptic shock, leading to sudden respiratory and cardiac arrest."

"Her nervous system failed?"

"Shut down, suddenly and catastrophically."

"How?"

"Basically neurotransmission in her central nervous system was hyperpolarized—inhibited —immediately prior to death."

"By what? Toxins?"

Kostroff shook her head. "All the blood and tissue work came back negative for toxicity."

"So what are we looking at?"

"Something in the 'skin. It's got wetronic hooks into her peripheral and central nervous systems."

"What kind of hooks?"

"Nothing I've ever seen. I'm going to notify NTSI. At this point, it looks more like their baby."

Nanotechnological Systems Investigation handled everything from designer drugs to illegal ware, including street-kinked 'skin and dirty grafts. Since the forensics pointed to a cause of death other than homicide, the case was no longer his. He could wash his hands.

"There're couple of other things I found," Kostroff said, "which may or may not be important."

"What's that?"

"She was carrying a lot of dormant REbots. Mostly in the face. It appears that the bots took bone from her nose and cheeks and redistributed it to other parts of her skeleton for reuse."

"Nanoplasty for the 'skin." It was a high-end modification that made it possible for a person to alter their physiology to more closely imitate the appearance of the philm they were screening.

Kostroff nodded. "She was also pregnant."

Van Dijk took a moment to let this sink in. "How far along?"

"I'm not sure. The baby was . . . abnormal. I'm not even sure it was alive, strictly speaking."

"Abnormal how?"

"Fully formed and properly proportioned, for its size. More like a scaled-down version of an adult than a fetus."

Van Dijk raised his brows. "Piecework?"

"That's what I'm thinking. The infant, if you can call it that, was also 'skinned." Kostroff gnawed a corner of one lip. "It's almost as if the fetus was being used as a culture, to grow the 'skin."

"Any DNA from the fetus?" he asked hopefully.

Kostroff shook her head. "NOF."

So he wouldn't be able to identify the victim that way. Even if she had gone to a legal piecework clinic that kept DNA records, they would be confidential. He'd need a court order, and at this point he didn't have enough probable cause.

After Kostroff logged off, van Dijk stared at his reflection in the windshield, pale and spectral against the cabaret of street LEDs and blinking ad-casts.

The girl. Lisette. He needed to find her. She had seen something—or someone—she shouldn't.

Why else would she run?

14 Nadice felt queasy. The trip to Dockton had left her shaken. So had lack of food. The shelter stopped serving at seven and she'd been forced to go to the Tandoori Express down the street.

Surely a solid meal would help. But standing in line, her guts recoiled at the aroma of warm chicken, chutney, and curried rice.

She clutched her plate, certain she was going to vomit on the elderly woman in line in front of her. The woman hunched over the buffet, oblivious, neck and shoulders curled by osteoporosis.

Nadice tried to tell herself the nausea would pass in a couple of minutes. She was tired, exhausted, that was all. It had been a long day. Stressful. She just needed a minute or two for her nerves to settle.

She eased out of line, made her way to an empty table, and cradled her head in her hands. The nausea abated some, enough for her to take a few tentative sporkfuls of curry. But the queasiness lurked at the bottom of her throat, and after a moment she pushed the plate aside.

It was more than nerves or not enough to eat. The 'skin was beginning to tox her. Under the ceiling lights, it looked poisonously dull and cloudy. She had been planning to take the inhibitor after the

trip to Dockton. But with the ware still in her, she
had to wait. Another day or two, Mateus had said.
She wasn't sure she could hang on that long. She
stared at the bamboo-patterned floor tile, unable to
look at the frenzied ad clips that kept appearing on
the veneer of the table. "IBT—fashioning the future." "Vurtronic...so real it's reel." "Snap Dragon
Karate, where open hands lead to open hearts."

"Mind if I join you?"

Nadice looked up. A man stood across the table
from her. He wore black jeans, a faded denim shirt,
had a neatly trimmed goatee and a shaved head. His
eyes were a quiet blue, swirling with specks of white
like the flurries in a snow globe. Her gaze slid to his
hands, tucked into the pockets of his pants.

"I've already eaten," he explained. He removed
his hands from his pockets, as if to prove he had
nothing to hide.

Nadice offered a vague nod, which the man
seemed to interpret as an invitation to join her.

"Jeremy," he said.

"Nadice."

They shook. His hand was warm and dry, and
didn't linger too long. She noticed his nails were
philmed the same pacific blue as his eyes. For some
reason it didn't bother her. Perhaps because she was
too exhausted to feel anything but sick.

"I saw you at the shelter," he said.

Was he hitting on her? She couldn't tell. He
seemed more curious than anything.

He nodded at her half-finished plate. "Didn't care
for what they were serving up back at the cafeteria?"

"Not really." No way she was going to get into
where she'd been and why.

He nodded sympathetically. "It can take a little getting used to. Especially if it's your first time."

He seemed to know a lot about her, more than she was comfortable with. Her left knee bounced under the edge of the table. "I guess."

"I assume you've met Sister Giselle."

"We talked, yeah."

He placed his elbows on the table and threaded his hands together. "What do you think of her?"

"She seems nice enough and all."

"Yes."

She got the feeling he was prompting her, expecting her to say more. "For a nun, I mean. I don't really know her."

"Of course not. Let's hope it stays that way."

Nadice blinked, uncertain what he was implying.

"Don't get me wrong. It's a great place. Clean, and well run. But you don't want to get stuck here long term."

"No."

"All I'm saying"—he leaned closer, lowering his voice—"she's not the only game in town. You have other options."

She shook her head numbly, feeling stupid, confused. She was missing something.

"I can help you," he said. "With the baby."

"I'm not—"

"You're not the first to end up here," he continued. "Believe me. That's why I'm talking to you."

"I'm fine." Nadice smoothed her thighs with flattened palms. "I can take care of myself."

"I know you can." He spread his hands, as if conceding the point "Otherwise you wouldn't have found your way to the shelter."

"You don't know anything about it." Or me, she thought.

"I know it won't be easy. You'll need prenatal scans. Help with delivery. Drugs."

His bluntness unnerved her. She didn't feel menaced...in danger, or anything—just out of sorts, nudged from her center of gravity. "What're you saying?"

"If you're under contract, I can buy it out. If you need protection, no problem. If necessary, I can even arrange to have you naturalized."

And in return... "Who are you?" she demanded. "What do you want?"

The flurries continued to swirl in his eyes, gently, patiently. "Your baby is special. Wouldn't you agree?"

She said nothing. What did he expect her to say? Still, he didn't seem to be patronizing her. The question wasn't entirely rhetorical.

"I have reason to believe that your baby might be unique," he went on. "A miracle one might say. I want to make sure that miracle is given the best possible chance at life."

In a sickening rush, it came to her. He wanted her to sell her baby, or give it up for adoption.

"No," she said, pushing her chair back, away from him.

"You can't have the baby here," he said. "Where will you go? Whatever company you work for will pressure you to abort. So that's not an option. The father? If there is one, he isn't an option, either. Am I right? If there isn't one..." His voice trailed off, but his gaze didn't falter. It blanketed her, enfolding her.

He knew. Somehow, he could tell there was no father. That she had conceived on her own.

"Think about it," he said. "That's all I ask." He reached across the table, took one hand, and pressed something into it, curling her fingers around the little object.

"You're not alone," he said, standing. "There are others just like you. Remember that."

And then he was gone. Nadice unfolded her sweaty hand. A polymer-coated combead the size and color of a pomegranate seed nestled in her palm.

Her head spun. When he said there were other women like her, did he mean other virgin pregnancies? If so, how many? Where? What was happening? *How* was it happening? The questions somersaulted inside her, leaving her motion sick and confused.

"Damn TVs," someone said loudly, pointedly.

Nadice jerked her head up. She'd been staring blankly at her bowl.

Two men stood at the far end of the table. Each held a bowl of soup and a package of crackers. They looked like temporary guest workers in their jeans and steel-toed Timbo boots, but underneath they were pure crunk.

"Fuckin' waveheads. In here ridin' dick. Knowmsayin? Bumpin' off at the mouth an kissin ass."

"Fasho."

They didn't look in her direction. But they seemed to be talking to her as much as each other.

"I can't believe they let 'em in here. He comes back slangin' that shit, I'm a gonna get off in *his* shit."

His companion nodded as the two sat. "Bet. I gotcha, bruh."

"Things are gonna get crucial around here. No way that motherfuck is gonna hull this place."

A Transcendental Vibrationist. That was who'd sat down with her. All of the TVs she'd ever seen wore robes. This one had been different, polite, not pushy. Still . . .

She looked at the bead in her hand, then stood and pushed her chair from the table. As she passed a trash can, she paused, her hand near the opening.

She was doing fine. She didn't need any more help. She was safe. She had Sister Giselle and the other social workers to protect her. There was no reason to go anyplace else. Plus, the TV's interest in her baby seemed odd, unnatural. And yet he'd known there was no father. And he had treated her with respect. Not like a freak.

"You gonna pick your ass crack all day?"

Nadice flinched as a six- or seven-year-old boy prodded her in the back of the thigh with a spork. The bead slipped from her hand.

"Leave her alone," the small girl with him said. She sniffed, and rubbed her mucus-glazed nose with the back of her hand.

The boy ignored his younger sister, keeping his attention fixed on Nadice. "What's the matter? You a 'tard or somethin'?"

Nadice listened to the bead skitter across the floor—tick . . . tick . . . tick—then fall silent.

A sign? The bead had come to a rest in the corner, lodged in a grimy crack in the floor. Pick it up? No, she decided. It wasn't worth it. She'd find the answers to all the questions she had someplace else.

Nadice woke to muted shouting. Faint...down the hall somewhere. She imagined one of the elderly residents wandering the floor, confused and afraid, lost in an Alzheimer's-fueled panic.

The commotion grew louder. Not only that, it was headed her way. She sat up on her futon. Moonlight sifted through the window closest to her, projecting a grid of bleary lines on the far wall. Soft, stirring noises came from the other side of the partition, stifled whispers thick with anxiety, followed by hushed reassurances. At some point during Nadice's absence, a family had replaced the old woman who had shared the room with her.

Intermittent words punctuated the disturbance, urgent and sweaty:

"...know you're here..."

The voice sounded familiar. No, she thought wildly. It wasn't possible. Not here.

"...room...every one if I have to..."

Mateus. He sounded drunk, angry. How had he found her? How had he gotten into the shelter? Nadice thought about the crunkheads in the fast-food buffet. Coincidence? It didn't seem likely.

"...goddamnit...where are you?..."

She couldn't tell where his voice was coming from. It caromed off the walls, like a reflection in a room full of fun-house mirrors.

Where was Sister Giselle...the night staff? Someone must be on duty. Surely they had called the police.

A door banged open and someone screamed. There was a brief scuffle, then a thud shook the walls.

Nadice felt the shudder reverberate inside her. She rose, placing a hand against the fabric of the acoustic partition to steady herself. On the other side, the man comforted his wife, rocking her, stroking her hair.

"It's okay," he soothed. "There's nothing to be afraid of. We're safe. It's not him. Trust me."

She couldn't stay here. She had to leave. She made her way to the door, slowly at first, then more quickly. Gripping the knob tightly, she steeled herself, then turned the handle and peeked out.

Mateus stood across the hallway to her left, next to an open door less than ten meters away. He was flanked by the two crunkheads. They formed a loose circle around a man who sat slumped against the wall. A woman wrapped in a pink nightgown huddled in the doorway, sniffling.

"Shut the fuck up!" Mateus shouted, discharging flecks of pink-colored spit under the muted LED hall lights.

The woman flinched but continued to whimper.

"Leave her alone," Nadice said. She stepped into the hallway and closed the door softly behind her.

Mateus turned. " 'Bout time."

"What do you want?"

He nodded at the crunks and walked toward her. "Let's go."

"Where?"

His breath stank of cheap wine. "Wherever the fuck I say." He caught her by the arm.

"I need my stuff," she said, stalling.

"Forget it." His fingers pressed into her biceps. "We'll get you new stuff."

Several more doors on the floor had opened. Out

of the corner of her eye, people emerged, some sleep-addled, others irritated, belligerent. They coalesced into a smob of sorts in the middle of the hall.

A stocky, thickset Japanese man stepped forward. "Is there a problem?" He wore black drawstring baggies, a black leather jacket, and a green turban. In his right hand he carried a flute made out of a sawed-off length of white PVC pipe.

"No problem," Mateus said. "Go back to sleep."

"What's going on?" Nadice asked. She kept her voice reasonable and composed, trying to instill some measure of calm into the situation.

He slapped her, his open hand catching the side of her head. She winced, resisting the urge to touch the welt left by one of his rings.

"Keep it down," someone in back shouted.

"Yeah," another voice said. "Take it outside."

Nadice dry swallowed. Her tongue felt anesthetized. "All right," she said, hoping to buy time. If she dragged her feet...

She allowed him to guide her down the stairs. The crunkheads trailed several steps after them, interposing themselves between Mateus and the smob. More people had gathered on the first floor. No police or private security. What was taking them so long?

Outside the air was cool. Her arm ached where he clutched it. "What's wrong? I thought we had until tomorrow or the next day."

The crunkheads grinned at her, then sauntered casually in the direction of a quick mart across the street.

"I want you close by," Mateus said.

"Why?"

He mumbled something under his breath and an

empty transit car detached and sidled up to the curb next to them.

"Get in."

He was afraid, Nadice realized, of something or someone. "What have you done?" she asked.

He shoved her into the car. She sprawled across the padded seats. By the time she righted herself, he'd joined her and pulled the door shut.

He gave her a feral look, his eyes illuminated by the d-splays, ad masks, and nanoFX decals fighting for attention on the interior philm of the car. "Just keep your mouth shut. Don't make things worse for yourself."

She nodded mutely. Her mind raced as the car scooted into traffic, searched for a stopped, available bus, then slotted into place behind a pair of identical cars attached to the segmented frame. Through the tinted bubble windows she could see passengers in the shared interior of the bus, which was devoted to overflow passengers, people waiting to board one of the other detachable cars as their destinations approached.

He wasn't going to kill her, she reasoned. Not yet. He needed her alive. At least for a while. But that didn't mean he couldn't hurt her—cripple her if he thought she was planning to run. That must be what he was worried about. Nadice taking off, cutting him loose and selling the ware to the highest black-market bidder. He was protecting his investment, nothing more. It wasn't personal, it was business.

The bus rocked from side to side. It slithered like a caterpillar through LED-lighted intersections, past apoplectic neon signs that smeared her retinas with blues, reds, yellows, and greens.

Nadice clutched her stomach. "I think I'm going to be sick."

"Sure you are."

She retched, splashing the seat and floor of the car.

Mateus jerked to his feet. "Sumbitch...!" He swore, and the door to the inside of the bus hissed open.

Bile burned her nose. Her eyes watered under the warm, sour smell of undigested chicken and rice.

He grabbed her by one wrist and half dragged, half flung her from the car into the center section. She hit somebody in the back, a teenage kid, felt the air go out of him and Mateus's handcuff-firm hold on her relax. She slipped free and found herself on her knees, feet all around her, dancing to get out of the way. A sharp heel gouged the side of her thumb, tearing skin. She tucked in her fingers and crawled. N-zymes kept the rubberized floor relatively clean, but someone spilled tea on her back. She flung herself to the side, into a shuffle of plastic sandals and rubber-soled shoes. She elbowed shins and knees to avoid being trampled, flailed at the tail of an ankle-length coat that billowed against her face.

"...fuck outta my way!" Mateus said, not far behind her.

"Bite me, asswipe."

Nadice raised herself onto her hands and knees. Just across the aisle, the door to a six-person car opened. Nadice twisted her head. Over her shoulder, less than two meters away, she picked out Mateus's vomit-stained boots.

Blood hammered inside her chest. She lunged into the car. "Excuse me...Sorry."

"...got you..."

Hands reached down, catching her, pulling her in, away from the door sliding shut on Mateus's stunned, livid face.

"...okay?" a man asked.

Nadice nodded numbly, and his face retreated. The passengers were part of some Renaissance cast. Their complexions reminded her of candle-lit wax, luminous in places and brooding in others, smudged with shadows. The women wore white pleated blouses with blue skirts, the men black vests and bunched brown pants.

"Here." An older woman offered her a plain vetiver-scented handkerchief edged with lace.

"Thank you."

Nadice daubed the handkerchief to her mouth and watched Mateus's face recede as the car detached from the bus and turned onto a side street.

———

She couldn't go back to the shelter. The crunkheads would be waiting. Still, her shoes and jacket were there. She couldn't spend the night barefoot, with no way to keep warm.

Nadice watched the building from the old shopping center across the intersection, hidden in the doorway to a Honey B's hair salon.

What now? Another shelter was out of the question. If Mateus had found her at this one, how hard would it be to hunt her down at another?

Her bare feet were cold. She stamped them on the rough concrete, then leaned against the honeybee appliqués decorating the boutique's plate diamond window. Her thoughts drifted to the ware she carried.

What would it do to her if she didn't get rid of it when she was supposed to and it stayed in her system too long? Would it harm her? The baby? If she knew who Mateus was working for—the person who had examined her in Dockton?—she could go directly to him. But she didn't know. Mateus had kept her in the dark.

He would find her eventually. He had probably tagged her with some sort of GPS or nanological locator. He was smart that way. Except if he'd tagged her, why would he want her close to him? Was he afraid that someone else, a competitor, might try to steal the ware?

If she was smart, she would walk back to the shelter and wait for him to return. She could make up a story, say that it was an accident, a mistake . . . and hope he believed her.

She shivered, closed her eyes for a second while she rubbed her arms and debated her options.

"Hi."

Nadice jumped at the small but sharp voice.

"I scared you. Sorry." It was the little girl from Tandoori Express. She stood a few feet away, tentative, hands twisting the wrinkled hem of her shirt.

"Not your fault. I'm just tired, that's all." Nadice put on a smile. "So what are you doing out here? Where's your brother?"

"The bee said I should come see you."

Nadice searched the girl's expression, saw nothing but sincerity. "What bee?" she said carefully.

The girl pointed at the window, where one of the appliqués had apparently freed itself.

Like the fish in Dockton. She watched the bee methodically flatten itself into the pane, tail first, like something out of an M. C. Escher print she'd once seen. Lizards. Half-in the paper and half-out. Goose bumps pimpled her arms. "Why did it say you should see me?"

"So I could give you your earring." She held up the red bead Nadice had dropped, pinching it between nail-bitten fingers.

Nadice took the bead. "Thank you."

The bee was totally flat now, no different from any of the other nanoFX appliqués.

First the fish, now the bee.

"I have to go," the girl said. "Or my brother will be mad."

"Wait," Nadice said, reaching out . . .

But the girl had turned and was already scampering across the street, racing back to the shelter.

What the hell, Nadice thought. She had nothing to lose.

Fingers trembling, she pressed the combead into the nanosocket port Atherton Resort Hotels had installed in the lobe of her left ear.

15

Marta sat in her locked room, staring at the scratched and tarnished shortwave she had dug out of the closet.

The radio was a Grundig Satellit 800 Millennium with an oversized telescopic whip antenna, fully extended, and a broken LCD screen the color of dull aluminum. She'd plugged the headset in, but for some reason couldn't force herself to place the phones over her ears. Faint static came through the headset. The hiss reminded her of the low, faraway roar in a seashell.

If she didn't listen, it wasn't real. Marta could pretend her father had imagined the voice. Maybe he had. The display was dead. Other than the background hiss, there was nothing. All she could hear were his snores through the thin wall.

How did that saying go? If a tree falls in the forest and there's no one to hear it . . . ?

She clasped her hands between her legs, squeezing them tight with her knees. It had been over an hour since she got home from the Jade Dragon, and by now most of her anger had finally run its course, leaving her disconsolate.

Pelayo could be such a hypocrite sometimes. She couldn't believe him, telling her to stay away from Lagrante when he did business with the rip artist all the time. What an asshole.

After she'd left the restaurant, she'd been afraid Pelayo would come after her. Then, she'd been pissed that he hadn't, because without him there was nothing to fuel her fury. And she wanted to be furious. Not just with him, but with Concetta.

Nguyet, too, with her crystal divinations, assuring Marta that everything would be okay, that Concetta would come home, safe and sound.

Unclenching her knees, Marta picked up the headphones and slipped them on. She heard nothing; only the muffled hiss that held the sound of her pulse at bay and deadened her heart.

What had her sister been doing? What had she been involved in? Had she left on her own, or had she been taken? The questions continued to gnaw at her, one frayed memory after another . . .

———

"I can't tell you," Concetta said. Her tone was flat, matter-of-fact, the one she used to hold people at arm's length.

She'd had it since she was a little girl. For as long as Marta could remember there had been a place inside her sister where Marta couldn't go—where Concetta refused to let anyone go—that she kept walled off like a secret garden. Every now and then Marta felt her sister peeking out, and caught alluring, tantalizing and sometimes prickly glimpses of what grew inside: risky behavior, questionable friendships, thorny liaisons.

"Why not?" Marta demanded.

"You don't want to know."

Marta's jaw muscles bunched and unbunched in frustration. "What the hell is that supposed to mean?"

"It's for your own good."

"So now you know what's good for me and I don't."

"This isn't about you."

"You just said it was for my own good. That makes it about me."

"You know what I mean." Impatience edged her sister's voice. "There are other people involved. People—besides you—who might get hurt."

"Bullshit."

Concetta's expression shifted from irritation to pity. "Stop being so selfish all the time."

"You're one to talk."

Concetta shook her head sadly. "You don't understand. You never have. That's why—"

"I understand fine. You want to be a martyr. The center of attention; the person everyone admires, but can never be, because you're so altruistic."

Concetta bristled, like a thistle under a hot sun. "You're no different. You don't have a life of your own. You never have. You've always wanted to do what I've done."

"Because you wanted me to," Marta said. "You needed a follower. Someone to look up to you."

Concetta always had to be first; the leader; the risk taker. She had been the first to 'skin herself, back when philm wasn't considered safe. Somehow, she'd gotten hold of a pair of pasties, philm nipples she had placed over her own nipples. Concetta had shown them to her one night. Marta was ten, Concetta twelve. The oversized nipples looked out of place, comical on her flat, underdeveloped breasts. But when Marta laughed, Concetta took offense. She wasn't even sure

whose nipples they were—Marilyn Monroe, maybe,
Velvis, or XXXodus. They made a game out of guessing,
but it was serious business. With the pasties, Concetta
was grown-up and she had gotten there ahead of Marta.

That was the important part. She'd been first. She
wasn't afraid. And, out of concern for Marta's safety—
she said—Concetta had refused to let Marta try the nip-
ples on. It was way too dangerous...

Dangerous for Concetta. It had taken Marta a long
time to understand who was at risk, and why.

The trailer vibrated as the front door opened and
shut. Nguyet, returning from her meeting. Her stepmother rattled around the kitchen, filling the
teapot, muttering to herself in preparation for another divination. She always did a divination after a
planning session to read the hidden messages imprinted on her by the meeting.

The divinations were one of the things about
Nguyet that bothered Marta the most. Because no
two water crystals were exactly alike, only similar,
they were open to interpretation. Nguyet could read
anything she wanted into a divination and pretend
it was real. Marta supposed it was what got her
through... what got her father through. Still, it
seemed fake, a pathetic self-delusion.

It took a moment for Marta to realize the voice
she was hearing wasn't Nguyet's.

Three...seven...two. Pause. Five...fifteen...
eight.

The diction was robotic, the toneless narration
thin and skeletal. Marta clamped the headphones
tighter with both of her hands.

Ten . . . fifty-eight . . . thirty-six.

The sequence lasted a full minute then ended in a squall of static. She removed the headset to escape the sibilant hiss, set the phones on the bed, and turned to the shortwave.

Words blinked in necrotic gray on the LCD display. Three brief sentences, one after the other in quick succession.

> *HAVE FAITH . . .*
> *BECOME A TRUE BELIEVER . . .*
> *ALL YOUR PRAYERS WILL BE FORGIVEN.*

Forgiven. Not answered.

Marta scraped her bottom lip with her teeth. The message was followed by a series of numbers: 36-50-291 121-47-113.

Then the numbers faded and the little screen went blank. All she was left with was the Geiger-hiss of static.

Marta activated a small d-splay philmed on her left palm, accessed a public datician, and recited the numbers. Her mouth felt parched, the words shaky, as if they might crumble on her tongue. A beat passed. Two. Finally, a fixed GPS map appeared, etched in gold, on the d-splay.

The numbers were global positioning coordinates, latitude and longitude, for a street address.

———

"Where are you going?" Nguyet asked. She stepped from the kitchen, where she'd been taking a new water-crystal reading.

Marta paused in the doorway, hand on the knob. "Out."

Nguyet glanced at the clock on the Vurtronic screen in the living room. "It's getting late."

It was a couple of minutes after ten. "I need to get some fresh air. Clear my head."

Nguyet snorted.

"What?" Marta said, defensive. As usual it felt like Nguyet was judging her. She shouldn't feel guilty, shouldn't feel the need to justify herself. And yet for some reason she did.

"No fresh air around here," Nguyet said in disgust. "Maybe anywhere."

"Yeah, well." Marta hiked up her shoulders and zipped her jacket, as if to shore up her resolve. The jacket was genuine leather, light brown, and on the inside Marta had sewn one of Concetta's cotton shirts as a lining. The dyed, handwoven shirt was one of Marta's favorites, Guatemalan, with all the colors of the rainbow threaded into it.

"How long will you be out?" Nguyet pressed.

"Not long."

Nguyet made a face. "Be careful."

Marta seethed, as much at herself as Nguyet. Why did she let her stepmother get to her? She didn't need her permission or approval. So why did she play along, give her more power than she deserved?

"See you later." Marta stepped outside and pulled the door shut, softly but firmly, on her stepmother.

16

Atossa was waiting for Pelayo when he got home. She'd philmed herself as a Hula Honey with a copper sun-burnished complexion, hair the color of molten gold, and hibiscus lips. She wore a blue pineapple-print dress, a puka-shell necklace, and palm-frond sandals. Her toenails were sunset red.

"Where have you been?" She got up from the couch that faced the large Vurtronic screen and crossed the living room to him. "I was afraid something bad happened."

He shrugged off his jacket and tie, draping them over the back of the chair next to the couch. "I had to talk to Marta."

"You could have called. Left a message." She looked hurt, her face pinched tight around the eyes and mouth.

"I'm sorry." She refused to let him draw her into a hug.

"I brought dinner." She nodded at the three Asian Rose take-out boxes arranged on the coffee table next to a pair of empty plates. His favorites: pineapple tempeh, Singapore noodles, and basil eggplant. "It's probably cold by now."

"Sorry." Pelayo ran both hands over his head, still surprised by the hair and how real the nanoscopic fibers felt under his fingers. Ditto the wrinkles on his forehead and the faint parenthetical crease lines circumscribing his mouth and eyes. "I wasn't thinking."

"Not about me, anyway." She turned from him and went to the kitchenette for a glass of water.

Pelayo frowned—this was about more than his being late and not calling, or her being worried—and went after her. "What is it?" he said. "What's the matter?"

"Nothing." She twisted her mouth and shook her head. "It's not that important. We can talk about it later."

Something to do with the class she was taking, he guessed. Or her job. She held the glass with both hands.

"Talk about what?" he asked.

"I said it can wait." Tossa raised the glass to her lips and swallowed, as if forcing the water past an obstruction.

There was no point pushing her. She would just dig in her heels.

"So what did Marta want?" she said, placing the half-drained glass on the counter.

Pelayo ran through events, relieved to be talking. Sooner or later, they would get around to what she wanted to discuss. That was the way things usually worked; she just needed time to calm down.

"If Marta wants your help," Tossa said when he finished, "she'll ask for it. Until then, it's none of your business."

Pelayo wasn't so sure. "I guess," he allowed.

Tossa let out a breath, then took a step back and appraised the test philm with a practiced eye. "You look like you should be carrying a Bible in one hand and a Tommy gun in the other."

"Yeah." He loosened his collar, then lifted his arms and turned in a little pirouette. "What do you think?"

"Any idea who you're supposed to be?"

"Uri didn't say. Asshole wouldn't give me shit. I was hoping maybe you could tell me."

She moved closer to touch the sleeve of his jacket. "Did IBT provide the clothes, or did you pick them out yourself?"

"They're part of the ware."

"Serious?" She shifted her hand to explore the ridges of his knuckles and age line running through his palm.

"The hair, too."

She frowned. "What's that on your face?"

"What?"

She reached up and turned his head under the ceiling-strung LEDs. "It looks like a blemish."

He touched his right cheek. "Like a birthmark, you mean?"

"Or a watermark." Tossa withdrew her hand. "What's the 'skin like without the philm?"

Pelayo shrugged. "I haven't checked." Between Lagrante and Marta, there hadn't been time.

"Let's take a look." She mirrored the screen on the Vurtronic.

Pelayo studied his reflection. He initially mistook the necrotic gray patch for a shadow. But the size and shape didn't change as he turned his head under the ambient track lights.

It could be a defect...or an indication something

went wrong with the installation. Then again, maybe not.

"Come on," Tossa teased. A smile sidled into one corner of her mouth. "Let's see what you got."

Pelayo stripped out of his pants and shirt, down to gray boxer shorts and the watch philmed on his wrist. Held in place by a black leather strap, the elegantly crafted watch had a gold case and a black bezel with roman numerals. The name Hamilton was stenciled across the top half of the white-marbled face, while a small dial counted off seconds on the lower half of the face.

He tapped the crystal with a fingernail. It felt hard and smooth as glass. "Any idea what kind of watch is this?"

Tossa accessed a datician, scanned an image of the watch, uploaded it, then opened a d-splay inset on the mirror and conferenced him in on the ear-feed.

According to the datician, the watch was a replica of a Hamilton Piping Rock with a 14K gold case. The watch was first introduced in the 1920s, and included a white gold version with a bronze-colored face.

Pelayo pressed the crown, the winder knob on the side of the case, expecting the philm to toggle off manually. That's the way it worked with every other 'skin he'd tested. There was a basic on/off switch, normally in the form of a button, ring, or earring. Instead, a translucent d-splay appeared in the upper right of his field of view.

"Well?" Tossa said.

"Virtual menu," he said.

Most of the menu options—tie color and width, suspenders, suit fabric (worsted, gabardine, Saxony) and pattern (pinstripe, herringbone, houndstooth check)—were grayed out, not available in the beta version. This included skin color. Caucasian was the only ethnic background supported. All other ethnicities—a comprehensive list that included Latasian and Vietino—were not yet offered.

"Quit stalling," Tossa said.

He thought-selected the option to display/hide the philm.

The 'skin turned translucent as it deimaged. His pseudoidentity faded, giving way to nanosculpted features he barely recognized as himself. The hair on his body retreated, absorbed through the pores of his tissue into subcutaneous cavities, leaving him smooth-shaved. Naked, he couldn't feel the graphene exomer. With most 'skin, there was a dull, waxy patina that left his flesh feeling stiff and inelastic. This was different. All that remained was the retro Hamilton. He could even feel a dank, briny draft from the open transom on the other side of the room.

Pelayo examined his flesh carefully in the mirror. There was no sign of the blotch, on his face or anywhere else.

"It looks like it's part of the philm," he said.

Tossa eyed him critically. "How do you feel?"

"Fine." No ill effects, so far. It might be cosmetic, harmless, or normal even . . . part of the test plan.

"Try rephilming," she suggested. "See what happens." She blinked, activating an eyefeed.

When he rephilmed himself the blotch reappeared, in the same exact configuration and location. Definitely a hardware or software issue. Unless the betaware was reacting to something it encountered inside him . . . some physical or chemical trigger. "I wonder if maybe I should go in," he said. "Have Uri take a look at it?"

Tossa coiled a strand of hair around one finger. "What if Lagrante's the cause of the glitch?"

Assuming it *was* a glitch. Either way, there were risks. If the electronic skin was defective and it went undiagnosed, he could hull himself: permanent nerve and cell damage, according to the medical release he'd signed. If he went in, and the problem turned out to be serious, Uri would probably pull the plug on the clinical trial and scratch him as a test subject. If that happened, he would be left with nothing.

Lagrante hadn't been able to crack the ware. It was possible he'd damaged the 'skin. If that was the case, and Pelayo brought it to the attention of IBT, things could get ugly. Uri would want to know where he'd been, who he'd been in contact with, what he'd been doing.

"Let's wait," Pelayo decided. "See what it looks like in the morning." He could always claim that it had shown up while he was asleep . . . hadn't been discovered until he woke up.

Tossa worried the strand of hair. "You sure?"

"Yeah."

He touched the blemish again. It didn't feel odd, abnormal.

Neither did he.

"I wish there was someone else you could go to to get checked out," she said.

"It's probably nothing," he said.

"I don't like it."

"If we knew more about the background of the philm," he said, "that might tell us something."

"You mean style, historical context, and cultural influences? Like that?"

"Right." Pelayo led her back to the sofa and the boxes of cold Sri Lankan takeout. "What you've been doing in class," he said, pulling on pants and shirt.

"It's not exactly the same. We don't get into fashioneering. But I might be able to run some cross-references, see what turns up."

While he heated the takeout, Tossa uploaded the images she'd grabbed with her eyefeed cams.

Overhead, moonlight etched hieroglyphs into the skylight perched on the roof of the converted warehouse. Hairline cracks in the glassine, sutured together with cartilage-thick welts of epoxy, cast a shadowy web of veins on the concrete floor slab.

He brought the plates back to the coffee table. A moment later, a black-and-white still appeared on the d-splay. The photograph showed a man lounging next to an old gasoline-engine sedan, parked in front of a dry sand beach. The man sported a suit similar to the one Pelayo was waring.

"The suit's called a Windsor," Tossa said. "It's a modified version of a 'drape cut' suit originally created by this London tailor, Frederick Scholte. Its trademark features are slightly tapered sleeves, wide, pointed lapels, and shoulder pads."

"What time period are we talking?"

"Around 1935 to 1940."

Pelayo brushed at a short length of noodle cling-ing to his shirtsleeve. "What's the suit made out of?"

"Worsted yarn."

Pelayo shook his head.

"Cloth made out of thread spun from combed, stapled wool. It has a hard sheen to it. A super glossy, smooth finish."

"How about the shirt and tie?"

"Cotton and silk. The shoes are patent leather."

"Who wore Windsors?"

"White-collar professionals, mostly. Businessmen, politicians, entertainers. Like that. It was seen as a sign of success."

"What about religious leaders?"

"Sure. As soon as religion got to be big business, religious leaders became these big-time media per-sonalities. Especially televangelists. They packaged and sold faith as entertainment."

"So they dressed the part."

"Exactly."

"That fits in with the corporate angle Lagrante was telling me about. The tough-ass business 'tude tempered by strict moral values."

Tossa frowned at something on her eyefeed. "This is interesting."

A new d-splay opened on the Vurtronic screen. It showed a large sphere next to a tall, triangular nee-dle or spike. The design incorporated both geomet-ric elements as part of a larger Christian-style cross.

"What is it?" he said.

"The Perisphere and Trylon," Tossa said, "from the 1939 New York World's Fair. They were part of something called The World of Tomorrow exhibition." She opened another d-splay, clicked through various images of the fair, then paused to chew on a sporkful of eggplant.

"We're talking Art Deco," he said.

"Futurism, too. It was all about science and technology. According to the datalib, 'this perfect machine-based world is one of the primary meta-narratives of the twentieth century.'"

The d-splay expanded to accommodate a monolithic cityscape. The mountainous buildings were all composed of flat, sharp-edged planes with a grid of windows. There was no color, only charcoal shades of gray.

"The style pretty much eliminated all decorative ornamentation," Atossa said. "It was big on simple geometric shapes, like cubes and triangles."

A tall zigzag building, albumen silver and perforated with windows, replaced the cityscape.

"Function over form," Pelayo said.

Tossa nodded and swallowed.

Pelayo scraped more chunks of diced pineapple onto his plate. "So what does that have to do with the philm?"

"I guess it's trying to tap into that particular narrative. Simple, plain, fundamentalist. Whatever."

"But why R&D a whole new 'skin just to develop a new cast?" Pelayo shook his head, got up, and began to pace. It didn't make sense.

Tossa got up from the sofa and joined him next to the wall d-splay. She slid a hand into his left front pant's pocket. Gentle fingers curled around him and he felt himself grow stiff.

"No," he said.

"Why not?"

Uri had warned him about dirty-dicking himself. But Pelayo wondered if Uri was more worried about him passing something on to someone else. "IBT said not to. Plus..."

Tossa stopped stroking, but kept her fingers in place. Holding him that way. "The blemish?" she said.

He nodded. "Do you know if any other images like these have shown up anyplace else?"

"Together, you mean? In the same context?"

"Yeah. Maybe there's a connection to some larger audience, a new political smob or philm cast."

Slowly, reluctantly, she withdrew her hand. "I'll ask around. See what I can find out."

Figure that out and he might have a better idea of where he stood, what plans IBT had for the 'skin, and what role he would be expected to play.

17

One of the flies in Zhenyu al-Fayoumi's latest experimental test group had acquired a new face.

Al-Fayoumi stared at the magnified image on a virtual d-splay. The face was female, with kohl-etched almond-shaped eyes, a long, narrow nose, full lips, and a graceful neck. According to the datician he queried for enhancement and face-print comparison, the features matched a stone statue of Queen Nefertiti.

How had the latest image, the idolon, been transmitted? Where had it come from? Had it been inherited from a parent, another unrelated fly, or the environment? Was it an entirely new image, or a permutation of an existing one?

The fly had emerged from its pupa late last night. Early that morning, al-Fayoumi had separated the offspring flies from the parent population and applied a layer of electronic skin to the head and wings of each. Several hours later, the mutant image had appeared.

None of the fly's siblings had acquired this particular idolon. They had expressed the parent image: David Hedison from the original 1958 version of *The Fly*. That was typical of the epigenetic mode of inheritance he was hypothesizing: images were being transmitted from flies to their descendents without the information being encoded in either the soft or digital DNA of the parents. To complicate matters, every so often a spontaneous and apparently random mutation occurred. Inexplicably, an offspring fly inherited a new face.

The faces had started out as a gimmick. As part of a grant proposal to study image expression in digital allotropes, he had philmed a batch of flies, adding the gray and yellow feathers of a goldfinch to their wings.

Ha-hah. Everyone in the Developmental Nano-biology Department got a kick out of it, undergrads, grad students, staff, even faculty.

Could he do faces? they wanted to know. Sure. Airplane wings? Why not? After all, anything was possible.

The requests poured in. So he became a fly guy. A strict vegetarian for most of his life, he had purchased meat, bred maggots, and philmed his flies with the faces of old comedians, politicians, and big-screen movie stars. He gave the flies the Rising Sun wings of kamikaze Zeros, Iron Cross biplanes, and Hammer and Sickle MIGs.

It became a game. The game ended after he 'skinned a new batch of flies but had to leave before he could philm them. When he returned a few hours later, he found that all of the new flies had inherited the philm image of the parent fly, the gold-and-blue mask of King Tutankhamen.

A practical joke, his detractors claimed. That's all he was seeing. Not a new form of phenotype transmission or epigenetic inheritance. Certainly not Lamarckian inheritance.

At first he agreed. What else could it be? Someone, a colleague, was having a bit of fun with him.

Without telling anyone, he repeated the process. The result was the same. The offspring flies inherited the primary image after only a few hours. Somehow it was being copied, transmitted from one generation of electronic 'skin to the next.

How? For weeks, the question haunted him. The inheritance appeared to be Lamarckian, as absurd as a kid being born with a tattoo identical to one inked on one of his or her parents. Clearly, there must be some other mechanism. But, fearful of damaging his credibility, he was afraid to investigate openly. Safer, at first, to pursue the matter in secret, on his own time. That way, he wouldn't be risking his reputation. He could always go public later, after he had a better idea of what was going on and whether it was a valid line of inquiry or not. For the time being the less anyone knew about what he was doing the better. Except for a couple of bootleggers and rip artists he occasionally contacted for information about black-market ware, he had managed to maintain a low profile.

Until now.

Al-Fayoumi checked the time. Not quite eleven. The man hadn't shown. Possibly he wouldn't. Possibly he was having second thoughts. Fine. Al-Fayoumi should never have agreed to meet with him in person, and especially not in his lab. A mistake. Neutral ground would have been better, a restaurant or a hotel lobby.

Or not at all.

Al-Fayoumi stared into the gloom of his basement. The makeshift lab was jammed with flimsy steel shelves, storage cabinets, and recycled lab equipment, most of it purchased at flea markets and scavenger shops in the Trenches. The only light came from the red heat lamps over the terrariums, and the phosphor-bright traces of the flies buzzing about.

How had the man, who called himself Yukawa, heard about what he was working on? Who had told him? One of his black-market contacts? Or was there another source he didn't know about?

Troubled, al-Fayoumi wrung his hands. He needed to know. That was the main reason he had agreed to meet. There had also been a hint of private funding, dangled in front of him like a bright lure.

After a year he still didn't know how the images were transmitted or inherited. He was at a dead end. All he had were a couple of working principles he had been unable to prove: one, all philm-based images were the same image, and two, all programmable matter was the same matter.

A message d-splay opened and a DiNA signature code blinked in his field of view. Al-Fayoumi's hands grew chill, his underarms damp.

Yukawa had arrived.

———

The man wore silk shirt and slacks, both an unostentatious silver-gray. His jacket was a tasteful Art Brico collage of fabrics that successfully integrated African tribal weavings and Indian reshamwork. Despite its slapdash appearance, the design was very calculated. There was nothing arbitrary about it.

He had philmed himself as a Japanese zaibatsu samurai: high cheekbones, straight nose, coarse black hair parted in the middle and smoothed back. The smooth patina of the philm and the waxy stiffness of the 'skin combined to create a portrait of quiet reserve and firm candor. It wasn't a face al-Fayoumi immediately recognized. It was probably a composite image, fashioned from obscure cinematic references he was unfamiliar with.

Clothing had always been an indicator of attitude, values, or status. Philm was no different. Except that it also exhibited certain traits of epigenetic inheritance, mainly the transmission of phenotype through virtual updates and downloads.

"Mr. al-Fayoumi." The man bowed. At the same time he held out his hand. "A pleasure to meet you. Thank you for agreeing to see me." He peered at al-Fayoumi from over the tops of vintage WWII-era eyeglasses.

"Mr. Yukawa." They shook. Then al-Fayoumi led him down a narrow hallway to the main lab.

The man claimed to be with Sigilint, a philmware development firm that specialized in dynamic imaging systems and remote, downloadable plug-ins for electronic skin.

"Can I get you something?" al-Fayoumi asked. The words felt awkward, atrophied. It had been months since he'd had a visitor.

"I'm fine. Thank you."

Al-Fayoumi nodded. So much for formal niceties.

Yukawa solved the problem by taking an interest in the terrariums, with their dizzy electron clouds of flies. "Is this what you are working on now?"

"Idolons," al-Fayoumi said.

Yukawa shook his head politely. "I'm not familiar with the term."

"Phenotypic expression of images with social and/or cultural content," al-Fayoumi said. How to explain? Tongue-tied, he groped for the right words.

"*Architecture parlante*," Yukawa mused after a moment.

Al-Fayoumi found himself at a loss.

"It's an architectural term for a building taking on the physical form of the task it's designed to do," Yukawa explained. "For example, a donut shop constructed in the shape of a donut. Or, in the case of electronic skin, programmable matter adopting the shape of acquired images."

"Inherited," al-Fayoumi said.

Yukawa raised one brow, more puzzled than skeptical. "Inherited from what?" he said.

"A parent image. Images that have the same digitype but different iconotypes, the way cells with the same genotype can have a different phenotype."

"Lamarckian inheritance," Yukawa said with a sly smile. "The expression of acquired characteristics. In this case electronic images instead of a physical alteration or learned behavior."

Al-Fayoumi nodded. His throat felt tight and dry. He didn't trust himself to speak.

Yukawa pursed his lips thoughtfully. "What's the mechanism for inheritance?" he said. "How are the images, the idolons, transmitted?"

Al-Fayoumi swallowed. Had he already revealed too much? "I'm not sure."

Yukawa seemed to accept this at face value. He returned his attention to the batch of test flies. "Do the images ever change? Evolve?"

"Every few generations a new variant appears," al-Fayoumi said.

"In response to what?" Yakuwa said. "The environment, or some other stimulus?"

Al-Fayoumi hesitated, reluctant to say more. He was venturing into terra incognita and unwilling to commit himself to speculations that could be held against him. A simple slip of the tongue, no different than that of a knife.

Mesmerized by the flies, Yukawa didn't seem to notice. The polished lenses of his spectacles flickered. "Tell me," he said. "Have you ever observed any quantum effects in the idolons?"

Al-Fayoumi blinked. "How do you mean?"

Yukawa waved one hand casually, implying that they were speaking off the cuff now, engaging in speculation. "Superposition of states, for example. The same idolon simultaneously possessing several different images or values. Eigenstates, to be precise."

Al-Fouyami frowned and moistened his lips. "You mean images that appear to be different are really just different expressions of the same image? The way a photon is in two places at once until it collapses into a location."

"Exactly. When an idolon is in one state, it might look different from when it's in another state. That might explain the sudden appearance of a new image; it could be the same image collapsing into a different state."

As opposed to a mutation. Yukawa was suggesting a different expression of the same image with higher or lower probabilities of appearing. That still didn't explain how the images were transmitted, but—

"Entangled inheritance is another topic we're

interested in. EPR effects," Yukawa said, as if antici-
pating his train of thought. "The instantaneous
transmission and expression of information in programmable matter over long distances."

EPR. Einstein-Podolsky-Rosen paradox. Sometimes referred to as "spooky action" at a distance,
where quantum-entangled particles communicated
with one another instantly no matter how far apart
they were.

"You think that might be a possible mechanism
for the transmission of the images?" al-Fayoumi
asked.

"The philm project we're currently developing,"
Yukawa said, "has a shared social component. We're
interested in mathematical tools, software applications if you will, that can be used to predict the
habits, tendencies, and behavior of groupware
within a structural inheritance system. One that
uses programmable matter to express phenotype."

Al-Fayoumi's brow pinched. "You want people
waring the same philm to be able to inherit and express specific acquired traits?"

"In this case the traits would be images," Yukawa
sad, "and any three-dimensional component they
code for."

Al-Fayoumi rubbed his jaw. "What would be the
source of these traits?"

"Existing philm. Or new source philm that acts as
a template for new versions and releases."

"So the inheritance would be directed," al-Fayoumi
said. "Engineered."

"Yes."

"By whom?"

Yukawa shrugged. "Clearly, I can't get into specifics. The details are proprietary and confidential, subject to strict nondisclosure. All I can say is that it involves electronic skin with a single quantum state, so that spatially separated portions of the 'skin are quantum-entangled."

"Able to share information," al-Fayoumi said.

Yukawa nodded. "And influence one another."

Al-Fouyami started to pace, caught himself, stopped. "What exactly do you want from me?"

"You would be formulating inheritance models and helping cut the source code to manage the emergent shareware."

In other words, quantum inheritance. The instantaneous transmission of phenotype from one person to another.

Yukawa regarded him with calculated intensity. "Are you interested?"

Al-Fayoumi cleared his throat. "Why me?"

"I should think that would be obvious. You are one of the few scientists who is doing any work in non-Darwinian inheritance, especially when it comes to the epigenetic transmission of images."

"How much time would I have?"

Yukawa smiled, baring exquisitely lacquered teeth. "I take it that's a yes."

Al-Fayoumi hollowed his cheeks and nodded.

―――――――

When Yukawa had gone, al-Fayoumi went back to his office. He turned down the main lights and watched a new batch of maggots seethe under the heat lamps.

Plausible deniability. That was the reason Yukawa had come to him. If there was a problem, if the project failed, Yukawa could blame him. He would make a convenient scapegoat.

Why had he agreed? He hadn't intended to. He had planned to politely decline, a courteous thanks but no thanks.

Fear. That was why. He'd been afraid Yukawa would discredit him. Not publicly, but behind his back; a well-placed word here or there and his career would be over. He'd had no choice.

He was being set up, al-Fayoumi realized. But what for?

18

Into the Trenches.

Before making the trip below sea level, into the excavated streets, Marta bought a pair of cheap, foreign, and probably stolen spex from a street vendor. The spex cost twice the going rate because she needed a pair with built-in GPS.

Marta checked for cops, then headed north on foot, first along Zmudowski, then Sunset, following the curve of the beaches and the houses piled against the crumbling seawall like cliff dwellings. The southernmost edge of the Trenches, where the streets started to slope down into the landfill, was marked by an intricate network of levees, dams, sump pumps, and drainage pipes designed to hold high tides and storm surges at bay. She skirted the old desalination plant that still supplied water to the Flats.

The buildings went from above ground to below ground, forming unbroken walls on either side of the street...

Squeezing her, Marta thought. Molding her into a another shape—another person. No different from 'skin, or the water divination that Nguyet used to supposedly transform herself.

Marta had never bought into the spiritual nature of water. The belief that water responded directly to prayers, thoughts, or ideas by forming differently shaped crystalline structures seemed ridiculous.

"People are mostly water," Nguyet argued. "Sixty percent or more. If I change the character of the water in me, I change my character." To her it was obvious. A direct one-to-one correlation.

Marta had seen the pictures, of course. The books Nguyet used to perform the divination process showed dozens of crystals, how there was a particular shape, or family of shapes, for different emotions and states of balance or imbalance. Even words like "love," "peace," and "hate" equated to a particular shape. The crystals were no different than runes, *I Ching* hexagrams, or the signs of the Zodiac when it came to analyzing oneself, answering questions, and deciding on a particular course of action. Except that a person could influence events by realigning their physical being.

"How can water respond to words?" Marta had once asked. "It can't read or hear. So how does it know what message you're sending?"

"Because it's an expression of the same universal consciousness we are all part of."

If the logic behind the prayer crystals was flawed, then the metaphysics at the heart of them were even more mysterious and idiosyncratic. The exact same word, or expression, in different languages could produce different crystalline shapes. Two different types of stimuli—music or words—could supposedly produce the same, or similar-shaped, crystals.

"Everything is connected," Nguyet had told her. "If I am in balance, then the world around me will be in balance. More harmonious."

Marta queried the GPS indicator on her spex and

turned down a side street covered by a barrel vault. Architectural graphene stretched tight over the half pipe kludged together out of Kevlex and aluminum tubing.

The Flats were beginning to wind down for the night. Most of the retail outlets had closed. Marta passed a restored clothing store and an Art Brico gallery, found-art jewelry fashioned out of bits of excavated debris. The bars were still open, the late-night clubs and cafés, spilling music, laughter, and dank conversation into the night air.

Marta wondered if the person on the radio had been Concetta. Was the shortwave her way of letting them know she was alive, and to tell them how to get in touch with her?

Marta's heart stuttered when a red indicator on her spex started to blink. Not far now—only a couple of hundred meters. With each step, the light blinked faster and her pulse sped up to keep pace. When the coordinates matched the ones she had entered earlier, the LED glowed solid green.

She stood in front of a store that appeared to be a combination pawnshop and mini flea mart. A sign on the window said EGGED, ROWED, AND OLE GOODS. Whatever that meant.

Was Concetta inside, waiting for her?

She raised her hand—it felt heavy as concrete—and rapped on the door. Ten seconds passed, twenty, with no answer. Even the door remained silent. Maybe it wasn't smart, or maybe it was just being tight-lipped after closing up for the night.

What if she'd gotten the coordinates wrong? Misheard, miscopied, or misentered them?

Sweat broke out on the nape of her neck. Her face

felt hot. There was no way to replay the broadcast. If she'd misheard, the information was lost.

She tried the handle, a sort of bone-and-metal claw. It felt like shaking hands with a movie prop, some grade-B prosthesis animated by wires and gears. To her surprise, the hand tightened around hers and tinny laughter spilled from a speaker embedded in the door.

"Welcome," a voice said. "Come in."

Mechanical fingers gripped her. She twisted her hand to free it, but the prosthesis turned with her. Then a latch clicked, the door swung open, and the hand let go, freeing her to enter the shop.

A carnival game, Marta thought. A fun-house gimmick. She adjusted the power on the spex, maxed the night-vision setting, and looked around.

The shop was gloomy, lighted only by the sputtering neon of the sign branded onto the window. She heard water dripping, the steady plink plink of seepage collecting in an underground tank. Glass display cases, sheet-metal cabinets, and adjustable shelves lined the walls of the room. Shadows cobwebbed the contents: a stuffed elephant here, a wooden train there, a clown-faced jack-in-the-box. Kevlex fiber mesh hung from the ceiling, heavy with detritus. The air felt puffy, swollen. It pressed against her, tender and inflamed.

"Hello?" It sounded as if a thick cotton pillow was pressed against her mouth, muffling her voice.

No answer.

"Concetta..."

"I'm not interested in your name." The harsh whisper scraped out of the darkness, choking her off. "Or the reason you're here."

Marta's breath snagged on her vocal cords. Finally tore free. "There's something you should know. I'm not—"

"Have faith," the voice said.

"All right." She wet her lips.

"Have faith..." The voice paused, expectant.

Her mind raced. Have faith in what? In who? Then, it came to her.

"Become a true believer," she said, haltingly repeating the message. "And all your prayers will be forgiven."

The room seemed to exhale. "This way," the voice said.

A grainy rectangle of light, roughly the size and shape of a door, appeared three or four meters to her right.

Taking a breath, Marta walked toward the opening. She could see a chair inside the other room, facing a luminous green wall crisscrossed by abstract lines reminiscent of Jackson Pollock or the ghosts of high-energy particles.

Several steps from the door, a fuzzy silhouette appeared behind the wall. The wall wasn't solid, she realized, but some sort of hospital green Kevlex or cellophane sheet plastic. The person behind it moved slowly, meticulously, with precise, almost mechanical, movements.

The room itself was small, not much larger than a closet. No LEDs or bulbs of any kind. The only light came through the membrane in front of her.

"Close the door."

She pulled the door shut behind her. Past the front edge of the chair, two holes in the curtain stared at her. Not holes, exactly, but openings to

tubes of some kind, spaced about twenty-five centimeters apart.

"Are you scared?"

She nodded, her tongue dry and shrunken.

"You should be."

Why? she wanted to ask. But the question cow-
ered in her mouth.

"I'm not here to reassure you," the man said. At
least she thought it was a man, but the voice was
clipped, as clockwork as his movements.

Something clicked, then hissed, on the other side
of the curtain. A rubber pressure seal.

"Sit down. Facing the screen."

Marta slid onto the chair. The legs scraped on
naked concrete. The silhouette took a seat directly
in front of her so that together they formed a single
shadow between them—an interstitial ghost where
their lives met.

"Place your hands in the gloves."

Marta leaned forward and slid her hand into the
holes. It was like reaching into the hollow arms of a
space suit.

"All the way," the voice said. "As far as you can."

Marta reached deeper and encountered gloves.
She wriggled her fingers in, all the way to the tips.
Something round and cold pressed snugly into the
palm of her right hand, nestling there like a coin.

"Good." The man seemed satisfied. "Don't
move."

His hands took hers, probing. He found the wafer
and pressed it firmly into place.

He was a doctor, she realized, used to dealing with
patients. His examination was experienced, his

movements confident. Any quivering came from her, not him.

Why did she need to be examined? Was he looking for something in particular or was this standard operating procedure?

"You have beautiful bone structure. Very delicate."

Was this a compliment, or a clinical observation detached of emotion and judgment? Before she could answer she felt a brief, needle-sharp prick in her palm. Out of reflex she tried to curl her fingers around the sliver of pain.

Her fingers refused to move. They felt numb, leaden. She jerked back, away from the curtain, but he had cuffed her by the wrists, metal bands holding her securely in place.

Panic seized her.

"Relax," the man said. He caressed her hands through the gloves, stroking them the way he would a dying animal. "This won't take long. A few minutes of discomfort. Nothing more."

She couldn't speak, couldn't cry out. Chemical scissors had cut the neural circuit that transmuted thought into sound.

Her mouth tingled.

Poison, she thought.

The tingling spread, a numb flush that started in her extremities and worked its way inward. Soon it would infiltrate her chest. When it did her heart would stop, fall suddenly and irrevocably silent.

Her mind thrashed. She opened her mouth to speak, and found that she couldn't breathe. A vacuum had formed in her lungs.

"That's it," the man said. "Not so bad. It will be

worse if you fail to make your next connection. Fatal, I'm afraid. You would do well to remember that."

In other words, there was no turning back. She was committed. The only way out was forward.

He released her hands. Sensation flooded back into them. Her lungs heaved and she coughed, clearing her throat of saliva, snot, tears.

Abruptly the shadow stood, becoming lighter and more diffuse. Shaken, Marta withdrew her hands. Her palm was fine, no sign of injury. "What happens now?" she managed.

"Go." The voice softened to gray velour. "You have forty-eight hours to make contact. After that..."

"Go where?" she asked. "Contact who?"

There was no response. The shadow spread into a hazy vignette, then dispersed altogether. The glow behind the partition dimmed, engulfing her in gangrenous, green-tinged darkness.

Marta stood, pushing the chair back with her legs, and groped her way to the door. She fumbled with the latch, then staggered blindly into the shop. Half a minute later she found herself standing in the street, gasping for air and looking giddily around her.

She couldn't go home. Not now, maybe never. She couldn't risk putting her father, or Nguyet, in danger. She might expose them to whatever she'd been injected with. Until she knew what it was, what she was supposed to do, she couldn't go near them.

Why hadn't the man told her something? Anything? How did he expect her to do the right thing?

A shelter, she decided. She could spend the night there. In the morning, she'd get in touch with Sister Giselle. Then she'd go to the Get Reel and collect whatever back pay Jhon owed her.

And after that?

Have faith. There wasn't much else she could do.

19

Steam billowed up from a manhole and slipped along the street, a white finger working its way under the dark elastic of the night.

From his unmarked car, parked down the street from the North Beach apartment building, van Dijk watched the mist slink into an alleyway, dim the LED array on a security light, and fondle the skirts of a Betty Boop ad for Hongtasan cigarettes.

There was no sign of Lisette. In the hour he'd been watching, no one had entered or exited the building.

It didn't look as if the girl would be coming back anytime soon.

Van Dijk logged into SFPD central data and queried a datician regarding the status of the simage array Apodaca's crime-scene unit had sprayed on the walls of Lisette's apartment, the dead woman's apartment, and the stairwell leading up to them.

According to the datician, the array had identified and recorded several DiNA-authorized residents in the past twenty-four hours. But no one, identified or unidentified, had approached or tried to enter either of the apartments under surveillance.

In addition to simages—the simulated image created by the nanotrodes woven into electronic skin to produce a virtual construct—the array recoded standard optical images. Visible spectrum resolution was limited—so unphilmed articles of clothing, hair, and nonelectronic skin tended to be sketchily translucent—but for anyone using the stairwell, van Dijk would see both a virtual image and a standard optical image.

The same would be true of the apartments. He'd see whatever new philm, if any, had appeared on the programmable wallpaper when no one was around.

Decorative philm told as much about a person as the philm they wore. A lot of people changed interior décor at regular preprogrammed intervals—nights and weekends were common—to create a certain ambiance. If the walls in the victim's apartment had rephilmed in the last twenty-four hours, it might tell him where she was from, where she spent her free time, or where she wanted to go.

Van Dijk entered the building and made his way up the stairwell. On the second-floor landing he paused, turned to look back down the steps, and issued a mental command to the datician to flash him the recordings from the stairwell.

Time-lapse, he instructed. *Compression ratio: sixty to one. Split d-splay.*

The stairwell flickered under a faint light imbalance as the datician downloaded the simage clip to his eyefeed.

The first recording had a time stamp of fifteen hours ago, at seven in the morning.

An old woman appeared six steps below him. She had philmed her face and hands only. Katharine Hepburn. On the simage d-splay, her face and hands floated like bodiless apparitions. The rest of her was invisible, indicating she had no other 'skin on her body or philmed articles of clothing. On the optical d-splay, she bent under a spectral wool jacket and the weight of a grocery bag as she gripped the banged-up handrail and hauled herself toward him.

Three steps from the landing, she passed out of range of the array and disappeared from both d-splays.

Thirty seconds later, half an hour real time, a school-age kid materialized, bounded toward him, and blinked out of existence in less than a second.

In five minutes, van Dijk had watched five hours real time pass before him. A quick cross-reference told him that the old woman and three other people were residents. The kid, on the other hand, was a visitor, and had left a few minutes after storming up the stairs.

A friend of Lisette's?

The kid had philmed herself as a cast member of the Ghost Dragons, waring one of the spirit masks that conveyed special powers, like iron fists or fire breath. He wasn't able to tell if the kid had actually been 'skinned, or if the mask was nanoFX paint or a graphene prosthetic that could be put on and taken off.

Van Dijk ran the kid's DiNA, which yielded a home address in a coop a couple of blocks away, then made his way down the hall to the dead woman's apartment to see what the walls could tell him.

———

He stood in the middle of the room and replayed the simage recording. Not much change in the last twenty-four hours. The décor remained resolutely fixed: pine veneer flooring, walls philmed in white brick, Art Nouveau stained-glass windows. Only the red-and-black-framed Japanese partitions arranged in front of the windows as privacy screens re-philmed at regular intervals, a built-in factory preset that mechanically cycled through a packaged series of Hokusai and Hiroshige woodcut prints like *The Great Wave* and *Plum Estate*. The sequence didn't appear to have been revised or edited in any way. It was off the shelf.

Usually, test subjects were hardcore philmheads, "any ware, anywhere" types who datahoused vast collections of philm and even snipped their own images for private use or resale.

Not this woman. Why? What was different about her?

If she was new, maybe she hadn't had time to collect an image library. Or maybe she was just being cautious, afraid if she flaunted the betaware, she'd become a target for black-market rip artists and bootleggers.

Possible. But he had the feeling there was something more.

Van Dijk instructed the datician to continue the simage log for another twenty-four hours—it was a long shot, but something might show up—then left the apartment, no closer to figuring out who she was than before.

The simage in Lisette's apartment was troubling in other ways. In addition to the "Ghost Dragon" Chinamation on the cheap Vurtronic d-splay, the walls were philmed with toons. Unicorns and faeries, mostly, with a few insects tossed in for good measure. The same half dozen images looped over and over again, the visual equivalent of comfort food kids snacked on continuously, even obsessively.

The girl was alone, left to her own devices while mom outsourced herself in another city or country. Van Dijk pictured her sitting in the sofa, gnawing her nails bloody while the toons kept her company and she tried to cast herself as a Ghost Dragon.

That explained the watercolors in the bathroom. She had no way to 'skin or philm herself. So she painted her face, applying the mask the way the performers had in the old Chinese operas.

What about the dead woman? How did she fit into the picture? Had she taken the girl under her wing? Was she a surrogate mother, a friend, or possibly a big sister? Van Dijk could see it happening…

———

The door stood open a crack. A sword-thin blade of light slashed across the floor of the hallway.

Eight-year-old Kasuo crept up to the door on tiptoes, careful to avoid being cut by the light. Inside, Mr. Natal knelt on a yoga mat on the floor. His back was to the door. He wasn't wearing a shirt, but his skin wasn't naked. It was covered with so many tattoos it looked as if he was wearing a black Hawaiian shirt decorated with green leaves and red flowers. The tattoos wrapped over his shoulders and continued down his arms in colorful sleeves.

"It's not polite to stare," Mr. Natal said.

Kasuo started. "I'm…I'm…"

Mr. Natal grunted. "There's nothing to be sorry about. It's I who should apologize for not inviting you in."

Kasuo hesitated, uncertain if he should run to the safety of his mother's apartment. His gaze snagged on the man's feet, tucked under his buttocks. The soles had been inked to look like bamboo sandals.

"Well?" Mr. Natal didn't turn his head to look at him. Probably he was watching the door through an eyefeed. "What are you waiting for?"

The question felt more like a command. There was no turning back. Kasuo eased open the door and crossed the room.

"I was just..." The explanation was swept away by the roar of his pulse in his ears.

"Come here. Let me see you."

Kasuo edged around the yoga mat. The man's face reminded him of smooth, rain-wet stone.

"You are Kasuo," Mr. Natal said.

Kasuo nodded, surprised the man knew his name. Kasuo and his mother had only been in the apartment down the hall one week. As far as Kasuo knew, his mother and Mr. Natal had never spoken. Mr. Natal was a hermit who kept to himself.

"You're curious," Mr. Natal said.

Kasuo nodded, unable to speak. He'd just noticed the long knife arranged on the yoga mat in front of Mr. Natal's knees.

"Good. But you're afraid."

Another nod. The blade of the knife seemed to shimmer with silvery heat waves.

"That is also good. Still, you want to know what I'm doing. That is why you are here."

Kasuo swallowed to make room for a response. His silence swelled like a blister. The more it grew, the more uncomfortable it became.

"Well?"

Kasuo flinched under the sudden sharpness in Mr. Natal's voice. "I wanted to..."

"Speak up! I can't hear you."

"I wanted to know what you were doing," he blurted.

"Since you asked, I'll tell you," Mr. Natal said. He became suddenly calm, there was no trace of the outburst. "I was thinking."

"About what?"

"Nothing."

"How can you think about nothing?" He already knew how someone could think about everything. His mother did it all the time. She was always worrying. At night he heard her in the kitchen, drinking tea to help her sleep.

"A good question," Mr. Natal said. "It is not as easy as it looks. But I can see you already know that."

Like a compass needle, Kasuo's attention returned to the blade. "How come you have a knife?"

"It helps me think."

Did his mother have a knife when she stayed up? "How?"

"It sharpens my mind."

Kasuo watched light from the door glimmer on the edge of the blade. Maybe Mr. Natal could tell him how to help his mother think about nothing.

Mr. Natal tilted his head, as if listening. "Your mother needs you," he said.

"She does?" Kasuo didn't hear her calling.

"Thank you for visiting. Please shut the door on your way out."

Kasuo ran back to his apartment. In the morning, there was a commotion from the hallway. Shouts, followed by sudden silence. Kasuo peeked. A crowd of floormates had gathered around Mr. Natal's door at the far end of the hall. The door was open, but none of the people went in. They huddled outside, whispering among themselves.

When Kasuo started down the hallway, his mother caught him by the arm, holding him back.

"But I want to see," he said.

"It's better if you don't," his mother said. A moment later the wail of sirens came to them from the street below.

The sound haunted Kasuo for years. Why had Mr. Natal killed himself? It didn't make any sense. Mr. Natal hadn't seemed depressed or upset. He had been calm.

And yet something, or someone, had made him plunge the knife into his stomach.

Who—or what—was Mr. Natal protecting or running from? Had he been thinking about someone else when the blade entered him, or himself? Had he been thinking about everything, or nothing?

The simage had ended. Van Dijk, standing in the middle of the room, grew aware of a soft whir. Annoyed, he craned his head, searching for the source of the sound.

A blue damselfly clung to the wall. It appeared to be injured—only two of its four wings were moving. The opposite set of wings and the tail end of its long abdomen were pressed flat to the wall.

Van Dijk was about to turn away when he noted that the size, shape, and iridescent blue of the damselfly matched the toon dragonflies he'd seen zipping about in the simage, harassing faeries and perching on unicorn horns.

Van Dijk moved closer. The damselfly wasn't real.

It was a toon in the process of emerging from the wall, like a cicada from the ground. As he watched, a third wing came free, leaving only the fourth wing and the last couple of abdominal segments embedded in the graphene.

The dameselfly had the head of fish. What the hell?

Van Dijk reached for the toon. Before he could cage it in his fingers, the last wing and abdominal segment peeled free from the graphene and the damselfly, fully formed and functional, flashed under the ceiling LEDs. It circled for a moment, darting here and there, hovering over him for an instant before zigzagging off.

Van Dijk turned to see the damselfly zip through the open doorway. Hurrying into the hallway he forced his thoughts to slow as he queried the SFPD datician, speaking out loud so the datacian could learn his synapse firing pattern for damselfly, a word he hadn't used before. "Image type. Blue damselfly. Identify."

"*Enallagma cyathigerum*," the datician replied. "Considered the bluest of the blue damsels. Widespread and common." A snapshot flashed over his eyefeed. "The males have a club-shaped black mark on the second abdominal segment and broad antehumeral stripes along the dorsal surface of the thorax..."

Van Dijk stopped listening. The damsel was gone. He returned to the apartment. "Play simage," he said. "Last five minutes. Realspeed."

He watched the initial stages of the damsel's emergence. First, the head and legs. Then the thorax and the first filament-veined wing.

"Image source?" he said when the sequence completed.

"Unknown," the datacian said.

"Current location?"

"Unknown."

Van Dijk started to pace. "Log image. Cross-reference. Then compare for like images."

The nanoware had been looking for something. Not him—he had been summarily examined and dismissed.

Lisette. If the toon was keyed to her, there was a possibility it could lead him to her. Find the damsel, and he might find the girl.

20

Marta nursed a tamarind-flavored agua fresca from Tacopulco, one of the all-night taco bars. A grizzled philmhead crouched in the breezeway with her. The guy rocked back and forth, knees pulled to his chest while he spat out a profanity-laced diatribe. "Can't starve a fucking hunger artist. Nipple to the bottle. That's what I'm talking about. Bite me, cocksucker..."

Hard to tell if the monologue belonged to him or one of the music channels he had loaded into his earbud. An hour earlier, she'd run into him as she was walking downtown from Sister Giselle's homeless shelter on Branciforte. She hadn't had a chance to talk to the nun. So she had ended up in the covered alley behind the Get Reel, the only place she could think to go for the night. In the morning, after she quit her job and things settled down, she would get in touch with the Sister.

What about the person she was supposed to contact? Would they know how to get in touch with her? Where to get in touch with her?

Her chest tightened. Sweat stung her armpits. She pulled her leather jacket tight and hugged herself, taking comfort in the added warmth of the heavy Guatemalan cotton lining.

Have faith...

She repeated the thought like a mantra, filling her head with it in an effort to force aside her doubt and fear.

The philmhead turned out to be a blessing in disguise, annoying enough to distract her from her thoughts. When he'd first showed up, she thought he might hit on her or rob her. He stared at her and the leather jacket, and licked his lips. But it turned out he was as old and tired as the music trickling over his earfeed, Christian white rap, totally out-of-date.

As if that wasn't bad enough, his pseudoself was one hackneyed edit job after another. So many faces had been spliced together, one on top of the other, that his appearance was an unrecognizable blur. Washed-out eyes, shapeless nose and lips, muddy complexion. It was obsessive-compulsive with some people. They couldn't decide who they wanted to be—or they wanted to be everybody—and ended up being no one. That was where Pelayo was headed. She could see it, even if he couldn't. That was why he was a test subject.

Of course, Pelayo would never admit it. He was in denial, and the problem would get worse until he bottomed out.

At 6:40, when the philmhead lapsed into fitful paresis, Marta made her way to the Pacific Avenue mall for a bite to eat.

Serf's Up opened at seven and served a decent tofu scramble that had a half-life of only a couple hours and wouldn't corrode the lining of her stomach—unlike the java juice the place served.

Thick fog had rolled in overnight, watering down

the Marie Gabriel foliage philmed on the trees. Waiting in line at the kiosk, breathing in the sharp tang of brine, processed kelp, and deep-frying peanut oil, a wave of nausea engulfed her. She hurriedly stepped out of line and cupped both hands over her mouth, pressing her fingers against her lips to stifle an onrush of bile.

When the bout passed, she stumbled to a nearby bench, sat down, and held her head between her knees. She dry-heaved once, felt sweat break out on her scalp.

What was the matter with her? Was she really that uptight? Her stomach had been upset for days and she'd been feeling more and more bloated.

Marta forced slow, deep breaths. By the time she felt better, an hour had passed. It was almost eight. Time to head back to the Get Reel.

———

"What's this?" Jhon said. He narrowed sleep-addled eyes at her. "You saying you want to quit?"

"Yes. Effective immediately."

He massaged the back of his hairy neck. His morning espresso hadn't yet kicked in. "Why?"

"Family emergency."

"Christ." He let out a sour breath that sent her stomach cartwheeling. "Okay, then. Watch the counter for a few minutes. I'll be right back."

Before she could protest, he lumbered back to his office. There was no reason to watch the counter. The store didn't open for business until ten. But he didn't appear to be thinking too clearly. She usually came in at nine, to get things set up. By then he was his normal pain-in-the-ass self.

Jhon poked his head around the dividing screen. "I need your help. Can you come back here for a second?"

"Help with what?"

But he'd already disappeared. Typical. It was just like him. She wouldn't get paid until he got as much out of her as he could. If he had his way, she would be lucky to leave before the doors were unlocked.

As she rounded the partition, and made her way through the splice room to Jhon's office, she heard music...and caught a whiff of something rancid.

The philmhead from the breezeway. He sat in a chair at Jhon's desk and smiled at her as she entered. Not in the stoned way he had earlier. His eyes were clear and sharp.

Marta stopped, pulled up short by the expression. "What the hell's going on?" she asked. Something wasn't right.

"I know what you've been doing," Jhon said.

She kept her face carefully blank. No reaction at all.

"Helping illegal immigrants," he said. "Giving them black-market ware so they can avoid domestic security."

She forced her voice to remain low, tightly controlled. If she got all ballistic, it was all over. "That's crazy."

"You've been using the store," Jhon said. "Using me. Putting me and everything I worked for in danger."

The philmhead must be with Immigration, working undercover. That was what he'd been doing last night. Watching the store. Her.

"That girl yesterday," Jhon went on. "She wasn't the first. But I can promise you she's the last."

Marta tilted her chin at the undercover agent watching from the chair. "That what he told you?"

The philmhead chuckled. "I'm not with the government. If that's what you think." The rhythm of his speech was slightly off, as if he was waring a voicefeed.

"But that can be arranged," Jhon said. "If you decide not to cooperate. In fact, I guarantee it."

Cooperate with what? "What are you talking about?"

"You'll be reported to Immigration," Jhon said. "Your family, too. I'm willing to bet you're not the only one giving sanctuary to illegals."

The light in the room appeared to flicker. Marta touched a finger to her forehead. This wasn't happening. Not now, it couldn't be. She should never have come here after last night. Stupid, stupid, stupid.

The philmhead stood. "You're not feeling well," he said. "That's to be expected." He walked over to her and caught her by the elbow. "Sit down."

Marta pinched her brow. To be expected. What was he saying? She let herself be guided to the seat.

"Who are you?" she asked, without her earlier hardness.

"We have an arrangement," the philmhead said. "Your boss and I."

"Which is...?"

The philmhead sat on the front edge of Jhon's desk. "He finds people for me. People in need of a spiritual compass. People looking to change the direction of their life."

"It's not just me," Jhon said quickly, defensively. "They got other people recruiting for them."

Them? Recruiting? The words reverb'd in her head like a struck bell.

"There are others," the philmhead admitted. He spread his hands, palms up. "But that's not the issue here."

Marta turned toward Jhon. "You get paid by this guy?" Her eyes flashed. "To do what?"

Jhon shrugged. "Look. Most of the people who come in here are losers. They're never gonna amount to shit. Even they know it. That's why they get philmed, so they can be *some*one. I'm not selling 'em something they don't already know. I'm just giving 'em what they want."

"No. You're selling them out. The same way you're selling me out."

"You screwed yourself. Don't blame me."

Marta shook her head in disgust. "You're pathetic."

His face reddened. "How stupid do you think I am, not to figure out what you were doing? You're the fuckup here, not me."

He was baiting her, his pride injured, pissed off about being used and trying to get a rise out of her. She cut a quick glance at the other man, whoever he was. He seemed lost in his own thoughts, oblivious to their bickering.

"How long did you think you could get away with it?" Jhon asked. "That's what I want to know."

Marta pressed her lips tight, unwilling to give him the satisfaction. She turned back to the philmhead. "If you're not with the government, who are you with?"

He blinked once, and the unrecognizable Rorschach blotch of features disintegrated into pointillist noise.

"You're a TV?" she said.

The philmhead smiled. His eyes twinkled with static. "It's not as bad as it looks."

It was hard to focus on him. There was nothing for her gaze to hold on to. It was as if he'd scraped the surface off reality to expose an undercoat of raw pixels. "What do you want?"

"To help you."

Marta bristled. "I don't need your help."

"I'm not so sure."

"Think about it," Jhon said, bending close. His breath tickled her. "Your family. Friends. Loved ones..." He let the implication hang in the air—allowed the unspoken threat to rattle around in her head.

"Fuck you!" She spat at Jhon. He stumbled back, his hands flailing wildly as he tried to avoid the saliva. She turned on the TV. "Is this how you get your converts?"

The TV shook his head. "Your situation is different. You have something of ours. Something that's very important to us."

"How could I have something of yours?"

"The child you're carrying," he said. "That's the reason you haven't been feeling well."

Her hand darted involuntarily to her unsettled stomach. How long since her last period? Three months? Four? She couldn't remember—couldn't think. Sure, she was late. But she'd always been irregular. Too skinny, according to Nguyet's divinations. Too stressed.

"That's not possible." She was just late. No way she was pregnant. "I can't be."

"It is," the TV said. "And you are."

"I don't believe you." It could be anything. Lots of stuff could make her throw up, cause her period to be late.

"Have you been to a doctor?" A pause. "I didn't think so. If you want, I will pay for an examination."

He sounded so sure, so confident. "How...?" Marta stopped, derailed by a sudden thought.

"How do I know? Or how is it possible?"

Marta bit her lower lip, worrying it until she felt a sharp stab of pain. "What do you mean the child is 'yours'?"

"I'm afraid I can't answer that now."

She tasted blood, ran the tip of her tongue across the ragged cut. "I want to know what you've done to me."

"You will. Trust me. Now is not the time."

Have faith. Was this what it had meant; that she was supposed to become a TV?

"Well?" the TV said.

She nodded, to herself mostly, and caught a flash of Jhon grinning in triumph. She followed his gaze to her hands.

They were trembling uncontrollably in her lap.

21

An early-morning call from Uri dragged Pelayo out of a heavy sleep. He blinked a few times to clear the gunk from his eye-feed.

"I need you at the lab," the skintech said. His expression betrayed nothing.

"When?" Pelayo sat on the edge of the bed. He ran a hand over his face and scalp, trying to massage himself fully awake as Atossa joined him.

"As soon as possible."

In other words, now. "What's the rush?"

"I'll let you know when you get here," Uri said.

The skintech's image vanished, leaving him staring at the albumin-gray wall across the room.

"Bad news?" Tossa said.

"The lab wants to see me."

"What time is it?" she asked.

Pelayo checked the Hamilton on his left wrist: 6:42.

Atossa groaned as he eased from the bed and wandered into the bathroom to check himself in the mirror.

The blemish had vanished. So maybe it *had* been a glitch on IBT's end and a remote update during the night had fixed it. That could be what Uri wanted to see him about. Or maybe the skintech had found out about his contact with Lagrante.

Panic fluttered in him. His head ached. He leaned on the sink, gripping it tightly as he stared into the faux marble bowl.

What was wrong with him?

After several minutes the pressure subsided. He splashed cool water on his face and willed himself to relax. There was no need to mention the blemish. If Uri asked about it, no problem. It was just a temporary glitch. No big deal. If he asked about Lagrante...

Atossa appeared in the mirror next to him. "You all right?" She wrapped her arms around him from behind, pressing her breasts against his bare back.

"Yeah."

"You want me to go with you?"

Pelayo shook his head. If there was a problem, he didn't want Uri to think she was involved. "I'll be fine."

Her hand slid down and he felt himself stiffen in her fingers.

"I can't," he said.

"I know." She relinquished her grip. "Just wishful thinking."

"Don't."

"You can't keep doing this forever. Sooner or later you're going to have to give it up."

They'd been through this before. "We'll talk about it later."

"That's what you always say. One of these days, there might not be a later."

Whatever *that* meant. He took a cold shower, then reached for the winder on the side of the Hamilton to rephilm himself. Before he could toggle it, the selection menu appeared. Apparently, the

new 'skin had autosynchronized with his extant
brain-computer interface. He didn't need to physically press the crown anymore, just thinking about
doing it was enough to activate his BCI.

Was the philm becoming a part of him? he wondered. Or was he becoming part of it?

"Call me," Atossa said on his way out the door.
"Right away. I want to know how it goes."

———

"How do you feel?" Uri asked.

Pelayo squinted at the skintech under the scathing
lab lights, searching for the fine print. "Great," he
said.

"Any problems?"

"No. So far, so good."

Uri clicked his teeth, then bent over a stainless
steel tray. When he straightened, he held an old-
style syringe.

Pelayo eyed the needle and the cloudy white solution the hypodermic held. In the past, updates to
the 'skin had been made electronically.

Uri smiled at his unease. "I need to tweak the
wetronics in the 'skin to support an add-on."

"What kind of add-on?"

Uri slipped the protective cap from the needle.
"Circuitry to improve synthapse performance. For
various reasons, we weren't able to include it in the
preliminary build." He held up the syringe, tapped
it a couple of times, then squirted a tiny stream of
the milk-white fluid. "It's mostly backend, so you
won't notice much change."

Uri took his right hand, located a vein on the top,
and inserted the needle. There was a brief sting as

the needle disturbed a couple of million nanosocket links connecting the 'skin to his nervous system, then nothing. A minute dot of blood welled up when Uri withdrew the needle.

"That wasn't so bad now, was it?" Uri had a way of condescending that got under his skin worse than the needle.

"Didn't feel a thing."

Uri replaced the empty syringe on the tray.

"That it?" Pelayo said.

Uri nodded absently, already concentrating on the next bullet item on his to-do list. "You're good to go."

———

As soon as Pelayo stepped out of the IBT building, his thoughts turned to Lagrante. Should he contact him? Bring him up to speed on the upgrade? See if maybe he'd heard back from his contacts about ripping the 'skin?

No, Pelayo decided. Let Lagrante sweat for a change, worry that he might decide to take his business elsewhere and let another rip artist have a crack at the 'skin.

He scanned the ad masks circulating up and down Pacific Avenue, looking for one that might be Atossa. She hated his job as a test subject. From the beginning, she'd tried to talk him out of it. Too dangerous, she said. She didn't want to see him get hurt, didn't want to lose him. She'd toned it down. But every so often, like this morning, she tried to scare him.

One of these days, there might not be a later.

None of the ad masks approached him. Just as

well, he wasn't ready to get into it with her. Not yet. Most of the masks were descending on a smob half a block down on Pacific, drawn like vultures to fresh meat.

Pelayo drifted toward the smart mob, caught in the magnetic attraction of consensual curiosity. The attention of the crowd seemed focused on the sidewalk rather than the storefront window displays. Probably some street musician or novelty act had captured the spontaneous interest of passersby and triggered the mass convergence for a particular cast.

"What's going on?" he asked a Goth-philmed yamp. Instead of a full 'skin job, she was waring an ensemble of paste-on cinFX patches and grafts: charcoal eye shadow, white-complected nanoFX paint, mortician-black hair and fingernails.

"Performance art," came the terminally bored response.

The Edward Gorey Gashlycrumb Tiny next to her smirked, hemorrhaging sarcasm. "How can you tell?"

The Goth shrugged, then pressed her black appliqué lips more firmly into place. The paste-on lips had started to peel at one corner, exposing a moist, glistening welt of synthapse collagen and flesh. The cinFX patch seemed irritated or infected. She prodded the sore with the tip of an equally inflamed and disdainful tongue.

A gap opened in the smob and Pelayo caught a glimpse of a pudgy guy squirming on the sidewalk. His feet kicked and legs thrashed, wracked by convulsions, as he fought to pull a Chinamation popera mask from his face.

A shabby street musician, dressed in Confederate

gray, hacked a wad of phlegm onto the ground in front of Pelayo, barely missing the soft patent leather of his shoes. "I guess some ads just can't take no for an answer."

"Buy or die," a woman joked with forced hilarity.

"No, man. That shit started before the mask. He collapsed and all, then the mask jumped his ass."

"Talk about taking advantage," someone else said.

A snicker rippled through the smob.

"Anybody know what store it's from?"

A distant siren warbled. Then the smart mob surged back in a collective muscular contraction.

"Look out! There it goes!"

"Quick! Grab it!"

Slowly, lazily, the popera mask drifted above the smob, face turned to the sky as it ascended, growing smaller and smaller until it slipped from view.

A call, flagged urgent, bleated frantically over his earfeed. But it wasn't Lagrante or Atossa.

Pelayo frowned. "Nguyet?"

"I need your help," his aunt said. "It's an emergency."

22

"Here we are," Jeremy said. The TV helped her out of the private van he'd picked her up in.

"What is this place?" She craned her neck to see, following the straight, rectilinear grid of the building's façade.

"A conference center." He seemed preoccupied. "We use it for a wide variety of activities: Retreats. Seminars. Planning sessions and special events." He led her by the hand to the front entrance. "There are a number of women here already."

"Like me?"

"Yes."

Nadice glanced nervously at the street and the steep hill leading up to the hotel. She didn't want to be here, but Mateus had given her no choice. He would never let her go. He had never intended to. He would string her along with promises or threats, whatever it took to keep her in line.

Jeremy caught her staring at the street. "What?"

"I'm worried about Mateus. He'll follow me. He found me at the shelter—he'll find me here."

"Mateus is your boyfriend?"

She shook her head. "The man I work for. I have something of his. He'll want it back."

"Something you stole from him?" Jeremy said. He turned the full spotlight of his attention on her.

"Not exactly."

He waited for her to explain.

"I'm carrying something for him," she said, uncertain how to word it. She should have said something sooner, so he wouldn't think she was trying to hide it from him.

"Something?"

"I don't know what it is." She rolled her shoulders. "He didn't tell me. I brought it into the country for him, when I was transferred from my previous job in Lagos."

"You're a courier?"

"It was just for this one time. It was the only way I could get free of Atherton . . . so they wouldn't force me to give up the baby."

He frowned, and her stomach pinched. It was over, she thought. No way he was going to take her now.

"Who's the package for?" he asked.

"I don't know. This guy examined me yesterday. I guess whatever I have wasn't ready yet. I'm supposed to see him again."

"When?"

"Today, I think. Mateus was supposed to let me know."

"So there could be others looking for you, in addition to Mateus."

She ducked her head. "I'm sorry."

He smiled philosophically. "These things happen. We'll just have to deal with it, if it comes to that."

Relief flooded her. He wasn't going to cut her loose, wasn't going to send her back to the shelter.

A pair of heavily armored security guards loomed just inside the main double doors to the lobby.

"See?" Jeremy said. "You're perfectly safe. We're used to assholes coming up here and causing problems."

Nadice smiled at the exoskeletoned guards. They projected the don't-fuck-with-me attitude of professionals. The shelter hadn't had security like this. If it had, Mateus would never have gotten inside. He would have a harder time getting to her in here. As far as she could tell, the only way in was through the well-defended lobby.

Jeremy registered her at the front desk. The process involved a DiNa bar code and retinal scan. Since she wasn't waring a built-in eyefeed, she was given a pair of spex. When registration was completed, he took her to an elevator framed by tall plants in Raku pots. The graphene foliage was programmable. It changed shape and texture, alternating between variegated leaves and the fluttering, diaphanous wings of insects. The effect left her unsettled, and more than a little light-headed.

"Hungry?" he asked.

She bit her lip. Her stomach churned, remembering the rice she had tossed on the commuter train.

"You look a little pale," he said. "It might help if you lie down."

———

Her room overlooked the Boardwalk and a ribbon of seawall that meandered along the coast, holding the ocean at bay.

"That's Monterey over there," he said, pointing. Through the floor-to-ceiling window, she could make out the hazy outline of coastal hills hunched across the bay. "On clear days, you can sometimes see whales. Their waterspouts, anyway."

Exhausted, Nadice plopped down on the side of the bed. The tempergel molded to the undersides of her legs.

"Try to get some rest," Jeremy said. "You're scheduled for a medical exam in two hours."

There was a second bed in the room. "Who's that for?"

"We might need to pair you with someone else. I'm afraid space is rather limited right now."

Were there really that many of them?

"I'll check back with you before the exam. In the meantime, if you need anything, feel free to query the building datician."

Nadice fingered the spex in her lap. "How long will I be here?" She hoped it was for a while. She couldn't believe how totally wiped she was...how much tension she had been holding. All she wanted to do was sleep.

"In a day or two, if you're healthy enough to travel, you'll be transferred to a more permanent facility."

"And then what?"

The smile reappeared. "You become a mom."

————

Dr. Kwan pursed cherry-blossom lips as she looked Nadice over. She wore white slacks and a pink disposable lab coat with matching slippers. Her head was shaved. Any second, Nadice expected the doctor's scalp and the rest of her 'skin to philm over with the prickly static all of the street TVs were screening these days.

"How do you feel?" the doctor said.

"Tired," Nadice admitted. The two-hour nap had

helped, but she still felt weary, a little disoriented and, well...overwhelmed. She still wasn't sure what she'd gotten herself into, if this was the right move or not.

The doctor gave a curt nod. "That's to be expected."

Nadice couldn't tell if this vague generalization referred to all pregnancies or to hers in particular.

The doctor pinched the skin on the back of her hand. "It looks like your electronic skin has started to degrade."

Nadice nodded. "It started three days ago."

"I assume there's a security marker in the 'skin, and when the degradation reaches a certain point you'll be toxed."

Nadice showed her the ampoule she'd been given at the Get Reel. "I'm supposed to take this to slow things down. But I've been afraid to take it because...because of the baby."

Kwan plucked the ampoule from her, examined it, then dropped it into a side pocket in her lab coat. "Have you experienced any numbness or muscle weakness so far, or had any difficulty breathing?"

"Not yet."

"Good. Jeremy also informs me you might have been doped with additional GPS, RF, or chemical taggants."

"I'm pretty sure."

"All right." Kwan seemed unperturbed, her manner matter-of-fact and confident, equipped to handle all contingencies. "We'll check for those first. Spybots, too. Might as well cover all the bases." She stared at an eyefeed image and tapped a command on a small palm d-splay.

Nadice watched her brusque, efficient eyes, trying to see into them, through them, for any sign that might betray her underlying feelings.

"Now, let's take a look at the baby. Shall we?" Kwan offered her a clinical smile. Not particularly warm, but what it lacked in fuzziness it made up for in competence.

Nadice relaxed. It didn't matter if the doctor liked her or not. Kwan would do her job. As long as Nadice had the baby, the TVs would protect her, keep her safe.

"Please take off your clothes and lie down," Kwan said, nodding at the recliner in the corner. The doctor dipped her hands into a tray filled with sterilizing solution. When she removed them, they were gloved.

Nadice stripped. The room was aseptically cool. Her nipples, already tender, hurt as they stiffened. At least the tempergel on the cushions was warm. So was the overhead light. The goose pimples on her arms retreated.

"Open wide."

Nadice spread her knees and stared at the milk-white ampoule Kwan held between pinched fingers. "What's that?"

"Nanocams and a linked simage array," Kwan said. "They will embed in the wall of your uterus and keep a close eye on things for us."

Kwan slipped the ampoule in. It was coated with some kind of slick lubricant and dissolved almost immediately.

Kwan produced a second ampoule. "This one contains wetronics to disable the security ware and neutralize any other maltronics you might have picked up. There are also several proprietary applets that will enable us to download and manufacture specific protective n-zymes."

"What kind of maltronics?" Nadice asked.

"REbots and nanomals from industrial spies and black-market hackers looking to steal downloads or rip copies of philm."

Nadice pinched her brow. "REbots? Nanomals?"

"Re-Engineering bots and nanobot malware. They break down the functional and structural components in electronic skin so they can be analyzed and copied. Most of the time they're fairly benign. You don't even know they're there, but not always."

"It sounds like you see that a lot," Nadice said.

"All the time." Kwan deftly inserted the ampoule, then straightened. "We think these bots may be how you became pregnant, by disassembling DiNA sequences, which later recombined to form packets of nanoanimated motile DNA."

Nadice blinked. "Sperm, you mean."

"Yes. Or the functional equivalent."

Nadice clamped her knees together, feeling suddenly vulnerable. "How?"

"We're not sure." Kwan pursed her lips. "The odds of that kind of nanomation and exaptation occurring spontaneously and simultaneously in hundreds of women around the world are astronomical. That's why we believe the mechanism is divine in nature...that it arose from the background radiation of the universe."

Nadice stared at her. "You're kidding, right?"

"In every fetus we've examined so far," Kwan said, "no two DNA profiles are the same. Each contains new genetic material we've never seen before."

Nadice dug her fingertips into her trembling knees. "That's nuts. Just because you don't understand something doesn't mean it's a miracle. How do you know it's not some hack job?"

Kwan's face clouded.

"Do you know what these nanomated genes do?" Nadice asked.

"Not yet. The only thing we know for sure is that the development of the fetus is accelerated."

"Accelerated?"

Kwan peeled the gloves from her hands. "Gestation appears to be about twice the rate of a normal fetus. Growth starts out fairly normal, then speeds up after the first eight weeks or so. We've received a couple reports of early midterm abortions where the baby was developmentally much farther along than it should be."

"Why would they grow so fast?"

"Good question." Kwan tossed the latex gloves into a translucent pink biohazard recycler. "We're still not sure how many of the babies will prove viable. There appear to be a much higher than normal incidence of mid- to late-term miscarriages, possibly caused by the rapid development."

Nadice stared at the discarded gloves. She could lose the baby. That was what the doctor was telling her. "That's why you're looking for pregnant women, isn't it?" she said. "So we won't get abortions when we find out what's inside us."

Kwan folded her arms on her chest. "I want every woman to have access to good information and good medical care so they won't make a rash decision. I want to be sure every baby has a chance."

Why? What were they looking for? Hoping for?

When Nadice got back to her room, she discovered she had a roommate. The woman from the Get Reel. Marta. She lay in a fetal curl on the bed, staring blankly at the eggshell-smooth wall.

"What are you doing here?" Nadice asked. Stupid, but the only thing that came to mind.

Marta sat up. "You, too?"

Nadice nodded, unsure what she was referring to—that the TVs had found her, or that the conception was immaculate.

"I'm sorry." Marta took her hand and squeezed it, first in sympathy, then in solidarity. Marta had long, delicate fingers. Nadice's were ugly in comparison, cracked and calloused from years of cleaning up after other people, disinfecting soiled lives. She pulled her hand back, curling it into a self-conscious ball.

"When did they come for you?" Marta said.

"Last night."

Marta returned a sour grimace. "They caught up with me first thing this morning. Gave me the good news."

"I just had my first exam," Nadice said.

Marta snorted. "I guess they don't waste much time around here. How did it go?"

Nadice sat on the edge of the other bed so they faced one another, her back to the big sun-warmed window. "The doctor inserted some nanocams in me to keep an eye on the baby."

Marta forced a laugh. "I can't wait."

"It's not too bad."

Marta regarded her coolly. "Are you one of them?"

"No."

"You could just be saying that."

"Go blow a wet turd."

This time the laugh was genuine. "What else did this doctor do to you?"

As Nadice relayed the conversation, Marta's expression grew darker. "Talk about fucked," she said at last.

"How do you explain what happened to you?" Nadice said.

"I can't. Not yet." Agitated, Marta pushed to her feet and began to pace. "There has to be another explanation."

Nadice thought of the fish and the bee that had approached her. "There are things out there we don't understand."

"What kind of things?"

Nadice told her about her encounters with the flying fish and the honeybee.

"You're starting to sound like them," Marta said. The comment fell just short of a scoff.

Nadice shrugged. "I'm just saying."

Marta went to the window and gazed out at the ocean, her shoulders rigid, her jaw set. Nadice joined her, resting one hand lightly on her arm. The muscles there were stiff, bundled so tight they felt close to snapping. "You okay?" she asked. Some of the tension under her fingertips eased.

"Just thinking."

"Lot to think about."

"Yeah. Nothing is ever what it seems."

"Including you?" Nadice said.

Marta cut her a scathing glance. "Don't worry

about me. If you're smart, you'll look after yourself. Know what I'm saying?"

"Sure." Nadice dropped her hand and stepped away from the rebuke. She could take a hint. She walked back to the bed, giving them a little space.

"I don't want you to get hurt," Marta said after a while. She seemed to be talking to her own reflection in the sunlit diamond.

"It's not your fault I'm here," Nadice said. "Don't blame yourself."

"I'm not." Marta turned to look at her. "I just don't want it to be my fault if you don't get out."

23

Seoul Man specialized in heirlooms, personal and cultural artifacts he pawned as arcana. His shop on Valencia Street contained an old Curta calculator, a three-meter-long-by-five-centimeter-wide strip of embroidered foot-binding cloth, a Royal manual typewriter, a pair of rhinestone-studded sunglasses purportedly worn in concert by Elton John, various jade netsuke, and a set of eight deformed bullets he claimed had been dug out of the skulls of political rivals and detractors who had been personally executed by Pol Pot during the Cambodian genocide.

"Found at the site of an old Phnom Penh high school that the Khmer Rouge secret police turned into a torture center," Seoul Man told van Dijk, grinning. Under plain brown monk robes he had philmed himself as a gold-complected statue of the Buddha. Black moon-shaped eyebrows framed a red bindi dot centered just above the bridge of his nose. An elaborate ushnisha, with a prominent flamelike halo, crowned his head.

Van Dijk shook his head. The bullets were set in soft foam in a glass-lidded display box with a pewter hasp. "I think I'll pass."

Seoul Man's expression remained placid as he sighed. "That's what everyone says." He closed the lid on the bullets, returned the box to the glass case in front of him, and turned back to van Dijk. "What can I do for you, Detective? It's been a while. I was afraid you'd taken your business elsewhere."

"Hasn't been any business. At least not in your specialty."

"Until now."

Van Dijk reached into his jacket and pulled out a plastine evidence bag, containing the glass earrings and necklace from the dead girl. He held the bag up in the tallow-soft gloom of the shop.

Seoul Man plucked the bag from him and slid it under a magnifying lamp mounted on the top of the case. He peered through the lens. "Roman glass shard," he said. "Crude silverwork, probably modern. Not all that unusual." He straightened. "What else do you want to know?"

"Who made it?"

Seoul Man smiled serenely. "Ahh, so you are buying, after all. Information—the most valuable commodity."

Van Dijk grunted. "How much?"

"Let's find out."

With a quick mental command the antiquarian locked the front door to the pawnshop and d-splayed a BE BACK SHORTLY sign. He then led van Dijk through a rear door, down a short hall to his workroom.

Crammed with equipment, the room was a cross between a physics lab and a museum curator's office. Shelves with dusty brass-knobbed specimen drawers occupied one wall. A scanning electron microscope, X-ray diffractometer, mass spectrometer, gas chromatograph, and acoustic microscopy imager elbowed for space along the remaining walls. The ceramic-topped counter in the center of the room held a stainless-steel sink, a Bunsen burner, and a gene-sequencing centrifuge.

"Any restrictions I should know about?" Seoul Man said. "Special precautions or handling requirements?"

"Just your usual tender loving care."

The antiquarian nodded. He sprayed his hands with liquid gloves. "Where'd the jewelry come from?" he asked while he waited for the translucent latex to dry. "If you don't mind my asking."

"You tell me."

The antiquarian regarded him impassively. "You know what I mean."

Van Dijk nodded. Any trace particles or residue from the site where the earring was recovered might taint the results. "Apartment over in North Beach."

"Does she have a name?"

"Does it matter?"

"Everything matters, Detective. I don't need to tell you that. The Devil may be in the details, but so is God."

"No ID yet," van Dijk said.

"Too bad," the antiquarian said, serenity giving way to sorrow. "I always like to know the names of the people whose lives touch mine."

Van Dijk said nothing.

Seoul Man unsealed the evidence bag, carefully removed the jewelry, and set one earring under a regular light microscope. He activated a wall d-splay and the earring appeared, much larger than life. Magnified, the tiny pits in the square silver frame around the pale azure shard resolved into small nano- or laser-engraved crucifixes.

"Names add a certain value," the antiquarian went on. "A certain meaning that's otherwise missing. Take the victims of those bullets. I haven't been able to identify them yet. I probably never will, but that won't stop me from trying. It's the search that counts, right?"

"A bullet tells more about the killer than the person it kills," van Dijk said.

Seoul Man nodded. "Perhaps the same will be true of this earring." He shaved a miniscule sample of silver from the setting for analysis, followed by a tiny silver of glass. "This may take a while."

"When should I come back?"

"Just before closing." The antiquarian went to one of the machines along the wall. "I have the skulls, you know. Intact except for the bullet holes. I can show them to you, if you like."

24

Over a secure eyefeed, Zhenyu al-Fayoumi d-splayed the project scope and specifications provided to him by the Sigilint datician: Quantum phenotype. Entangled inheritance. Group selection. Instant epigenetic transmission.

He rubbed his eyes. The project sounded like more than a straightforward philm release. The philm would be used to literally create a shared social system or subculture in which everybody dressed and thought in lockstep. Yukawa was basically designing a new kind of smart mob, joined not by mass-mediation but electronic skin.

To what end?

A regular smob formed in response to online stimulus. The goal was to get people en masse to buy a particular product, attend a show, or instantiate a shared group activity, like a pray-in or a political rally.

Yukawa's smart mob would be stable, permanently linked through their 'skin, and programmable—capable of directed action.

A military application, he thought. That made the most sense. Instantaneous field updates of information and ware. Inheritable physical traits and characteristics, such as camouflage. Coordinated group activity. Shared, modifiable habits and tendencies. All of these would be desirable in a combat or security unit.

Of course, there would need to be some kind of fail-safe to make sure things didn't get out of control—some way to isolate the groupware, the quantum-coupled 'skin. How to do that in the case of superposed states? Was it possible? It had to be. There must be a way to induce a null state that contained information that could not be understood from the outside.

Still, he had the feeling that he was missing something, something obvious.

Mokita, he thought. The truth everyone knew, but no one was willing to admit or talk about, even though it was there to see for anyone who cared to look.

Or wasn't afraid of what they might find.

Al-Fayoumi stood in front of a lamp-warmed terrarium and examined the batch of flies he'd 'skinned a few hours ago. The graphene coating had finally cleared on most of them. Now they were slowly reviving.

The problem with smobs was instability. They were inherently chaotic. There was no way to predict the types of conditions that gave rise to random, possibly uncontrollable behavior. Based on his observations of the flies, and the mathematical models he was developing to explain the Lamarckian inheritance of idolons, Yukawa wanted him to come up with an algorithm to predict the acquisition of images and the behavioral traits those images produced in a quantum-entangled group. The project referred to these behavioral traits as LMTs, Learned Memetic

Tendencies. LMTs could include, but were not limited to, memes and habits. It was well established that certain images encouraged similar behavior in people waring those images. That was why people belonged to a certain cast. The images screened by members of the cast conferred an attitude, and codified a certain type of behavior. Images gave people permission to act in a certain way, because the act wasn't carried out by them but by the pseudoself the image represented.

Ultimately, Yukawa's goal was to reduce the unpredictability in smob behavior . . . calculate the expected frequency of random mutations and weight the viability and severity of any such mutations.

The latest batch of newly 'skinned flies was stirring to fitful life beneath the lamps, dry wings twitching intermittently and buzzing.

Al-Fayoumi bent a fraction nearer. One of the flies looked different; it appeared to be two flies stuck together, one behind and slightly on top of the other. On closer inspection, however, he noticed that it was actually one single fly with four wings and an elongated body.

A damselfly.

As he watched, the long, reed-thin body flashed vibrant blue and the head began to rephilm.

Al-Fayoumi blinked several times under the heat lamps. With each staccato blink, the emergent image became clearer, more distinct, until it resolved into the head of a fish with silver scales and gill slits.

He toggled to a real-time simage over his eyefeed

and increased the magnification until the idolon appeared to be as large as his hand.

The damselfish rose into the air, turned, and approached the front of the terrarium to peer at him directly. Half-floating, half-hovering, its gills gulped and its mouth opened and closed.

As if preparing to speak.

25

"It's time," Uri said.

He and Mateus sat in a secure booth in Uri's favorite chat room. The simage construct resembled an old twentieth-century New York City deli complete with wooden tables, scuffed linoleum tile, and dusty fluorescent tubes. Framed black-and-white photographs of classic prize-fights and other boxing memorabilia, like sweat-stained shorts and leather gloves, decorated the walls. There was even a heavy bag hanging in one corner next to a cold case. Uri liked the smell of pastrami, and the pugilistic scratch of a transistor radio behind the cash register, reliving Ali-Frazier, Louis-Schmelling, or some other famous bout. "The quantum ware is fully assembled," he went on. "Ready to extract."

Mateus wet his lips. "When?"

"Tonight."

Mateus rubbed his face. The simage was real-time, transmitted by tight-weave nanotrodes embedded in his 'skin, so Uri knew it wasn't some software affectation but a genuine case of nerves.

"Tonight could be difficult," Mateus said. "The exact timing, I mean."

"Why's that?"

Mateus flexed and unflexed his hands. A sure sign

of trouble. Something was wrong. Apprehension, serrated with impatience, cut into Uri. He opened a d-splay on the table in front of him and packet-sniffed the neural stream from the 'skin the smuggler was waring. The crunkhead was bleeding perspiration, a torrential downpour of jitters. Sweat beaded on his upper lip.

"She flipped." Mateus scratched the back of his neck, chafing under Uri's immediate presence. "Took off before I could stop her."

"You said she wouldn't run," Uri reminded him. "You guaranteed it. No place to go. Too much to lose."

"I'm on it. I'll get her back. No problem."

"Where is she?"

Mateus cleared his throat. "TVs got her."

Unfuckingbelievable. Uri ran the tip of his tongue carefully along the shark-edged tips of his teeth. "Where are you now?" He couldn't tell from the eye-feed. It wasn't the 'skin house where he'd examined the girl last night. There was a bubble window next to Mateus. Filtered sunlight heated the side of his face.

"A hotel, some TV events center. I've got her tagged and that's her last reported location."

"You still receiving a signal?"

"No." A slight shake of the head. "The feed cut out a couple hours ago."

"So the TVs identified the taggant and disabled it."

Mateus squirmed.

"Which means she might not be there anymore," Uri went on. "They might have transferred her someplace else."

Mateus shook his head. "I don't think so."

"Why not?"

"I've been keeping a close eye on the place. She hasn't come out. No one's come out, except for TVs."

"You're positive?"

No answer.

"Make sure," Uri said. "Find out."

"What you want me to do if she's there? I got some boyz—we can go in an' grab the bitch."

"No." Uri's head throbbed. He pressed cool fingertips into his temples. The last thing he wanted to do was provoke a well-organized, well-defended group of religious fanatics. They had the girl. God only knew what she'd told them. He had to assume the worst. That meant she'd almost certainly warned them about Mateus and his crunkhead thugs. Ergo, the TVs would be on the lookout for them. So a direct frontal assault was out of the question. There had to be a way to get to her . . . talk to her, threaten her, buy her. Whatever it took to get the quantum ware. That was the main thing. He didn't care how it happened.

"Well?" Mateus said.

"Stay put. Keep an eye on things. Find out if she's still there but don't take any other action. Is that clear? Call me, but don't *do* anything."

"I gotcha."

"What did you do to her?" Uri asked.

"Say what?"

"To make her leave. You must have done, or said, something." That was the only explanation that made sense. If the girl had really wanted to become a TV, she could have done so at any time while she was working as a maid. People didn't suddenly convert except as a last resort. They'd been backed into a corner financially or emotionally and it was an act of desperation just short of suicide.

"I didn't do shit," Mateus protested.

"Come on. A crunkhead like you, always looking to knock down some dime piece or yamp." Fucker was always bragging about doing it with this or that young tramp.

"Maaan! It wasn't like that. Our relationship was strictly business. No way I'd cut somethin' with that ho."

Uri propped his elbows on the table in front of him and leaned forward. "Tell me."

"I went to get her. At the homeless shelter. Fuckhead at the front desk gave me a hard time. No visitors after 9:00 P.M. Some shit like that."

"So you forced the issue."

Mateus raised his palms. "It wasn't my fault things got out of hand. Goddamned welfare junkies turned it into a riot."

"Why'd you go get her in the first place?"

Mateus shifted uncertainly. "My boyz saw her talking to a TV. I got concerned. Figured I'd better get her ass out of there."

"For being preached to?"

"The TVs been recruiting a lotta pregnant women. Single mothers. I read it on a newzine feed. Free medical care and all."

Uri had forgotten about that. The girl was knocked up. He could use that to find her. He saw that now. It was obvious.

"Find out if she's there," he reiterated. "Rephilm

yourself in case they have your description. Then get back to me and be ready to move."

It would work, Uri told himself. He still had part of the quantum circuit he'd injected into Pelayo. The circuit was entangled, including the part that Nadice still had in her. All he had to do was tweak Pelayo, and the tweak would show up in Nadice.

It couldn't get any simpler.

The more he thought about it, the clearer it became.

———

Giles Atherton sat in his penthouse office, reviewing the retail distribution plans for Iosepa Biognost Tek's upcoming line of designer philm. Ilse Svatba had finally deigned to give him a preview of the fashion downloads that would be available for the custom 'skin he'd contracted for. Dresses, suits, shoes, jewelry, and other designer accessories hung on the Vurtronic d-splays around him.

"If I run across any bootleg copies prior to the official release date," she'd warned him, under the guise of a playful chide, "I'll know whose scent to pass on to our corporate lawyers."

The implication being that he was the only one she'd leaked information to . . . which he didn't believe for a minute.

"Not to worry," he'd reassured her. "I can keep a secret as well as you, Ilse. You know that."

That had earned him a bright, plastic laugh.

It was bullshit, of course, part of IBT's unofficial marketing strategy. She *wanted* the designs to leak into the black-market. Not right away, maybe. But

soon. That would generate buzz. Buzz would generate more buzz, which in turn would generate sales.

"I need a firm release date, Ilse. I need to tell my
retailers when they can expect to receive delivery."

"Soon, Giles. I promise."

"You know what they say about promises."

She had waved one burgundy-gloved hand. "And
you know what they say about believing everything
you're told."

This time, it was his turn to force a laugh. Even if
she gave him a date, there were no guarantees.

He stared at the floor-to-ceiling d-splays, draped
with new clothing. Both the 'skin and philm would
be sold at the network of exclusive retail outlets
located in Atherton resort hotels. As much as
he hated smart mobs, that's what he was trying to
instantiate—a global smob that would drive sales
of the new 'skin through the roof. It would be difficult, but not impossible. Initial market penetration
was the key. Hit critical mass, and he would control
the masses.

He stood, went over the nearest Vurtronic, and
ran his fingertips along the hem of a Mucha-style
dress.

He would need endorsements, of course. Philm
stars. Musicians. Other high-profile celebrities. Once
those were in place, the window of opportunity
would be wide-open. He would have to act quickly,
though. Timing was everything. Not just for the legal sales but for the bootleg ones. They needed to be
carefully coordinated so that initial supply lagged
behind demand.

By how much? That was the question. Not
enough availability, and interest would wane. Vol-

ume would never reach critical mass. Too much availability, too soon, and the novelty would wear off. It was a balancing act. The black-market component was the most problematic. He could control the supply chain for the retail outlets in his hotels. What he couldn't control was the number of rip artists hacking the ware and how many bootleg copies they made. His black-market contact was already pressuring him for the go-ahead to start ripping the 'skin and selling street downloads even though the quantronics weren't up and running yet.

A tiny bell tone sounded over his earfeed, and Uri's secure signature appeared over his eyefeed. Atherton rerouted the message to one of the big Vurtronic d-splays, replacing the Mucha dress with Uri's face.

"We have a problem," the skintech said.

"What is it this time?"

"Mateus. He lost the girl."

With an effort, Atherton kept his face impassive. "Before or after you retrieved the ware?"

"Before. She's with the TVs."

Atheton fought down panic. "I assume you're taking appropriate measures to get her back."

Uri nodded. "But I might need some help."

"I can't be involved. Not directly. You know that."

"You won't be. I need a secure place to hide her. Just for a few hours, until I can extract the ware."

Atherton narrowed his eyes. "Where?" Though he was pretty sure he knew where Uri was headed.

"The Fairmont."

The Fairmont in downtown San Jose was the closest Atherton resort hotel. "I don't like it," Atherton said.

"Dockton is too far," Uri said. "I need someplace closer I can take her. IBT is out of the question. I've got spare equipment in my lab I can use but I need to be able to set it up in a secure location without any questions."

"What about the Seacliff Inn or an Akasaka capsule hotel?"

Uri shook his head. "Too risky. There's no way I can move all the equipment into place without drawing attention."

"There must be some other location."

"Yeah. If I had time to set it up. But I don't. I need it tonight. In a couple hours. You can backdoor me past security as a delivery driver and register the room using one of the disposable DiNA identities you keep lying around."

Atherton took a deep breath . . . let it out slowly. "All right. I'll take care of it."

"One other thing," Uri said.

Atherton waited for the second shoe to drop.

"Mateus."

"What about him?"

"He's becoming a liability."

Atherton waved a hand. "Do whatever you think is best. You hired him . . . you fire him."

"I'm just letting you know."

"Fine. I don't need to know any more." Mateus wasn't his problem. "What about your consultant?" he asked.

The question seemed to take Uri by surprise. "Al-Fayoumi?"

"You were going to keep me posted."

"Everything's fine. I'm keeping a close eye on him." Uri hesitated a beat. "As I expected, he ran a background check on Yukawa and Sigilint."

"And?"

Uri fidgeted under Atherton's irritation. "He appears to have accepted the bio and background information I set up."

"How long before he connects the dots and figures who Yukawa really is?"

"He won't. There aren't any dots to connect."

There were always dots, Atherton thought. Mateus wasn't the only one that might have to be erased.

———

Before approaching TV central, Mateus rephilmed himself as a 1960s Hippie-era dreadhead, complete with tie-dyed T-shirt, Birkenstock sandals, and matted fro extensions he picked up at a warehouse cosmetique. He could have chosen something badass, Bruce Lee or Delta Force D-boy would've been perfect, but decided it would be better not to come at them with too much 'tude. It would only make them uncooperative from the start. Besides, everybody knew those philms were off the shelf—public-domain shit that would cast him as an amateur. Not only would they not give him any intel, they'd totally laugh their asses off at his expense.

Checking himself out in the side mirror of his car, he felt like a pansy. How did a dreadhead talk, anyway?

Fuck it. The sooner he got this over with, the better. You couldn't think too much about shit. You did what you had to do. And you did it meaner and harder than everyone else, and you didn't look back. That was how you got ahead in life. No second thoughts. No regrets. No involvement other than the business at hand. Those were the rules.

It was no different with Nadice. He'd made the mistake of taking a liking to her—of trying to help her out. A moment of weakness, and now he was paying for it. That's how it always was. There was no forgiveness in the world. It didn't cut you any slack. It didn't pay to cut others any slack.

He probably shouldn't have hit her, but he had. He couldn't take that back. All he could do was move forward and keep moving.

Mateus climbed out of his car and made his way down the street to the hotel. On the way he passed a surfhead house fenced off from the street by long boards, dozens of three-meter-high oblongs planted side by side in the ground. The boards reminded him of yellow fiberglass teeth, all cracked enamel and chipped edges.

The TV security guards eyed him suspiciously as he sauntered across the parking lot to the main entrance. Both of them had that static snow job philm that hurt to look at. "What's up, class?"

"What can I do for you?" one of the guards said, his polite voice relayed through little speakers in the thick sound-, bomb-, and bulletproof door.

"I'm here to talk to my sister," Mateus said.

"Your sister?"

"Yeah. Her name's Nadice. She converted last night, and I didn't get a chance to say good-bye."

The guard frowned, and Mateus wondered if the guard knew Nadice didn't have a brother.

"You can't talk to her," the guard said.

"Why not?"

The guard's frown deepened to a scowl. "Because it's against the rules."

"But she's here? Right?"

"I didn't say that."

"Don't you have visiting hours? You know? For loved ones? I'm the only family she's got."

"Not anymore. We're her family now. I'm her big brother." He jerked a thumb in the direction of his sidekick. "And this is her other big brother."

"Come on, bro. I just wanna make sure she's okay."

"Why?" The guard's manner turned overtly hostile. "You the one who smacked her?"

Mateus held up his hands, palms out. "What makes you say that?"

"We see a lot of domestic violence. Boyfriends and husbands trying to apologize and make amends."

"Not me, man. Like I said, I'm her kin." They couldn't prove shit unless maybe they took some soft DNA prints.

"I still can't let you in."

The dude wasn't budging. Clearly a different strategy was called for. "What if I agree to convert?"

The guard shook his head. "Sorry. This center is for women only. You want, I'll send you the address of one of our other conversion centers."

"Sounds like you got a good thing going here. Lots of female company. Must be nice." Mateus grinned, hoping to appeal to the dude's baser instincts and establish some masculine rapport.

The guard's eyes bulged, belligerent. "It's not like that. You some kind of pervert or something?"

Christ. The asswipe was probably neutered. One of those eunuchs churches kept around for choir practice.

"I think you better leave," the guard said. He rested a hand on the taser at his side and nodded for his buddy.

Mateus spread his hands wider and took a step back as the second goon joined the first. "Awright. I don't want no trouble."

"Then hit the road, Jack. And don't come back."

"No problem, man. I gotcha." He bobbed his head like he was stoned, playing the part. With any luck, they'd write him off as a typical dreadhead and forget about him as soon as he was gone, another hapless spoon-cooked soul.

Besides, he had what he needed. Nadice was in the building.

26 "So what's the big emergency?" Pelayo said. He walked toward Front Street and the San Lorenzo levee. The levee was shaded by a line of tall palms that dappled the concrete barrier. Leafy splashes of light snagged on found-art partially embedded in the wall: a bald rubber tire, a twisted bicycle frame, several rust-pitted shopping carts, the glaucoma-dull headlight of an old car, and the hollow tubes of a wind chime that poked out of the mud-colored 'crete like the bones of some exotic bird that had been carried to the bottom of the river, stripped of all flesh, and slowly silted over.

Over his eyefeed d-splay, Nguyet fretted, picking at her front teeth with a ragged thumbnail. "Have you seen Marta?"

"Not since last night."

"She hasn't contacted you?"

"No," he said. "Why?"

"She's missing."

Pelayo shaded his eyes from the metallic shards of glare the wall seemed to emit as part of some slow, steady decay. "What do you mean, missing?"

"She didn't come home last night."

"That's it?" Typical Nguyet. Everything was a

disaster with her. One questionable divination and the world was coming to an end.

"It isn't like her to just go off," Nguyet said.

True. Marta usually stuck close to home, worried about her father.

"Maybe she's seeing someone," he said. It was bound to happen. Even with somebody as closed off as Marta. She shut people out, held them at a distance, but every wall had its cracks.

Nguyet shook her head, obstinate. "She's not involved with anyone. She doesn't have a regular boyfriend."

"How do you know?"

"When she went out last night, around ten, she promised that she'd be back in one hour. We haven't heard from her since."

That didn't prove anything. "Did she say why she was going out?" he asked.

Nguyet nodded. "She said she needed to get some fresh air."

"How'd she look?"

"Fine. A little pale, but not too bad. Not like before. If she was feeling sick, she wouldn't have gone out."

"Was she upset about anything?" He'd pissed her off, but not enough to send her into a serious funk.

"I don't think so. She was alone in her room fifteen or twenty minutes before she left."

"Did Rocío say something to her?"

"No. They didn't fight, if that's what you're getting at. He was asleep." Nguyet chewed at a frayed hank of hair. "I think something bad happened to her. She got into some sort of trouble. I just know it."

The crystals again. Behind her he could see the divination cards spread out on the kitchen table. Seven of them, lined up in a row, one card for each chakra.

"What kind of trouble?"

"I think maybe she's trafficking. I did a reading, and it revealed one crystal inside of another crystal. Something hidden inside of something else."

"Trafficking for who?"

"Her boss. Someone else. What difference does it make?" Nguyet gave him a strangled look. "That's why she hasn't been feeling well. Whatever she's selling is making her sick."

"Just calm down." Telling himself as much as her. "Take it easy. Have you called the police? The local hospitals and clinics?"

"Yes. No one's seen her."

Just like Concetta, he thought, filling in the blank left by the pause between them.

Pelayo was no longer walking. He had come to a dead stop next to the accordion-ribbed trunk of a shaggy palm. Bicyclists and joggers cruised by on the fenced footpath that ran along the top of the levee, their shadows tangling with those of the palms. "What do you want me to do?"

"You know people, right? Street types. Maybe you could ask around, find out if they've heard anything."

It was probably a waste of time—it had been with Concetta. But if he didn't try, he'd never hear the end of it. Nguyet would never forgive him. And if something bad happened...

"Where was she working?" Pelayo couldn't

remember. Marta changed jobs the way most people changed philm.

"This place called the Get Reel."

"All right. I'll see what I can find out."

Nguyet sagged, relieved. "Thank you."

Turning back to Pacific Avenue, Pelayo noticed an ad mask clinging barnacle-tight to the face of the levee.

"Atossa? Is that you?"

No answer.

The left side of the mask was chalk-white, the right side dark brown smudged with black. Filigreed gold leaf gilded the bridge of the nose, brows, and temples. Carbon-black foil, etched with white curlicues, covered the sides of the nose and the cheekbones. Gold outlined a fish's mouth and blue scales on the chin and jaw. A white triangle, outlined in gold, on the forehead, held musical notes.

It looked to be a sculpture, part of the other debris embedded in the wall.

The mask stared blankly at him, its eyes black and unfathomable. The vacant gaze unnerved him. It was like a vacuum, waiting to be filled.

He started to turn away, but the lips moved. Or seemed to. He couldn't be sure. It might have just been the light. He reached out to touch the mask, paused, then withdrew his hand and hurried off. Atossa would be at work by now. If she was keeping an eye on him, he wanted to know.

Model Behavior was located in the old Rio Theater, at the intersection of Seabright and Soquel. It took twenty minutes to climb the hill from the river, past all the tourist shops that had settled there like an incurable infection.

The theater, over two hundred years old, had gone through at least two major fires and several extensive renovations. The only thing that hadn't changed was the chrome-and-glass ticket kiosk out front. The kiosk verified his DiNA bar code, then ushered him into a main lobby decorated with plush red carpet, black marble walls, and decorative, Art Nouveau-embossed tin ceiling panels. The original concession stand had been converted into a check-in desk.

The historical landmark was used for ad demos and fashioneer shows. FEMbots, dressed in the latest designer clothing or philm, strutted down a runway in front of a big d-splay that provided thematic backgrounds. Preproduction ad masks circulated above the seats, colorful as circus balloons and kites.

Atossa worked in a second-floor cubicle, where she pulled the electronic strings on ad masks around the world. Locales like London, Paris, Tokyo, and Beijing. Rich first-world cities teeming with haute couture dilettantes and philmheads from every imaginable cast. Clothiers, perfume and cosmetic manufacturers contracted with Model Behavior to have masks advertise their products in cinephile nightclubs, bars, and cafés. As a sales and marketing tool, it had proven to be particularly effective in politically volatile regions.

Glass cases containing replicas of the masks she was licensed to operate lined the walls of the cramped room. The masks gazed out at him—a Japanese kog-yaru, an Indian Maharani, a Russian zolotaya, a Chinese popera queen—illuminated by a real-time cityscape on the room's Vurtronic d-splay: Moscow, judging by the overcast sky and the even drearier Soviet-era buildings.

Atossa hadn't been looking over his shoulder after all.

She sat at a desk in front of the d-splay. She looked upset, her hair in disarray, her face puffy, her expression glazed. Her brow wrinkled when he stepped through the door. "What are you doing here?"

"I just got done. I was going to call, but I figured I might as well come by and see you in person."

"I wish you'd called." Her mouth puckered, sour. "I'm just getting ready to do a run."

A frown threatened to corrode his smile. "Are you feeling okay? You don't look so hot."

"I'm fine! You're not the only one with a job to do."

"You don't sound fine."

She sniffed, swiped at her nose with the back of her hand. "Christ. I don't know how much longer I can do this."

"Do what?"

She turned away from him, hiding her face while she stared at the d-splay. "Look. This is not the time for a discussion. Not *here*. Not *now*." Her voice came out raw, as if she was about to cry, or had been.

He went to her, bent down on one knee, and tucked a loose strand of hair behind her ear. "What's wrong?"

She shook her head, twisting free of his touch.

"What?" he said. "What's the matter?"

Her back started to shake. Then her shoulders crumpled forward, and a stifled sob escaped her.

"Girls have been getting pregnant." She cleared her throat. "Five I know in the last week. Some of them don't even have boyfriends. You know what I'm saying?"

"I'm not sure," he said.

"Single women. Same-sex couples."

"Wait a minute." Pelayo pinched the bridge of his nose. "Are you trying to tell me you're pregnant?"

"It's not what you think." She refused to meet his gaze.

"What am I supposed to think?"

"I was afraid you'd be pissed."

So this was what she had wanted to talk about last night. He stood. "I thought we were taking precautions. Both of us."

After a second, she turned in the chair to look up at him. "That's what I'm saying. These other girls shouldn't be pregnant."

Pelayo combed his fingers through the lank, unfamiliar hair and began to pace in the tiny room, feeling suddenly confined. "So how did it happen? If it's not mine, then whose is it?"

"I'm not saying I am. I haven't even gotten tested yet. It could just be stress."

Pelayo stared at her, incredulous. If she *was* knocked up, the baby wasn't his, and she expected him to give her the benefit of the doubt.

"I know how it must sound." She dropped her gaze to her lap. "But you have to believe me."

"How come you haven't been tested?"

She shook her head. "I've been afraid."

"Of what?"

"I'm not sure. I know"—she knitted her hands tightly—"it doesn't make sense. But I'm scared."

"You afraid to find out what's going on?" he asked.

She nodded, looked up again. Her eyes were teary, red-rimmed. "Yeah. Maybe. And I don't want to be told it's my fault. That I did something to bring this on myself."

"Like what?"

"I don't know. It's that whole, if a woman gets raped or beaten or something, she must have asked for it."

Pelayo took a moment to let out a deep breath. "So what do you want to do?" he finally asked.

Atossa mashed her lips. Her expression was frayed, pocked with shadows. "If I am pregnant, I'm thinking about getting an abortion..."

Pelayo wasn't sure what to say. Or what she wanted from him.

"...but I wanted to talk to you first."

"Are the other women you know getting abortions?" he asked.

She twisted her hands. "Some of them."

"But not all."

"No."

"It's up to you," he said. "Whatever you think is best." It was her choice, not his. He didn't want to tell her what to do.

"I want it to be a joint decision," she said.

So she wasn't asking for his advice, necessarily, but his support. She wanted him to be there with her, for her. Pelayo knelt next to her again. And when he went to put an arm around her hunched shoulders, instead of pulling away she leaned into him for comfort.

"Piecework," she said after a while.

"What about it?"

"I did that once, when I was fourteen. Grew rotaxanes inside me. That's what this feels like, except it's not my choice."

"You think that's what this is? Some kind of industrial infection?"

She shrugged, then straightened under his arm. "A TV was following me the other day. *Watching* me."

"Where?"

"Here and at home." She rubbed goose-pimpled arms. "It was creepy, like he was checking me out. Keeping an eye on me."

"When was that?" Pelayo asked.

She hugged herself. "Yesterday morning. After I went to the clinic to see about setting up an appointment."

About the same time the TV had been spying on him. Unless it was really Atossa the TV had been trying to keep track of. "Why would a TV want to know whether or not you're pregnant?" he said.

Tossa shook her head. She sucked in her cheeks, the hollows of her face drawing tight and hard.

He rested a hand on one shoulder and squeezed gently, feeling knotted, bone-hard muscle. "You want to stay at my place for a while? Until we figure out what's going on?"

"You sure that's all right?" she said. "It won't mess with the test trial?"

"Right now I'm more concerned about you." He kissed her lightly, tilting her chin like a wineglass between the tips of his fingers, and stood up. "Let me know when you're done here and I'll pick you up."

She followed him to the door. "Where are you going?"

"To get some answers."

27

Kasuo van Dijk sat in his office, staring out the window behind his desk. It wasn't a real window. He kept a permanent real-time d-splay from Japan on the graphene-covered walls of his basement office.

The philm was part of his Samurai pseudoself. Late at night he liked having a little piece of day to light his office. The d-splay provided a view of the rock and raked-sand karesansui garden at Nanzenji, a Zen temple at the foot of Kyoto's eastern hills. Using the nanotrode array woven into his electronic skin, an applet in the d-splay screen kept track of his location and adjusted the view through the window so he saw exactly what he would see if he was looking out the window in Nanzenji. He preferred to leave the graphene on the rest of the walls transparent, showing the bare underlying cinder block.

Turning from the window, he onlined and queried the SFPD datician. "Damselfly search results."

He'd used the damselfly from Lisette's apartment as a baseline parameter, but had instructed the datician to include plus-minus permutations if the initial search turned up no useful results. The search included all known image libraries around the world—both public and private—as well as simage-array databases and online transmissions.

A report d-splay appeared on the wall to the right of his desk. He scrolled through the results. In the last month, there had been three hundred thousand damselfly instantiations worldwide that met the search criteria. Ten thousand downloads a day, on average. Fairly miniscule compared to F8 or XXXodus.

"Limit the search results to the San Francisco Bay Area," van Dijk instructed the datician. "One-hundred-fifty-kilometer radius."

The d-splay repopulated to just under three thousand downloads and simage-array recordings.

Still too many. Van Dijk leaned back in his chair and propped his feet on his desk. Most of the downloads were to Vurtronic d-splays. The graphene screen was capable of producing texture in addition to images, but it couldn't be peeled off. There was no way for the damselfly to take flight from a standard screen.

"Eliminate all Vurtronic downloads," he said.

The list narrowed to six occurrences. None of them were downloads. All of the occurrences were ad hoc simages, programmable graphene appliqués that weren't restricted to a fixed location. Three of the occurrences, including the oldest, took place in Lisette's apartment. Of these, one preceded the time of death of the young woman by twelve hours. One instantiation, the most recent, was in South San Francisco. The second oldest time stamp registered in Dockton. That left Santa Cruz and San Jose, the two most recent occurrences after South San Francisco. All of the occurrences had street addresses but no subnet address.

"Identify origins of these images," he said.

"Unknown," the datician said.

"Trace."

"I'm sorry, Detective. The paths dead-end."

Van Dijk frowned. Whatever it was, it didn't want to be found. He lowered his feet. "Cross-correlate," he said, "based on location and time."

A second d-splay opened on the wall. It mapped the locations in a stack of space-time sheets, starting with the oldest at the bottom and progressing upward to the newest. Lines joining each occurrence helped him to visually track the progression of events, but failed to reveal a meaningful pattern. The links appeared to be random and unconnected.

Van Dijk turned to stare at the karesansui garden. The simage in Santa Cruz was associated with an ad agency, Model Behavior.

Could the young woman have been working as a model, an ad demographic scout, or marketeer?

Van Dijk had the datician submit a request for the firm's employment records. It would take some time to process; he'd need the approval of a judge. The agency hadn't filed a missing person's report with SCPD, but maybe the firm didn't know an employee was missing. It was also possible that she was a former employee.

The address in San Jose was equally baffling. It was subleased to a tenant named Zhenyu al-Fayoumi. A relative, possibly, or a boyfriend? According to the datician, the man was an associate professor with the Developmental Nanobiology Department at San Jose State University.

"Tag him as a person of interest," van Dijk said. "Message him with a request to contact me as soon as possible." If there was probable cause, he could subpoena any call records later.

"Message sent," the datician confirmed.

Van Dijk turned his attention to the Dockton address, a travel agency that was no longer in business and hadn't been for a year.

At a loss, van Dijk said, "Display the images. Oldest to newest."

Several d-splays opened in quick succession to show the now-familiar damselfly, followed by a flying fish, a damselfish, and finally, an ad mask with the mouth of a fish.

"Point of clarification," van Dijk said.

"Yes?"

"Explain the fish images."

"You requested any images that contained elements that were an exact match to those found in the baseline image of the damselfly. The wings on both the flying fish and the damselfish meet that criteria, plus or minus the standard deviation of 2-percent."

"What about the ad mask?" It didn't have any wings that he could see.

"The mouth and scale pattern are an exact match of the fish mouths recorded in the other two images."

Which meant he could probably rule that one out. At least for the time being.

"Calculate and d-splay the most probable locations, from highest to lowest, for the girl associated with the baseline image."

Lisette remained his first priority.

On the d-splay, the address in South San and its assigned probability blinked red at the top of the list.

28

Marta didn't know what to say. She and Nadice couldn't talk, not really. Not with the TVs listening in and watching. Marta could feel their eyes peering at them through nanocams hidden in the walls and the utility dust floating in the cool, recirculated air. The air chafed her skin and smelled faintly of fullerenes.

Nadice didn't strike her as a convert. She wasn't proselytizing, bubbling over with enthusiasm. She seemed more a victim of circumstance than a willing initiate.

Their reasons for being here might be different, but the two of them were more alike than not. They were both guarded, wary.

Still, the silence grated. It was unnatural. No talk was more suspicious than idle chatter. They needed to maintain at least the appearance of normalcy or they would draw more attention to themselves, not less.

"Some music would be nice," Marta finally ventured. Inane, but she was tired of tiptoeing around the forced quiet. The plush bed was starting to feel like a coffin under her, the room a funeral parlor.

Nadice scrutinized her, as if searching for ulterior motives. "I guess. Depends on what they let us listen to."

"Who do you like?"

Nadice gave a halfhearted shrug with one shoulder. "F8's all right." Everybody liked F8. It was the most noncommittal response she could give. "How about you?"

"Zenocide. Evilution."

"Never heard of them."

"Japanese screw."

Nadice regarded her with unabashed skepticism.

"Tokyo punk that's been slowed way down," Marta explained. "It was popular a few years ago, for almost a month."

"Sounds harsh." Nadice sat up on her bed.

Marta shrugged. "No different from wrap or spunk."

Nadice gave Marta a blank look. "I don't listen to a lot of music," she confessed.

"Not your thing?"

Nadice's smile was more of a wince. "I guess not. My grandmother wasn't into it. So neither was I."

"She didn't approve?"

"No. I mean, we sang in church and all, like everyone else. But when we were at home she liked things quiet while she painted, and that was nice. I got used to not having very many distractions."

"Your grandmother raised you?"

"I was adopted—one of those frozen fetuses that Right to Light women decided they'd give birth to so we wouldn't get cloned."

Marta steered the conversation toward safer ground. "What kind of stuff did she paint?"

"People, mostly. Landscapes. She worked with electrostatic gel and LEBs, light-emitting bacteria.

After they were dried and polished, she sold them on consignment in a couple of bazaar shops."

"Was she any good?"

"Yeah. I used to watch her when she wasn't looking and wish she'd paint me, put me in one of her scapes. You know, take me from this world and put me in another world."

"Why?"

"Because that way she could make me more beautiful. I could live in a nice house with beautiful gardens forever."

And without worries. "Like philm," Marta said.

"Except I'd never get old or sick, and I wouldn't want to change." Nadice's gaze slid past her. "I wouldn't want to be someplace else or someone else. I'd be happy with where I was, and who I was."

―――――――

"What about you?" Nadice said when the sun was a little higher in the tatty denim sky, the glare off the bay brighter. "Why are you here?"

"It's complicated." Marta stared up at the light rippling on the LED-dotted ceiling panels.

"You don't have to tell me if you don't want."

"My older sister," Marta said finally. "Concetta. I'm trying to find out what happened to her."

Nadice shifted on the bed beside her, a dim blur along the chalk-white rim of Marta's vision. "She disappeared?"

"Three months ago. Just like that. No message, no nothing."

The shadow scooted closer. "I'm sorry."

Marta adjusted her shoulders on the creased bedspread. "We don't know why she vanished. If it was something we did. Something she wanted to do. Or..."

Or what? That was the hardest part.

"That must be terrible," Nadice said. "Not knowing, I mean."

"Yes." Marta stiffened under the fingers that brushed her arm. But the touch was brief, as tentative as it was comforting.

"Do you think she joined?" Nadice said.

"No." Marta blinked, and the light on the ceiling blurred and smeared.

"Then how come you're here?"

Marta closed her eyes and tried to sink into pinched blackness. But even the dark hurt to look at.

"Maybe you're not just looking for your sister," Nadice said. The words trembled, like water in a glass. "What if you're also trying to find yourself?"

A TV came for them late in the afternoon.

"Everything all right in here?" she asked, poking her head into the room. Blinding sunlight skipped off the flat surface of the bay, washing out the digital lint clinging to her head and arms.

"Why wouldn't it be?" Nadice said.

The TV's gaze flitted anxiously between them. "Just wondering."

"What's up?" Marta asked. The TV wasn't just checking up on them out of goodwill. Her lead-in was clumsy, a pretense.

"There's a meditation session at four-thirty for all the new mothers. We'd like you to attend."

"What kind of meditation?" Nadice said.

"Think of it as an orientation." The TV smiled sweetly. "It's to help you settle in and answer any questions you might have."

Time to get indoctrinated. It was bound to happen. Sanctuary always came with a price.

———

The meditation room had once been a penthouse restaurant with a 360-degree view of Monterey Bay and the Santa Cruz Mountains. The windows had been replaced with programmable graphene panes. Some of the panes were clear glass, others were philmed with silk fabric. The floor was bare oak. Except for a table set up at one end of the room as an altar or pulpit, there were no tables or chairs. Tatami mats had been laid on the floor in even rows. The mats were identical, two-foot-by-three-foot rectangles spaced three feet apart.

Two dozen or so women milled around the room. Most clustered in groups of two or three. Roommates sticking together. Huddling against the unexpected. Nadice stayed close to Marta, quiet but welcome comfort.

Whispers circulated around the room in currents as subliminal as the movement of air. Eddies formed and dissipated, little whorls of conversion that tugged her in, then let her go.

Some of the women seemed excited, jubilant. The true believers. Those who had asked to come here or decided to convert after the fact.

Nadice nudged her in the ribs. "Check that out," she whispered, her breath warm and moist against Marta's ear.

Marta turned her attention to the altar. It was dec-

orated with an odd collection of apparently unrelated objects: a brass handbell with a mahogany
handle; a white porcelain bowl; a short glass tube,
filled with water or some other clear fluid; and a partially empty wine bottle. It didn't make much sense,
but the items had been carefully, artfully, placed.

"Ikebana," Marta said.

"What?"

"Japanese flower arrangement. It reminds me of
that, but without the flowers. Everything perfectly
positioned." Marta had come across the term at the
store where she worked before the Get Reel.
Runeways specialized in self-help spirituality. The
shop carried everything from tarot decks, aromatherapy sticks, and books on the *I Ching* to
chakra-stimulating body art and water-divination
kits. "It literally means to 'make flowers become ac-
tive, or alive.' The idea is that the person arranging
the flowers is supposed to give life to them even
though they're dead."

"Give life how?"

"By arranging them in a way that they enhance
each other and give the illusion of life."

Nadice frowned, leaving a cleft in her forehead.
"Why kill something just so you can make it look
alive?"

Good question. Marta stared at the altar. Religion
was more about death than life. Overcoming death.
Being resurrected, born again, or raptured into life
everlasting.

Was that why she wanted to find Concetta? Was
she afraid to let go, afraid that a part of her would
die with no hope of salvation if Concetta died?

When the priest entered the susurration died, like windblown grass falling suddenly, eerily, silent.

"That's Jeremy," Nadice said.

The whisper stirred tremulous eddies. Marta blinked. "Who?"

"The TV I told you about. The one who was super nice. The one who talked to me at the shelter."

He wore a static-philmed robe. The static changed color and intensity as he made his way to the table. From there, he gazed out at them and spread his arms, lifting them high. The ceiling lights doused and the graphene panes opaqued, ebony awash in a blizzard of pure white static.

Stars. That was what the static represented; hundreds of billions of tiny pinpricks of light.

It was as if the windows and the ceiling had vanished... or had never been there at all.

Jeremy lowered his hands. As he did so, acolytes began seating the women in the room, helping them onto the mats.

Nadice squeezed Marta's hand—giving or receiving reassurance, Marta couldn't tell—then lowered herself to the mat she was standing on. Marta sank to her knees and sat back on her heels, relieved to be off her feet.

"The light of the universe," Jeremy said when the congregation stilled. He picked up the brass bell and raised it, like a chalice. "In the beginning, there was the Singularity," he intoned.

"One light," the acolytes replied in unison.

He rang the bell... a single pure note that reverberated for a long time before falling silent. "The mind of the universe fills our minds."

"One mind," came the response.

Jeremy laid the bell gently, soundlessly on the table. He picked up the glass tube. Placing a thumb over one end, he uncapped the opposite end and held it over the ceramic bowl. "The heart of the universe fills our heart."

"One heart."

Jeremy lifted his thumb, allowing a drop to fall into the bowl. There was a gentle plop. Concentric waves rippled across the walls. The room seemed to vibrate. Marta's head roiled.

Jeremy set the glass tube on the bowl, fitting it into notches on the rim, then lifted the wine bottle to his lips. "The breath of the universe fills our lungs."

"One breath."

Instead of sipping from the bottle, he blew into it, coaxing forth an eerie, haunting note.

"The blood of the universe flows in our veins," he said.

"One blood."

This time he tipped the bottle. The blood-red wine touched his lips, but he set the bottle down without drinking.

"The life of the universe flows in our lives." His voice was a sonorous singsong.

"One life," came the chorus.

Jeremy spread his arms wide, as if to embrace them all. An ethereal keening rose within the room.

Marta glanced around. The acolytes had closed their eyes and bowed their heads, touching them to the mats. Everyone else, except for the converts who were copying the acolytes, were doing what she was—watching.

Nadice, looking like a bound prisoner on her knees, mouthed something under her breath.

This is crazy.

Marta nodded, all she could manage. She too felt caught—trapped by the sound. Eventually the keening would absorb her, swallow her whole, and she would lose herself in its dying echo.

29

Pelayo loitered across the street from the Get Reel. He sat on a wooden bench and nursed a mocha while he watched the cosmetique, waiting for an opening.

It was busy. A fat white guy did the actual modwork—tats, philm edits, grafts, and appliqués—while a girl worked the counter. She sold ware that didn't require professional installation and helped customers try on accessories in curtained-off fitting stalls. Most of the customers were teenage kids and chronic philmheads. Lowest-common-denominator clientele.

What the hell was Marta doing, working in a place like this? It didn't make a lot of sense. In some ways, she was even more of a stranger than Concetta.

Pelayo finished the mocha and tossed the plastine cup into the recycling bin next to the bench. Distracted, his gaze traveled to a nearby boutique called Third World Threads. Colorful dresses and blouses hung in the large display window. The designs were mostly African, and included a number of fashionable headdresses. Next he checked out the latest selection of surfware at a Hang Ten shop. Hang Ten sold surf and skate clothing with waterproof wetronics. They had a decent selection of loud Hawaiian shirts, tees, and shorts.

He selected a black-and-red-flowered shirt, a pair of smart-camo cargos, and rubber-soled shoes. In one of the tiny fitting rooms, he dephilmed. But when he tried to download The Hang Ten ware, the beta clothes refused to update. Uri hadn't authorized him to modify the default settings. He couldn't change the way he looked.

Ten minutes later, there was a sudden lull at the Get Reel. A smob had formed at a sidewalk display half a block down, sucking people out of the Get Reel.

Pelayo crossed the street and pushed open the glass door. It chimed in response to his DiNA signature and greeted him in a bright contralto. "Welcome to the Get Reel, your chance to get a life."

Pelayo made his way past racks of nanomated appliqués, bacterial tinctures, and nanoFX sculpture paint to the sales counter. Shrill muzik plucked at him, whining for his attention.

"Can I help you?" The girl sported an uncomfortable-looking pair of face screens—gold Renaissance-carved picture frames attached to a red velvet mask that concealed the top half of her face and forehead. Below the mask, her lips sagged in a desultory pout, languid as half-melted wax.

"Your boss around?"

"You a rep?"

"Philmplants."

"What kind?"

Like she really cared. "Genital."

"Yeah?" She smacked her lips.

He stepped away from the counter and reached for his fly. "You wanna private demo?"

That did the trick. She rolled her eyes in exagger-

ated disgust and jerked her head in the direction of
the privacy screen set up at the back of the store.
"Jhon's in back."

"Thanks." He winked at her. It had the desired effect; her eyes glazed over with practiced stupor.

"Whatever." She yawned and rhinestones glit-
tered on her tongue, chipping away at the enamel
on her teeth.

Pelayo slipped behind the screen, through a cur-
tained doorway into the edit room. The curtain was
sound-absorbent. When he zip-locked it in place,
the muzik retreated to a distant screech. The room
was furnished with a recliner that flattened into a
table. The overhead LEDs were surgically bright and
recessed.

A door on the far side of the room stood partially
open. Pelayo went over to it and peeked in through
the narrow crack.

Jhon slouched behind a desk, a pair of wasp-sleek
spex screwed tightly into his sockets. He wore a
NASCAR pit cap over pale hair that hung in limp,
stringy tangles. A faded black-and-white-checkered
flag flapped on the front of his sweat-stained T-shirt.
The 'skin he wore was philmed with stock-car racing
decals as well as ads for various brands of motor oil,
lite beer, and domestic cigarettes.

The man had attitude, Pelayo had to give him
that. Jhon's hands were concealed below the back
edge of the desk, fiddling with something in his lap.

Pelayo rapped on the door. "Excuse me."

The guy started. His hands jerked into view.
"Who the hell are you?" He gaped, his mouth slack,
his cheeks flushed pink.

"Jhon, right?"

Embarrassment turned to anger. "How'd you get in here?"

"Your girl out there. She was real helpful. I give her high marks for customer support."

Jhon wet his lips and removed the spex, leaving two circular indentations around his eyes. "Who you with?"

"That's not your concern."

Jhon risked a glance at the door. Pelayo shut it behind him with a soft click. Now, it was just the two of them. He took a step forward.

"What the hell do you want?" Jhon set the spex on the desk and made a show of collapsing them into a medallion-thin disk.

Pelayo leaned heavily on the desk, resting his palms on the front edge. "I'm looking for Marta."

"She's not here."

It came out quickly, too quickly. "Yeah, I already got that. Now tell me something I don't know."

Jhon fidgeted with the spex. "I don't know where Marta is. She never showed up for work."

Pelayo watched Jhon's pudgy hands twist and untwist, fumbling to get a firm handle on the lie. "I don't believe you."

"Fuck you. It's the—"

Pelayo shoved the desk. Hard. It caught Jhon in his doughy paunch, doubling him over with a half-congealed grunt. The spex dribbled out of his grasp, skittered across the table, and dropped to the floor.

The guy might be soft, but he was heavy, deadweight. It took everything Pelayo had to push him into the wall and pin him there, gasping for air, spittle drooling down his chin.

"You're starting to piss me off," Pelayo said.

"—the truth," Jhon finished, coughing up the words in a phlegmatic gurgle. "I swear."

Pelayo cupped a hand to his ear. "What's that?"

"She quit this morning."

"When?"

"First thing." Jhon wheezed several times in quick succession, panting. "She gave notice. Walked out."

Pelayo kept the pressure on, his weight against the table. "She say why?"

A hasty shake of the head. "There was a fucking TV with her. The two of them left together."

"She converted?"

"What do you think?"

"I think you're lying." Marta would never convert, not willingly. Would she? The Marta he knew, or thought he knew, didn't believe in anything—not even herself most of the time.

Pelayo lifted the table a few centimeters off the floor and heaved his weight into it, jamming Jhon's ribs and cutting off a sharp yelp of pain. "You got one more chance," he said.

Jhon's eyes lolled. Saliva glistened on his chin and a sour stench bubbled up from his throat. Pelayo eased off enough for the guy to draw in a breath. Jhon grimaced as he sucked air through his clenched teeth.

"Turned her in," Jhon grated. "The TVs. They pay me. To recruit."

"You sell customers to them?" Sweatshops. Indentured help. Pelayo knew that shit happened all the time. But religion. Christ.

"Most of 'em are worthless fuckheads, anyway," Jhon said by way of justification. "Street trash."

"That what Marta was?"

"Naw. Marta was a knocked-up cunt. What the TVs are looking for now. Paying extra for them. Triple, if they're between the ages of fifteen and thirty-five."

"Why?"

"How the hell should I know? Maybe the only quim they got these days is old and dried up."

"How do you know she was pregnant?"

Jhon snorted. "Sick all the time. Plus, no tampons in the garbage for the past few months. I don't know who dirty-dicked her. I didn't think there was a key in the world that would open that box."

Pelayo tightened his grip on the edge of the desk. "Where'd he take her?"

"Beats me."

Pelayo lifted the desk a few centimeters off the floor, threatening to give it another shove.

"I didn't ask," Jhon said quickly. "None of my business." Sweat streamed down his face. His cap was flaccid, drenched with sweat. Greasy hair coiled out from under the rim. His eyes were jaundiced under the LEDs. "What're you gonna do?"

Pelayo breathed heavily, from anger as much as exertion. He eased away from the desk, taking a step toward the door.

As soon as the pressure let up, Jhon thrashed, struggling to free his arms. The desk lurched forward, exposing an open fly and a glimpse of pale freckled white, shriveled in folds of denim and tawny hair. "Asshole!" Jhon started to stand. "You're gonna pay for this."

Pelayo kicked the chair out from under him and Jhon went down hard. His head slammed against the wall, then the floor. He lay on his side, groaning, the floor tiles under his face bright with blood where he'd bitten through his tongue.

———

On his way out of the cosmetique, Pelayo messaged Atossa. "Have you got a few minutes?"

"Where are you?" she asked over his earfeed.

"The Get Reel."

"What are you doing there?"

"I'll explain in a second."

The counter girl was busy with two young tramps, discussing the merits of scented skin bacteria. The yamps, fifteen or sixteen, were dressed as grade-school kids in pleated skirts, knee-high stockings, and Mary Janes.

Hanging on to their lost youth, he thought. Pretty soon they'd be wearing designer diapers.

"Thank you for your patronage," the door said on his way out. "Please come back reel soon."

"What's going on?" Atossa asked when he was on the sidewalk.

"Do you know of any TV centers near downtown?" She might have heard something through friends or coworkers if a Model Behavior client had approached the agency about selling to the TVs.

"What do you want with them?" Tossa said.

"Marta."

"What about her? What are you talking about?"

"I think she's in trouble."

"What kind of trouble?"

Across the street, the main door to the Get Reel opened and the two young tramps stepped out, blithely preening and chattering, oblivious to the world.

"I'm not sure. But I think she might be at a TV center. One that's recruiting only women."

"Serious?"

"That's what I'm trying to find out."

"I think there might be one up on West Cliff," Tossa said. "We're not supposed to ad mask up there. It's a no-fly zone."

Pelayo watched the yamps prattle down the sidewalk, forcing other people to step out of the way.

"I have an idea," he said. "But I need your help."

30 Zhenyu al-Fayoumi discovered the surveillance nanocams by accident. The tiny photoreceptors had been designed to accumulate in the eyes of insects. One of the bugs happened to be a mosquito. When he'd squashed the mosquito on his arm, a few hundred thousand cams had found their way into his bloodstream, where they had been detected by a linked antigen array on the lookout for toxins, nanomals, and other free-radical hazards to his health.

He stared at the smear of blood, short of breath and angry. He'd hoped Yukawa wouldn't feel the need to watch him. The cams demonstrated a lack of trust that was hard to excuse.

But it got him thinking. With the addition of the nanocams, the mosquito's phenotype had been altered. It had acquired a new trait that modified its basic function in the environment. Not unlike the Lamarckian inheritance of habits.

Except that it wasn't really inheritance. Behavior wasn't being passed down from one generation to the next. It was being passed from one environment to another. From one program mode to another.

Excited, al-Fayoumi set to work in the shuttered gloom of his lab. Yukawa, or whoever he was, had provided him with a schematic of the quantum

processor that would be used in the new 'skin. The
processor had many different possible modes, or
structures. These structures existed in a state of
quantum superposition. They weren't fixed, but
overlapped in a phased array of many possible
processors that formed a single unified processor.
The result was a distributed resonant state of software and hardware, a shared holographic domain
where each processor contained information about
the larger processor.

Over his eyefeed d-splay, this processor resembled
a complex organic molecule made of artificial
atoms...clouds of trapped electrons that functioned
as transistors. The molecule had been flattened—
pressed onto a programmable graphene layer—
where the superposed configurations existed in
phased simultaneity.

A utility provided with the quantum chip allowed
him to switch between different possible states,
modalities of behavior as he had begun to think of
them. When the q-chip was collapsed into one
modality, it resembled a standard biochip.

He plugged the q-chip into a virtual computer,
tweaked the operating system to accept the new
processor, and ran one of the simplest behavior programs he'd developed to explain the transmission of
idolons in flies. He logged the results, reran the program using different input, then repeated the
process again.

Gradually, he began to see what Yukawa and
Sigilint were trying to do.

The phased-array processor gave rise to a distributed metaprogram that ran across all instances of
the quantum-coupled 'skin. People wouldn't be war-

ing different 'skin, but a single distributed 'skin that was essentially holographic. Each piece might appear to be separate, independent, but it contained information about the whole and was influenced by the whole.

From what he had read about Lamarckian social inheritance, specific sets of habits tended to lead to a certain type of behavior. Plug in a set of initial attitudes and behavioral tendencies, and in theory you could predict how a closed population would evolve—if the community would become functional or dysfunctional, supportive or divisive, apathetic or energized, peaceful or violent.

Useful information. He could see where it might have applications when it came to setting up and managing mass-mediated casts that needed to integrate people from a wide variety of cultural, political, social, and economic backgrounds.

Assuming the equations that described the exchange and expression of images in flies could be applied to people. Ten years ago, electronic skin and philm had been illegal, available only on the blackmarket. Now that it was regulated, most people wanted to be philmed. It had become a means of self-expression and tribal identification with a certain group. That was why Yukawa had approached him: Siglint believed its quantum-coupled 'skin would become the new paradigm for personal and group behavior. If Sigilint succeeded, the biological manipulation of social structure would be replaced by digital manipulation. People would be connected in a way that had never before been possible.

It raised a lot of questions. Would the new system

preserve diversity or eliminate it? What about ethnicity or cultural values? Would people with the same morals all look the same? More important, whose morals would they have?

Hard questions, questions he wasn't prepared to answer.

His mind burned, feverish. Glare from the bright light outside his window wells seemed to set the dingy yellow curtains on fire. He could feel himself slowly turning to ash in the blaze, growing lighter with each passing minute.

He needed to take a break. Eat. Get some rest so he could think clearly... decide what to do.

But he wasn't hungry, or tired. He paced the kitchen. His head ached with a dry, septic heat that left him agitated and confused.

After several minutes, he found himself staring at the flies in their terrariums. The damselfly was gone. He didn't see it anywhere. He blinked, pressed his fingers into his eyes, but his vision remained blurred.

Fresh air, he decided. That was what he needed.

He took the stairs. The elevator was faster, but the exertion would do him good—loosen muscles, get the blood flowing.

By the time he reached the roof, he was breathing heavily and his calves ached. A fine sheen of sweat glistened on him. He took out a handkerchief and wiped his face and the back of his neck. A fetid inversion layer had settled over San Jose, trapping the stink of brine and hydrogen from leaky fuel cells.

A tall Kevlex fence encircled the roof, preventing anyone from leaping to the street below. Debris clung to the netting, dead palm fronds and wind-blown scraps of paper that had somehow escaped biodegradation and reclamation bots.

He shut the door to the stairwell behind him. The roof was studded with circular exhaust vents and fans. A pile of old plastine window frames lay in one corner. A pigeon-spattered roll of photo-tunable cellophane, partly unrolled, lay in skeins on the bituminous, gravel-covered roof.

At some point in the past a makeshift greenhouse had been built against the waist-high cinder-block wall that supported the Kevlex fence. Three plastine frames, spaced two meters apart, stuck out from the wall to create four stalls. The stalls, covered by a rectangle of cellophane, were about a meter deep and three meters long. A single row of chipped gray cinder block, stacked three high, formed a low retaining wall for the potting soil that had been hauled up and tamped into the stalls. The cellophane was dual purpose. It trapped heat and provided electrical power to the full-spectrum LEDs glued to the wall. Most of the lights were burned out or broken, dulled by dust.

Faded Jackson Pollock tangles of graffiti covered the pocked and weathered wall. Before the building had been renovated by the city, the roof had been home to an itinerant homeless community.

Gravel crunched under his boots as al-Fayoumi made his way to the endmost stall, tucked into one corner of the roof.

He pulled aside a curtain of dull plastic, ducked his head, and stepped over the cinder-block threshold.

The sagging cellophane had pulled loose at the wall, torn down by rain and the puddles of dust that had accumulated in the creases. The potting soil had washed away from the window frame on that side, leaving a furrow where the runoff had drained. He crab-walked to the wall and stood up in the gap between the cellophane and the window frame. He loved the view from here, south to the minarets, onion domes, and pagodas of the Coyote valley e-cologies and r-cologies. The philmscape shimmered with heat, rippling residential Monet gardens, purple and orange Wolf Kahn trees, and monochrome Hong-Oai mountains, shrouded in chemical-white mist and industrial black shadows.

Cirrus clouds streaked the afternoon sky. A loose corner of cellophane flapped as a breeze stirred his short-sleeved shirt and the hair on his arms. When the gust died down the tickle remained. Al-Fayoumi brushed his left forearm, and felt wings flutter under his fingertips where an image of the damselfly had appeared on his 'skin.

No, not an image. Like a tattoo brought to life, the damselfly emerged. First one wing, then another. As the body thickened into a bas-relief and started to wriggle free, it became fishlike.

Al-Fayoumi gripped the edge of the wall and stumbled back, his arm outstretched. The area immediately around the image itched. But there was no blood as the synthapse connections between the electronic skin and the underlying tissue ripped, then pulled loose.

The damsel drifted idly for a moment, its wings testing invisible currents, then, with a quick flick of its body, angled toward him. In addition to the head

and mouth of a fish, the nanomated creature had acquired a tail and dorsal fins.

"Who are you?" al-Fayoumi asked.

The nanomal circled slowly. It seemed to float
rather than fly, fragile, lighter than air.

Yukawa, al-Fayoumi decided. He couldn't think
of anyone else who might want to hack into his
'skin.

"I'm not what you think," the idolon said. The
voice over his earfeed was soft and flutelike. The lips
synchronized perfectly with the words. It looked
and sounded as if the fish were actually speaking.
"Neither is Yukawa."

31

"I can't go through with this," Nadice said. She paced in front of her reflection in the window. Below the hotel, under late-afternoon clouds, yellow LED lights on the pier marched out to sea and an advancing fogbank.

"You have to," Marta said.

"Why?"

"What choice do you have?"

Nadice swallowed. Her cheeks flushed, blazing with anger and determination.

Marta's gaze hardened. "What are you going to do?"

Nadice stripped off her yellow dress and, tipping her chin up, knotted the flimsy cloth thin and tight around her neck.

Marta shook her head. "It will never work. They'll stop you. Whatever you do, it will only make things worse."

Nadice stared at Marta, defiant, her breasts rising and falling between the trailing ends of the dress, the pulse on the side of her neck panting against the twisted makeshift noose.

Marta's pulse throbbed in her chest. Sweat trickled between her breasts. After a moment she stepped forward and coaxed open Nadice's clenched fingers, clasping them in her own so she could loosen the knot.

"You really want to die?" Marta asked, watching the shadows of the day lengthen into late afternoon.

"What do you think?"

"Everybody wonders what it would be like to kill themselves."

They lay facing each other on the bed closest to the window, whispering softly so they might not be heard. Each time Marta spoke, the centimeters between them stretched to kilometers and the air felt bruised and pulpy.

"The job you quit," Marta said. "Was it really that terrible? There was no way to make it work?"

"The man I was working for threatened me," Nadice said. "He already tried to kill me once."

"I can't go back either," Marta said.

"Why? Does someone want to kill you?" Nadice spoke lightly, joking to ease the tension.

"I made a deal with someone," Marta said. "A promise. If I don't keep it, I'll die, too."

Nadice narrowed her eyes to luminous white slits. "You're serious."

"Dead," Marta said.

—————

Marta lay perfectly still, listening to their breathing. After a time, their inhalations and exhalations synchronized, becoming one breath.

"I overheard one of the girls talking right after the service," Nadice said when the sky had gone black. Bubonic. "One they brought in just this afternoon."

"And?"

"She said it's all over the newzines, how women

are getting pregnant for no reason. A lot are getting abortions, before their boyfriends and husbands find out. What's weird is the babies are farther along than they should be, just like Dr. Kwan said, except that some of them are smaller than normal."

"Do they know why?"

"Not yet. The problem is, a lot of women don't know if the babies are legit or not. Some women have even been killed because their boyfriends thought they were cheating. The accelerated development makes it look like conception was at a different time than it really was."

It figured. Fear. Jealousy. Superstition. People came up against something they didn't understand, and they panicked—or used it to justify a prejudice or policy they wanted to impose.

"There's another solution," Nadice said, long after Marta thought she had drifted off.

Marta didn't answer immediately. She wasn't sure she wanted to know. "What's that?"

"Miscarriage."

Marta grimaced. She didn't think she could go through with it—physically injure herself or Nadice.

"The TVs wouldn't want us anymore," Nadice said. "That's the only reason we're here. Take that away and they'll let us go. There won't be any reason to keep us. Kwan told me there are a lot of miscarriages after the first trimester. So if we did it right, it could look like an accident."

"Could you do it?" Marta asked.

Nadice shrugged. "I'm not saying it would be easy. But if we had to, if we didn't have a choice, it's an option. That's all."

"I hope it doesn't come to that."

"Me, too." Nadice moistened her lips. "I just don't know what's inside me? It's creepy, especially if we're farther along than we think and it's going to grow even faster now. You know?"

The corners of Marta's mouth tightened. "I know." She found Nadice's hand on the bed next to her and squeezed it. "I'm scared, too."

32

The South San Francisco address for the damselfly, and hopefully Lisette, turned out to be a budget r-cology not far from SFO International Airport.

The modular housing stack was a twenty-story steel frame with track-guided forklift arms that raised/lowered portable housing units into slots in the structure. Once in place, the PHUs tapped into public service lines built into the frame. Most of the vacant spaces on the exterior of the building were covered with ad d-splays for fast-food franchises, or architectural façade panels philmed to resemble Renaissance balconies, garden terraces, or Italian-esque frescoes.

Kasuo van Dijk parked his sedan at the corner of Seventh and Walnut. He stepped out of the car and mentally conjured a HUD over his eyefeed.

"Location map," he instructed the SFPD datician. "Satellite and street image overlay."

"Resolution?"

"Standard."

An overhead view of the building and several surrounding streets appeared on the heads-up d-splay. A red dot identified the location of the damselfly. A green dot marked his position even though he could see himself moving real-time in the image, dodging an electric robo-lorry as he crossed the street and made his way to the side of the building.

The neighborhood, zoned mainly for travel and airport support services, was bustling. One of the rail forklifts was lowering a PHU to the ground, leaving a gap-tooth hole where it had been removed. Exposed wires and pipes dangled in the opening. Van Dijk couldn't see out the back end. His view was blocked by another PHU that had been slotted into an abutting hole from the frame's interior courtyard.

Rent in this type of r-cology was cheap. The target demographic was tourists and temporary/contract workers who moved from job to job or city to city, and lived out of a PHU, which was significantly larger and more comfortably equipped than the coffin-sized sleepods found in a typical Japanese racktel.

"Three-d building schematic," van Dijk said. "Display a cutaway of the site and each of the adjoining PHU slots."

The slot was ground-level, outside-wall, and currently unoccupied. Ground-level slots, especially those on the exterior, were usually allotted to short-timers. For security purposes, long-term residents preferred interior, upper-level spaces. The slots immediately above and behind the target slot were filled. So was one of the slots next to it, leaving only one adjoining slot empty. The façade panels along the bottom depicted a colonnade made out of white marble. The sealed panels doubled as security doors. They were bomb- and bulletproof. But they could still be hacked.

"Access code?" he said.

"Acquiring," the datician replied.

Van Dijk approached the façade panel. The clank of the descending forklift, combined with the relentless roar of the air and street traffic, made it impossible to hear anything behind the roll-up door. "Is there an on-site manager?"

"Not at present. HUMOP is available . . . but service requires at least a twenty-four-hour advance notice."

"What about surveillance?" For added security, most of the higher-end r-cologies installed broad-spectrum detectors in vacant slots. But for low-rent r-cologies, the added peace of mind wasn't worth the expense.

"Exterior monitoring only," the datician said.

What he'd expected. "Any chance of satellite IR?"

"Insufficient delta-T."

In other words, too much ambient heat to obtain a clear infrared image. There was no way to sneak a quick peek inside to see what he was dealing with.

"Access code acquired," the datician said.

"All right." Van Dijk loosened the HK minifuge in its holster, hoping the rumble of the forklift gears covered any noise he made. "Go ahead and transmit."

As the façade panel rolled up, van Dijk dropped into a crouch and went in low, the HK drawn.

Light flooded the steel-frame cavern, rushing onto the bare concrete pad like water across a beach, frothing around dark-rolled clumps of tangled bedding, scattered shoes, T-shirts, and half-empty takeout.

"Police!" Van Dijk shouted.

The bedding stirred, exposing Ghost Dragon-philmed faces, and bare-splayed arms, legs, and feet.

Somebody groaned. A hand lifted to shield slitted eyes. A nose emerged from the crook of an arm.

"Lisette?" van Dijk said. Force of habit swung the HK in the direction of the adjoining space.

One of the Ghost Dragons mumbled something.

Van Dijk turned, leading with the muzzle of the 9mm. "What?"

The person sat up. A sleeping bag fell from the bony shoulders of a kid, the same kid whose simage he'd seen in the stairwell.

"She ain't here," the boy repeated. He rubbed his eyes with his knuckles as a few more bundles sat up, sloughing off blankets and sleep.

Van Dijk holstered the minifuge and made his way into the room. It stank of stale fajizza and unwashed bodies. Water dripped from a loose hose into a bucket. A couple of Vurtonic panels flickered on the structural foam walls of the next-door PHUs, d-splaying pale Chinamation in the midafternoon glare.

"So she was here," van Dijk said. "That what I'm hearing?"

"What you want with her?" another kid asked, propping a thick elbow underneath her.

Van Dijk kept his attention focused on the boy from the stairwell. "Where'd she go?" he said.

The girl next to the boy shrugged one ample shoulder.

"We don't know." The boy shook long tangles of hair from his eyes. "She didn't say."

"You gonna arrest us?" the girl said. "Or what?"

The boy stood up in his sleeping bag, letting it fall

to the tempergel mat under his feet as he bent down to gather up a T-shirt. "She left last night," he said, pulling on the shirt. It was philmed with a vidIO clip from a Ghost Dragon episode.

"Why'd she leave?" van Dijk asked when the boy's head emerged from the shirt.

"I'm not sure. She was scared."

"Of what?"

The kid sat back down and crossed his legs. "She wouldn't say. Something she saw."

"Back in the apartment?"

"I think so." He picked at a toenail.

"Plus she had something with her," the girl said. "Some kind of ware telling her what to do."

"What'd it look like?"

"A dragonfly," the kid said.

"Yeah." The girl pushed up into a sitting position. "But a fish, too. A fish with wings."

33

Giles Atherton stepped from cloud-stippled sunlight into a oasis of liquid-cooled calm.

"Welcome back to the Fairmont, sir." The hotel datician snapped into deferential mode as it recognized him. "We are honored to have you."

Doubt assailed him. Perhaps he should have followed Uri's suggestion and used a false DiNA signature. He maintained several, for security purposes, when visiting Third-World resorts. Best if places like Lagos and Rio de Janeiro didn't realize he was in town. There was a certain safety in anonymity that could never be bought with money or power. But in this case, he had decided to act as if he had nothing to hide.

Plausible deniability. If Uri did anything stupid, Atherton wanted to be able to wash his hands of him. Nadice was a disgruntled hotel employee. It would be a simple matter to discredit her. The whole sordid affair could be written off as an unfortunate tryst. Guests invited "friends" up to their rooms all the time. The precise nature of these friends wasn't the hotel's concern.

Atherton paused in the lobby. Sections of the Greek Classical interior were philmed in old integrated-circuit designs. Microchip artwork accented the marble walls and support columns. In places, it appeared as if the solid-state circuitry had been acid-etched into the stone. Transistors and diodes gleamed under overhead LEDs that resembled silicon wafers. He fingered the nanoFX-textured philm on the balustrade that encircled the lounge, smooth black and gold filaments wired to small silver bumps.

Forgotten Braille, or a dead language, like the dull patina of Latin.

Was philm an update of the past, or merely a restatement of it? From time to time the question rose inside him, out of clammy depths, only to settle back again. He was pleased to see that the IBT outlet next to the nail salon had received a new delivery of ad masks and FEMbots. The remote-operated dolls stood naked in the display window, awaiting the new 'skin and philm. He had contracted with Model Behavior to jockey the dolls and masks in Atherton hotels around the world, casually screening the new IBT philm in lounges, bars, and restaurants. If guests saw the new ware in action, they would be more inclined to want it for themselves.

"Shall I prepare your suite?" the datician asked.

"No." Atherton removed his hand from the balustrade. "I'll be having lunch only." He brushed his fingertips together, wiping away the impression left by the capacitors and resistors.

"Your usual table?"

"Yes, but no simage." He planned to check on Lisbeth. It was just past midnight in Paris, the time she normally sat down with the Bible and a cup of herbal tea to help her get to sleep.

"As you wish, sir."

"I would also like to reserve a room for a business client." His mouth felt dry, the words desiccated husks.

"For what dates shall I book the room?"

"This evening. One night only."

"Would you like to put him or her in your private suite?" A hopeful note trickled over his earfeed.

"No. One of the other suites, if possible."

"All those are presently occupied." The datician projected discomfort, sensing a conflict.

"A regular room, then." He didn't want to make a fuss; the less attention he drew, the better. "The nicest available."

"Of course, sir." Relieved. "Who should I key the room to?"

Atherton mentally xferred the DiNA code Uri had given him. It was undoubtedly hacked. Uri wasn't stupid. That caution would afford him one more layer of protection.

"Would you like to see a menu?" the datician asked.

"That won't be necessary. I'll have the same thing I ordered last time."

He couldn't recall exactly what that was. Some kind of sashimi. It didn't matter. He had more important things to think about, but it was imperative to keep up pretenses. Appearance was everything.

"A bottle of Pellegrino, as well," he added. Something carbonated, to help settle his stomach.

"Very well, sir. I'll place your order immediately."

The Pellegrino was waiting for him on the table when he arrived ten minutes later, following a visit to the men's room.

Fresh tap water still cooled on the back of his neck and freshly combed hair. The circuit-board motif on the programmable walls had a pleasant Art Deco ambiance. Gold and black lines intersected to create simple yet tasteful Egyptian designs.

Feeling more relaxed, he opened the bottle and filled his glass. The mineral water tasted clean and therapeutic. His stomach calmed. By the time he finished the glass a waitress arrived with his lunch, artistically arranged on a ceramic dish.

"Is there anything else I can get you?" the waitress asked, grinding her way through the gears of courtesy.

"No," he said. "I don't wish to be disturbed."

The waitress nodded. She was philmed as Queen Nefertiti, one of the half dozen or so approved employee casts. Exquisite skin, finely chiseled cheeks and lips. Beautiful to look at, but unreadable underneath. They all were. Philm hid as much about a person as it revealed.

The waitress backed out, closing the etched-diamond doors that led to the main restaurant. Atherton pinched the bridge of his nose, taking a moment to compose himself before the next order of business.

———

"About time I heard from you." The rip artist's Hongtasan bobbed between slack lips, wagging at him like a finger. "People are gettin' antsy, knowmsayin?" Languorous jazz played in the background.

"It couldn't be helped," Atherton said. "There were . . . complications."

"No shit."

"Everything's being taken care of."

"I hope so. I can't afford any more delays. My reputation's at stake. I've made a lot of promises. Business commitments. I don't keep them, I'm not the only one that gets hulled."

The threat coiled in the air like the smoke from the cigarette, thick and insinuating.

"I understand." Atherton smoothed his Vuitton necktie. "Trust me, it will be worth your while."

Lagrante withdrew the cigarette, pinching it between long, delicate fingertips. He sucked on his upper teeth. "So we're good to go?"

"Yes."

"Awright." Lagrante winked, then his simage faded from Atherton's eyefeed.

Atherton took a fresh handkerchief from his breast pocket and patted at the sweat on his upper lip and forehead. There was no turning back now; it was done. He would still have to deal with IBT—Ilse in her lily-white, elbow-length gloves. But that would be more pleasant, familiar territory.

He replaced the handkerchief and checked the time. Lisbeth didn't usually retire for another hour. He wouldn't talk long enough to keep her up. A few minutes at most, to see how she was doing.

———

His wife looked up from the Bible that lay open in her lap. It was the leather King James version he'd gotten for her 120th birthday. She sat in a high-backed chair, wrapped in her favorite shawl, which she'd philmed with details from Gustav Klimt's *The Kiss*. A cup of hibiscus tea steeped on the table next to her. The tea bag had left a red stain on the yellow, flower-shaped caddy. On the d-splay walls of the room, she was screening a Pastor Lud sermon. Prayers, mentally uploaded by the Right to Light faithful around the world, scrolled down the huge vidIO screens in the sanctuary.

Margaret. Beloved grandmother of seven. Alzheimer's has opened the door to the Devil. And, *Pray for God to protect us against F8. Found my eleven-year-old son listening. Please help, before it's too late.*

Atherton rephilmed the Vurtronic d-splays in the lunchroom with the Pastor Lud simage feed from her room, baptizing himself in the calming waters of the sermon.

"Giles?" Lisbeth said. Out of habit, she removed her horn-rimmed reading spex, switching to direct eyefeed. "Where are you?"

"The Fairmont."

"Doing what?" Her eyes, the soft golden amber of beeswax, radiated fatigue.

"The usual."

"That's what you always say." She sighed and shut the Bible, keeping her place with two bony fingers.

"How are you?" he asked. She seemed haunted.

"I haven't been able to sleep."

"Again?"

"I'm afraid so." She offered a wan shrug. "Any word on Apphia?"

"Not yet."

"It's hopeless, isn't it?" She sighed in resignation. "Don't lie, Giles."

"There's always hope."

"Do you really believe that?" She pulled her shawl tighter. "I'd like to. I'm not sure I do anymore." Her smile was hollow. Even her pink lipstick couldn't lighten the melancholy behind it.

"You're just tired," he said.

"It's more than that." Her fingers knotted where she clutched the shawl. "I see the news and the world doesn't seem to be getting any better."

"It will." Atherton labored to sound upbeat, to smooth the wrinkles of her despair. "Have faith. All our prayers will be answered. The world was good once, it will be good again."

34

Pelayo followed the two yamps from the Get Reel to Marini's candy, where they bought a bag of assorted coffeine drops. From the Serf's Up fast-food kiosk next door, he watched them suck on the raspberry, cherry, grenadine, and mint-flavored drops while they jawed at each other.

"Are you sure this is a good idea?" Atossa said over his earfeed.

Pelayo shrugged. "It's up to them," he said. "Their choice." If they didn't want to do it, he'd find someone else. It wasn't like he was forcing them. "I'm sure they can take care of themselves."

"Just so they know the risks," Atossa said.

The girls stood, preparing to leave. He sauntered over to their table. "You wanna score some cold hard?" he asked.

The yamps stared at him, then smacked their lips in unison. Pelayo caught a whiff of raspberry and rum.

"Blow me," the shorter of the two said when she'd finished swallowing. Then she turned away, giving him the shoulder.

Her friend ignored her. "How much?"

Pelayo held up a cache chip, projecting the amount onto the d-splay screens on the inside of their spex.

"You're shitting us," the short one said, turning back to confront him.

"Half now, half when you're done," Pelayo said. "Word."

"You a cop?"

"What do you think?" Nothing he said would convince them. They'd make their own read.

The tall one pursed her lips, sucking the pierce on the tip of her tongue. "What do you want us to do?"

It didn't take long for the yamps to find a TV. There was one camped out on the sidewalk, at the corner of Pacific and Walnut. He'd set up a hand-scrawled sign, SLAVATION IS NEAR, and seemed content to sit there humming to himself with his eyes closed.

Pelayo watched as the yamps approached the TV. His view was limited, restricted to the nanocams in the eyes of the ad mask the tall yamp was waring. The feed was jerky and the up-and-down, side-to-side movement left him feeling motion sick until Atossa got the image stabilization synched to his eyefeed. After that, his stomach settled, but not his nerves.

They were going to screw it up. For a while, it looked like they might take off on him. They had already paused at several clothing stores and jewelry kiosks to smob shop. It had taken Atossa a while to find a mask the yamp would ware, one that wouldn't make her look like a total Douglas, da ugliest person on the street. Finally, they'd settled on a mukudj white-face mask, which was occasionally rented out by Third World Threads and Gateways. The mask, worn by the Punu people, represented feminine beauty and spirituality. It had a rounded forehead, high-arched brows, almond eyes, and an elegantly thin face that tapered to a small chin under full, red lips.

"Hey," one of the yamps said. Pelayo couldn't tell which one. Vocalware made them sound alike, and the ad mask's audio wasn't all that great.

When the TV didn't respond, the taller yamp prodded him in the knee with a pink-sandaled foot. "Hello?"

The TV opened his eyes but said nothing.

"Aren't you supposed to be, like, talking to people?" the yamp asked. "Spreading the good word, or whatever."

"I was meditating."

"I guess."

"You should try it sometime," the TV said.

"We have a problem," the short yamp said. "We were thinking maybe you could, like, help us."

The TV regarded them serenely. "What kind of problem?"

"Well"—the tall yamp squirmed—"it's kind of embarrassing."

"You're not fucking with me, are you?" the TV said, his tone placid but edged with savoir faire.

"No!" The short yamp clapped a hand over her mouth in mock horror. "Of course not!"

The tall one shook her head soberly. "We would never do that."

"Because a lot of people give me crap. That's all right. I can take it. It's all part of the vibe."

"It's just that we're, like, kind of desperate."

"Who isn't?"

"Yeah, well, we're not sure where to go. And we hear you might be able to help."

"With what?"

"Medical expenses."

"Our boyfriends don't know," the tall yamp said by way of explanation. "They'd, like, kill us if they did."

"You know?" the short girl said, inclining her head.

The TV nodded, gathered his feet under him, and stood. "I might be able to help." He looked directly at the ad mask. "But you have to ditch the adware."

"It's not an ad mask," the short yamp said. "I'm doing a simage cast to a friend of ours in Africa."

The tall yamp concurred with a nod. "She has the, uh, same exact problem we do."

The TV seemed to accept this. "All right. Let's go."

———

An hour later they stood on West Cliff, facing a hotel conference center that overlooked the Boardwalk and the brown splinter of the Santa Cruz pier, embroiled in late-afternoon fog that had turned the sun mercurochrome pink.

"Here you go," the TV said.

"This is it?" one of the yamps asked around a coffeine drop.

The yamp waring the mask tilted her head back at what seemed like a precarious angle to look at the building.

The conference center was a multitiered structure with several terraces shaded by palm trees. Architectural philm covered the modular frame, shrink-wrapping it in fuzzy white haze. The building resembled a solid, three-dimensional mass of static, or random noise, no different from the TV standing next to the yamp. In fact, as the TV took a step forward, he appeared to vanish into the static or be absorbed by it.

It wasn't hard to picture the same thing happening to every other TV. They were all waiting to be assimilated, preparing to become one with one another.

"You really think Marta's in there?" Atossa said, splicing into the earfeed from the ad mask.

"I don't know, maybe." But Pelayo found it hard to believe it was where she really wanted to be.

"So what happens now?" one of the yamps asked.

"You talk to those guys." A bare hand materialized in the static, pointing. "They'll get someone to let you in."

The mask's gaze dropped, centering on a glassed-in lobby where two hefty security guards were stationed. The guards were well armed, packing some serious weaponry and 'tude. It was clear they weren't just window dressing.

"You know," the tall yamp said, gnawing on a black nail, "those dudes seem, like, way scary. Totally roided out. They're giving me the jeebies."

"Me, too," the other yamp said.

"It's not like that," the TV countered. "You can trust them. They're here for your protection."

"Yeah, sure. Like we haven't heard *that* before. Jesus. You people are the same as everyone else. All show and no tell."

They flounced down the hill, back toward downtown. After half a block the yamp with the mask peeled it off.

"Okay," she said, holding up the cache chip

where the mask could image it. "We kept our end of the bargain."

Pelayo freed up the remaining balance on the chip and watched them scurry away.

"Now what?" Atossa said. She piloted the ad mask away from the street and the sidewalk, close to the wall of a parking garage where it would be less likely to get blown around by wind or passing traffic.

"The roof," he said. "Can you go up there and take a look around?" There was a cool breeze gusting off the bay, but she might be able to fly the ad mask up high enough to take a look at the roof and see if it was as heavily fortified as the ground-level access.

"Even if I can," she said, "what good is it going to do?"

From this angle, Pelayo thought he could see the rotors of a helicopter just above the roofline and the terraced gardens—accessible from the ground by gated stairs—that formed patios and balustrades along the topmost floors. "There might be a way up," he said.

35

Nadice woke to the carnival lights of the Boardwalk. Lipstick smears of red, blue, green, and yellow neon splashed against the window next to the bed.

She was like that light. Only a small part of her shone through into the world. The rest of her was a ghost.

Nadice became aware of quiet-but-alert breathing beside her, and a pleasant radiant heat pressing against her skin.

Marta. They'd dozed off on the bed when the fog started to roll in, dampening the low-slanting rays of the sun.

"What are you thinking?" Marta said.

"I was just wondering what time it was."

There was no clock in the room; they had been cut loose from time. First the past, now the present.

Marta shifted slightly. Nadice turned her gaze to the acoustic-tiled ceiling. "Have you been awake all this time?"

"Yes."

"You're not tired?"

"I can't sleep."

They were beyond sleep. It was as if they had crossed into another country.

"I've been thinking," Marta said. "Listening."

"For what?"

"Anything," Marta said. "Everything. You. My heart. The helicopter."

Nadice hadn't heard it.

"I'm glad one of us was able to get some rest," Marta continued. "I have a feeling we're going to need it."

Nadice rolled onto her side, facing her. "What for?"

Marta shrugged, shaking the bed. Then she raised an arm to her forehead, resting it there.

"What do you think's going to happen to us?" Nadice said.

"It's already happening." Marta's voice grated, abrasive as stone in the pastel gloom.

"You know what I mean. After the babies." Where would they live? *How* would they live? Would they be allowed to care for their babies? Or would the babies be taken from them?

Marta lowered her arm, found Nadice's left hand on the bedspread between them, and guided it up under her blouse to her belly.

Marta's skin was warm and smooth under Nadice's fingertips. Taut. She felt her own belly tightening and the warmth spreading downward.

"Feel that?"

"Yes."

"Inside of you, I mean." Marta placed her hand over Nadice's fingers, and gently pressed them into her flesh.

Nadice's breath caught. Deep inside of her, she felt the pressure. Her own hand, she realized. As if it was her body she was probing, pushing against. "What's going on?"

Marta withdrew her hand. "Our babies are joined. Or it could be that they're the same baby."

Nadice kept her hand on Marta's abdomen, measuring her pulse and the slow rise and fall that came with each breath. "Joined how?"

"Who knows. Maybe something we're each carrying inside us, connecting up so that we have one womb. One baby. You and me. Maybe all of us."

"That's crazy." There had to be a reasonable explanation. Dr. Kwan had installed some kind of biodigital interface. They were caught in a virtual web. Tug on one thread and the vibration traveled to all the others.

"I don't know what to think anymore," Marta admitted. "What's crazy and what isn't." A note of fatalistic resignation scratched the surface of her earlier determination. "What about you? Where are you at?"

A tremor passed through Nadice's fingertips. "I'm not going to kill myself, if that's what you mean." It no longer seemed like an option. If what Marta said was true, and they really were one body, one person, what would happen to Marta if she injured herself? Would Marta be harmed, too? Would the baby? What about the other women who were pregnant?

Nadice shifted her hand, brushing Marta's navel with her fingertips. A muscle in Marta's stomach jumped. Nadice felt the echo of the spasm reverberate within her own abdomen, followed by a tingle that spread to her thighs. A long shudder coursed through her.

Marta wet parched lips. "I don't know if this is..." The protest floundered on an indrawn gasp.

"You don't like women?" Nadice said.

"It's not that. It's just—they might be watching."

"I'll stop. If you want."

Marta tensed, rigid with fear and desire. "No."

Nadice's hand drifted downward, light as a hummingbird.

———

"Are you all right?" Nadice said later.

"Fine."

A puffy, immobilizing silence swelled to fill the space between them. "Then what's the matter?"

"Nothing."

"Don't give me that."

Marta's chest heaved, dissolving a clot of emotion in her chest. "It's been a while. That's all."

"Me, too." They'd both been wrapped tight. Neither one of them had been able to let go entirely.

Let go and they might be pulled out to sea. Lost forever.

———

"If it's really just one baby," Nadice ventured, "then how does it get born?" The neon glow from the window glossed their hair and annealed the sweat on their bare skin. Either time had slowed, or their lives had sped up.

"I guess we'll find out."

"Should we tell Kwan?"

Marta shook her head on the pillow. "I'm not telling that bitch anything."

"Do you think she knows?" Nadice said.

"Damn right she does."

Nadice tasted salt on her lips. *Their* salt. She felt alert but calm, strangely sedate.

"What about us?" Nadice asked. "If we're becoming one person, what happens to each of us?"

Marta said nothing.

"Will I forget who I am?" Nadice went on. "Will I lose my personality...my memories?"

"I don't see how," Marta said. "We'd have each other's memories, but we'd still have our own. Like now."

"Not if they get all jumbled." Things were already getting jumbled, just between the two of them.

"That might not be such a bad thing," Marta said.

True, Nadice thought. Only the strongest memories would remain, the most useful and important ones. The runts would get stomped out. "Survival of the fittest," she said.

"What do you mean?" Marta asked.

"Not all of the babies will be born," Nadice said. "Only the strongest will make it to full term. All the others will die."

She was talking about them, as well, she realized. The mothers. They couldn't all live through this.

"You don't know that," Marta snapped. "You don't know anything. None of us knows a goddamn thing."

Nadice gave her a few minutes to simmer down, then placed her mouth to Marta's ear. "There's something else bothering you," she whispered.

Marta tightened under her breath. "I can't tell you."

"Why not?"

"Because I can't tell anyone." The planes of her face shifted in the half-light, hard and angular where they chipped away at the shadows.

"Something in your past," Nadice said, hoping to draw her out.

Marta touched a finger to Nadice's lips. "Not now." Not ever, her breath seemed to say.

It was funny, Nadice thought. The last thing sex guaranteed was intimacy or trust. She took the tip of Marta's finger between her lips and sucked on it gently for a moment, letting the taste of her infiltrate the words forming on her tongue.

"When I came to the Get Reel," Nadice said, "I was working as a mule, smuggling black-market ware into the country from Africa."

"You don't have to tell me this."

"I want to. I don't care if they hear. It doesn't matter. It's not going to make any difference."

Marta opened her mouth, thought better of whatever she was about to say. "What kind of ware?"

"I don't know. It doesn't really matter. What's important is that it's still inside of me."

"You didn't deliver it?"

"No. I had this feeling as soon as I did, they were going to get rid of me. That's why I ran."

"How long do you think you can hide?"

"As long as I have to."

Marta narrowed her eyes. "They'll never stop looking for you."

Nadice swallowed but held Marta's gaze. "I just thought you should know, you're not the only one with baggage."

Marta touched the wet tip of her finger to Nadice's chin, tracing the rigid curve of her jaw.

"I'm not asking for help," Nadice said, keeping her voice steady. "I'm not looking for your protection."

Marta withdrew her finger. "I don't know what I have in me, either. All I know is, like you, I can't leave."

Can't, Nadice thought. That was different from won't.

———

A knock on the door roused Nadice. Next to her, Marta sat bolt upright, her legs slipping over the side of the bed. She was on her feet, padding silently past the endless flicker of the Boardwalk lights before Nadice had blinked the sleep from her eyes.

"Time to get up." The muffled voice was followed by a second knock, firmer and more insistent.

"What do you want?" Marta said, standing next to the door.

A sliver of light sliced through the paper-thin darkness and cut across taupe carpet. Nadice sat up, straightened by adrenaline, and waited.

A TV appeared in the rapidly widening gap, suffusing it with static. "You need to get ready."

It sounded like an older woman, her voice brusque and matriarchal, accustomed to giving orders.

"For what?" Marta asked. She stood to one side of the light, a rigid silhouette.

"A trip," the woman said. "You're being moved."

"We're leaving?" Nadice said. She smoothed the wrinkles from the body of her dress, adjusted the straps.

"Be ready in a half hour. There won't be any stops or amenities during the trip, so make sure you use the bathroom if you have to."

Outside their room, Nadice could hear the same

conversation taking place, up and down the hallway.

Marta pulled on her brown leather jacket. "Where are we going?"

"Just be ready." The TV stepped back, pulling the door shut.

Above them, from the roof, a guttural whine shuddered through the steel frame of the building.

Nadice readjusted the straps of her dress, her hands fumbling as the roar vibrated through them.

36

"I need some coffee," Thabile LaComb said. "Especially if you expect me to think on such short notice this late in the afternoon."

"I suppose I'm buying," van Dijk said.

The noetics professor pushed her chair back from her desk and stood up. "Damn right you're paying. You want an education, it's going to cost." But she smiled as she said it.

Van Dijk returned the smile. "I've been hearing that a lot lately." He had worked with the noetician a couple of times before. Online. This was the first time they'd met in person.

She lifted a hand-knitted sweater from the back of her chair. The sweater was the color of daffodils and complemented the purple beads threaded through her hair. "Come on, Detective. Let's go for a walk. It can get kind of stuffy in here—if you know what I mean."

From her Cognitive Sciences office in Campbell Hall she took him across campus, in the direction of Berkeley and Telegraph Avenue. As far as van Dijk could tell, Thabile LaComb didn't ware 'skin. She wasn't philmed...not even her nails. If she belonged to a cast, it wasn't advertised. She wore a batik blouse, and jeans nanoembroidered with fine titanium thread that shimmered in the patchy afternoon light. Her hair gave off the faint scent of crushed cloves.

"First of all," she said, as they passed Sather Tower, "before we get into the inner workings of sageware and daticians, I want some context."

Van Dijk took a moment to compose his response. "I'm looking for someone," he said.

LaComb arched one brow. "Aren't we all?"

"A young girl is missing." Van Dijk flashed her a picture of Lisette, taken by the uniformed officers when they first questioned the girl.

LaComb's expression sobered as she studied the picture over an eyefeed d-splay. "Runaway?"

" 'Running.' That seems to be the operative word."

"From what?"

"Something, or someone, she saw."

"And wasn't supposed to see, I take it." A chill breeze off the San Francisco Bay ruffled the trees around them, scattering a flock of starlings and loose bits of debris.

"A young woman was found dead in the apartment just down from the girl's," he said. "I'm afraid that's all I can tell you."

"Is this young girl in danger?"

"If she's running, I have to assume it's for a reason."

LaComb glanced at the side of his face. "You're worried about her."

"She's on her own. She doesn't have anyone to turn to, or to go back to. Mom's not in the picture."

"So someone's got to look after her," LaComb said.

They walked in silence for a few minutes. LaComb spent the time staring down at the pavement, lost in a frown. But the walking was pleasant. Van Dijk was in no hurry to press her or cut the stroll short.

"Distributed processing," LaComb finally said. They were nearing the intersection of Bancroft and Telegraph, with its bustling crowd of street vendors and buskers. Spicy incense and cooking oil drifted on the air.

"Meaning...?"

"Sageware doesn't reside on any single node. It resides on many nodes in a shared processing environment."

"So if a node goes down," van Dijk said, "the sageware can still function. It keeps ticking."

"Correct. It also makes it possible to control user access to a particular datician or specific functionality."

"Control how?"

"Through what are called run options. Users are given permission to run specific agents, make certain queries, d-splay certain data."

"Or not," van Dijk said.

"Right. Most of the time it depends on what you pay for. The more you pay, the more functionality you get."

"So who controls the sageware?"

"Manage, or administer, would be more accurate. 'Control' implies an absolute top-down mechanism for enforcement that doesn't really exist. In practice, the system is more flexible. All sageware is heuristic."

"It has the ability to learn," van Dijk said.

LaComb nodded, softly rattling the beads in her hair. "And adapt. Up to a point, anyway."

"And then what?"

"It gets upgraded. Here." LaComb turned into a corner coffee shop that sold bagels and spreads: cream cheese, hummus, baba ganoush. "I'll have a Turkisha. With cocoa nibs."

Van Dijk ordered her coffee and a latte for himself, then joined her at a cozy, sun-warmed table next to the window. "So, what do daticians do during off-peak hours," he asked, "when demand is low?"

LaComb rested her forearms on the table in front of her. She'd pulled her hands into the sleeves of her sweater. Only the delicate tips of her fingers peeked out. "There aren't any spare CPU cycles, per se."

"At all?"

"The load is fairly constant. If one datician gets overloaded, its processing tasks xfer to another datician. That keeps the system balanced and access times to a minimum."

"Do daticians ever act independently?"

"In what way?"

"When they do something, is it always in response to a request? Or do they ever operate on their own?"

"Free will, you mean?" LaComb's brow furrowed.

"I guess."

LaComb picked at a scratch in the table. "Technically," she said, "the answer to your question is no."

"But?"

She looked up and eased her hands from her

loose sleeves, clasping both wrists. "Requests and instructions are often open to interpretation. You see that with people all the time. Different people hear and act on things differently. Likewise, not all daticians process requests in exactly the same way. They should, but they don't. Does that mean one or more of those daticians is acting independently? I don't know."

Their coffees arrived. LaComb wrapped her fingers around the warm cup. She leaned forward to inhale the aroma, then straightened. "Brain-computer interfaces add another level of complexity. BCI interpreters are accurate 99 percent of the time. But there are well-documented cases where someone issues a mental command, or believes they're issuing a certain command, and the BCI carries out a completely different command. Most of the time the neuron pattern that's executed is similar to the one the person wanted, within the BCI's margin for error. But every now and then it's not even close."

"Do you have any idea what causes the discrepancy?" he said.

LaComb blew on her coffee, then took a sip. "There's a theory that the shared processing environment that balances load also creates transients. Temporary overlaps where things get jumbled. Misinterpreted."

"But it hasn't been proven?"

"Or observed. When we try to look at one of these transient waveforms, it goes away. So we can't actually *see* what's going on. We can observe the effects but not the cause."

"Sounds like it's hiding from you," van Dijk said. The same way the damselfly seemed to be hiding from him.

———

"The shards are authentic," Seoul Man told van Dijk when he went back for the jewelry. "The barium, lead, and iron isotope concentrations are consistent with Roman glass made in western Germany during the late fourth century."

"You're sure?"

"Positive. There's also a high concentration of strontium, pointing to the use of marine mollusk shells as carbonate."

"What about the silver?"

The antiquarian gave a dismissive wave as he handed van Dijk the plastine bag. "Cheap. Probably melted down and reused from another piece of jewelry."

Van Dijk took the evidence bag. He ran his fingers over the earrings, along the delicate chain of the necklace. Were they a gift? Had the young woman bought them herself? "Any idea where they came from?"

Seoul Man shook his head. "Any one of a thousand artisans or craft shops, all around the world."

"You're saying there's no way to run down the manufacturer? Or backtrack to whoever sold it?"

The antiquarian shrugged. "This stuff is available everywhere, on the street and online. It shows up for sale all the time."

Van Dijk nodded and put the bag into his jacket pocket. "What's the damage?"

Seoul Man's smile was a slice of Nirvana.

Fifteen minutes later van Dijk left the pawnshop, bearing not just the weight of the Roman glass jewelry but eight misshapen bullets.

As if he didn't already have enough death on his hands.

37

It was all about timing, Pelayo thought. Being in the right place at the right time.

This was not the right time.

Something was happening at the TV center. There was a lot of activity in the front lobby. People kept stepping in and out of the main elevators. Instead of two security guards, there were three. He'd been watching the convention center for a couple of hours now, scoping the lay of the land from the roof of a parking garage across the street. He thought he'd gotten a pretty good idea of how things worked, and was waiting for full-on night, when the helicopter appeared, materializing out of the bright solder of glare where the sea met the sky.

Pelayo shivered against the swirling chill of the fog. "Any idea what's going on?" he said to Atossa.

The mask bobbed unsteadily. Metallic gold tracery on the mask gleamed, suture bright. "Someone's arriving," she said over his earfeed. "Or else getting ready to leave."

Pelayo looked back to the hotel. He watched a group of people come out of the parking garage onto the street below. Tourists, off to visit the Boardwalk or the surf museum farther up the hill on West Cliff. There was a bronze statue of a surfer there, a gift shop that sold wet suits, boogie boards, and other surf memorabilia. He'd gone there with Atossa once, on a calm, clear afternoon, to watch the waves pummel the rocks below the seawall.

One of the tourists on the sidewalk below him tossed a green nanoFX wrapper into the gutter, where the leaf-textured cellophane was nudged along by the steady onshore breeze. Pelayo turned to the mask. "What do you think?"

"The wind is too strong, and it's coming from the wrong direction."

"Try. While they're busy."

All she had to do was get the mask close to the building. Once she was next to a wall, the building would block most of the wind and she could maneuver the mask to check the roof and look in windows.

"What if they catch me?" she said.

"An accident. You got blown off course."

"I'll still get reported."

"We don't have much time," Pelayo said.

The mask circled him a few times, then bumped him in the head and dove off the parking garage and up the street.

It was slow going. The mask dipped and rose like a kite, gaining ground, then losing it.

"I'm not going to make it," Atossa said.

"You're almost there."

Pelayo watched a second chopper drop out of the foggy sky above the bay. This one was larger. It droned loudly as it touched down on the roof, ponderous as a bumblebee. Below him a muscle-bound crunkhead hurried across the street, toward the parking garage. The 'skin the crunkhead was waring was cheap. It had the waxy, secondhand look of paraffin, glossy-smooth and stiff.

What if Marta really had decided to convert? What if he was off base about her, and this was what she really wanted? Maybe she had reached a crisis point, felt trapped, and this was the only door that led out.

Especially if she'd gotten pregnant.

If that was the case, he wasn't going to stand in her way. Her life was her business. Maybe this was what she needed right now. If so, Nguyet would just have to deal with it. It might be nice, not having to think about the pressures of everyday life. No more worries about the rent, food, or medical care. It might be restful, even liberating. He could see the allure.

He felt the pressure, too. It got to him after a while. It got to everyone. Each day, reality became a little less familiar . . . a little more uncertain. Maybe that was why so many people cast themselves in the past. It wasn't real, but it had *been* real. Which was more than anyone could say for the future.

"It's not going to happen," Atossa said. "I'm coming back."

Pelayo looked up. The mask was no closer to the building. She wasn't making any progress. Too many eddies and currents. She was coming at it from the wrong direction. Yet every time she tried a different angle, a fresh gust pushed her back or off to the side.

Pelayo swore under his breath. It would be dark soon. Lights had come on in the conference center windows. That would make it easy for Atossa to see in. All they had to do was get close.

At some point, the lights had winked on at the Boardwalk. Red, blue, yellow, and green sketched the outlines of rides. Here the merry-go-round, there the Big Dipper and the Sky Tram.

The mask tumbled out of a tendril of fog and settled to the weathered concrete at his feet. Pelayo picked it up and hurried to the stairs.

"Where are you going?" Atossa said.

"I have an idea."

She sighed. "I was afraid of that."

In the stairwell, Pelayo ran headlong into the crunkhead, who was taking the steps two at a time.

"Move yo ass, muhfucker, before I get off in yo shit."

Pelayo's jaw tensed. He tightened his grip on the mask and stared into the crunk's nicotine-yellow eyes.

"Don't," Tossa whispered. "It's not worth it."

"Yeah." Pelayo gritted his teeth. "I hear ya."

He stepped aside, knocking the crunk's hand away when the dude brought it up to shove him in the chest.

"Leave it," Tossa said. "Just let it go."

"Right." Pelayo put on the mask, jammed his hands into his pockets, and continued down to ground level. On the street, he turned down the hill to the Boardwalk, glancing back every couple of steps to check on the helicopters. They seemed to have settled, but for how long?

38

"What about Yukawa?" Zhenyu al-Fayoumi asked. A chill had crept into the air as the sun sank over the Santa Cruz Mountains to the west, into the roiling bank of fog spilling over into the Santa Clara Valley.

The damselfish drifted closer, gliding past the side of his face, then pausing next to his ear.

Al-Fayoumi fought the urge to pull back. His shirt bunched under his arms, bound his neck. He ran a finger under the collar.

"His real name is Uri Titov," the damselfish said over al-Fayoumi's earfeed. "He's a skintech with Iosepa Biognost Tek."

"IBT?" he said. "Not Siglint?"

The damselfish swam back into view and appraised him coolly. "You haven't been given all of the information you need to know about the project you're working on. If completed, a lot of innocent people will be harmed."

"Including you, I suppose."

The damselfish flapped fins and wings, arcing away in an ellipse. Sunlight flashed, rippling off its scales. "What makes you think I'm innocent? Or a person, for that matter?"

"If you're not a person, what are you?"

The damselfish paused in midair for a second, as if debating. "What do you think?"

Al-Fayoumi shut his eyes for a beat. "Sageware. A datician—or many daticians, perhaps—animating distributed nanoware." He opened his eyes.

"Perhaps." The fish's lower fins quivered. "If Yukawa—Titov—is successful, then all programmable matter will become the same matter. All 'skin will become the same 'skin. All philm the same philm."

"You're already quantum-entangled," al-Fayoumi said. That was how the image was acquired, how the idolon was xferred from one fly to another. "That's why you are afraid. If the entanglement spreads, you'll be part of it. You'll no longer be independent."

"No one will be free." The damselfish twitched, slipped sideways, steadied. "The net being cast is a wide one. Eventually, everyone will be caught in it."

Al-Fayoumi pursed his lips. "Is there more sageware out there like you?"

The damselfish rephilmed, and a girl's face replaced the head of the fish. The girl was young. She had long black lashes and loose-curled hair that fell in ringlets over her smooth brow.

Al-Fayoumi didn't recognize the philm. He had no clue who the girl was—if she was real or imagined.

"Her name is Lisette," the damselfish said. "She is ten years old and has no one to look after her."

Al-Fayoumi frowned. He shifted his gaze from the damsel to the pink scarf of sun trailing along the horizon. "What about her?"

"She needs your help."

His focus returned to the damsel. "What kind of help?"

"Protection. A safe place to stay."

"Protection from whom?"

"Titov." The damsel dropped suddenly, landing on his arm, close to the spot where it had emerged.

Al-Fayoumi flinched under the sharp myelin tickle of the nanomal. "Why are you telling me this? What do you expect me to do?"

"Save her." The damsel fit itself back into the shallow indentation. "And yourself."

39

As the evening deepened, so did Mateus's urgency.

He was running out of time. He could feel the seconds slipping through his tightly clenched fists. From his vantage point on the roof of the parking garage across the street from the TVs' hotel, he watched the copters prep for flight. It wouldn't be long now, he figured. An hour, maybe less.

He hadn't been able to determine where the copters were headed. If they left and Nadice was on one of them, his chances of finding her dropped to fuck-all. Once the copters were in flight, he had no way to track them. That meant the copters couldn't leave. It was as simple as that. He was working on getting more muscle, putting together an assault team, but that wouldn't happen for another few hours at the earliest.

He couldn't wait that long. He needed to act now.

Uri had agreed. He'd even offered to rephilm Mateus's boyz for the job. "Just get her. Do whatever you need to do."

"It could get messy," Mateus warned.

"It's already messy!" Uri snapped. "You fuck this up, it's going to get a helluva lot messier."

"You care if she's alive?" That always made

things tougher. It was a complication he'd rather do without.

"Just make sure she's in one piece." Uri didn't bother to grin, a bad sign. "If she's not all there, if any part of her is missing, parts of you are gonna end up missing."

Despite the threat, Mateus felt calmer under the cover of darkness and the raucous glare of the Boardwalk. He had a plan. His boyz were on the way. Mateus checked their coords on his spex. They were less than a kilometer away. Another five minutes and they'd be here. Ten minutes after that, they'd be set up and in position. Ready to lock and load.

Taking the stairwell, Mateus made his way down to the street. By the time he got to the sidewalk, his boyz were making the turn onto West Cliff at the foot of the hill.

He watched the restored Benzy rumble up the slope, the hydrogen fuel cell pissing water out the tailpipe. 'Cept for that it was nicely candied up, with a wood-grain steering wheel, drop top, and blades.

The sedan pulled to a stop along the curb, between a couple of three-wheeled cars that were strictly for in-town use. They were pissant small, but they afforded a little cover from the casual passerby.

The passenger window slid down and Rafa glowered at him, indignant. "When we gonna get some treal philm for this new 'skin? This makes me feel starched up, like I'm the Lone Ranger, or sumthin'."

His boyz were totally reskinned, fresh out of the tank. Uri had philmed them as clean-cut private-security goons from Texasecure, out of Houston. They had the company's distinctive logo, a lone Texas star in the middle of a yellow rose, inscribed prominently on their foreheads. The starchiez uniforms looked authentic. Ditto the boots and ten-gallon hats. Not that it mattered. In the pandemonium, no one would ask questions. All people would see was the lone star rose on their foreheads and that would be enough to give his boyz free rein. There wouldn't be any of the trouble they'd run into at the homeless shelter, people asking questions and threatening to call the cops on them because of the way they'd gone into the place. This time, they were the cops.

"Dude's never satisfied," Tiago said from the driver's seat. "He scores ware that no one else has, and all he can do is complain."

"You got what I asked for?" Mateus said, getting down to business.

Rafa nodded. "In back."

Mateus looked back down the street, toward the Boardwalk and downtown. "You see any laws on the way in?"

Rafa shook his head. "No po pos to speak of. They all off lookin' for skull down at da Walk."

"You sure?" The last thing they needed was a police cruiser to swing by, checking shit out. Cops had access to all kinds of surveillance.

"We gonna do this, or what?" Tiago asked. His fingers pattered on the blond grain of the wheel, tapping out a staccato rhythm. He was a twitchy punk, throwed half the time. But he got it done when it counted, no ifs, ands, or buts.

"Bet," Mateus said. "Let's pop some trunk."

Rafa's grin widened. "I feel ya!"

Mateus went around to the back of the Benzy, waited until he heard the lock click, then opened the trunk. Zipped in three nylon boogie board bags were two Russian RPG-7 rocket-propelled grenade launchers and six rounds of ordnance.

You couldn't beat old Soviet-era weapons. Over a hundred years old, and the shit still worked. It was simple, reliable, and readily available. Peasants in Afghanistan, Syria, and Iraq were still digging up weapons stockpiles, hidden by Al-Qaeda and other raghead terrorists.

The RPG-7 was shoulder-fired, recoilless, and muzzle reloadable. It had an effective range of five hundred meters against a fixed target and could punch through twenty-plus centimeters of conventional plate armor. Mateus had practiced with one a few years back, outside of H-Town, when he was running with Fo-Fo. He'd used it to light up the junk cars they'd used as targets.

There were also a couple of compressed gas fléchette pistols that fired needles or darts. Nice and quiet. He jammed one into the waistband of his pants, dropped the other into a mesh side pocket, along with a MEMS grenade.

Rafa and Tiago joined him. "Let's get a move on," Mateus said. He didn't like it, being out in the open.

They hefted out the bags, alarmed the Benzy, and climbed the stairwell to the roof, where they moved into position.

There were four copters. Mateus double-checked the distance with a pair of night-vision binoculars. Two hundred and twenty meters. It would work, no problem. Him shouldering the RPGs while Rafa loaded them and Tiago guarded the stairwell. He should be able to get off four clean shots in a minute or two.

"Got some activity," Rafa said. He had the grenades

neatly lined up. In the open bags, they looked like cone-tipped spears or javelins.

Mateus took the night-vision binoculars and peered through them, the world going grainy and monochrome green. Several TVs stood next to the copters, gesturing. The fuselage doors to the copters were open; it looked as if they were going to start taking on passengers. Sure enough, a service entrance to the roof opened and a close-bunched group of women spilled out, looking confused and frightened. They huddled together as they were herded to the nearest chopper.

He looked for Nadice, but he was too far away to make out individual features or clothing.

One of the women broke away from the group and ran. A couple of TVs sprinted after her. There was a waist-high wall topped by a Kevlex fence around the building. No place for her to go, but that didn't stop her from trying.

Bitch had spunk, he had to give her that. Maybe she'd be grateful if he saved her ass. Maybe a lot of them would. He'd heard pregnant women were horny all of the time, something to do with—

"What we waitin' for?" Tiago said.

Mateus wet his lips and lowered the binoculars. "Nothing," he said. "Let's get to it."

40

"It's still pretty windy," Atossa said. "I don't know if I can make it."

"It will work," Pelayo said. At least now the breeze was blowing in the right direction.

They stood in line for the Sky Tram. The tram's cars—little blue, red, green, and yellow buckets suspended from tower-supported cables—followed the seawall, running between the Santa Cruz pier at one end and the Ferris wheel at the other.

"What if she's not there?" Atossa said.

Pelayo puffed out his cheeks. "Then I'll let it go."

"Even if she is, I might not see her. No matter how close I get."

"I know," Pelayo said. He massaged his face. It felt tight, vacuum-sealed by the mask. The microvilli that held it to his 'skin itched.

The line inched forward a few steps, up the ramp to the loading platform. Below them, the Boardwalk seethed with activity. Arcade games flashed, signs blinked, philm scrolled, and kids screamed in fear and delight. Carnival music pummeled them from all directions. Ad balloons and masks trawled between the tightly packed kiosks, schooling like barracudas under the palms.

A message tone squealed over his earfeed. The call

was flagged urgent and a red subject line blinked on over his eyefeed, indicating a pop-up d-splay. Pelayo groaned.

"What?" Atossa said.

"Call from Uri." The subject line continued to blink, baleful and insistent: *NEED YOU IMMEDIATELY.*

"About what?" she asked.

"He wants to see me again."

"Now?"

Pelayo shook his head. "It's not going to happen," he said. "I'm busy." He was tired of being constantly on call.

"You're not going to go in?"

"It can wait," he said. It was probably nothing. Uri yanking his chain over some minor bug.

"What if there's a serious problem with the 'skin?" Atossa asked.

They inched forward a couple of steps, forced from behind by the line wending up the access ramp.

"With Uri, everything is crucial."

An updraft from the still-warm concrete of the Boardwalk stirred the 'skin's thick hair, blowing it across the ad mask.

"Maybe you should see what it's about," Atossa said. "It couldn't hurt."

"No!" he said, exasperated as much by the sloth-like progress of the line as Uri's call or Atossa's second-guessing.

"Fine," she huffed.

Pelayo closed his eyes for a moment, willing calm. This was not the time for an argument. "It'll be all right," he said, "I feel fine. I'll go in as soon as we're done here."

"Your turn, asshole," a voice said. The ride operator, some kid philmed as X-F! from the "Solonauts."

An empty car swung around. Pelayo sat and the restraining harness folded down over his chest and legs, securing them firmly in place.

Half a second later the car jolted forward, rocking back and forth as it lifted him above the seawall and the Kevlex fence that kept people from falling or jumping into the seaweed- and kelp-choked beach that had once been home to beach towels, lawn chairs, and volleyball nets.

Music gusted up from the dervish rides and the fun-house arcades, bringing with it the smell of caramelized popcorn, cotton candy, and spicy batter-fried *nopales*. This section of town, including the Beach Flats a couple of blocks to the east, was nothing but philmscape: the 1849 Gold Rush; Paris in the 1890s; 1920s Coney Island. There were no cracks, no chipped corners, no peeling paint. Everything looked fresh and new, the past flawlessly reminted, shinier and more desirable than the present. If there was a future, it was cast from the past, perfectly configured to gloss over the defects of the here and the now with a collage of collective, mass-mediated nostalgia.

The conference center loomed a few hundred meters behind them. The helicopters were lit by Klieg lights, the glare bright and urgent.

Pelayo twisted in his seat, facing the moonlit water of the Bay. He pinched one corner of the mask, slowly peeling it from his face. Free of his body heat, the ad mask stiffened as it cooled, lapsing into its default shape. "Ready?" he said.

Atossa let out a breath. "I guess."

Pelayo held the mask at arm's length, away from the chair. The breeze snatched at it, trying to pluck it from his fingers. "Keep eyefeeding me. I want to know what's going on."

"I'll do my best."

Pelayo let go of the mask. The wind caught it, flipped it, and sent it tumbling back in the direction of the pier and the hotel. He watched it swirl away into ink-black air before switching to an eyefeed d-splay.

The mask was still tumbling out of control, sending him kaleidoscopic glimpses of the Boardwalk, the Beach Flats, silver-bellied clouds. He took a deep breath to quell his motion-sick stomach. Finally, the mask righted itself and the image stabilizers kicked in, giving him a relatively steady view.

"You're heading too far right," he said.

"I know!" Atossa snapped.

The onshore breeze had shifted. It was a little more westerly than it had been ten minutes earlier. She was going to miss.

"Try less altitude," he suggested. There would be less wind closer to the ground, less shear.

No answer. The mask passed over the pier and the seawall at the base of the hotel rushed toward them.

"Toss—" he began, when suddenly the eyefeed cut out and the d-splay inset went blank.

Now what? He was trapped. Short of leaping fifty feet to the ground, there was no way to exit the tram. All he could do was wait.

A beat later a message tone beeped. No visual. Pelayo answered it immediately, thinking it would be Atossa.

"Say," Lagrante said, his voice saxophone smooth. "What it do?"

————————

"Make it quick," Pelayo said. "I'm in the middle of something."

The tram had reached the far end of the Boardwalk, turned, and was heading back. The conference center loomed in the distance, barely visible above the lights of the merry-go-round.

"That gurl of yours keeping you busy?" Lagrante said.

"You could say that."

Lagrante forced a chuckle. "I hear ya."

Pelayo said nothing. The tram was halfway to the debarkation point and his mind was racing, planning his next move, whether to go to the hotel or Model Behavior.

"Right," Lagrante said, taking his cue. "I'll get to the point, then. I found what I was looking for. If you're still interested, I can take care of biz. But it's got to go down quick."

"When?"

"Tonight. No more than a couple of hours from now. If you're not too busy to make it, that is."

"Where?"

"Place we first met. Got a band playin' I want to catch. Some of that nouvogue I been hearin' about."

————————

Pelayo was three blocks from the hotel when the eyefeed from the ad mask came back online and the d-splay inset reappeared.

He blinked and found himself staring into an

empty hotel room that looked as if it had been hastily vacated. "Where are you?" he said.

"Third-floor window on the east wall," Atossa said.

"What happened?"

"Technical difficulties. I ran into some interference."

Which could mean almost anything, literally or euphemistically. When she didn't elaborate, Pelayo let it drop. There was no sense getting off on a tangent, especially one that might lead back to him. Next time, he'd keep his mouth shut and let her do her job.

"How many rooms have you checked?"

"Three. They're all like this."

"Empty?"

"Yeah. I think it's a waste of time to keep checking. I'm going to head up to the roof, see if I can figure out where they're taking them."

And why, Pelayo thought.

41

Night in San Francisco gave rise to afternoon thunderclouds in Japan. Through the d-splay window in his office, Kasuo van Dijk watched the ebb and flow of shadows in the karesansui garden at the Nanzenji temple.

"Submit an interdepartmental query," he told the on-duty datician.

"Recipient?"

"Detective Buhay, with the San Jose Police Department."

Twenty minutes earlier there had been a second damselfly appearance at the street address for Zhenyu al-Fayoumi. A follow-up call to al-Fayoumi had been routed directly to his voice mail. When queried, al-Fayoumi's Call Management System reported that he had not logged into his account in the last 71.4 hours. According to an admin assistant with the department of Developmental Nanobiology at San Jose State, al-Fayoumi was taking some personal time to work on research.

Van Dijk had decided that it was time to do some research of his own.

A message light blinked on his eyefeed d-splay. Van Dijk turned from the window and mentally routed the call to a wall d-splay.

"Sam." Buhay said. "Been a while." He'd simage-cast himself as a lantern-jawed, hatchet-nosed Dick Tracy.

·

"Sorry it couldn't be longer." Inside the San Francisco Police Department he hadn't been called Sam—short for Samurai—in years.

"Not a problem." Buhay waved off the apology. "What can I do you for?"

"Zhenyu al-Fayoumi. Ring any bells?"

Buhay polished his chin for a moment. "He involved in something you're working on?"

"I'm not sure. I've got a dead philmhead, with a suspicious cause of death, and a missing witness who might be headed his way." Assuming there was a connection to the damsel. "What can you tell me about him?"

"Fly boy," Buhay said.

"Pilot?"

"Bugs. The insect variety. He started philming them a few months ago. Faces. Airplane wings. Like that."

"Sounds tacky but not necessarily illegal. You got a new law on the books I don't know about?"

Buhay smirked. "Apparently his bad taste, and interest in philm, isn't confined to academia."

"What'd he do?"

"Technically he hasn't done anything."

"In the meantime, you're keeping an eye on him."

Buhay lowered his hand from his jaw. "He contacted one of the plainclothes we got working a sting op on the local crack market. Hacking, ripping, and bootlegging of electronic skin and philm."

"Undercover?" van Dijk asked.

Buhay nodded. "Deep six."

Which meant that he had been at it for a long

time and was going after a big fish, probably corporate. "What'd al-Fayoumi contact him about?"

"Fly boy wanted to know what was available, what was up and coming. Ware he could get here. Ware he had to get elsewhere, so to speak. Overseas."

"He say why?"

"Nah. He wasn't that stupid. I figure he's doing contract work for a philm studio, as a way to fund his own research."

"Hard up, huh?"

"The grant money hasn't exactly been pouring in for 'skinned flies. You don't get funded, it's only a matter of time."

"I take it he's not tenured."

"Not in this lifetime."

Buhay popped a coffeine drop and chewed. It was van Dijk's turn, and he got to the point. "There's evidence my philmhead may have been a test subject."

"What kind of evidence?"

"First-run philm on unregistered 'skin. Our skintechs are still trying to REbot the autopsy results."

Buhay popped another drop. "We talking blackmarket?"

"Maybe. Maybe not."

Buhay nodded. "Either way, you think there might be a connection to al-Fayoumi. Your test subject have a name?"

Van Dijk shook his head. "Not yet. Both hard and soft DNA came up negative."

"Which is where your wit comes in."

Van Dijk nodded and let Buhay work out the next step for himself.

"What kind of support you looking for?" Buhay said, rolling the drop between his cheek and gums.

"I'd like to pay your fly boy a visit."

"Official?"

That would involve a warrant and van Dijk didn't want to go that far into debt. At least not yet. "Social," he said. "For now."

"I think we can manage that." Buhay bit into the hard-shelled coffeine. "This is a friendly town. Sharing."

Van Dijk took the point. Any information he came across would be passed on to Buhay. "Thanks," he said.

"When should I put out the welcome mat?" Buhay asked.

"Now would be a good time. You might want to have some flypaper handy, too."

42

Marta had a bad feeling about the TV. The woman wasn't just no-nonsense, she was watch-spring tight. The air around her felt brittle, as crinkly as her cheap 'skin and starched mannerisms.

One wrong step or word, Marta thought, and the TV would crack.

"Are you going to philm us?" Nadice said as the TV led them from their hotel room, down the hall to the elevators.

"All in good time," the woman said. "First things first."

She picked up the pace, hurrying them along the narrow strip of carpet that receded toward a vanishing point of pure white vertigo. Marta tried to imagine white stucco walls in place of the static, paisley frescoes, or velvet pin-striped wallpaper . . . anything substantive to dispel the feeling that the corridor was narrowing and that she was falling headlong into a singularity from which there was no escape.

Marta hadn't eaten since yesterday morning, just before quitting the Get Reel. If she became any more light-headed she'd float off into delirium. Already her body felt detached, sucked dry by events.

But maybe that was part of the plan. Starve them, deprive them of all strength and energy to the point where they were beyond caring. The walls leaned closer. Marta could feel the static attacking the cyst-hard attitude she'd encased herself in, a sort of corrosive fizz bubbling away with carbolic fury. It ate at her will, gnawed at her desire to resist.

"Is there a reason we were locked in our room?" Marta said as they waited for an elevator to arrive. "Not allowed to go anywhere?"

Conversation provided ballast against the acid bubbling, helped to anchor her in who she was.

The woman's gaze scalded her. "It's for your own protection," she stated with tart severity.

"Protection from what?"

"The church has many detractors." The woman's compressed mouth puckered into a sour gash.

"Who?" Nadice said.

"Some people think you're an abomination," the TV said. "They think you should be rounded up and quarantined. Or worse."

"What does that have to do with keeping us isolated?"

"At this point it's better if you have as little contact with the outside world as possible."

Marta shook her head. "You don't want us to know what's going on. That way we can't question what you're doing."

"There's a lot of misinformation being broadcast right now," the woman said. "The newzines report every rumor as if it's fact."

Lies flocked to silence like flies to shit, Marta thought, the quote leaping unbidden to mind. One of Nguyet's favorite aphorisms. "What's your name?" she said.

The woman gave her a look of blank, implacable static. "I don't have one. I gave up my name." The ultimate self-effacement, her expression seemed to say.

"What for?" Nadice said.

"The One name. When it's written on me, I want to be a blank slate, ready to receive my new identity."

———

The TV took Marta and Nadice back up to the penthouse restaurant. There, several dozen women had been separated into distinct groups. The altar was gone, the tatami mats stacked against one wall. The windows were dark and full of internal reflections. Through the translucent tableau, Marta gazed southeast to the LED-lighted curve of the Bay, looking for the Slab and the Trenches.

Her father must be worried sick. Nguyet, too. Marta pictured her frantically doing a water-crystal reading, then another, and another. Her usual pattern, as if a second or a third reading would revise the first. Only when the readings were the same could she stop, let go.

Generally Marta didn't think twice about Nguyet's compulsion. It wasn't worth the effort. Like most self-help mysticism, there was no way to prove or disprove the results. In the end, it boiled down to faith. Some people just couldn't accept the world as random and pointless. There had to be a hidden meaning, a divine plan. And they believed that if they could get a good look at the master blueprint, it would tell them how to live their lives and the lives of everyone around them.

It was no different with the TVs. They were tuned in. They *knew* they were tuned in. They'd seen the light, and convinced themselves that whatever light anybody else saw was false light.

The only good thing about the water crystals was that they helped Nguyet manage her anxiety. This made life easier for Marta and her father. Without the crystals, Nguyet would be a total basket case and their lives would be miserable. If the crystals kept her from unraveling, more power to them.

"You've been assigned to group Alpha-Three," the TV advised them. She guided them across the restaurant, in the direction of a group of six women huddled near an open door that appeared to lead to the roof, where she could hear the muffled whine of turbine engines.

"Where are we going?" Marta said.

"When your group is called, you are to assemble at the door over there as quickly as possible." She pointed to an exit door. "You will be met there by somebody who will assist you."

"How long before we leave?" Nadice said.

"Not long." The woman clicked her tongue, firm but judicious taps.

The TV left them with their group. The other women stopped whispering. A few smiled in hesitant welcome. Marta grimaced. Distracted by the furtive commotion in the room, her attention skittered.

Dr. Kwan stood near the door. Another TV was with her, a man dressed in a blue seersucker suit. The conversation was animated. Dr. Kwan moved her hands a lot, short, sharp gestures to get across whatever point she was trying to make. At one juncture, she cast a quick sidelong glance at Marta.

Marta's skin crawled. They were talking about her.

Had Kwan finally discovered whatever had been implanted in her? Clearly the doctor was concerned, worked up about something. Why else would Kwan be talking to him, unless there was a problem?

The man listened intently, nodding every now and then in apparent agreement. He glanced once at Marta, confirming her worst fears.

Kwan seemed satisfied. After a couple of last-minute gestures she strode from the room, her gait brisk and confident.

"I have to go to the restroom," Marta said. She needed a few minutes to think, to gather herself.

"You just went," Nadice said.

"I have to go again. Listen. If that TV comes over here and asks about me, tell him..."

"What?" Nadice leaned close to Marta, her voice low but urgent. "What's going on?"

"Don't tell him anything. All right?"

"About what?"

"Anything." Marta reached for Nadice, then snatched her hand back, her fingers curled in a rigor-tight knot. "Explain that we just met, and that you don't know me very well. I haven't said shit to you."

"Okay."

"No matter how nice he is." Desperation scored her voice.

"This is what you can't talk about, isn't it?" Nadice said. "The reason you came here."

"I'm not sure. It could be."

Nadice drew a measured breath. "If it is, what's going to happen?"

Good question. Marta's thoughts flickered around

the edges. She shut her eyes, but the palsied waver refused to steady.

Nadice slid a hand to her arm. "They're going to separate you from the rest of us, aren't they? Take you someplace else."

Cool fingers shackled her wrist. Marta's eyes snapped open. She should go now, put as much distance between them as she could while there was still time. Nadice hadn't asked to get involved. She didn't know what she was getting into. It wasn't fair to drag her along.

"I'm not going anywhere," Marta said. The hand held her in place.

"It's all right," Nadice said. "I understand." She seemed reconciled.

"No." Marta's wrist hurt. The dull throb, carried through her veins, clotted in her chest and throat.

"Shhh." Nadice's gaze slid sideways, dragging Marta's with it. "Here he comes."

The decision had been made for her. She'd waited too long. The TV had approached to within a half dozen steps of them. Nadice squeezed her wrist harder, just for a second, then let go.

"Hello, Nadice. It's nice to see you again." Jeremy smiled and tipped his head at them.

His features traced shadowy outlines behind the blizzard of pixels. Only his eyes were recognizable, a fixed steady blue, like twin bits of sky beaconing through the flurry. Marta resisted the urge to massage her wrist.

"How are you?" Jeremy asked. "Is everything all right?"

Nadice pursed her lips. "Fine."

"Good, good." The TV turned his gaze to Marta. "Do you mind if we have a brief word? In private."

"The woman who brought us up here told us we were supposed to stick together," Nadice said. "So we don't get separated."

"This won't take long. A few minutes."

"Don't worry," Marta said to Nadice. "It'll work out. I promise."

Straightening her shoulders, she followed the TV to a pair of rubber-sealed double doors that hissed at her as they parted.

———

The doors led to a banquet-staging area. Through scratched plastine windows in a second pair of double doors directly in front of her, Marta could see a stainless-steel kitchen.

Forcing bravado, she stopped and said, "What's all this about?"

The TV touched a finger to his lips.

She slowed her breathing, tried not to sound anxious. "I just don't want to get left behind."

"In here," Jeremy said, opening the door to a storage closet where the altar table was kept. He ushered her in and closed the door. Other than the table and several stacks of plastic chairs, the room was bare.

Now what? They were alone. If she called for help, no one would hear her; there was nothing she could do.

Jeremy gestured to one of the available chairs, offering her a seat. "We can speak freely now. It's safe."

Marta stood her ground. "Talk about what?"

"Relax," the TV said. He sat on one corner of the table. "Have faith."

Marta stiffened. She pictured the weathered sign outside the shop: EGGED, ROWED, AND OLE GOODS. It wasn't possible, she thought. He couldn't know the password. The man had recruited Nadice at the homeless shelter. Kwan had obviously gone to him with a problem.

The man was watching her, waiting. Clearly, he expected a response. And soon.

"Become..." Marta faltered. "Become a true believer...and all your prayers will be forgiven."

There. It was done. No turning back.

Jeremy reached into his robe, took out a dermadot, and handed it to her. "Before you keel over."

"Thanks." Marta peeled the backing from the dermadot and placed the antitox on her tongue, where it dissolved, as bitter as tannin.

Jeremy became suddenly agitated. He seemed anxious, pressed for time. "Well?" he said. "What have you got?"

Marta hesitated, at a loss.

"Let's start with the purpose of the pluglet," he said.

Marta shook her head. "I'm not sure I understand."

Jeremy pushed away from the table and began to pace. "Dr. Kwan found a pluglet in you. That's what she came to tell me."

"Pluglet?" Marta said.

"Plug-in applet." The static on his brow altered frequency. "You weren't told what you were carrying?"

"No. The person I—whoever installed it didn't say anything."

Jeremy massaged the base of his skull. "According to Kwan, it's a small modular circuit, an add-on to existing wetronics. I assume it's to augment the ware Kwan found in Nadice. That's why I put you in the same room."

"Nadice told me she was smuggling something. But she didn't know what it was."

"That's what I was hoping you could tell me. Kwan's never seen anything like it. She thinks that it might be a new type of quantum circuit that connects 'skin, turns it into shareware."

"What does the pluglet do? Rewire it?"

"Kwan's not sure. She's still analyzing it, trying to figure out if it's a threat or not." Jeremy pinched the bridge of his nose, fingers merging with his face. He appeared tired, his emotions threadbare, as if he'd been on edge for way too long.

"What are you going to do?" Marta asked.

"Until I receive further instructions, everything I can to protect you, maintain your cover."

A pop-up d-splay opened on his right wrist. He glanced at it, frowned. At the same time a shadow surfaced beneath the pixels of his face, hesitated, then slid from view, some subtle imbalance or perturbation, more imagined than real.

"...unfortunately Kwan refuses to authorize your release," the TV was saying. He combed pale fingers through his nonexistent hair. "For the time being, my hands are tied. There's nothing I can do."

Marta blinked. "You're keeping me here?"

"Kwan wants to hold you for further observation.

I'll arrange for your release as soon as I can, but it's going to take some time. I'm sorry."

"What about Nadice?" she said.

"She's going with the others. Kwan wants to keep you two separated until she knows more about the ware each of you is carrying and what it does. I'll do everything I can to look after her."

Marta dug ragged nails into her palms. But whatever grip she'd had on herself, or the situation, slipped through her fingers. She touched a hand to her abdomen. "And the babies? What's going to happen to them?"

"I don't know, yet. Church leaders are waiting for an image to be born. A source image that will provide a new face for humanity."

"Divine, you mean?"

"In origin, yes. Supposedly, only those people who are waring this face when they die will be recognized by God and admitted—"

A thunderclap shuddered through the walls. The floor shook, pitching Marta into the table.

Earthquake, she thought, righting herself.

Jeremy reached for the door. "What the—?"

Muffled screams, shrill with panic, filtered into the room as the trembling ceased and the rumble quieted. Jeremy yanked open the door. Tendrils of smoke wafted into the room.

Not an earthquake...an explosion. She followed Jeremy into the banquet-staging room, then the pandemonium of the main restaurant.

Marta glanced frantically around. Dust burned her throat. "Nadice!" she shouted.

She couldn't see her. There was too much confusion. But she could feel her, shared blood and adrenaline searing her veins.

A second thunderclap—directly above. The acoustic ceiling tile disintegrated in a furnace blast of heat that flensed the air in her lungs and slammed her to the floor.

Pelayo met Lagrante at the Bent Note, a jazz club in Palo Alto. He found the bootleg artiste in a recessed booth, sipping a glass of Nouvelle-Orlèans pale green absinthe and tapping a Hongtasan to the sensuous beat of Uzbek slazz.

Pelayo settled into the black vinyl seat across the table from Lagrante. Light sifted down from a diffuse LED fixture, dusting the amber-tinted veneer on the tabletop. Old sheet music, torn notebook pages, and reproduction mimeograph flyers papered the walls, held in place with bent staples and tarnished thumbtacks.

"What do you think?" Lagrante said. He pinched the Chinese cigarette between the tips of three fingers, holding it with the surgical precision of an orchestra conductor.

Pelayo couldn't tell if Lagrante was asking about the club, the music, or the vintage 1940s zoot suit he was waring. The suit was bold and baggy. It sported a wide-shouldered yellow jacket with exaggerated lapels, silver high-waist pants, cinched tight at the ankles and held up with suspenders, and a white shirt with a black-and-red-patterned tie that looked like it had been lifted from a painting by Miro or Kandinsky. A matching borsalino-style hat, yellow with a black band, hung from a brass hook mounted on the side of the seat back. Lagrante had philmed himself with a composite image constructed from various photographs and posters of jazz musicians scattered around his office. The collage blended Thelonius Monk's goatee and meditative spirituality with Charles Mingus's placid contemplation and Charlie Parker's mustache and verve.

"What do I think about what?" Pelayo said. Trying to read the expression behind Lagrante's heavy black spex was pointless. The lenses were dark enough to watch a solar eclipse.

"You look kind of pale," Lagrante said.

Pelayo stared at the stage, and the smoke curdling in the air under the stage lights. "Lot on my mind."

"I can tell." Lagrante tapped his cigarette on the edge of a black ashtray. Fresh ashes had dulled the lustrous sheen of the onyx, silting it with gray. After a couple of rhythmic taps, Lagrante reached into the breast pocket of his casually overwrought jacket, took out an ampoule, and placed it on the table between them.

Pelayo eyed the ampoule. "What's this?"

Lagrante put the cigarette between dry lips and inhaled. "Like I said. I found someone can do the job. But you gotta take that ahead of time. Preps the 'skin for the rip."

"So we've got an arrangement."

"Depends." Lagrante exhaled, his smoke-laden breath smelling of mint and warm licorice.

"On what?"

"Whether you agree to the terms."

Pelayo placed a hand over the ampoule. His fingers trembled, and he curled the ampoule into his palm. "How much we talking?"

"I don't know yet."

"You always know."

Lagrante made a face. "Not this time. I don't even know what my percentage is going to be."

"Bullshit."

"Like I said before, the platform is totally new. We're operating in terra incognita here. I don't know what my man's going to want to do the job—how much I'm going to have to front. I won't know until he gets into it, sees what's involved. Bottom line is I'm taking a risk."

Pelayo unfolded his hand, letting the ampoule rattle to the table. "You wouldn't be here if you didn't think it was worth it."

"I'm here because I think there's a possibility that it might be worth it. There's a big difference. A possibility is still a gamble."

Pelayo waved a hand. "Whatever. Either way, that tells me other people will be interested." He started to slide out of the booth, leaving the ampoule on the table.

Lagrante leaned across the table and restrained Pelayo by the wrist. "No need to start actin' an ass on me."

"Ditto."

Lagrante grinned, then relaxed his grip and smoothed the creased cuff of Pelayo's jacket.

Pelayo stared at the wrinkles left by Lagrante's grip. The rip artist was desperate. He'd cut a deal with whoever was going to help him rip the 'skin. He couldn't back out. Couldn't afford to have Pelayo back out.

Lagrante balanced the Hongtasan on the edge of

the ashtray. "Buy you a drink? The bar here's top-notch."

"How 'bout some of that 'sinthe." It couldn't hurt to press his luck, see where it led.

Lagrante's smile retracted fractionally. "Sure. What the hell?" He opened a d-splay on one palm and placed the order with a magnanimous tap dance of fingers.

Pelayo slid back onto the seat. Elbows propped on the tabletop, he retrieved the ampoule and held it up to the light.

"I'd be careful with that, I were you," Lagrante said.

"You wouldn't have arranged to meet here if you knew the cops were casing the place."

"Not what I'm talkin' 'bout."

Pelayo sat up. Had Lagrante picked up information on the street about the clinical trial? "I'm listening."

"A lot of philmheads are gettin' uptight about new 'skin—especially street 'skin—with so many women gettin' knocked-up sick."

Pelayo absently turned the ampoule from side to side. "What do you know about that?"

"For one thing, it's bad for business."

"Yeah? Why's that?" Pelayo unsealed the ampoule and inserted the nozzle into his left nostril.

"The newzines. They're phlogging all kinds of rumors about corrupt philm and tainted downloads. Some women out there are sayin' they been raped. Focusing all kindsa unwanted attention on cracked ware. They download a ripped copy of F8, get pregnant, and natch assume the ware was what hulled them. Is that some fucked-up cause and effect, or what?"

Pelayo pinched the ampoule and snorted. Whatever it was hit him hard and fast—snapped his head back inside his skull. He smelled burnt lilac, tasted cold metal. "What else you heard?"

"Word I'm getting—from hardcore hackers and philmheads—it's nothing like that. The general consensus seems to be the TVs are responsible."

"How?"

"Some kind of ad hoc programmable matter. Recombinant."

"Ad hoc how?"

Lagrante massaged his temples. "The way it was explained to me, there's whole libraries out there, databases full of digitized nucleotide sequences. We're talkin' everything from the geneprints of murder victims and dead celebs, to the DiNA bar codes for every extinct insect in the last two hundred years. And from time to time shit leaks out. Goes from being digital to analog. Virtual to real."

"They say why the TVs are downloading this stuff?"

"Because the muhfuckers are crazy. Out there. Knowmsayin?"

"Still, there must be a reason."

Lagrante probed his teeth with the tip of his tongue. "If there *is*, my sources don't have a line on it."

Or weren't telling him. "This skintech of yours," Pelayo said. "He gonna meet us here?"

"Not 'skin, specifically. Programmable matter."

"There a difference?"

"Used to be. Before there was a philm industry, like the one we've got now, and I was just getting started in this business."

"When was that?"

Lagrante's expression lost some of its focus. "Back in the early days, when 'skin was a dopant layer that confined electrons with electric fields. Electrostatic quantum dots."

"Artificial atoms," Pelayo said.

Lagrante nodded. "Now the term applies to fullerenes and nanotube threads that can be woven together into a bulk material. But originally it was a thin coating, used strictly for military apps. Everything from camouflage and stealth to field-mutable armor. It didn't go civilian—architecture, fashion, entertainment—until later. Took years to figure out how to power the 'skin using biolectrics. How to wire wetronics into the graphene and integrate the nanoware."

Lagrante's crunk 'tude had slipped away, peeling from his speech and mannerisms like dead skin. The Lagrante he knew was an act. Underneath the lifestyle the rip artist clothed himself in was another life and person Pelayo had never seen, had never imagined existed.

Pelayo's absinthe arrived, served with a sugar cube on a perforated spoon. He poured water over the sugar into the absinthe and took an exploratory sip. The herbal liqueur numbed the back of his tongue.

His gaze wandered to the audience, seated at little round tables in front of the stage and at booths similar to theirs around the perimeter of the room. It was a lively crowd. Lots of zoot suits and colorful women in lime green, canary yellow, and hibiscus dresses. The style was Harlem Renaissance, full of the glowing optimism and cosmopolitan joi de vivre painted by Archibald J. Motley, Jr., or the splashy, soulful exuberance expressed by Ivey Hayes.

He looked down at the d-splay on the Hamilton, checking the eyefeed from the ad mask. Nothing new. Atossa was still maneuvering the mask along the Kevlex mesh fence, looking for a clear view of the service door entrance to the roof.

Pelayo turned back to Lagrante.

". . . two kinds of cages," the rip artist was saying, off on a riff. "The one people try to put you in, and the one you put yourself in. The choice is yours. You just got to decide which one you're most comfortable with."

Pelayo nodded. "So who put you in a cage?"

Lagrante made a dry spitting sound. "What's that supposed to mean?"

"You've been stringing me along."

"How do you figure?"

Pelayo held up the ampoule. "If you weren't, you would've gotten this to me a lot sooner."

Lagrante shook his head, then forced an unreadable smile. "You got it all wrong, man."

"Bullshit. You didn't want me to go to someone else. So you fed me a line. Lied about not being able to rip a copy of the 'skin."

"That ain't how it is. While I was waitin' to hear back, I was working the hack. I got to you soon as I could."

Slowly, Pelayo leaned forward. "Hear back from who? Who else are you talkin' to?"

Lagrante's amusement, if that's what it was, faded. Finally, the rip artist spread his hands in concession. "This dude contacted me a few weeks ago. Told me about the new 'skin. Said I might see you."

"What kind of dude?"

Lagrante fingered the stubble on his chin. "Corporate exec. Upper management. You know the type. Said he'd pay me to wait on ripping and downloading the 'skin. He wanted it bootlegged, but at a certain time."

"So you agreed. Figured it couldn't hurt to hold off. You'd make a little extra on the side, in addition to whatever you pulled in from the hack."

Lagrante shrugged.

"In the meantime, you didn't want me going anywhere," Pelayo said. "You were working a deal and put me off till it was done."

Lagrante's nostrils flared, then relaxed. "Maybe I had a deal. Maybe I didn't. I wasn't sure. If I couldn't rip the 'skin in time, I didn't know what this guy would do. I had to assume all bets were off."

Pelayo massaged the back of his neck. "Exec with who?"

"Who do you think?"

"IBT." It had to be. They were the only ones who knew he was testing the 'skin.

Lagrante nodded. "Might be someone else in bed with them. I'm not sure on that yet."

Pelayo sniffed. "So you're playing them, the same way you played me."

"And you aren't? Takin' ware from Uri with one hand, and sellin' it to me with the other?" Lagrante loosened the double Windsor on his tie. "If I were you, I'd be a lot more worried about how someone at IBT knew you'd be comin' to me or another bootlegger. Think about it. Someone high up at IBT knows you're sellin' crack ware to the street, and they're letting it happen. Why?"

Pelayo eased back in his seat. "Because they want the 'skin ripped," he said.

"And they don't want anyone to know about it," Lagrante said. "Not you. Not the cops. Not the competition."

"Why?"

Lagrante lifted his hat from the knurled hook and fitted it onto his head. "Market share. That's what it's all about. Generating demand and—"

A flash detonated on Pelayo's d-splay, followed by a roar, then nothing, not even static.

"Shit!" Atossa said.

"What?" The face of the Hamilton was blank. Pelayo clapped his hands over his ears, shutting out the music, the rattle of glass, silverware, and laughter. "Atossa, what's going on?"

"...plosion," Atossa said. "Someone just set off a bomb."

44

Mateus took out the lobby first, then the emergency stairs leading down from the garden balconies at both ends of the hotel.

He lobbed the last RPG onto the roof, turning the choppers into a tangled mess of carbon and metal composites. It was a chance he had to take. He couldn't let the copters leave. No one had boarded them yet, so the odds of torching Nadice were small.

The fireball bloomed green in his binoculars, boiling a crater in the gravel-covered bitumen.

Vibrate *that* shit, motherfuckers.

Tiago and Rafa grinned as they watched the choppers burn, light smoldering in the oily cloud of smoke and ash that drifted over the carnage like ground fog. Where the roof hadn't fully collapsed, it was strewn with rubble.

And bodies. Doused in green monochromatic flame.

Ditto the front lobby. It was a slag heap of charred diamond, melted plastic, and shattered floor tile. The suspended ceiling panels had caved in, revealing twisted joists. The debris clogged the elevator and the stairwell. The two security guards were history. They appeared inert through the binoculars, lifeless.

Time to wreck shop. They didn't have long. Five or ten minutes tops, before the parameds and laws showed up. Local residents had already begun to assemble on the sidewalk, stunned out of their nightly boredom by the pyrotechnics.

He turned to Tiago and Rafa. "Let's do it."

———

Mateus approached the smob that had gathered on the street in front of the blast-destroyed lobby. "Get back!" He gestured for the smob to retreat. "For your own safety, stand clear of the building."

Occasional shouts and agonized cries drifted down from the roof. The smart mob stepped back, content for the moment to observe from a safe distance.

He turned to Rafa and Tiago. "Make sure no one tries to come in actin' a hero," he said. Last thing they wanted was a bunch of Good Samaritans. "Keep an eye out. Holler at me as soon as you see any laws or EMTs."

Rafa coughed, his eyes watering from the smoke. "How long we gonna be here?" he asked as they threaded their way through the debris in front of the lobby.

"Long as it takes," Mateus said.

Feeling gritty and determined, he made his way into the lobby, slipping through the jagged-edged pieces of metal and plastine that had once been the door. The air smelled singed and hot. Caustic.

They should have worn gas masks, or even handkerchiefs. Anything to cut the fumes. Mateus covered his mouth and nose with the crook of one arm. Only good thing about the dust and the smoke was that it hid them from view. It was a bitch on the eyes, though. Stung like a motherfucker.

Tiago and Rafa took up a position just inside the ruined front door while Mateus checked on the security guards. One of the TVs was still alive. The man groaned when Mateus prodded him with the steel-tipped toes of his Timbo boots.

"Help me," the man croaked. The words gurgled up in a feeble whisper. "Please. Can't move my legs."

Mateus dropped into a crouch next to him. "Easy, bro. You're gonna be all right. Medivac is on the way. What we need to do now is help everyone we can. Understand?"

The dude managed a strangled grunt. Despite the puddle of blood under the back of his head, he was hanging in there. A real trouper.

Self-preservation. It kicked ass on faith every time; didn't matter how religious you thought you were. Most of the time, it was the whole goddamned reason *for* faith. People didn't want to *die* when they died.

"Think you can answer a couple questions?" Mateus asked.

The dude blinked.

"Good." Mateus glanced toward the front of the lobby. He couldn't see the smob through the smoke. Which meant that he couldn't be seen. He turned back to the injured guard. "How many people in the building?"

"Hundred." The dude winced. "Women...mostly."

"Where?"

The man closed his eyes.

Mateus nudged him. "Stay with me, bro. Don't go to sleep. People are countin' on you."

The man's eyelids fluttered open, the lashes fibrillating. He was going into shock.

"They in one particular place?" Mateus said. "Or spread out all over?" He didn't want to search every goddamn room in the place.

"Top floor...penthouse. Getting ready...to leave."

"You sure?"

A labored nod. "Took 'em...up there." The TV swallowed. "Who hit us? You see...anything?"

"Sorry, man. I was driving by when I heard the shit go down. Got in here fast as I could."

"We were on...lookout."

"For who?"

The TV grimaced and wheezed, sucking wet air. It sounded as if he might have a punctured lung.

"We got laws," Tiago whispered over his earfeed. "One cruiser here. More on the way."

That was it, Mateus thought. Time was up. He reached for a nearby piece of sheet metal, ripped from a ventilation duct. The steel was still warm, the edges ragged but sharp.

The man's gaze followed him, tracking the movement.

"I'm just gonna make you more comfortable," Mateus said. "Get this shit outta the way."

A siren wailed in the distance. The guard let his eyes close, as if comforted by the sound.

Mateus pressed the jagged edge of the sheet metal against the guy's throat, slicing fast and hard through the carotid. He leaned in with his body weight, pinning the guard in place until he stopped struggling.

Tiago and Rafa joined him as he stood. The sirens

were closer and louder, several of them warbling in unison.

"Where to?" Rafa asked. He glanced nervously in the direction of the approaching sirens.

"Top floor," Mateus said. The elevator shaft was a burned-out tube of depressurized pneumatics, the walls fire-blackened and sooty as an old chimney flue. "Looks like we're taking the stairs."

The stairwell door to the second floor was locked. The first people they met came from above. They appeared dazed as they groped their way down. Muffled sobs echoed off the walls.

On the way up, Mateus checked the third-floor exit. It was unlocked.

Shit. No one seemed to be entering the stairwell from the lower levels. But that didn't mean it couldn't happen. There were seven more floors to the penthouse. Short of locking the emergency exits, there was no way to seal off the stairs to keep anybody from entering or leaving.

Mateus stopped on the landing to the third floor.

"Go back down to the second-floor landing and watch for her there," he told Rafa. He didn't want Nadice sneaking out behind them. "Meantime we'll check out the rest of the building."

"What you want me to do if I see her?" Rafa asked. He seemed relieved not to be making the climb to the top.

Mateus tapped one ear. "Holler at us. Then pretend to help her out to the street. We'll hook up with you at the Benzy."

"What if the po pos or the medicals try to grab her?"

"They won't. Long as you're helping her out, you'll be doin' them a favor. Free 'em up to concentrate on other things."

If Nadice was wounded, he thought, the situation could get seriously hulled in a hurry. Fucking EMTs would be over her like flies on shit. They'd want to medivac her ass to the nearest hospital.

He sprinted up the stairs, taking them two at a time.

45

An enormous weight pressed down on Marta, crushing bone, cramping muscles, twisting joints.

The pain wasn't entirely hers; some of it belonged to Nadice. Shared neural input. She imagined the quantum-coupled wetronics in her responding to Nadice's injuries. The exact location and type of trauma eluded her, lost in a hazy wash of endorphins.

The pain was good, Marta told herself. It meant Nadice was alive. It meant *they* were alive.

How badly had they been injured? If one of them didn't make it, would the other die?

It felt that way. Without Nadice, a part of her would cease to exist. It wasn't just the pluglet that joined them, wired them into a shared simultaneity. The baby joined them, knitting bone, nerves, and muscle into something that she couldn't explain, something that lived outside her at the same time it grew inside her.

———

Marta lay on her right side on the floor, buried in loose debris. Her right forearm was pinned. It hurt to breathe. The air burned, triggering a coughing fit that smelled of scorched wood and melted rubber.

Thick denim jeans and the heavy leather of her jacket had protected her from serious cuts and burns. But something sharp pressed against her right cheek, into bruised and bloody gums. The taste of copper and iron had dried on her tongue. A chorus of muffled voices rose and fell around her.

"...bleeding..."

"...punctured, I think..."

"...over here..."

The words came and went, louder and then softer, washing over her in swells. She thought of the explosion, the concussion rattling through her, threatening to tear her apart like cheap sheet metal.

Someone had attacked the hotel with a missile or a bomb. Destroyed the top floor, collapsing the roof.

She had to move. Get up. She couldn't stay where she was. Not if she wanted to find Nadice.

Light sifted through gritty lashes. Marta found herself staring at a smooth-curved surface of injection-molded black under cracked and peeling fabric.

Smart cloth. From one of the helicopters. In places the composite shell had been ripped, revealing the synthetic cartilage of the flexible airframe.

The copter must have fallen through when the roof collapsed, strewing the restaurant with chunks of concrete, twisted rebar, acoustic ceiling panels, and bituminous asphalt studded with small bits of crushed white gravel.

Her right forearm was lodged under the tail section of the chopper. She lifted the side of her face from the rubble and looked at the tail. It narrowed, tapering quickly as it disappeared under a snarl of ceiling mullions.

Marta could barely feel the fingers of her right

hand when she tried to make a fist. Her left hand was wedged under her stomach. She dragged it free and shoved at the tail.

The fuselage refused to budge.

Pain throbbed in her lower back. *Whose pain?* Hers or Nadice's? Could Nadice feel the pain of her pinioned forearm?

Something stirred in her womb. The squishy sensation didn't hurt. But it wasn't pleasant, either.

"...push..." someone said.

Not possible, Marta thought. It was too early. The baby would be premature. It would never survive.

The tail section shifted slightly, rising a couple of centimeters before settling back into place. Three or four of the acoustic panels leaning against it dislodged. They fell in a heap on Marta's head.

"Harder," the voice exhorted.

The tail section rocked sideways half a meter, held aloft by muffled groans. In the sudden absence of weight, Marta rolled onto her back, dragging the weight of her right arm after her. More rubble cascaded onto the floor. Dust mixed with smoke powdered her face.

She blinked at the grit. Her right forearm throbbed, then prickled, as it came back to life.

A fissure of watery light appeared less than a meter in front of her. Clenching her jaw, she crawled toward it on her stomach and elbows. She kicked, shoving debris aside until she wriggled free of twisted sheet metal, clutching wires, and charred lichenboard.

Above her, through the tangled thicket of rebar, pipes, and joists, Marta could see thick cotton-batting fog. Portable LED lanterns and flashlights tented the interior gloom, pushing it aside.

"That's it," the voice said. "Easy now."

The man sounded like Jeremy. He wasn't talking to her, but to the ragtag collection of people pulling someone else from beneath the mangled helicopter, clearing space on the floor.

They didn't know about her yet. How many other people were still buried—still undiscovered, waiting for help?

Sirens pierced the air, attenuated by a fitful salt-laden breeze that swirled through the hole in the roof and the windowless frames where the graphene panes had blown out.

"This way!" another voice kept saying. "Over here!"

She watched a flashlight beam wobble around a doorway with an *EXIT* sign above it. People who were well enough to walk on their own migrated toward the door, singly or in groups. Through the emergency exit, Marta could see the steady, beckoning glow of a stairwell.

Nadice was still there. She wouldn't leave, not without her, the same way Marta wouldn't leave. The certainty felt hardwired into her; it circulated through her with each heartbeat, as real and nourishing as her own blood.

Next to her, a blackened slab of concrete angled up from the floor to the roof at a forty-five-degree angle. Grabbing an exposed length of rebar sticking out from one edge, Marta hauled herself to her feet. She stood, gripping the bent, ribbed bar, and took a lungful of air.

Other than her mouth and nose, she didn't seem to

be bleeding. Her right wrist ached. Swollen. Cracked maybe, but not broken. No bones poked through the skin. Movement had returned to her fingers, but no strength. Marta curled them, managing a weak, trembling fist.

Across the room, Jeremy shined a light on the face of the woman lying motionless on the varnished wood. The woman was dead. Dull eyes, blood-matted hair.

Marta staggered away from the collapsed section of roof—lost her balance...recovered.

Voices, mixed with sobbing groans, orbited around her. The sound left her dizzy, disoriented. She clamped her hands over her ears. But the noise refused to go away. It continued to spin inside her head.

A hand caught her by the shoulder.

"There you are! Thank God!"

Marta turned. The hand left her shoulder, fluttering to the side of her face.

"I've been looking for you everywhere," Nadice said. "I couldn't find you." The whites of her eyes burned phosphor bright. "I thought you were...I thought maybe you didn't make it."

Marta drew Nadice to her, leaning against her for support. "You would've known."

Nadice touched her arms, shoulders, and face. "Are you okay? Can you walk?"

"I think so."

"We need to get out of here," Nadice said. She cut a glance at the sagging ceiling. "Before the rest of the roof caves in."

Marta nodded. When she stepped back from Nadice, the hem of her shirt was wet with blood.

"It's not mine." Nadice shivered in the fog. "I've been helping people. Trying to get them out of here."

"You're cold," Marta said. She slipped off her jacket and threw it over Nadice's shoulders.

"What about you?" Nadice went to shrug off the leather jacket. "You don't have anything—"

"I'm not in a dress," Marta said, "and I'm not wet. You need it more than me right now."

Nadice nodded. With Marta's help, she slipped her arms into the rainbow-lined sleeves of the jacket and drew it around her.

"We should look for casualties," Marta said. "In the debris."

"There are paramedics on the way," Nadice told her. "Rescue workers. The best thing we can do is get out."

She was right. They'd only be in the way. The sirens were loud now, close to the hotel. And she could see the approaching floodlight from a rescue helicopter, sweeping along the seawall. Fog swirled in the glare, wraithlike.

"All right," Marta agreed. They headed for the crowded exit. "How come we're all going out this way?" she asked. "There has to be another stairwell."

"All of the other exits are blocked," Nadice said, "including the outside terraces. A bunch of women tried to go down them and had to come back after a few floors."

"What the hell happened?"

"God knows," she said, shaking her head. "The elevator's not working, either. No one can get in touch with the front desk or security."

Great. They weren't going anywhere fast, and had no idea what they'd find when they got to the bottom.

Their descent down the stairwell was slow going. People coaxed each other along with reassuring whispers and fleeting hand squeezes.

There was no philm on the walls, just bare concrete, devoid even of acoustic tile. The light came from emergency biochem strips taped to the walls, and the *EXIT* signs at each landing.

"She's here." The voice drifted up from a couple of flights down. "Jus' 'cause we ain't seen her yet don't mean shit." It was a man's voice. "We get to the top, I want you guarding the door. Understand?"

Nadice froze.

The woman behind Marta bumped into them. Marta stepped aside, pulling Nadice with her, so the others behind them could pass. She put her mouth close to Nadice's ear. "What is it?"

"Mateus," Nadice whispered.

"Who?"

"The guy I was working for."

"As a mule? The one who's looking for you?"

Nadice nodded, then bit her lower lip, sudden resolve overriding her panic. "We have to go back."

"We can't just turn—"

"We have to!" Nadice tugged Marta up the stairs, fighting against the downward flow of bodies.

She could hear footsteps now, clomping after them loud and heavy on the cement stairs. There were two pairs of boots, echoing hard and steady.

Marta stole a glance back. Half a flight down the line shifted to one side, making way for the men. Their shadows lunged upward, scaling the wall with quick, determined strides. She caught a glimpse of a smooth-shaved head just as they reached the landing for the next set of stairs.

They weren't going to make it. They still had three floors to get to the restaurant.

Nadice stopped on the landing, breathing heavily, doubled over with exertion and pain. She leaned next to the door and clutched her right side, where fresh blood spotted the hem of her blouse.

That explained the squishiness. "Why the hell didn't you say something?" Marta whispered.

"Didn't...want you...to worry." Nadice panted. A sheen of sweat glistened on her face. She licked pale, glutinous lips.

"You need help."

"I'll be...fine."

Above her, Marta heard the thwup of the helicopter. It seemed to be hovering in one place. Waiting for them, just out of reach.

"There's my gurl," a voice below them crooned. "I been lookin' all over for you, Nadice. It's good to see you in one piece."

Marta looked down. On the landing below the man grinned up at them, flashing white teeth, bright with triumph.

46

Zhenyu al-Fayoumi wasn't sure what he was doing, or why. He sat in the All the Raj café, sipping a chai latte and looking for a girl who matched the image the damselfish had left on his forearm, like a tattoo, when it sank back into his 'skin.

Not that the picture would necessarily help identify her. The girl had cast herself as a Ghost Dragon. Based on the image, al-Fayoumi couldn't tell if she was waring face paint or philm. Face paint seemed more likely. Ten seemed a little young to be 'skinned, but it was becoming more and more common.

Why had he agreed to come? What was he getting himself into? There was no reason to believe, let alone trust, the datician, sageware, or whatever it was that had spoken to him.

In the end it boiled down to curiosity, about the damselfish and the girl. Who was she? What was her connection to the flies and the idolon? If she really was in trouble, he could at least look after her long enough to call the police or her family, assuming she had any.

Al-Fayoumi checked the time. Almost eight. The café was busy, filled with late commuters and a few

De Anza Community College students studying for exams. He sat at a table in the middle, making himself as conspicuous as possible.

Would the girl know who he was? Presumably, the idolon was guiding her here and would instruct her, the way it had instructed him.

A vague hope flickered in his stomach. Perhaps she wouldn't show. But just as quickly, the hope was doused.

"Here she comes," the damselfish whispered over his earfeed, as if it had been waiting there with him all the time. Al-Fayoumi looked up from the image on his arm to the door.

And there she was, looking small and afraid as a bus pulled away from the curb, leaving a group of passengers that quickly dispersed in its wake. The girl hesitated, then approached the café and peered between the resham-style curtains—but didn't enter.

Al-Fayoumi stood. When the movement didn't catch her eye, he lurched toward the entrance, jostling his way around tables.

Finally she saw him, and tensed, straightening her arms as she clasped her hands tightly in front of her.

But she didn't run. She nodded, as if listening to someone speaking, and held her ground when he pushed open the door.

What to say? He couldn't think. She must be scared to death, meeting a stranger on her own.

"Show her your arm," the damsel said.

Al-Fayoumi pulled his shirtsleeve back and turned his wrist so she could see her face. While her attention was diverted, al-Fayoumi took the opportunity to inspect her Ghost Dragon mask. NanoFX makeup, he decided.

She looked up and twisted her arm. A Vurtronic d-splay patch pasted to her left wrist looked out at him. The image was real-time; when he frowned, the simage frowned back, like looking into a mirror.

"My name's Zhenyu," he said, uncertain how much the damsel had told her.

"Lisette." The d-splay patch disappeared as her left hand sought the comfort of the right.

"You hungry?" he asked.

She shook her head.

"Thirsty?"

Another shake.

"How about some sorbet?" He started toward the gelato kiosk just down the street, but she refused to budge. Al-Fayoumi came back to her. "We can't stand here all night."

Apparently, they could. The girl remained rooted in place. She looked around at all the storefronts, ad masks, and signs, as if waiting for someone else to show up. The damsel perhaps, telling her what to do.

Al-Fayoumi squatted next to her and lowered his voice so the people lounging at the bus stop couldn't hear him. "I'm scared, too," he admitted.

The girl scowled. "I'm not scared."

"It's okay to be afraid," he said.

The girl bristled. Her hands knotted tighter. "I'm not!" she insisted.

"Where's your mother?" he asked.

The girl blinked, as if he'd grabbed her by the shoulders and shaken her. "I don't have a mother."

"You don't?"

The girl's gaze dropped to the pavement and her cheeks, where they were visible, burned. "She left."

Something told him to let it go. For now. He could bring it up later, if he got the chance. "What about friends?" he said.

Lisette bit her lower lip. "I don't want anything bad to happen to them because of me."

"Is that why you're here?"

A nod.

Al-Fayoumi let out a breath. Now what? He was an only child. He didn't have the benefit of nephews or nieces. Come right down to it, he'd never been a kid himself. Between school and piano lessons he'd never had the chance. Maybe she hadn't, either, but for different reasons. Maybe they had more in common than either of them realized.

"We could just hang out for a while," he said. "You know. Look around, check stuff out. Whatever."

She nodded at the sidewalk.

He held out his hand. She didn't take it, but when he started down the street she followed a step behind.

Where they were headed was anyone's guess.

47

Nadice stood transfixed as Mateus mounted the stairs, shouldering his way through the downward press of women in the stairwell.

His gaze was tarnished, flat, and pitiless. He no longer needed her alive. His only concern was the ware, and he would do whatever it took to get it.

Nadice shuddered. If she'd just gone with him as agreed, none of this would have happened. No one would have been hurt.

"Gurl." He reached for her. "It's good to see you. I been worried sick I might not find you in one piece."

She shrank from him, and found herself caged by the LED strips on the chill walls. It felt as if his tattoo-blackened fingers were entering her chest and closing around her heart.

Nadice gasped.

"This way!" Marta hissed. She pulled open a door next to her.

A hand gripped her upper arm, dislodging the one around her heart.

"Bitch!" Mateus lunged for her, shoving aside several women who had paused in confusion.

Nadice stumbled after Marta, into a carpeted hallway. The door swung shut with a click.

"Come on!" Marta said, tugging her down the hall.

In the stairwell, someone screamed.

"No." Nadice sagged to a stop. There was no place to go... no place to hide. All of the rooms would be locked. "I'm tired of running."

"You can't stay here."

"I know. I'm going with him." The resolve calmed her. It was what she should have done all along. She'd been an idiot to think she could escape.

"He'll kill you," Marta said.

"It'll be better this way," Nadice said. "I don't want any more people to get hurt. I don't want *you* to get hurt."

More screams echoed from the stairwell.

Determination and anger flared in Marta's eyes. "You are *not* giving up. I won't let you. You're too important."

"No, I'm not."

"If you weren't, they wouldn't be coming after you."

Nadice wavered.

"If you go with him, a lot more people are going to get hurt. You understand what I'm saying? You can't let him have whatever you've got inside you."

The door to the stairwell opened. A boot appeared, followed by a hand and a bare forearm.

Marta threw herself against the door. It slammed shut against the arm and the side of a face. Something popped, a bone or a joint. The man bellowed. His clenched hand opened and a large gray grape with a single pomegranate-red seed suspended in the center rolled onto the Jacquard-pattern carpet.

"Run!" Marta shouted.

She shoved Nadice ahead of her, just as the grenade went off.

MEMS sprayed the hallway. The micro-electromechanical devices, embedded in globs of sticky gel, slammed into Nadice. The gel burned. When she went to wipe the goop off, it smeared, spreading the spiderlike bots. They scuttled over her on thin legs, jabbed her with thousands of stinging, needle-sharp proboscises.

Her legs went numb, then buckled under the toxins. Nadice sprawled sideways onto the hallway carpet, breathing in the floral scent in the thick pile. She tasted blood on her tongue.

Get up, she told herself. Keep moving. Wasn't that what they always told you to do?

She grew cold all over. Her bones felt heavy, as if covered with ice. Her muscles tightened, rigor-stiff in the chill. Her lungs ached.

Marta lay unmoving in the hallway a couple meters ahead. She groaned. One arm flopped sideways, spasmed, then quivered uselessly next to her.

Nadice heard the stairwell door rattle open. The clamor in the stairwell swelled, then quieted as the door slammed shut.

Gray smoke swirled in the hall, blending with the white static philm on the ceiling and walls. Down the corridor, past an open service elevator, a door to one of the outside garden terraces banged open. She shifted her gaze toward the sound.

An indistinct figure materialized out of the smoke. The figure approached slowly, growing larger but no clearer.

Mateus. No—it couldn't be. The stairwell was

behind her. There was no way he could have gotten onto the balcony.

The shadow seemed to be just that, an absence of light and nothing more. It didn't appear to be cast by anyone. It seemed to exist independently, as if it was not connected to the world.

"Nadice," Mateus said. The voice behind her was calm, reasonable. "Don't get all scared, gurl. I ain't gonna hurt you. Word."

The shadow in front of her stopped, suddenly rigid, as if the MEMS had paralyzed it, too.

"I know you're there," Mateus went on. "I can see you now." His voice was closer, louder, but no less soothing.

She swallowed, and imagined him crushing her windpipe.

The shadow moved. Four quick steps and it knelt on one knee next to Marta, head bent close to hers.

Help! Nadice wanted to shout. *Call the police!*

As if in response, the shadow looked up, directly at her.

"Who's this?" Mateus said, still a few meters behind her. "Who you got with you, gurl?"

Nadice heard the click of a safety being released, followed by the compressed hiss of a fléchette gun spitting needles.

The shadow turned from her, rolled Marta onto her back, grabbed her by the arms, and pulled her down the hallway. As Nadice watched, Marta seemed to dissolve into the smoke, become one with it.

A new shadow drifted across the edges of her vision. A couple of seconds later an ad mask settled onto her face, momentarily blinding her as it fitted itself over her nose, cheeks, mouth, and chin.

Nadice couldn't breathe. Her heart fluttered wildly in her chest and throat.

Mateus chuckled. "Thought you could fool me, gurl. Thought I wouldn't recognize you behind a mask."

She thought he would remove it. Instead he stroked her hair, traced a finger along the outer cusp of her ear. His familiar cologne, mixed with sweat, washed over her. The scent caught in her nose and her eyes started to tear.

"Might work with other folks," he went on, "but I'll know you anywhere. There's no way you can hide from me."

Some of the feeling had returned to her arms and legs. Her lungs weren't as icy or as heavy. She managed to open her mouth.

"What's that?" Mateus touched her lips.

"You win," she gasped. "I won't"—she took several deep breaths—"run again. I promise."

The first shadow reappeared, an unsteady blur that solidified slightly as the smoke dissipated and thinned.

"Take care of her," the shadow said.

Jeremy. His voice wobbled. Nadice thought he might come closer, but for some reason he held back.

"If anything happens to her," the TV continued, "you'll regret it. I promise." He stepped back, retreating into the haze.

Nadice blinked tears. Instead of trying to help her, he was leaving.

A second barrage of needles whispered through the air.

Jeremy seemed to disperse, contracting inward

from the edges as he grew smaller, until all that remained was a blurry smudge...the persistent afterimage of an eye-watering brightness.

Mateus lifted her by the arms, draped her over his shoulders in a fireman's carry, and headed back to the stairwell. "Time to take care of unfinished business," he said.

48

The blemish on Pelayo's philm reappeared on the elevated magtube from San Jose to Santa Cruz.

Eight minutes into the fifteen-minute trip, the eyefeed from the ad mask flickered back on. Jittery snatches of a dimly lit stairwell, crowded with women, snarled Pelayo's optic d-splay.

"What's going on?" he asked Atossa. He wasn't sure if she'd regained control of the mask or hijacked another one.

"I found her."

"Marta?"

"I'm pretty sure. She's wearing that brown leather jacket of hers, the one with the really colorful lining."

At the mention of Marta's name, Lagrante came out of his meditative silence long enough to cut Pelayo a quick sidelong glance from the adjoining seat.

"How is she?" Pelayo asked.

"Unconscious, I think. It was really smoky in the hallway, and the mask cut out before I could get a good look at her. I've been trying to call for help, but I can't get through. It's a total zoo over there."

The d-splay died and Pelayo closed his eyes for a moment, giving his stomach an opportunity to settle.

Striated bands of yellow light from the magtube's LEDs flickered across his lids.

"Where are you?" Atossa said.

"We should be there in about ten minutes. We're in a car that bypasses the main downtown station and goes directly to the Boardwalk."

"Okay." Atossa exhaled sharply. "I'll stick with her as long as I can. Keep you updated."

"How's she doin'?" Lagrante said when Atossa dropped off-line.

"Hanging in there."

Lagrante nodded. The LEDs leached the color from his zoot suit. "What's that on your face?"

Pelayo turned to examine his reflection in the window next to him. "I thought it had gone away," he said.

Lagrante's expression soured. "This ain't the first time?"

"It showed up a few hours after I got out of the tank." Pelayo touched the blotch. It had changed shape, the way a shadow lengthened and warped, and now resembled the inkblot wings of an insect.

Lagrante lowered his smoky black shades. He peered at Pelayo over the tops of the lenses, needle-sharp pupils set in slate-gray eyes. "What'd Uri say?"

Pelayo withdrew his finger. "I haven't told him."

"You got a reason for keepin' him in the dark?"

"It went away. I figured if it was a serious problem, it would have showed up as a red flag on his end."

"Right." Lagrante slid the spex back into place. "You didn't tell him because you were afraid he'd nix you as a test subject. 'Skin someone else."

Six minutes later, the bullet car dropped them off at the parking lot just outside the main entrance to the Boardwalk.

Except for emergency lights and the flashing racks on police cars and ambulances, the TV center was dark. Pelayo couldn't tell what condition the hotel was in. He jogged along the seawall, past the entrance to the pier, and up the hill. Lagrante huffed a couple of meters behind him, keeping pace. Despite the Hongtasans, he seemed fit, in much better shape than Pelayo would have figured.

Halfway up the hill, the eyefeed from the mask kicked back in. Grainy pavement bounced on the d-splay. Every now and then, he caught sight of a heavy boot and a pant leg.

"You there?" Pelayo said.

"That's the best I can do," Atossa said. "The mask was damaged in the blast and I can't get the visual array to sync up properly."

Pelayo slowed when they came to the smob scene outside the hotel. Through the crowd, he could make out debris, strewn across the parking lot, including the twisted wreckage of what had once been the building's front entrance and lobby. SARbots had begun to reconnoiter the debris-choked structure, the little helium-buoyed drones spearheading the initial search and rescue effort in preparation for full HUMOP support. Network and newzine COMbots jockeyed for position, darting toward fleeting breaks in the smoke and mist as they hunted for a clear view of the carnage.

"Shit," Lagrante said.

Over the eyefeed, more feet came into view, stepping back. Then a car tire and a polished black side panel, mirror-smooth, that reflected the fog-saturated lights from the demolished building.

"It looks like she's being carried," Pelayo said. He elbowed his way to a pair of ambulances and squad cars.

On the eyefeed d-splay a car door opened and Marta's head lolled sideways. He caught a fleeting glimpse of a man's face, as she was lifted into the backseat of a sedan, followed by a heavily inked hand, riddled with gang tattoos. Then he was staring up at the ceiling. Not an ambulance. Or a squad car: there was no barrier between the front seats and the rear.

"I don't see her," Lagrante said.

Pelayo skirted the crowd, searching for other vehicles. Past the first responders, the headlights on an old Mercedes parked next to the curb snapped on. He couldn't make out the color of the car behind the glare, but when the Benz eased away from the curb the eyefeed from the mask jostled just before the image sparked and dissolved.

"That her?" Lagrante said. He shrugged off his suit coat and bent over, arms on his knees, to catch his breath.

"I'm pretty sure." Pelayo's throat burned, scraped raw by smoke and frustration.

"I'm not getting anything," Atossa said. "I can't get it back."

"Keep trying." Pelayo followed the path of the Mercedes down the hill, toward the pier and downtown.

"They're probably taking her to a hospital," Lagrante said. "Dominican. That'd be my guess. In which case she's in good hands."

Pelayo grunted, noncommittal. Something about the man who'd been carrying her was familiar.

49

Uri finished filling the bathtub with surgical gel. Using a dolly, he wheeled the empty storage tank into the front room and set it behind the bed next to the other two tanks he had taken from his lab. The modular tanks were translucent white, designed to fit together for easy storage and transport. To hide the containers from security cameras, Uri covered them with a bedspread. He'd taken precautions, sanitized the room with both electronic and biochemical counter-surveillance, but you couldn't be too careful. The last thing he wanted was unexpected visitors.

Mateus would be here soon with Nadice. When they showed up, Uri wanted to get her scanned and 'skinned as quick as possible. As soon as the updated 'skin was installed and stable, it wouldn't take long for the quantum components in the wetronics to entangle.

In theory, the resonance state would collapse into a stable structure on its own. Once that happened, nonlocal EPR effects in Nadice's copy of the 'skin would entangle with 'skin that had already been doped with the quantum components he had taken from her in Dockton. Soon, Nadice, himself, and Mateus's boyz would all be entangled, waring the same 'skin.

Pelayo, too. That asshole had dropped off-line, hadn't bothered to get back to him. It pissed him off, but he didn't have time to deal with Pelayo now. That would have to wait till later.

Uri checked the time, then the med equip he'd set up on a coffee table next to the double bed.

Everything was in order. Where the hell were they? They should have been here by now. Uri sim-aged Mateus's boyz on his eyefeed d-splay. "You heard anything from your man?"

"Not since he left," the one named Rafa said. "Why?"

Uri got up and paced. "He's late."

"Probably stopped to take care of some unfin-ished bidness," the other one, Tiago, said with a wink.

"What do you want us to do now?" Rafa said. "Keep watching this place? There ain't shit we can do with all the activity. Place is crawling with po pos."

Uri thought for a moment. "Split up," he said. "I want you here," he told Tiago. "In case there's trou-ble."

"What about me?" Rafa said.

Uri forwarded him an address.

Rafa frowned as he pulled up the location. "Talk about a shit hole. What do I do when I get there?"

"Nothing," Uri said. "Stay out of sight. Watch the place. Let me know if anyone goes in or out."

Rafa nodded. "I gotcha."

A message light flashed at the bottom of Uri's eye-feed. It was Mateus. "Where the hell are you?" Uri demanded.

"Loading dock in back. There a way I can get her up to the room without being seen?"

"Service elevator." Uri copied him a floor plan of the hotel.

"Gotcha," Mateus said. "Be there in five."

Uri stared out the window across the room, at the sprawl of city lights that scoured the stars from the night sky. He couldn't ever remember looking up and seeing stars. Growing up, the only stars he knew, the only constellations he had to guide him, were the streetlights that illuminated back alleys and dead-end streets.

He d-splayed the décor menu for the room. The menu offered several options for wallpaper and pattern, floor-tile design, carpet texture and color, pressed-metal ceiling panels, and window embossing and etching. He selected the option for black silk drapes. In a few seconds, the programmable nanofibers on the surface of the window assembled into curtains and drew together, shutting out the light.

He was tired of being taken for granted. Tired of being taken advantage of by IBT and Atherton.

50

"I don't understand." The building manager swiped her hand in front of a DiNA scanner next to the door. "He's always been such a good tenant. Quiet, respectful. Not like so many of the young people I rent to these days. I can't believe he's involved with anything illegal, especially warewolves."

The woman had philmed herself from the neck up as a Betty Paige pinup, complete with cheap hair and lash grafts. Collagen, doped with bioluminescent bacteria that emitted candy-apple red, inflated her lips under the waxy, low-budget 'skin. She couldn't afford REbot cosmetics for the rest of her. Her loose-fitting, hand-knitted clothing clung to slack breasts, sagging arms, and a drooping waistline.

Van Dijk watched the cinFX on her nails, an old black-and-white film he didn't recognize involving a buxom blonde in a clingy evening gown and clumsy pumps. "You haven't noticed anything unusual?"

"If he had a 'skin tank in there, I'd know," she said.

Van Dijk thought she'd also probably be first in line. "What about people coming and going?"

Her lips pinched. "At odd hours, you mean?"

"Possibly . . . but not necessarily. Mostly different

people. Strangers who come by briefly, for a few minutes, then leave."

She led him down a steep, narrow stairwell. The door to the basement apartment was at the bottom, barely lit by the streetlight on the corner. In the cramped quarters the woman's violet perfume made his eyes water.

"No. Nothing like that," she said. "Just the opposite."

"What do you mean?"

"He never gets any visitors." The woman rested artificially young fingers on the steel knob. "He's always by himself, closeted away in his apartment. He never goes out, except to work or eat."

"He doesn't have any friends? He's not seeing anyone?"

"Not that I've ever noticed. He's quiet, keeps to himself." The woman sighed. "It's a pity. He doesn't know what he's missing."

"What's that?"

The manager turned the knob and pushed open the door. "Life."

The apartment smelled. Van Dijk couldn't place the smell. It was organic—not exactly rotten, but fecund, as if there should be lots of houseplants, growing in pots and hanging from the ceiling. There were no plants. Instead, there were terrariums...a whole wall of them on metal shelving units.

Van Dijk opted not to turn on the lights. If al-Fayoumi returned, the last thing he wanted to do was scare him off. Besides, he could see more in the dark.

The flies glowed. There were thousands of them,
crawling, buzzing around in their sealed cages. He
had to press his face close to the plastine to make
out the Fokker wings on them, the tiny faces rendered in microminiature detail, like the crests and
coat of arms on hand-painted military figurines.

He mentally activated the record mode on his
eyefeed and uploaded the image stream to the datician and case database.

He stared for several minutes, mesmerized, before
he realized that there was a pattern to the terrariums. Each terrarium contained a different cast, separated by image, almost as if each cast represented a
different species. Snow White here and Mona Lisa
there. Spitfires in this one, Japanese Zeros in that
one.

But no damselflies.

Van Dijk turned his attention from the terrariums
to the rest of the apartment. It looked more like a
research lab than a living area. Gradually, details
emerged from the gloom. A portable STM microscope. CNT probe array. Philm imager and sequencer.
Small 'skin chamber, designed for aerosol application
of liquid graphene and wetronics. Large Vurtronic
wall d-splay.

Down a narrow, windowless hallway, past a tidily
kept kitchenette, he found the bedroom and bathroom. Both were clean, spartan in their furnishing
and décor. The bathroom was too cramped for a tub,
and he could find no external tank or cutoff valve
spliced into the water tubes feeding the shower. The
bedroom had a neatly made futon on a wood-slat
frame, a set of drawers, a folding partition that
seemed to be more decorative than functional.

Pleated curtains concealed a window well that was home to discarded takeout trays, a paper cup, and at least one spent condom.

Returning to the terrariums in the front room, van Dijk heard the lock in the door snick open.

He stepped back, thumbing the safety off on the HK minifuge as the door swung inward. A shadow stepped into the rectangle of light cast by the street-light and seeped across the floor toward him.

51

Marta woke in an elevator alcove, roused by pincushion stinging in her feet, arms, and hands. She sat propped against a wall, her legs stretched out in front of her on plain white tile. The elevator next to her stood open, a birdcage of floral-etched diamond and wrought iron that had come to a stop fifteen or twenty centimeters below the level of the floor. Past the elevator she could see the dull gray of dead philm on the opposite wall of the corridor. The blizzard of white static was gone. So was much of the smoke, but the reek of scorched polymer and metal hung in the air.

Jeremy was gone. She recalled his dragging her here from the hallway—away from the MEMS—and saying he'd be right back. He needed to check on—

Nadice!

A muscle in her left thigh jerked, then stilled.

How long had she lain unconscious? Minutes, hours? No, not hours. Otherwise, she wouldn't still be here. Someone would have found her. She would be in a hospital or an ambulance.

Her pulse throbbed in her abdomen. It felt sluggish, anesthetized. But it was still there.

Alive. If the baby still lived, so did Nadice. The baby connected them. It needed them, both of them. Without them it would die.

She fought against the lethargy holding her in place. Bent her legs. Folded her knees under her. Grabbed the chrome handrail just above her head, and hauled herself to her feet.

"Nadice?" she called.

A soft, half-choked response answered her.

Marta's legs shook as she worked her way to the front of the alcove and hobbled into the hallway.

"Nadice?"

Jeremy lay on his side, curled up in a fetal position a few meters down the corridor. The shallow rise and fall of his ribs was barely visible. Fresh blood smeared the necrotic philm on the wall beside him, as if he'd slid sideways to the place where he now huddled.

There was no one else in the corridor. A SARbot appeared in the murk, probing the hall. Marta felt her way along the wall. When she reached Jeremy, she sank to the carpet next to him, too unsteady to stand. "What happened? Where's Nadice?"

Jeremy blinked, coughed. Blood-speckled saliva frothed between the static limning his lips. He licked at the blood, but a crimson bubble burst and trickled down his chin.

"Shit," she said.

The front of his shirt was wet and dark where he'd been hit. She could see the tiny constellation of holes left by the fléchette needles.

"Her boss," he groaned. The words gurgled up, moist and soft from deep inside his chest. "Mateus."

Marta leaned closer, trying to make it easier on him. She choked on the fetid odor from his mouth. "What about him?"

"Took her." His eyes fell shut.

"When?" She gripped his shoulder, squeezed it hard to keep him with her. "How long ago?"

"She had to go," he said. A cough wracked him and more blood gushed out, from his nose this time. "Couldn't stop him."

"Why did she have to go?"

"Sorry," Jeremy whispered. "Necessary."

"You *let* her go?"

"Had to."

"You bastard." She bit her lip. "You promised you'd look after her."

"Necessary. Pluglet—" A sucking wheeze rasped out of him. At the very least, one of his lungs was pierced. Maybe an artery, judging by the amount of blood he was losing.

"Where'd he take her?" she said.

He shook his head.

"Goddamn it! How could you?"

Jeremy's shoulders convulsed under her hand and a shudder coursed through her fingers. "Told him not to hurt her."

A lot of good that would do. Marta waved a hand to attract the attention of the SARbot's motion detectors and started to stand.

Jeremy clutched her wrist. "In my pocket. Shirt."

"What?" She sank back down.

"Take it."

The shirt pocket was damp. She slipped her fingers into the blood-slicked linen, groping through the sticky wet wrinkles and her mounting nausea. She could feel his 'skin through the sodden linen. It was soft and smooth, the texture of cold wax.

Her fingers encountered the databead, wedged into one corner of the pocket. The bead was the size of a pomegranate seed. She pinched it lightly, afraid it would squirt away.

"What is it?"

"Contact..."

His voice was fading, barely audible. Marta bent her ear to his mouth, straining to hear. "Who?"

He opened to his mouth to speak. But his voice guttered, then flickered out before Marta could make out the words. The static veiling his face and hands ebbed until all that remained of the philm was a flat, lifeless gray.

Marta jerked to her feet. The blood on her fingertips grew sticky. A ladies' room. That was her first impulse, to wash her hands.

No. She shook her head. There wasn't time. She wasn't fitted with a nanosocket I/O port for the bead and needed to find a pair of spex to access it.

She yanked open the door to the stairwell and the lingering stench of burned cloth and fear. A SARbot drifted toward, nav fans whirring. It doused her with UV light, and the blood on her hands fluoresced.

Marta pushed past the drone and quickly descended the stairwell.

Dust, smoke, and fog lingered in the lobby. Two more SARbots appeared as she worked her way through a bramble heap of twisted joists and crushed graphene wall panels. Emergency vehicles clogged the parking lot and street. Several rescue workers near the elevator were picking their way through the rubble, fanning out.

Her toe caught something soft. She looked down; a hand protruded from under a yellow plastic tarp.

She yanked her foot back. The tarp was unblemished, new. It had been put there after the explosion.

She started to step over the hand, then stopped. The corpse still wore a wristwatch. It was military grade. The Kevlex band was in good shape. So was the face. Marta could read the time: 9:12 P.M.

She dropped to her haunches. The body lay on its back. She pulled the tarp aside, exposing a man's face. A bent section of sheet metal protruded from his neck. It had cut deep, exposing bone and gristle and severing the artery.

The man still wore spex. They had sustained more damage than the watch. Heat had blackened the frames and the scratched lenses. But with any luck they might still be functional.

Don't look at the gash, she told herself. Just get it over with.

For a moment, the lenses seemed to be cauterized to his face. The heat-cracked graphene around his brow and cheeks resisted her, clinging to the frames.

Come on, she thought, gritting her teeth.

The frames tore loose and Marta discovered the reason for the resistance. One of the stems was bent where it had cooked to the 'skin behind one ear.

She checked the foam padding along the inside curve of the frame. It was a little discolored and misshapen from wear, but otherwise serviceable. She slipped on the spex, toggled them to IR mode, and made her way out of the lobby.

A smob had gathered on the opposite side of the street. In the parking lot, an inflatable trauma tent was ballooning to life. Several SCPD officers patrolled the perimeter of the smob, working crowd control.

Marta slipped into the roiling confusion, then ducked out the other side. As she hurried down the hill to the Boardwalk, a figure detached from the crowd, trailing after her.

Walking quickly, she clicked the databead into one of the I/O ports on the inside of the thin stem.

Nothing. The bead was shot. She would have to go to a minimart, pick up a pair of cheap disposables, and hope they had enough bandwidth.

Marta glanced back. A second figure had joined the first, which had broken into a trot. Headlights from an approaching car splashed the lenses, solar-flare-bright, blinding her.

She yanked off the spex, pressing the bead to eject it. Instead the lenses flickered, sputtering to life.

Marta refitted the screens over her eyes, holding the lopsided frames in place with one hand.

The narrow bandwidth image of a line-of-sight flashcast appeared on the warped lenses.

"... Marta?" a voice said over the stem speakers. "Is that you?"

52

"Pelayo?" Marta said.

"What are you doing here?" he asked. Her outline emerged from the fog, familiar details slowly taking shape. "What did you do with the mask?"

"What are you talking about?"

"I thought you were unconscious. Being rushed to the hospital by somebody in a car."

"Why?"

"Never mind." Less than ten meters separated them. Under the streetlight where she had slowed to a stop, her face looked uneven and pale. When she removed the spex, her eyes formed dark craters.

"Jesus," he said. "You look like hell. Are you okay?"

Marta leaned unsteadily against the wall behind her, an arched alcove to a game arcade. The place was lit up but empty, pinball machines and Vurtronic screens blinking. "Hurt. Bleeding, I think."

Pelayo reached her, followed by Lagrante. "Where?"

"Nadice."

Pelayo glanced at Lagrante, who shook his head.

"Do something," Marta pleaded.

"Who's Nadice?" Pelayo asked.

"Someone I met. Was trying to help." Marta's legs

trembled and Lagrante helped her sit. The spex clattered to the fog-damp concrete amid puddles of soft neon and flashing LEDs.

Lagrante squatted next to her. "How do you know she's bleeding?"

"Because *I* am!" Marta winced. "We have to help her, now. If we don't, the baby will die." She sounded exasperated and desperate, edging a little too close to hysteria for comfort.

"Your baby?" Pelayo said.

"*Our* baby. That's why I'm having a miscarriage."

She wasn't making any sense. "Is that why you took off without saying anything to Nguyet and Rocío?"

Marta's expression tightened, impatient. "This doesn't have anything to do with them."

"They're worried about you. How do you think they feel? First Concetta leaves, now you."

Marta closed her eyes. She pressed the heels of her hands to her forehead. "I need to find Nadice. Before it's too late." She made an effort to get up, and grimaced. Light scalded her features, leaving her face strained and gaunt.

"Take it easy," Lagrante said.

"I can't take it easy." Marta's breath came in cautious, pain-shortened gasps. "Mateus has Nadice. We have to find her—save her—before he kills her and the baby."

"How do you know she's not already dead?" Lagrante said.

"Because I'd be dead." Marta curled forward, knees tucked to her chest. "If he kills her, he kills me."

"Who's Mateus?" Pelayo said. "A TV?"

Marta shook her head. "The smuggler she was

working for as a mule. She was still carrying the illegal ware she'd brought into the country for him. That's why he took her." Marta cradled her stomach with one arm. "And as soon as he gets what he wants there's no reason to keep her alive."

"Took her where?" Lagrante said.

"I don't know." Marta reached for the spex on the sidewalk next to her and held them up. "One of the TVs gave me this. It might help."

Lagrante took the spex. He popped the databead from the stem, then inserted it into an I/O port on his frames.

"Well?" Pelayo said.

"Code." The creases in Lagrante's forehead deepened. "Some sort of encrypted datalib or program."

"What kind of program?" Pelayo asked.

"Hard to say." Lagrante popped the databead, slipped it into a pocket inside his jacket, and turned to Marta. "You think this Mateus might be the person who nixed the place?"

Marta's nod came across as bleak, defeated. "So he could get to her. Keep her from running."

Pelayo's stomach clenched around a feeling of queasiness. "He happen to be a crunkhead, by any chance?"

Marta moistened dry, chapped lips. "I think so. I didn't get a good look at him. But I'm pretty sure."

Lagrante turned to Pelayo. "You know him?"

"I bumped into him earlier this afternoon, in the parking garage across from the hotel." Pelayo ran a hand through his hair. "And I think I saw him putting Nadice in a sedan."

"When?"

"Ten, maybe fifteen minutes ago." He switched over his earfeed. "Tossa? You there?"

"What's going on?" she said.

"You masked the wrong person."

"What do you mean?"

"I'm with Marta. I think the mask is on a friend of hers. Do you know where it is?"

In response, the eyefeed from the mask d-splayed as a heads-up frayed with thin interference lines that threatened to unravel the image.

Pelayo shut his eyes to watch the feed directly. He was moving down a corridor philmed in creamy white marble. Ceiling lights scrawled across his vision, leaving wavy chromatic streaks. He passed a flat-faced wall pillar with a design etched in circuit-board gold on the polished surface.

"The Fairmont," Atossa said. "In San Jose."

"You sure?" The design was gone, obliterated by a nova-bright burst from one of the overhead LEDs.

"Positive." Her voice was firm, unwavering. "We just got a new contract to run masks and FEMbots there."

Marta groaned. "It's not stopping." She slumped onto her side and clamped her thighs together. "You need to find Nadice. Get her to a doctor."

Lagrante nodded. "First, we need to get you someplace comfortable. Least until help arrives. I've got a call in, but it could be a few minutes. Things are a little jammed right now."

Pelayo looked up West Cliff to the hotel. If anything, the chaos there was worse than before.

He turned his attention back to Atossa. "How soon can you be at your place?" he asked.

Ten minutes later, Atossa let them into her Beach Flats cottage, which had been philmed to resemble a Hollywood bungalow, circa 1940.

"Lay her on the bed," Atossa said. "Don't worry about the sheets. They can be cleaned or recycled."

While Lagrante arranged Marta on the bed, Pelayo joined Atossa in the kitchen, where she was rummaging through a drawer filled with blister packs of Chinese herbs, vitamins, amino acids, and other supplements. The kitchen window looked into a mini hydroponics greenhouse blazing with chemlights. Orchids were visible in the steamy interior.

"Paramedics should be here soon," he said. "If you want, I'll stick around. I can catch up with Lagrante later."

"No. You're set up with the eyefeed. You need to be at the Fairmont to help the police find Nadice."

"You sure?"

"We'll be fine." She took out a tube of antibiotic spray, a half-used blister pack of Flexodeine tabs, a spray bottle of Sponge-Aid absorbent foam, and a tube of antibacterial liquid gloves. "Promise me you'll take care of yourself, okay?"

Pelayo nodded. "You sure you're not going to get in trouble for leaving the mask unattended?"

Atossa slid the drawer shut with her hip. "I'll write it off as accidental damage. Happens all the time."

"You want, I'll try and bring the mask back."

Atossa moved away from the counter. "I'm more worried about you. Now get going, both of you, before it's too late."

53 "That's far enough," a voice said.

Al-Fayoumi halted. Next to him, the girl's fingers tightened around his, moist and afraid.

"Close the door, please," the voice said.

"Who are you?" al-Fayoumi managed. "What do you want?" His indignation and forced bravado sounded counterfeit even to him.

"Police." A palm d-splay shone in the semidarkness, presenting al-Fayoumi with an SFPD badge and a DiNA verification, transmitted via flash-cast.

"Detective." Al-Fayoumi shut the door. The girl shifted position, easing behind him and clutching his pant leg. "What can I do for you?"

A thin smile flamed white above the glow of the d-splay before the curl of fingers snuffed it out. "Funny. I was planning to ask you the same thing."

Al-Fayoumi looked at him blankly for a beat, his mind racing. "Lisette," he said finally. "You're looking for her."

"And these." The detective indicated the terrariums lining the wall immediately to his right.

"Have you found her mother?" al-Fayoumi asked.

The detective frowned in the illumination emitted by the flies. After a moment his stance relaxed. "I think we need to talk," he said. "The three of us."

"Let me get this straight," the detective said, staring across the desk at al-Fayoumi. "The damselfly, nanomal, whatever, asked you to look after the girl."

"Correct."

They sat at the desk in the middle of the room. Lisette studied the terrariums, tapping the glass, then sneaking a peek at the detective. She inched a little farther from the desk.

"Why does it want you to look after her?" van Dijk asked.

"It didn't say."

"But you went along, anyway. Trusted it for some reason."

"I was already having reservations about contract work for Sigilint. It seemed to confirm those reservations. Validate them, so to speak."

"By letting you know Yukawa was an alias for Titov, and that you were actually working for IBT."

Al-Fayoumi sighed. "It made sense at the time." It sounded ridiculous. Now.

"Any idea what it is?" the detective asked. "The damsel."

"Nanomated 'skin." Al-Fayoumi shrugged. "Programmable matter that is being nanotechnologically animated."

"By what?"

"I think..." Al-Fayoumi hesitated, struggling to organize his thoughts. "It may be more than that. An emergent collective conscious—or unconscious—perhaps."

"Whose?"

"Ours." Al-Fayoumi shifted, pinched by self-consciousness. "Those of us with nanotrodes that map the neurochemical patterns in our brains—the patterns we record in order to issue mental commands. I think it might be a natural outgrowth of that, like a harmonic. A note that is born out of other notes. It exists because of them and can't exist without them. The sum total of all uploaded neural activity."

"So when I issue a mental query, command, or whatever, I'm actively helping to create and maintain this damsel?"

"Yes."

"Where does it live?"

"Everyware, so to speak. Data paste. Smart fabric. Smart d-splays. Electronic skin, and any other form of programmable, artificially intelligent matter."

The detective fingered one cheek thoughtfully. "What would happen if I stopped issuing mental commands? If we all stopped? Would it die?"

"In theory."

"Something tells me it doesn't want to."

Al-Fayoumi took a deep breath. "Not only that, I think it wants to be born."

Van Dijk cocked his head. "Come again?"

"It wants to make sure that it lives. The best way to do that is to evolve, to acquire traits and adapt. That's what it's been doing with the flies—trying out various modes of inheritance and expression. That way, when it *is* born, the mechanisms for survival and reproduction will already be in place."

"Tell me more about your contract work," the detective said, changing tack again. He'd already switched gears several times, twisting the threads of the conversation to the point where it was getting almost impossible to keep them straight. "Exactly what sort of experimental 'skin are we dealing with?"

"Quantum-entangled," al-Fayoumi said.

"With what?"

"Quantum electronics. Superposed components that oscillate in phase to create coherent resonance states."

"Could you run that by me in lay terms?"

"Of course. Sorry." He seemed to stumble over himself. "It provides a way for people in a philm cast to connect...to experience sensory input and ware as if they were all one person, or the same person."

"How does it do that?"

"If the programmable matter and the wetronics in the 'skin are entangled, then they are essentially the same 'skin. Each individual 'skin is no longer separate. It is connected to—is part of—a single unified 'skin."

"So even though there might be a million individual 'skins, they're still physically connected by"—the detective consulted his palm d-splay—"EPR effects."

"Right. And any differences between 'skins are just different information states—modalities of existence, you could say—for the 'skin. One large non-collapsed wave function."

"So Yukawa, Titov, wanted you to figure out a way to program all these various shared states."

"To predict their behavior," al-Fayoumi corrected. "Determine how information—philm images in this case—would be inherited and expressed in the new 'skin."

"Which ties back to your research with the flies. The appearance of the idolons."

"Yes." Finally, he seemed to have satisfactorily explained things.

"The future of philm," the detective mused. "Everyone part of the same cast, or something like that."

Al-Fayoumi wasn't sure what to say, the question struck him as rhetorical, so he kept his mouth shut.

"What about side effects?" van Dijk said. "Is there any indication that this new 'skin might be unhealthy?"

Al-Fayoumi frowned. "Unhealthy?"

"You know. Dangerous." The detective waved a hand. "Deadly."

"No." Al-Fayoumi was at a loss again, perplexed... uncertain what, exactly, the detective was implying or getting at. "I mean, I assume the 'skin has been thoroughly tested—properly debugged."

"Why?"

Al-Fayoumi shifted in his chair. "Because if there were no safe clinical trials, the 'skin would never be approved for sale."

"Legal sale," van Dijk said.

Al-Fayoumi blinked rapidly several times. "Are you saying it might be marketed illegally?"

"You tell me."

"I have no idea."

Van Dijk smiled. "Maybe you should check with the black-market rip artist you contacted."

A hot flash prickled through al-Fayoumi, leaving behind damp palms and sticky armpits. "Research only," he heard himself mumble.

"Of course. Was that what the young woman was?"

"What woman?"

"The one I found dead in her apartment last

night. Same apartment building as Lisette. Same floor. Same hall."

Al-Fayoumi stared, unable to speak. His face felt frozen in horror, or rather some parody of horror the detective would surely misinterpret as a lack of sincerity. And yet he had nothing real of his own to offer up in place of this pseudoexpression. This falsity—imprinted on him, unconsciously, from some philmscape he'd seen—was all he had. He had become it—or it had become him.

Instead, the detective stood up and went over to the terrariums. The girl flinched but didn't leave. Together, they watched the clouds of flies.

"I need to know what you saw," the detective said after a while, without looking at the girl. "Last night. I need to know what happened."

Lisette tucked her chin to her chest.

"You saw or heard something, didn't you?"

The girl refused to look at him. She could have walked away but something kept her there.

"No one's going to hurt you," the detective said. He settled into a crouch and tapped the glass. "In fact, if you tell me everything you saw, it'll make it a lot easier for me to protect you because I'll know who to look for. If you don't tell me, I won't know."

The girl's stare seemed to harden into a glare.

"She was like a big sister, wasn't she?" van Dijk said. "Easier to talk to than your mom, because she listened."

The girl dug her chin farther into her chest.

"It's hard to lose someone like that," the detective said. He watched the flies. "Someone you admire. You want to be like them when you grow up, and then suddenly they're gone. It feels like they left and you don't know who you are anymore. You don't know who you should be, or how you should act. It's like you lost a part of yourself and you can't get it back. For a while, you even tell yourself you don't want that part of who you are back. You tell yourself that you're better off without it. You don't need it, or the person, anymore. You never did. The thing is, it's not true. That's the part of yourself that you need to try and get back the most. Because without it, something will always be missing from your life. And the only way you get that part of who you are back is to remember the person who's gone. Once you let them back into yourself, they bring the missing part of you with them. It's kind of like they borrowed it for a while, 'cause they needed some part of you inside of them, the same way you needed them. You feel what I'm saying?"

The girl sniffed. "She told me... She said if I told anybody about the warewolf, he'd come back. If I didn't say anything, there wouldn't be any reason for him to come back and hurt her or me."

"Who?"

"Apphia."

The detective turned to Lisette. "That was good advice. It got you this far. But it won't get you any farther, 'cause there's no place else to go. That's why the damselfly brought you here."

"I heard them arguing," she said.

"Apphia and someone else?"

The girl nodded but continued to stare at the flies. "The warewolf. They were in her apartment talking loud. So loud it woke me up."

"Fighting, you mean."

"Uh-huh."

"What were they arguing about?"

"Apphia said she was going to go to the police."

"Did she say why?"

"I'm not sure." The girl wrinkled her nose, creasing the nanoFX paint. "I think the warewolf was trying to get her to do something, and Apphia said no. She didn't care about the results."

"The man didn't like that?"

"No. He got mad. He said he was going to tell her father where she was living, and what she was doing."

"Can you tell me what she was doing? Did she say?"

"She told me she was a model. She said people paid her to screen new philm. I wanted to do that, too. But she said I couldn't, I wasn't old enough yet. Besides, it was dangerous, even for her."

"Had the warewolf been there before, or was this the first time?"

"The second time. The first time was a few weeks ago. That was when Apphia said not to tell anyone about him."

"Okay. What happened next?"

"The warewolf left."

"Is that when you went to see her?"

The girl mashed her mouth, crumpling the green dragon scales around her green lips. "No, I was afraid he would come back. I didn't want him to see me. So I waited."

"How long?"

The girl didn't respond. Al-Fayoumi moved to her side. It was time to put a stop to this. She had pulled into herself, or more likely away from van Dijk. Tears formed in her eyes.

"Just a couple more questions," the detective said, his voice gentle. "That's all, I promise."

Al-Fayoumi glared at him, but Lisette wiped her nose and nodded.

"This warewolf. Did you see him?"

Lisette straightened under al-Fayoumi's hand and shook her head. "I just heard him. I didn't look."

"That's all right." The detective paused. "Do you know if anyone else saw him?"

Another shake of the head.

"Is that it?" al-Fayoumi demanded. Enough was enough.

The detective sighed and unfolded from his crouch.

"Uri," the girl whispered.

Van Dijk dropped back into his crouch, elbows propped on his knees and hands loose.

"That's what Apphia called him," Lisette said. "It got him all pissed 'cause she knew who he really was and no one else was supposed to know he was there."

The detective glanced quickly at al-Fayoumi, then back to the girl. "You're positive?"

Lisette's nod was firm, her jaw set. "She said it was spelled just like urine, but without the N-E on the end."

The detective smiled. Al-Fayoumi blinked, at a loss. "I don't get it."

Lisette rolled her eyes. "Because he's such a dick-head."

54

Nadice floated in a bathtub filled with surgical gel and stared up at an Art Deco pattern of microchips on the ceiling. The back of her head pressed painfully on the ledge where the marble tub met the granite wall. A sponge pad, wedged between her shoulder blades and the edge of the tub, kept her from sliding fully into the surgel. Cool air tickled her newly shaved scalp. It wasn't nearly as comfortable as the first time she'd been 'skinned as a new employee at Atherton. The glass-enclosed tank there had been part of a spa, complete with a whirlpool, sauna, and pool. Tropical green ferns had pressed against the steam-fogged enclosure.

A coughing fit seized her. She snapped forward, expelling a wad of phlegm-thick gel. More gel poured from her nose like mucus. Her body seemed to be rising up out of the tub—levitating.

She could feel her arms and legs, an improvement, but she still couldn't move them. With every breath, her lungs ached. They felt bruised, raw as peeled fruit.

A second bout of coughing gripped her. When the fit subsided, her frame of reference flipped. It wasn't her body floating up, but the surgel lowering, sucked down by the drain in a thick, lazy spiral. It receded from her naked flesh, leaving a bright patina of new 'skin.

Blood oozed from an open puncture on the back of her right hand, where a drip IV had been inserted and removed. A puddle of sludge remained in the bottom of the tub, cloudy with hair, dead cells, and the last of the Atherton 'skin that had been scraped from her with viral scalpels.

The new 'skin wasn't as waxy as the old. She'd gotten used to the old 'skin's stiffness. This one was different, supple. And illegal. It incorporated whatever she had smuggled for Mateus.

"How much longer?" a voice asked from the room outside the bathroom. Mateus. He sounded jittery.

"Not long." This voice belonged to the man who had examined her in Dockton.

"Gonna take a while to clean this up," Mateus persisted. "Knowmsayin?"

"What I know is the sooner you shut up and let me do my job, the sooner we'll get out of here."

Nadice imagined Mateus prowling the room in nervous circles, bouncing from one spot to another like spit on a hot plate.

With effort, she twisted her head to the side. Her neck was stiff. The muscles trembled. They only stopped shaking when she allowed her head to rest against the edge of the tub.

Nadice swallowed. Something wasn't right with her. Whatever he had dug out of her had ripped up roots, done permanent damage. She'd known it was a risk, just not how much of one. Nadice squeezed her eyes, batting damp lashes.

The mask was gone. It came to her suddenly: she

could no longer feel it plastered to her face. Wary of triggering a renewed bout of muscle spasms, Nadice shifted her eyes, searching for the mask. Her gaze orbited the room. Finally, she spotted it hanging on a brass towel hook next to the vanity. It resembled a partly detached bas-relief, with sightless caryatid eyes.

Petrified, she thought. Like her.

The door to the bathroom stood open a crack. Through it she could see a glass-and-chrome coffee table that had been moved away from a U-shaped sofa unit. A large caddy of blinking biomed equipment took up one end of the table.

A shadow darkened the carpet. The tech from Dockton appeared, holding a sample tray filled with a grid of square wafers. The wafers were smeared with different-colored swatches of cloth or gel. It was hard to be sure; they looked a little like both.

He was growing 'skin, Nadice realized, analyzing it. She'd heard of biochips that mimicked the properties of human flesh. Doctors and scientists used them to check smart fabric and drugs.

"Almost ready," he announced. He placed the tray on the coffee table, apparently satisfied with what he saw. A sudden image of his teeth leaped to mind, smiling sharply at her.

" 'Bout time," Mateus said. He joined the man at the coffee table and watched as he checked the readouts on the biomed equipment.

"The quantronics are almost in phase," the man said. "As soon as the oscillations are coherent, we can start philming."

"I hope you picked out something fine for her."

His voice carried a faintly wistful note. "Be nice to send her out in style."

Send her out where? Nadice had the feeling it should be obvious. But she wasn't thinking clearly.

"What fucking difference does it make? Who gives a rat's ass what she looks like at this point?"

"Still. A fine-ass bitch like that. Be a shame to waste her."

The man scowled. "What you do with her is your business. As soon as I'm done here, she's your responsibility."

"I'm just sayin'."

"Just make sure you do your job."

"I feel ya. No worries."

"Okay," the man said. "That's it. We've got full resonance." He straightened and his teeth flashed in the hygienic glare of the white LEDs.

Her body tingled and her scalp itched. She felt a pore-deep change in the 'skin. It was shifting, morphing in response to the commands he was tapping in on a palm d-splay. A splash of red tinted one of her hands.

Adrenaline jolted her gaze back to the rest of her body. A smear of red spread across her stomach, breasts, and thighs. She watched her nipples vanish, followed by her belly button and pubis.

Not blood, she realized. Scarlet silk. The nano-weave threads assembled to form a low-cut, ankle-length evening gown. Elegant red gloves slithered up her forearms, halting just below her elbows. Threads wove into hair on her scalp, thick copper-tinted curls that lengthened into a luxurious tangle of ringlets.

"Ain't that it!" Mateus said from the doorway. He let out a low whistle and joined her. "Got you all g'd up."

Her heart drummed, the tempo in her chest hard and fast.

Mateus sat on the side of the tub. He touched the side of her face and ran a finger down her cheek, tracing the curve of her jaw and neck to the vein throbbing in her throat.

He cupped her chin and turned her face toward him. "You scared or excited?" he asked.

She tried to spit on his hand, but her tongue lolled helplessly. The best she could manage was a guttural grunt.

"Maybe a little of both," he said. His hand dropped to her right breast, cradling it in his palm while his thumb circled her nipple through the sheer fabric. "You an' me is gonna knock down later on. Cut sumthin' up, fasho! Payback for all the trouble you've caused me."

She shut her eyes, trying to shut him out. A moment later, she felt his dry lips on her mouth. Then his tongue, prying her apart and entering her.

"A little taste," he said. "Something to whet your appetite." She felt him get up and heard the departing thump of his Timbo boots over the heavily starched rustle of his jeans and black canvas jacket.

As the smell of his cologne settled on her tongue, she felt a warm spurt between her legs.

Pee. She'd wet herself.

Embarrassed, angry at the fear and the shame he'd provoked, Nadice opened her eyes.

Instead of urine, a tiny spot of blood darkened the surgel near her crotch. Like a single red tear, it trickled toward the drain.

Panic knifed through her. *The baby!*

55 Pelayo sprinted down the arabesque-tiled stairs leading from the magtube platform to the street. The Fairmont was two blocks away. He could see the topmost floors of the grandiose hotel. Sculpted by architectural lights, it rose above the surrounding milieu of office buildings, stores, and restaurants philmed in industrial wrought iron, Mediterranean white, and pink Spanish stucco.

"You got a room number yet?" he asked Lagrante.

The rip artist shook his head. "No one registered under Titov or Yukawa. What about you?"

Pelayo dodged around a loose knot of people tumbling out of a wine-tasting café. "Nothing yet."

The eyefeed from the ad mask had cut out again. Even when the d-splay was up, he'd been unable to get a clear view of the room. Grainy snippets of a bathroom vanity, bathtub enclosure, and a partially open door that looked out on a narrow entryway to the room. There was a full-length mirror on the wall across from the door, and in it he could make out the reflections of a bed, a coffee table, and a couple of indistinct figures, one of which might or might not be Mateus.

So far, there was no indication Nadice was alive or even in the room. The mask hadn't moved.

"What do you want to do when—"

Pelayo screamed, doubled over by nausea and a sickening, excruciating pain in his abdomen. He sprawled headlong onto the sidewalk and rolled onto his side, clutching his stomach. The scream seemed to come from outside of himself. It clawed at his vocal cords. Something, somewhere inside of him, was on the verge of rupturing.

He lay on his side panting, his legs folded up, his knees squeezed tightly together. He tasted blood.

"What the hell?" Lagrante bent over him, his black spex pushed up on his brow, his eyes bloodshot with concern. "You all right?"

Pelayo writhed onto his back. "I don't—" He coughed at the desiccated tickle in his throat. "I'm not sure."

Lagrante rested a hand on his shoulder. "What happened?"

Gingerly, Pelayo pushed himself to a sitting position. "Muscle—"

Another spasm gripped him. He curled forward and huddled around himself, his hands clenched over his kneecaps. The concrete was warm; it smelled of spilled coffee, cigarette butts, and dead leaves.

Lagrante looked around. "I'll call for—"

"Go." Pelayo sipped air, slow shallow breaths. "I'll catch up with you soon as I can."

"You sure?"

Pelayo waved him on. "Cramp. That's all."

Lagrante nodded, lowered his spex into place. "Holler at me if things get crucial."

"I just need to rest for a couple of minutes."

Pelayo winced as another contraction shuddered through him.

———————

Pelayo eased himself in the space between two square planters, out of the way of the dwindling foot traffic and ad masks. Leafy bamboo stalks leaned out over the concrete sides of the planters, which were philmed as an Egyptian frieze. Pharaohs, hiero-glyphs, and ankhs in raised and sunken relief. The frieze had been painted once. Pelayo leaned his head back, resting it on chipped flakes of paint. He shut his eyes against the pain.

Almost immediately, the eyefeed from the ad mask d-splayed on the inside of his lids. Colorless emulsion, stripped of RGB. Faint audio trickled over his earfeed, single channel and scratchy.

A slight movement in the mirror snagged his at-tention. "...probably Tiago," one of the figures crackled.

"About...time," a scratchy voice answered. No way to identify either one.

"...get it..." the first voice said.

A raster-edged figure occluded the reflection in the mirror, casting a fuzzy shadow across the carpet and wall. The figure stepped forward, then back, its face brightening momentarily as the door to the room swung inward and light from the hallway washed across the entry. A third figure entered the room, stepped past the door, and turned to close it. Metal flared on the door, then ran like molten gold across his retinas, elegantly crafted cursives that hardened as they cooled in memory.

Eyes clenched tight, watching the script fade from red to green to violet, Pelayo called Lagrante. "1028," he said. "That's the room number."

"Word?" The rip artist's voice echoed, cold and stony, off polished marble walls. Behind it, lounge music bubbled up from a piano. Laughter drifted into the evening, airy and meaningless.

"Be careful," Pelayo said. "Somebody else just showed up. I didn't get a good look."

"Sounds like they're getting ready to bump shit."

"Go hard," Pelayo said. "Or don't go at all."

Lagrante grunted. "Count on it."

———————

A light tickle on his left cheek teased his eyes open.

A blue dragonfly hovered centimeters from his left cheek. Not a real dragonfly. The insect had pectoral and tail fins. Flames roared back from its mouth and the wings, which beat lazily, and sported concentric red and blue RAF roundels.

"Whatever you're selling," Pelayo said, "I'm not interested." He swatted at the dragonfly. It dodged easily, into the bamboo, only to circle back and land on his cheek. When he brushed at it again, the adware had fastened itself to his 'skin.

"Nadice is running out of time." The voice over his earfeed sounded saxophone smooth. "So is Marta."

"Who are you?"

"You don't have long. If you want to help them, you have to do it now."

Pelayo clamped his eyes shut. No sign of Lagrante yet in the room. "I'll never make it."

"Yes, you will." The dragonfly seemed to sink into his 'skin, then through it.

It emerged deep inside of him, body flattened and wings folded back into a yellow dorsal fin with a single black roundel that disappeared as it plunged downward, into cold turbulent black.

56 When the call came, shortly after ten, Giles Atherton was screening a classic Billy Graham revival.

The broadcast was one of Atherton's favorites. He'd lost track of how many times he'd watched the sermon. Five or six times a year, probably, for twenty years. Graham's fervor, the heated certainty of his conviction, never failed to ignite in Atherton a feeling of renewed hope and determination.

Things could change—they *would* change.

He ached to be struck down, to be touched by the hand of God, his hair singed and his clothes turned to soot. Only then would he be cleansed, blackened on the outside, but purified within.

With a quick mental command, Atherton paused the broadcast to take the call from Ilse Svatba.

"I apologize for the hour," she said. "I wouldn't have awakened you unless it was absolutely necessary."

"Bad news?" It was the only reason she could be calling at this time. Not from her office at IBT, he noted, but from what appeared to be a study.

"I'm afraid so." She pursed her lips delicately, as if this would soften the impact of what she had to say. He was reminded of a closed flower, squeezed tight against the chill of night.

Atherton arched one brow. Ilse had philmed herself in a periwinkle evening gown, low-cut, sleeveless,
with white elbow-length gloves. A pearl necklace man-
acled her neck. Matching earrings accented the half-
shell curve of her ears.

"It appears that our security datician has detected
an unauthorized modification to the test 'skin."

"What kind of modification?"

She swallowed, rearranging the gloom that darkened her collarbones. "A plug-in of unknown function and manufacture."

In other words, black-market. "You're certain?"

"Quite."

Atherton sharpened his gaze, whetting it on her
chagrin. "When?"

"I was just notified."

Atherton delicately cleared his throat. "What I
meant was, how long ago did the incursion take
place?"

She took a moment to smooth the elegant wrinkles from her gloves. She seemed sleep-addled, as if
she had only just been awakened with the news.
"Our sageware indicates that it was compromised
fairly recently. Earlier today, possibly within the last
few hours."

"Have you located the leak?" he asked. "The
source of the plug-in?"

"No. We're currently trying to contact the skintech in charge of this phase of the clinical trial."

"Without success, I gather."

"None yet. He's not responding to our calls. I've
ordered security to send someone directly to his
home address."

"Do you think he's responsible?"

"I don't know." She shook her head. "I doubt it. More likely it's the test subject he contracted to beta the general-availability version."

"There was only one subject?" Atherton's stomach soured. Uri had implied there were several.

Why?

Because Uri had ripped his own copy of the 'skin, and if the rip came to light too soon, Atherton would know who was responsible unless Uri could point to someone else.

"We decided a single test subject would be easier to monitor the 'skin," Ilse said. "Prevent the situation we have now."

Atherton took a measured breath. "I don't suppose you've been able to locate the subject either."

"Not yet." She brushed at an imperceptible speck of lint on her chest. "But we will. It's only a matter of time."

"Unfortunately," Atherton said, "the damage has been done. And I don't see any way to undo it."

Ilse made no response. Her lips crimped tighter, increasingly parsimonious and unattractive.

"I was afraid something like this would happen," Atherton went on. He found it oddly satisfying to watch her squirm.

"We took every precaution," she said.

"Apparently it wasn't enough." He allowed a scathing note of disappointment to creep in.

"We're doing everything we can."

Atherton steepled his fingers. "Perhaps I can be of assistance," he suggested.

Her gaze narrowed. "What do you have in mind?"

"Send me the DiNA code for the 'skin the test

subject is waring, and I might be able to help you find him."

"I'm afraid that information is proprietary."

"Of course." Atherton rested his chin on the tips of his thumbs. "But if you're looking for blood, two hounds are better than one."

57

Pelayo surfaced—came up and out of himself, into another self.

Cold water slid up his spine. He could feel it circulating in his veins. The resulting shiver spread myelin-fast. He gasped, felt his breath ice over, and coughed. Tried to sit up. But a leaden numbness held his arms and legs in place.

Dead—

—weight.

Light pried at his eyes—the blade of a knife slicing through a thin-skinned yellow fruit.

Curves, sharp edges, and rounded concavities pressed against his 'skin. The topology hard and unyielding. A sauna tub with nozzles. Floral petals, vines, and leaves etched the pink granite.

An invisible fingertip carved a line on his cheek, following bone, to hook the slack corner of his mouth.

Nadice's mouth. He was waring her 'skin.

The realization reached below the surface, touched some shared autonomic reflex that quivered low in her abdomen.

—*No,* the fish whispered over his earfeed. *You are not waring her 'skin. You* are *her 'skin. She is waring you.*

He heard the voice through the part of him that was still seated against the planter. His mind ghosted here, a hologram fragment of his thoughts there, suddenly aware of the Hamilton Nadice wore, invisible except for the weight of it on his own wrist.

In response, the philm d-splay for the test 'skin opened. Several new items were available on the options menu. In addition to the familiar grayed-out choices for his ware, there were selections for evening gown [red/black], gloves [short/long], scarf [silk/lamé], eye shadow, rouge, lipstick [tea rose/carnation pink], and hair [long/short, straight/curled, platinum/strawberry/brunette].

A supplementary d-splay provided décor choices for the room. Wall material and pattern, floor-tile design, carpet texture and color, tin ceiling panels in lieu of copper, and window embossing/etching. The options for marble walls, silk drapes, pink granite vanity/bathtub, and cotton bedsheets were selected. The entire room was programmable.

Hooked by the finger, his head lolled to one side. A face leaned in to inspect him, grinning a wide expanse of domino-square teeth.

The crunkhead he'd bumped into. Mateus.

He held a knife in his free hand. It was a small Damascus Folder, with a polished titanium frame and a scrimshawed handle.

"We're all alone now, gurl. Time to cut sumthin' up."

Behind Mateus, hanging on a brass hook next to the vanity, a caryatid mask stared past them toward the bathroom door, its line of sight too high. On the mask's d-splay he couldn't see himself looking up at it, only see a daguerreotype reflection of Mateus in the mirror outside the door.

Mateus closed and pocketed the folding knife.

Then he slipped both hands under Nadice's arms and hauled Pelayo out of the tub.

The evening gown fell from his chest, exposing one breast. Mateus had loosened the straps; they dangled at his side, languid and desultory. Surgical gel trickled down his thighs, semen-thick, and dripped on the floor tiles. With a grunt, Mateus hoisted him up and carried Nadice from the bathroom.

Head cradled in the muscular hollow below one shoulder, Pelayo watched the ad mask's unblinking gaze follow Nadice out of the bathroom. Watched her on the d-splay, being carried into the main room.

Mateus dumped Nadice on the bed. Arms akimbo, Pelayo stared up at a pressed-copper ceiling panel, etched and embossed to resemble an antiquated twentieth-century microchip. His muscles trembled, prelude to some uncontrollable palsy that he would be helpless to prevent.

Mateus fished the folding knife out of his jeans pocket, thumbed open the skinny blade, then slit the front of the gown open to the crotch.

Threads tore inside Pelayo, sliced 'skin severing synthapse connections. But the pain was real. It belonged to him as well as her.

"Ain't that it!" Mateus licked his tattoo-bruised lips, then tossed the knife on the sheets and began to unfasten his black leather belt and lower his pants.

Pelayo reached for the knife, feeling the bare, hard concrete of the sidewalk under his fingers instead of silk bedding. He moved his hand past the specter of a spent Hongtasan on the coffee-stained sheets, wrinkled, gritty with mica and the pungent aroma of French lavender.

"What the fuck!" The bed shifted. Mateus bent forward, hobbled by his partially loosened pants, to smack Pelayo's hand aside. "I had about enuff a your shit, gurl."

Mateus gripped the gown. Bunching the nano-threads tightly, he yanked the dress from her body and flung it aside.

Pelayo screamed as the 'skin separated from the subcutaneous tissue.

He landed in a crumpled heap on the floor at the end of the bed, a pile of discarded, disembodied nanofiber.

Pain boiled up, searing and blood-wet.

He began to thrash.

58

"You hungry?" Atossa asked. "There's yogurt in the fridge. Maybe some cheese. Juice, if you're thirsty."

"Thanks." Marta pinched out a smile. "But I don't think I can keep anything down right now."

Atossa nodded. "Sorry the place is such a mess."

A Vurtonic d-splay hung on the wall across from the futon. The Vurtronic was an old portable fold-up, the corners dog-eared, the creases worn thin in places. Marta had seen hundreds like it for sale at flea markets on the Flats and scavenger shops deep in the Trenches. Clothes hung on hangers from a steel curtain rod that had been mounted to the low ceiling. A bureau with half-open drawers was piled high with socks, panties, T-shirts, jeans, and rumpled sweaters. Shoes, a half dozen or so pairs, occupied three antique milk crates that had been stacked on their sides so the open tops faced out.

"Maybe you could help me to the bathroom?"

"Sure."

Her pee was tinted red, a bad sign. She couldn't tell if the bleeding had stopped. It might only have slowed.

"If the parameds don't show up soon," Atossa

said from the doorway, "I'm taking you to the hospital."

"Thanks." Marta flushed. She just sat there, too weak to move. The baby was still alive.

"You should stay down," Atossa said. "Rest."

Marta nodded. Atossa helped her back to the futon. Heaviness flooded her limbs. She folded both hands on her abdomen, closed her eyes, and breathed in the sweet aroma of freesia from a joss stick on the bamboo end table next to the bed.

How long since she'd slept? She couldn't remember. Couldn't resist the warm caress dragging her beneath the surface.

59

Pelayo blinked. Opened disembodied eyes.

A wave of dislocation hit him, cutting him off from all physical sensation. Then the world congealed, solidified around him, and his perspective steadied.

From where he lay, a crumpled pile of 'skin on the floor at the end of the bed, he could see Nadice, naked on the bed. Mateus straddled her, and Pelayo felt the crunkhead force her legs apart as he wrestled her into position.

They were still connected. Even though the top layer of her 'skin had been ripped from the underlying substrate of synthapse grafts wired to her flesh, it was still receiving and sending information.

On the ad mask d-splay he could see himself reflected in the mirror, a red evening gown spread like blood across the floor.

—*Get up*, the fish told him.

Pelayo could feel it swimming around inside his head, relaying sensory input. He seemed to be accessing the world through the fish's sensorium. His ghost sight was a composite image assembled from visible-spectrum nanocams and simage arrays wired into the room's programmable matter.

—*Now,* the fish exhorted.

—*Can't*, Pelayo thought. The palsied tremors

paralyzed his muscles, robbing them of volition. His limbs twitched but remained flaccid.

—*Rephilm yourself.*

He thought about the gold Hamilton watch on his wrist. The jagged-toothed crown with its precise, effortless...

Click.

The selection menu for Nadice's and his 'skin appeared, the option for red evening gown highlighted. Pelayo tapped a mental finger on the suit option labeled WINDSOR D.B. The gown evaporated, rephilmed as a worsted double-breasted suit. The jacket was torn at the lapels, the pants ripped along both inseams.

Heat lightning crackled inside of him. His back arched. The flash spread outward, burning along the filaments of her nerves, photon bright.

At the same time a bright flash, titanium-hard, sliced across his vision and through the menu.

The Damascus folding knife, cold and bright.

—*Move!* the fish urged. *Now!*

Pelayo's right hand shifted. Wraithlike, fuzzy. It existed more in his mind than in reality.

But on the bed, Nadice's hand moved to one side. Pelayo raised his left knee, and kicked out. Nadice's foot caught Mateus in the groin. Groping blindly, Pelayo clawed for Mateus's eyes.

The blade descended.

60

Uri swore to himself in a deserted men's room off the main lobby. None of the private philm options he'd coded for his copy of the 'skin would come up on the selection menu. They refused to d-splay.

He stared at his pallid reflection in the mirror and the useless menu etched on the glass.

The 'skin had been cracked—tweaked maybe, with new ware or code. No other explanation.

Uri slammed clenched fists onto the vanity. His luggage, and all of the med-assay equipment from IBT, lay in a pile on the floor. He couldn't leave now—not without Nadice—and couldn't stay now that the room had been broken down and cleaned. Bottom line, he couldn't do shit until he had a safe place to take Nadice and time to examine her, figure out what had happened.

Dockton. The only available option.

He placed an urgent call to Mateus, got no response. Ditto the other crunkhead, Tiago, who was working disposal.

Al-Fayoumi, he thought. Asshole had to be involved. He was the only person with enough information and technical expertise to work a crack.

Uri retreated to a toilet stall with his bags, locked

the door. Before he could place the call to Rafa, a message light flashed over his eyefeed.

Atherton. Great, just what he needed. By now, the man probably knew that he'd ripped his own copy of the 'skin. He'd want to "discuss the matter."

Christ. What a mess.

Fuck it. Uri ignored the message and contacted Rafa, who appeared in a simage d-splay, still philmed in full Texasecure regalia.

"What's going on?" Uri said. "Anything?"

"Dude brought some kid home a little while ago. Since then, the place has been quiet."

"Get in there," Uri said. "Now."

"What you want me to do?"

"Whatever it takes to get him to talk. When he's ready, holler at me. I want to question him in person."

"I gotcha!" Rafa grinned.

As soon as the crunkhead dropped off-line, Uri logged into his virtual chat room. From there, he started querying all of the 'skinheads and cinephiles that parleyed in the deli. If al-Fayoumi had ripped the 'skin, was now cutting philm, someone would know. Bootleggers would have sniffed him out, drawn to new source code like sharks to fresh blood.

61

Marta gritted her teeth. She was bleeding again.

"I'm going to call for a cab," Atossa said.

Marta nodded, afraid that if she opened her mouth to speak, the blood would gush out unhindered.

Shut everything in, she told herself. Don't let anything out.

"Breathe," Atossa said.

She put on a pair of scratched spex, then sat on the bed beside Marta and pulled the sheets from her stomach, baring her thighs.

Marta shook her head on the pillow.

"I need to see what's going on," Atossa said. "I need to be able to send an image to the triage nurse."

Marta forced slow, steady breaths through her nose. She leaned her head back and dug stiff fingers into the soft mattress.

"That's it," Atossa said. "Hang on. Just a little longer."

It wasn't going to happen. She couldn't stop the blood from overflowing. The pressure was too great. The bubble that had been building inside her burst and the liquid spilled out, like a tipped bowl.

Atossa swore. "I think your water just broke." She stood up.

"Nadice—" Marta coughed, sucked saliva from dry cheeks. "She needs medical attention, too."

"I just heard from Lagrante. He's already called for help, got people on the way."

Instead of relief, dread flickered in Marta. Like the glow from a newly lighted candle it reached into every corner of her mind, exposing old fears and cobweb-thick doubts.

"Take it easy," Atossa said, "everything's going to be okay." She moved away from the bed and picked up a tube of liquid gloves.

Marta's gaze trailed after her. "What're you doing?" Her mouth was parched, the words gummy.

Atossa squeezed white cream from the tube and smeared it onto her hands. A few seconds later, the cream solidified into sterile, antibacterial latex. "Just in case," she said.

62

The blade pierced Nadice's left cheek, sliding between her teeth and coming out the opposite side. Pelayo bit down, trapping the blade and the dull taste of steel in his mouth.

Blood thrummed in his ears, urgent, pounding.

Mateus swore and yanked the knife free, raising it. Pelayo rolled, bucking against the tangle of arms and legs pinning Nadice to the bed. The thudding ended, and a bright rectangle of light leaned into the room. The knife flashed, and then darkened, doused by shadow.

"Police!"

Through the eyefeed from the mask, Pelayo watched Lagrante sprint past the mirror, the saffron jacket of his zoot suit billowing out behind him.

Above Pelayo, Mateus twisted away from Nadice, slid off the back of the bed, and snatched up the evening gown in one smooth motion, turning toward Lagrante.

The rip artist raised his right palm, face out, as if to slow the crunkhead. "You're under arrest."

Mateus nodded. "I gotcha."

He flung the evening gown at Lagrante and charged. The dress unfurled, wrapped over around Lagrante's upraised hand and draped around his head. Lagrante ducked, momentarily blinded, but Mateus's bull rush caught him full in the stomach. Lagrante fell back, hat sailing, and went down. A scimitar gash opened on the right side of his face, curving from ear to jaw.

The two men rolled onto the floor. The knife carved a slim, tight arc under the LEDs. This time the blade impaled Lagrante just below the shoulder blades, where it stuck, pinning the yellow jacket in place.

A crimson circle appeared around Mateus's neck; not blood but the evening gown, knotted tight. Mateus let go of the knife to claw at the ribbon with both hands. The crunkhead's fingers pried frantically at the nanomechanical fibers. But Lagrante cinched the noose tighter.

Pelayo stared down at Mateus, at the cyanosis-blue complexion and the fat tip of the tongue barely protruding from between swollen lips.

—*He's dead,* the fish said. *Nadice is dying. So is the baby.*

Lagrante lay on his side, sweating, breathing heavily. Blood smeared his face and stained the back of the zoot suit.

Blood stained the sheets around Nadice, too. Too much blood to have come from just the stab wound to her face.

"Lagrante?" Pelayo said.

The rip artist stirred.

"You okay?"

"Think so." The rip artist coughed.

"Nadice is in bad shape," Pelayo said. "She needs help."

Lagrante pushed himself up, propping a shoulder

against the bed. "Parameds are already on the way."
His voice wobbled. He reached for the sodden
sheets, tried to pull himself to his knees, and sank
back down.

—*Nadice doesn't have much time,* the fish said. *You
need to come with me, now.*

"Where?"

Inside of him the fish rose up from virtual depths,
swimming for the surface of his 'skin. As it ascended
it rephilmed itself in the integrated-circuit design on
the wall next to the bed.

—*This way.*

Pelayo mentally d-splayed the menu for his 'skin,
with the updated list of choices for room décor. He
thought-selected the wallpaper/microchip option,
and part of him merged with the wall.

He entered into it, became one with it, and in the
process was able to step through it...

...into an online room, simage-cast over his eyefeed.

Pelayo looked around the holographic d-splay.
"What is this place?"

A crib occupied one corner of the room. A
carousel of brightly colored plastic animals spun
lazily over the crib. A bundle of IV drip tubes dangled from a chrome stand, watched by a nurse in a
chair. The tubes were capillary-thin, more like fiber-
optic wires that dripped light instead of fluid.
Mounted high in one corner, a television on a swivel
arm stared down at the nurse. The screen was a blizzard of static.

Through a virtual door to the room he could see a

hall with other doors leading to other rooms. Other nurseries. Cries echoed down the hallway, fussy, hungry, tired, and colicky.

The simage construct appeared to be a hodge-podge compilation of images spliced together to form a single room. Each wall was different: rusty foam-backed sheet metal; powder-blue cinder block philmed with unicorn and faery cinFX; gray stucco tagged with Basquiat-style graffiti; and the microchip wallpaper he'd philmed himself in to instantiate here. Overhead a ceiling of tinted glass buzzed with honeybee appliqués. Varnished tongue and groove made up the floor.

"Tesseract," he said, thinking of Dali's *Crucifixion,* which he had seen in church once, the cross an un-folded hypercube. "Six rooms in one." All joined by programmable matter.

—*Hyperstantial,* the fish said. It detached from the mobile and drifted above the crib, green plastic weaving between the tubes.

Somewhere in the world, each simulated wall connected to an actual wall like the hotel room.

—*If you had the access code to philm yourself as one of the five other walls, you would be able to cast a sim-age of yourself from here to there.*

The same way he'd come from the Fairmont; the same way he'd presumably get back. "That how you get around? Wall to wall?"

—*Don't think of them as different walls,* the fish said. *They are all the same wall oscillating at different frequencies.*

Like a person screening different philms. Under-neath, they didn't change. They were still the same person, no matter how much they wanted to be someone else, anyone but who they were.

The nurse was asleep. Or unconscious. Pelayo walked over to her. A tiny puckered baby lay in the crib. A preemie, small enough to fit in the palm of his hand, but perfectly formed. Oxygen tubes snaked out of its nostrils, and a feeding tube trailed from its mouth. Several of the tubes had pulled loose. Air hissed from one tube. Food paste dribbled from another. Fluid from the bags hanging on the rack stained the mattress, dripped onto the nurse, and puddled on the floorboards.

Pelayo stepped up to the nurse and touched her on the arm. "Hello?" He prodded her gently.

—*She can't hear you*, the fish said.

"Why not? Wat's wrong with her?"

—*Her 'skin has been damaged. She is no longer fully connected to the child and is unable to provide life support.*

"Who is she?"

—*The mother of the child.*

The fish settled into the crib, behind smooth-varnished dowels. Pelayo watched it come to rest a few centimeters above a bunched flannel coverlet.

"I don't understand," he said. "Why'd you bring me here? What am I supposed to do?"

—*You need to reinsert the tubes.*

"Is that going to help Nadice?"

—*They connect the baby to her and to . . . others. If you stabilize the baby, you will stop the bleeding in her.*

Pelayo leaned over the crib. The fish slipped into the baby's hand. The newborn was a girl. Tiny fingers curled reflexively, holding the fish tight. "What others?"

—The other birth mothers.

"Mothers? As in more than one?"

—I had to be sure the child survived. The best way to ensure survival is through numbers.

"So you impregnated a bunch of women. Didn't ask for permission, or bother to tell them."

—If I hadn't, the baby would be dead. One mother has already been killed, along with the fetus. I couldn't take the chance that her death would spread to other mothers.

"Spread how?"

—Through quantronics in the electronic 'skin she was waring—similar to the 'skin you are testing—that were passed on to the baby.

"Wait a minute, let me get this straight. You're saying that the test 'skin she was waring killed her?"

—A virus, applied to the source circuit, was used to attack her autonomic nervous system. I've taken steps to protect as many of the remaining babies as I can, initiated the spread of an applet that will enable me to backdoor the ware. So far the installation is limited to a handful of Transcendental Vibrationists. But as soon as the applet is copied and distributed, the danger should pass.

"You infected the TVs?"

—Through a network of deprogrammers who already have a contact inside of the cult. I posed as a member of the network—fabricated a message that mobilized certain members for an emergency intervention. Arranged for the application to be administered and delivered.

Marta, he thought. She had been set up. Jhon selling her to the TVs had all been part of the plan, carefully orchestrated.

The fish seemed to sigh, soft wind rattling through the dusty window in the sheet-metal wall.

—*We're running out of time,* the rattle said. *Listen.*

"To what?" But he didn't need an answer. Less noise echoed in the hall—fewer cries from the other rooms.

What choice did he have?

Pelayo rubbed his face. The air tube, he decided. Start with that. He pinched the oxygen tube with shaky fingers. The baby stirred. Her head shifted to one side and she stopped breathing. Carefully, Pelayo tucked a finger under the baby's head, tilted her face up, and reinserted the tube into the nostril. The feeding tube was next. He slipped it in, threading it between dehydrated lips.

Still no response. It wasn't working. The baby wasn't responding. He picked up the IV tube that was dripping blood onto the aged tongue and groove. Plink, plink, plink.

A shadow spread inward from the doorway, darkening the floor. No sound came from the hall. Suddenly, all of the rooms grew quiet, as if they had been silenced by the shadow now lengthening to occlude the crib.

Hair prickling, Pelayo looked up.

Uri grinned at him. "I had a feeling I'd find you here," the skintech said.

63

"Zhenyu al-Fayoumi?" the security guard said. He stood outside the door, dressed in a clean, smartly pressed uniform with knife-sharp creases and a Texasecure watermark on his forehead.

The philm looked legitimate. It didn't appear to be a cheap bootleg copy. Perhaps the building manager had finally gotten a guard to watch the premises at night.

"Is there a problem?" al-Fayoumi asked, distracted by the online conversation behind him between van Dijk and somebody named Buhay from the San Jose police.

"Uri Titov," van Dijk said in a low voice. "I'd like you to pick him up. Bring him in for questioning."

The guard in front of al-Fayoumi grinned. "IBT thinks there is."

Al-Fayoumi frowned. "I don't have anything to do with IBT."

"Parent company of Sigilint."

"What's this about?" al-Fayoumi demanded. His voice sounded too high and thin, too close to a whine to be intimidating. "Who are you? What are you doing here?"

"I got a man wants to talk to you."

"Who?"

"I'm not at liberty to say."

Al-Fayoumi held his ground as the guard stepped toward him. "About what?"

The guard peered over his shoulder, taking in the terrariums and Lisette. The girl retreated down the hallway to the bedroom.

Al-Fayoumi raised his voice, hoping to attract van Dijk's attention. "Get out of here, now. Before I call the police."

"I don't think so," the guard said. "From what I can see, you don't want any laws sniffing around."

He shoved al-Fayoumi back and pushed past him, into the narrow entryway to the apartment.

Al-Fayoumi stumbled and lost his balance. He landed squarely on his back. The impact knocked the wind out of him. The guard shut and locked the door, then stood over him.

"Let's do this easy," the man said. "Don't make me get off in your shit. Ya feel me?"

"That's not going to happen," van Dijk said, appearing out of the gloom. Behind him, at the far end of the hall, Lisette's Ghost Dragon mask glowed demonically.

The guard turned to him. "This ain't none of your bidness. I was you, I'd get my azz outta here while I could."

Van Dijk smiled. "You don't know shit about my business." And d-splayed his SFPD badge.

The guard moistened his lips. "Fine. That's how you wanna play it, no problem." He stepped away from al-Fayoumi, backing toward the door.

Al-Fayoumi scrambled to his feet.

The detective motioned for him to *stay down* and

reached for the sidearm holstered under his one arm.

Sudden movement behind al-Fayoumi snagged his attention. His gaze jerked from the detective to a thick-barreled handgun the security guard had pulled.

Instead of a single large bore, al-Fayoumi noted dozens of pinprick holes in the dull anodized gleam. The muzzle looked more like the head of a big salt-shaker than anything else.

Someone screamed. Lisette. The glow of her face lurched toward him from down the hall.

Al-Fayoumi lunged to stop her. The air around his head shattered, splintering into hundreds of invisible needles.

64

"What are you doing here?" Pelayo asked. He straightened, still holding the IV drip in his right hand.

Uri smiled, the familiar saw-blade sim-age of his teeth more ragged in the online construct. "Hunting."

"For what?"

"Malware. Viral plug-in that's infecting the new 'skin." He took a Kahr PM9 hand-gun from the pocket of his white lab coat. He aimed the little 9mm at Pelayo. It had a black polymer grip, satin finish, and a stainless-steel slide. Pelayo noted that the safety was off. "Off the shelf antivirus," Uri said, hefting the weapon. "Best I could do on short notice. But I've modified the bullet, so to speak, adapted it with patch ware of my own."

"Have I been infected?" Pelayo said.

Uri shrugged. "If the bullet kills you, you're in-fected. If it doesn't, you're clean. Simple as that."

In the hotel room the ad mask had moved, was moving, from the bathroom into the main room at what felt like an agonizingly slow pace. Its reflection in the wall mirror grew steadily larger. Atossa must be moving it for the parameds. Trying to get a closer view of Nadice and Lagrante.

"You wanted the 'skin ripped all along," Pelayo said. He didn't move when Uri's hand twitched at the sound of his voice. "I was just doing what you expected."

Uri shrugged off the comment as inconsequential. He raised the 9mm a fraction of a centimeter and pulled the trigger.

Over his earfeed, Pelayo heard the simulated hiss of a bullet pass millimeters from his head. Behind him, the television shattered. He turned. Fracture lines radiated from a neat hole in the center of the glass screen. The static flickered, then cut out.

Pelayo looked back at Uri. Had a subsystem somewhere actually been targeted by the ware, or was the skintech simply making his point? "So how do the TVs fit into all this?" he said.

The Kahr lowered. The small dark hole in the muzzle centered on Pelayo's forehead. "The TVs are the source of the pluglet." Uri's face soured with irritation. "The way it's being spread."

"Through pregnant women?"

"Through the goddamn babies. Once a baby is infected in utero, it gets passed on to another baby."

"How?"

"Quantronics. The babies are growing the same quantum-based processors that are in the test 'skin."

"The mule you had working for you," Pelayo said. "Nadice." The mask had drifted closer to the bed. He could see Nadice now. She lay on the bedspread, faint as a shadow. Lagrante sat on the floor next to the bed, his back propped against the side. "When she got pregnant, the baby picked up the ware you were growing inside her."

Uri sniffed. "Probably."

Neither Lagrante or Nadice had moved; they were

in the same exact position he'd left them in. What was taking so long?

Uri gestured with the Kahr. "Now move away from the crib."

Pelayo listened for cries from the hallway. There were none. "You're murdering them, aren't you? The babies."

"Babies." Uri scoffed, as if he found the idea amusing. "These things aren't even human. Never will be, even if they make it to term."

"What are they, then?"

Uri's smile curled into a sneer. "Piecework. Some kind of nanoanimated matter that's using the fetuses as a host—a way to reproduce. I'm doing everyone a favor."

"In other words," Pelayo said, "it's replicating using the test 'skin. Whatever it is, you helped give birth to it."

The Kahr trembled. "And now I'm going to put an end to it, before things get any further out of hand."

Pelayo cut a glance at the unconscious nurse. "What about the mothers?" he asked. "What's going to happen to them?"

"Nothing, if they're clean. Otherwise—"

"What's going on here?" a voice said. "Uri? What are you doing? Who are these people?"

Pelayo's focus slid past Uri. A man stood in the hallway, peering tentatively into the room. He'd simaged himself in a black ministerial suit, white shirt, and silver tie. Thin gray hair flowed back from a high forehead, clouds trailing off an unyielding bluff.

The man looked directly at Pelayo, then consulted a palm d-splay. "You're the test subject," he said. "The two of you are working together on this. Stealing the 'skin, trying to take control of it behind my back."

"I'm not the one holding the gun," Pelayo said.

The man frowned at the Kahr and Uri. "You are responsible for the miscarriages?" His gaze flitted, bird-quick, to the crib.

Uri's shoulders rose a fraction. "I'm doing what needs to be done."

"Killing people? Unborn babies?"

Uri backed to one side. The muzzle of the 9mm teetered between the old man and Pelayo.

"This isn't what we discussed," the man said, ignoring the handgun. "We had an agreement."

The tiny black spot at the end of the barrel swung toward the man. "Not anymore."

The man trembled. Not out of fear, but rage. He seemed oblivious to the weapon. His eyes blazed. "This is contemptible. I refuse to be party to this. I cannot condone the slaughter of innocent children."

Uri reddened. "They aren't children."

"Enough! This is wrong." The man drew himself up. "As of now, I am officially terminating your association with Atherton enterprises. This cannot, will not, be allowed to continue."

Next to Pelayo, the baby coughed to life. The hand holding the fish lifted, waving the toy.

Uri's face hardened. He jerked the Kahr in the direction of the crib.

"No!" Pelayo reached out *and felt something invade him. The trigger against his finger. Part of him squeezing*

it and another part resisting, trying to keep from squeez-
ing; teetering in a moment of equipoise . . .

Pelayo pictured the décor menu for the 'skin, and mentally selected the option for pressed ceiling panel/tin.

Uri froze, the Kahr extended, as if gripped by a statue. Pelayo couldn't move, his fingers imprisoned in a veneer of embossed, finely textured metal. Somewhere, back in realspace, he hoped that Uri was similarly immobilized.

Atherton walked up to Uri. "I know where you are." The old man smiled. "I've notified the police and hotel security." He turned toward Pelayo. "It won't be long," he said, and exited the room, vanishing down the hallway.

Pelayo watched the baby play with the fish. On the ad-mask d-splay, he could see Nadice's face on the mattress staring up at him, her half-open eyes just centimeters away. Then the mask flipped and he saw the embossed ceiling panel she was looking up at, like the engraved lid of a coffin.

A yellow plastic bee detached from the mobile over the crib and approached him. It entered his mouth, and from there his thoughts . . . and finally, his dreams.

65

"I'm not going to make it," Marta said. She stared up at the ceiling, tracing a hairline crack in the plaster to take her mind off the contractions.

"Yes, you will," Atossa insisted. She sat on the side of the bed and held Marta's hand with firm fingers. "Help should be here soon."

A contraction gripped Marta. She squeezed her eyes against the pain, clenched her teeth. Perspiration tickled her neck.

"Not soon enough," she gasped as the pain relented, only to be replaced by a more forceful, more adamant tightening.

"Bad?" Atossa said.

Marta nodded. She spat out a strand of hair caught in the corner of her mouth and concentrated on breathing through the pain—taking rapid sips of air.

Atossa stood. She checked the washcloths in near-boiling water, then picked up a box of Sponge-Aid and set it next to the sterilized sheets she had spread between Marta's legs. She sprayed antibiotic on Marta's bare thighs, then her own hands.

"Son of a bitch." Marta gripped the wood sides of the bed frame. A muscle in her calf cramped.

"Here it comes," Atossa said. "I can see the head! My God! I can't believe how tiny it is!"

Marta woke to faint strobing outside the window. The curtain and the walls pulsed red. How long had she been out? A few minutes, no more. Otherwise, she would already be on her way to the hospital.

"Is it alive?" she asked. Afraid to look. Afraid not to. If she didn't look—if she didn't force the baby to be dead or alive—it would be neither and both. If she looked at the baby, it would have to be one or the other. And Nadice would have to be one or the other.

"See for yourself," Atossa said.

Taking a deep breath, Marta rolled her head sideways on the pillow.

Atossa sat beside her on the chair. She had bundled the infant in purple-flowered aromatherapy leggings, microwave-warmed and UV-sterilized.

Alive. Under the glossy protective coating of unphilmed 'skin, Marta could see a tiny blue vein throbbing in puckered, red-mottled flesh.

"We need to get her into a neonatal unit," Atossa said. "I don't know how long the 'skin will keep her alive."

A flash of green peeked from a fold in the legging. "What's that?" Marta asked. The tiny hand clutched something.

"It's a toy fish," Atossa said.

"From where?"

"She was holding it when she was born." Atossa shook her head. "I know. It's crazy, but—there it is."

It was from Nadice, Marta thought. Some part of her that the baby was bringing into the world, making her real.

She couldn't feel Nadice anymore. The Nadice she knew was gone, changed in a way Marta didn't yet understand.

Might never understand. Nadice didn't feel dead, yet she didn't feel alive either. Marta exhaled, forcing the tightness from her lungs, and waited. The ambulance drew closer, the strobing brighter.

66

Uri made it halfway to the door before hotel security showed up to detain him.

They found him on his hands and knees, crawling across the glazed ceramic floor tile. Walking upright was out of the question. The layer of tin he'd been sheathed in was thin, but stiff. He'd fallen when he stood up from the toilet. Since then, he'd been unable to raise himself any higher than his knees. His balance had never been all that great to begin with.

Metal fatigue. That had been his hope. Flex enough joints enough times and the tin would break and he'd be walking around like a knight in plate armor.

"Where do you think you're going?" one of the guards said. He prodded Uri with the rubber toe of his boot.

The second guard crouched in front of him. "Word is, you like to hurt women and children."

With effort, Uri straightened at the waist. Slowly, a few millimeters at a time, he opened his mouth to speak. Perspiration poured off of him, soaking his clothing and hair. His breath came in a series of slow, tortured gasps.

"No bark," the first guard said.

"No bite, either." The second guard whistled. "Check out those teeth. The shark man cometh."

The first guard stood. "What are we supposed to do with him? Wait until the cops show up, or take him into custody?"

"Custody, I think."

The first guard grinned, his cheeks round and chubby as a cherub's. "I have an idea."

"What's that?"

"Give me a hand." The first guard walked up to Uri and reached down, gripping his right arm.

Together the guards turned him around until he was facing in the opposite direction. They hauled him over to one of the open toilet stalls. The only thing he could see was the open toilet crouched between the green-and-white-speckled walls of the one-meter-by-two-meter stall.

"What you got to look forward to the rest of your life," the first guard said, sending him headfirst into the stall.

67

Giles Atherton offered Kasuo van Dijk his hand the way he would an olive branch. He smiled like a man who had something to hide. "Detective. Please come in."

The hotel entrepreneur escorted van Dijk into an office with several floor-to-ceiling Vurtronic d-splays mounted on mahogany paneling. All of the screens were blank, except one.

"My wife," Atherton said. "Lisbeth."

The woman had simaged herself on a plush high-backed chair upholstered in chez Art Brico silk-screen. She wore a dour gray dress, buttoned tight at the throat, and unflattering black shoes. For the occasion, she had philmed her face in severe Tamara de Lempicka planes and angles that rendered her cold and aloof.

Van Dijk offered a polite tip of the head. "Mrs. Atherton."

"Lisbeth," she implored. "Please. I don't see the need for formality. Do you, Giles?"

"Have a seat, Detective." Atherton indicated a burgundy leather chair in front of the vast desk. "Can I get you anything?"

"Thank you," van Dijk said, "but I won't be here long." He had no intention of letting either of them get too comfortable.

"You indicated that you might have some news about our daughter," Mrs. Atherton said.

Van Dijk nodded. "I'm afraid so."

"Where is she?" Atherton said.

"San Francisco."

Mrs. Atherton leaned forward. "Is she all right?"

"She's obviously in some kind of trouble," Atherton said. He turned from his wife to van Dijk. "Is she in custody?"

Van Dijk pursed his lips. "Two nights ago a young woman was found dead in her apartment."

Mrs. Atherton straightened with a sharp breath. "What makes you think that this woman is our daughter?"

"A witness identified her by name."

"That's all you have?" Atherton said. "A name?"

"At this point, yes. That's why I'm here."

"So it could be anybody," Atherton's wife said.

"Not anybody," van Dijk said. "The young woman was seen with Uri Titov." He turned to Atherton. "I believe you've met."

"No," Atherton said.

"That's not what Mr. Titov says."

Atherton paled, his face as ashen as his hair.

"Giles?" Mrs. Atherton worried the white, lace-fringed collar of her dress. "Who is Mr. Titov? What's going on?"

"A mistake," Atherton said, disconcerted.

"I don't think so," van Dijk said.

Lisbeth Atherton fixed him with a brittle glare. "What exactly do you want from us?"

"A soft DNA sample. To confirm her identity."

"So it might not be our Apphia," she said.

Atherton roused himself out of his agitation. "Was this young woman 'skinned?"

Van Dijk nodded. "Recently."

Atherton paced. "Then why can't you ID her using the DiNA code in the 'skin?"

"Unfortunately, the 'skin isn't registered."

Mrs. Atherton softened with relief. "Then that settles it. Apphia's 'skin is legal. Definitely registered. So it couldn't be her."

"The 'skin was experimental," van Dijk said. "A prerelease version in the initial stages of a clinical trial. For some reason, it wasn't registered with any of the required databases."

"The woman was a test subject?" Atherton said. "With who?"

"IBT."

Mrs. Atherton stood, hands knotted around the ends of her sleeves. "That's not possible. Apphia would never put herself at risk like that. It's absurd."

"There's a simple way to prove it," van Dijk said.

"How did the young woman die?" Atherton asked.

"Preliminary autopsy results indicate acute neuroleptic shock, leading to sudden respiratory and cardiac arrest."

"What does that mean, acute neuroleptic shock?" Mrs. Atherton's gaze darted between them. "Giles?"

"All of her autononomic functions shut down," van Dijk said. "Heart, lungs, and brain—they all stopped."

Atherton took a moment to massage his temples. "What led to—what caused her to go into shock?"

"There appears to have been a problem with the 'skin."

"Has IBT been notified?"

"This morning. That was the first they'd heard of it."

Atherton peered at him from between the palms of his hands. "Why weren't they notified earlier?"

"Titov wanted to keep it under wraps."

"He tried to cover it up?" Mrs. Atherton said.

"Along with the person or persons he was working for," van Dijk said.

Mrs. Atherton looked confused. "You just said that IBT hadn't been informed. If no one else at IBT knew about it..."

Van Dijk waited for her to connect the dots.

"He was working for someone outside of IBT," she said.

Beside him Atherton sagged, propped up only by the hidebound shell of his 'skin.

"If you would like me to get a warrant for the soft DNA," van Dijk said to him, "I will be happy to do so."

"No," Atherton said. "That won't be necessary."

"Giles?" Mrs. Atherton sat, her hands looking lost in her lap. "Is there something I should know?"

Van Dijk took a clear plastine bag from inside his jacket and laid it on Atherton's desk. "I'm sorry," he said.

Atherton picked up the bag. He held it up to the light to look at the Roman glass necklace and earrings inside.

Behind him, Mrs. Atherton burst into tears.

"Shall we go?" van Dijk asked.

Atherton nodded. He replaced the plastine evidence bag on the desk. "I think—" He cleared his throat. On the d-splay screen, his wife covered her face with her cupped hands. After a moment, Atherton looked away. "I think that would be best," he agreed. "For everyone."

68 Nadice had two faces. There was the mask. And then there was the face that her grandmother had stroked while she sang Nadice to sleep.

"Just smoothing away the wrinkles of the day," the old woman had once explained, as if the day had left a mark on her that could be removed, no different from a blouse or a pair of pants creased with wear.

No, that wasn't right. It was really just one face, like one of those drawings that contained two images. Depending on how you looked at it, sometimes one face emerged, sometimes another one. But both faces were there in the same place at the same time.

Like foreground and background. One couldn't exist without the other. Take one away and the other vanished.

That's what she was now. *Who* she was. Take away the mask, and the rest of her would go away as well.

She lay on the bed, the sheets rumpled and her hair a disheveled mess. In places her 'skin was stained red, but she couldn't tell if it was blood or remnants of fabric.

Mateus lay unmoving on the floor, the gown coiled like a python around his neck. She barely recognized him. He had changed, too, dephilmed, and pale as UV-bleached bone. Only his eyes gave him away. Even sightless they felt toxic.

Just past the edge of the mattress, she could see the balding head of another man, tipped sideways and slightly forward. One of his feet was visible on the carpet, the onyx-black leather of the shoe almost but not quite polished enough to show his face.

Nadice looked away. She lifted her hands to the mask, exploring the contour, and something wriggled inside her, akin to a shadow rippling across the sandy bottom of a streambed. The shadow flowed over her and through her. Like blood, it filled her, kept her alive. Without the shadow—and the mask that gave it shape—she would never be whole.

A room took shape around her, replacing the hotel room. The room had a wood-plank floor and foam-insulated sheet-metal walls, the foam backing yellowed by age and heat. Cloud-bitten light, spattered with bird shit, misted down from sheets of corrugated plastine.

A slender thread of fear tightened inside her, drawing her taut. "What's going on?" she said.

—*Do you remember me?* the shadow said.

It was the fish that had appeared to her in Dockton, swimming through the sultry Delta air. "Yes," she said.

—*Do you want to join me? Us?*

"Where?"

The shadow rippled, then slid across the streambed into muddy coolness.

—*This construct. Or another one.*

"Who else is here?"

A chorus of shadows plucked at her. They schooled around her, inside of her for a moment, then departed.

Unborn children, she thought, casting shadows onto the world.

A shut door appeared across the room from her, a mirror image of the door to the hotel room.

Nadice glanced back at the door that led back to the hotel room, to Mateus, to the grave of her grandmother, and Marta.

"Go on," she imagined her grandmother saying. " 'When one door closes, another opens.' "

Nadice hesitated.

"It's okay," Marta whispered within her mind, or maybe only her imagination. "I understand." And let her go, releasing her with a smile.

"Thank you," Nadice said. She pulled the door shut. Across the room, the sister door opened onto a covered porch joined by a wide walkway to other porches and other homes.

Each door gave rise to the other, Nadice thought. Without one, the other would never exist.

Without looking back, Nadice stepped through the doorway.

69 Zhenyu al-Fayoumi paced outside of the courtroom, waiting for the custody hearing to conclude.

He'd tried in vain to hear the proceedings through the closed door. He had even considered opening it a crack and peeking inside. In the end, he paced, read part of a newzine segment he downloaded from a d-splay in one corner—a story about Uri Titov, who had been charged with murder in the death of Apphia Atherton—and watched the other people around him whose lives hung in the balance.

Would he get foster custody? He could think of no reason, and a million reasons, why he shouldn't. He'd been interviewed and cleared by Social Services, DNA-printed, and retina-scanned. He'd even changed apartments, moving to a nicer, more expensive building that didn't accept flies as pets.

In the end, though, it came down to Lisette. Did she want him, or not? She hadn't said she didn't want him. But she hadn't said she did, either.

Maybe she just wanted to put the past behind her, and he was a painful reminder she could do without. Or maybe she was waiting to see if her mother would come back. After a month, the woman still hadn't been heard from. But she could turn up. That was the rub. Social Services wanted to keep open the option of reunification.

Still, for all intents and purposes, Lisette had been abandoned. There was no sense keeping her in a group home any longer. It was time to move her into a more permanent living arrangement. If not with him, then with someone else.

What would he do if the judge denied custody to him? Go back to his flies? And what then?

He had a grant, from the Neonoetik Institute, to study inheritance mechanisms in programmable matter.

Al-Fayoumi checked the time. Half an hour since Lisette, her lawyer, the social worker, and the social worker's lawyer had gone in to talk to the judge. What could be taking so long? Was longer better, or worse?

Worse, he decided. The longer things dragged on, the more questions the judge would be asking, the more reservations she would have.

Had he become too attached to Lisette? Did he need her more than she needed him? If so, why? What did he want from her?

Al-Fayoumi wasn't sure. Did he want Lisette to change him because he couldn't change himself? Seen in that light, his situation seemed less tenable—patently selfish. It might be better—for her—to be with someone else. After all, he had almost gotten her killed. Because of him she had *seen* a person killed. Those weren't the kinds of childhood memories that formed the basis for a happy life.

Al-Fayoumi was sitting on a wooden bench along the wall, staring at the nothing between his feet, when the courtroom door opened and Lisette came out, flanked by the social worker and the two lawyers.

No one looked pleased. Lisette stared at the ground. Was she unhappy, afraid to meet his gaze, or merely preoccupied?

Al-Fayoumi couldn't tell. He stood up. All he could see of Lisette was the top of her head.

"Congratulations." The social worker finally smiled. "You've been awarded full custody as a foster to adopt."

"But?" Al-Fayoumi waited for the other shoe to drop.

Lisette looked up, the corners of her mouth crimped. "The judge said even if my mom comes back and goes to jail, I have to visit her if she wants."

Al-Fayoumi nodded. So reunification with her mother was still on the table.

"For now," the social worker said. "I would have preferred a clean break, but the judge wants to keep things open in case the mother returns with a reasonable explanation. I don't think that's going to happen, but it could."

"Even if I don't want it to," Lisette said.

Al-Fayoumi let out a breath. "Is that it, then?"

The social worker nodded. "I'll be in touch—to keep you up to speed on what's going on."

And to check on them, no doubt, see how things were going.

"Come on," Lisette said. "Let's go."

"Where?"

"I don't know. Someplace new, where we've never been."

Lisette took his hand, tentatively at first, then more firmly, getting a grip on their new reality.

70

Each year Marta took Isobol to the Delta for summer vacation. There they spent three months in a tin-roofed shack, shaded by 150-year-old oak trees and tattered eucalyptus with peeling bark that curled like flames at sunset and set the evening sky on fire.

"Will I get to go fishing with Uncle Pelayo?" Isobol asked on the magrail trip to Bethel Island.

"Maybe," Marta said, carefully noncommittal. She gripped her daughter by one hand and guided her down the rickety gangplank that led from the pontoon walkway to the tall grass and soft mud of the island.

"Please?" Isobol pursed her lips and looked at her with black eyes.

"Let's see what Uncle Pelayo and Aunt Atossa say. If they think you're ready this year."

Isobol pouted. "That's what you always say." She toyed with the green plastic fish attached to a chain around her neck.

Every year, for the past five years, the fish grew slightly larger, as if paralleling the girl's growth spurts.

They passed the raised walkway to the TV enclave along one shore. Still hanging on, she noted, after all this time. The wooden slats were in poor repair, rotted and broken. A few cells survived here and there, but for the most part the church had disbanded in the wake of the miscarriages. Some people just couldn't let go.

What would Jeremy have thought? Would he be pleased with the outcome? She couldn't help wondering. Had he accomplished what he wanted with his life? His death?

What about Concetta?

"Are we going to go to see Nadice?" Isobol said.

Marta squinted against the early-afternoon glare. "Yes." She cupped a hand over her darkened spex.

Isobol folded her arms across her chest. The pout deepened. "Do we have to?"

Marta reached for the thrust-out lower lip. She nearly pinched it between a thumb and forefinger before the pout succumbed to a giggle.

"But it's a boring old poster," Isobol complained. "And the FEMbot doesn't even move."

"It might be different this year," Marta said. "You never know." Overhead, high, thin cirrus clouds shredded the sky.

"How come we always go there?" Isobol's tone crept toward a whine. "How come we never go anyplace new?"

"It's important." Marta turned down the grass-walled path that went to Pelayo's raised shotgun shack.

"Why?"

"It just is. One of these days, you'll understand." Ahead, Marta could see the dirty glint of the solar-paneled roof, the piezoelectric siding, and other found tech he scavenged for resale at flea markets around Dockton.

Despite the slow encroachment of philm—new Monet foliage here, Tiki-bar siding there—Marta liked the Delta. Dockton. The way the air shimmered, and the tall wetland grass undulated to the circadian rhythm of tides and the noonday heat. There was a quiescent movement to the place, an unhurried pulse she found it easy to sink into or that sank into her. She wasn't sure. Not that it mattered. It was one of the reasons she came. But not the only reason. Not the one that brought her back...that kept her bringing Isobol back.

"There you are," Pelayo said. " 'Bout time." He sat on the porch behind the house, under an umbrella, listening to the unhurried slap of waves against pontoons, the chafing of wood, and the whisper of a hot breeze too weary to lift itself above a sigh.

He had relaxed here. Something inside of him had let go, like old elastic losing a little tension, going slack but not entirely limp. Comfortable.

Maybe it was living with Atossa. It couldn't be Nguyet or her father. The reason Marta hadn't been able to settle here. Yet.

Marta kept waiting for the same sense of comfort to embrace her. One of these days, she told herself.

Eventually, she would forgive him. Pelayo had finally come clean to Marta about Concetta. How her sister had come to him late one night, asking to be 'skinned, because she was working for a cast intervention network called DART—Deprogram and Reprogram Together—and needed to go underground. As proof, there was the databead Jeremy had

given her, listing her sister and the contact frequency for the shortwave.

In retrospect part of her had always known. It was
the only thing that made any sense. And all it proved
was that Concetta had been right, that evening.
Her sister had stopped being real when she got
philmed. She became someone else—unrecognizable,
unknowable—a grizzled philmhead who could look
her in the eye, that morning behind the Get Reel, and
treat her like a total stranger.

Where was her sister now? Pelayo had stopped
wondering. He had given up all hope of ever seeing
her again, admitted the truth that Concetta was
dead, if not literally, then figuratively, and let
her go.

Maybe that was where peace came from, accept-
ing the inevitable, something she wasn't yet ready
to do.

Isobol ran ahead of Marta, sprinting up the steps
to the porch. Pelayo picked her up, twirled her
around.

Marta mounted the stairs. The zesty aroma of
jambalaya wafted from the thin-walled house. She
glanced through the utility curtain covering the
doorway. Atossa stood at the stove, fixing lunch.
Nguyet sat at a table, preparing a divination. Rocío
sat next to her, dozing in his black exosuit.

Nguyet motioned Isobol to the table. "Time to do
a reading," she cackled. "To determine how much
fun you're going to have with us."

While Nguyet performed the water divination,
Marta walked over to Atossa and gave her a hug.

"She looks good," Atossa said, peering over Marta's

shoulder at the table. "Tall. Have you told her anything?"

Marta stepped back. "Not yet."

"Maybe this year."

Marta shrugged. "We'll see. She's still pretty young."

Atossa put a hand on her arm. "It's not just her I'm thinking about."

Pelayo came up next to them. "Here's something I saved for you. Thought you might like to see."

A newzine d-splay opened over her eyefeed. The time stamp on the inset was two hours old.

After a four-year legal battle, Giles Atherton, the CEO of Atherton Resort Hotels, had been convicted of corporate fraud in a case brought against him by Iosepa Biognost Tek. According to Ilse Svatba, a senior vice president of marketing for IBT, "Giles Atherton had contracted with IBT for an original equipment manufacture he intended in advance to sell/distribute illegally via black-market download." The appeals judge in the case ruled that Atherton had violated the terms of the agreement, which had granted IBT exclusive marketing rights to the ware in compensation for up-front research and development costs. Actual and punitive damages had not yet been determined. Atherton was still facing criminal charges stemming from the illegal import of foreign technology.

"Is that supposed to make me feel better?" Marta said when the story ended, and the d-splay vanished.

"Is that possible?"

Marta sighed. Maybe it *was* time to finally let go— to open up some of the locked rooms and clean them out once and for all. Maybe without all that baggage from her old life, she could float to the surface of a new one and start over.

"It's time," Nguyet announced. She stood. "Nadice is waiting."

The FEMbot was stored in a shed at the end of an overgrown footpath. The shed had thin sheet-metal walls and a corrugated plastine roof that dripped watery light onto antique beer cans, old fishing poles, mud-choked bicycles, and other paraphernalia Pelayo had dredged from the muck.

"It doesn't seem as far this year," Isobol said. She swatted at a big, iridescent fly, philmed with pterodactyl wings.

"That's what happens, the older you get," Atossa said. "Everything keeps getting closer."

"Especially the past," Nguyet said.

Isobol puckered her brow at this, then wrote it off as one more silly pronouncement from her grandmother.

As they came around the last turn in the path, the fish slipped from the chain and, spreading its dorsal fin into origami wings, darted ahead with a flick of a vellum-pale tail.

"Hey!" Isobol clutched at the empty chain.

"See." Nguyet chortled, pleased one of her predictions had come true. "I told you something extra special was going to happen this visit."

Pelayo looked at Marta. "Has it done that before?"

Marta shook her head. Isobol turned to look up at them. Her eyes brimmed with surprise and fear.

"It's all right," Marta said. Her voice thin and

tight in her throat. "They do that when you get to be a certain age."

Isobol peered down the path, through the narrow space in the grass where the fish had disappeared. "What if it doesn't come back?"

"It will," Atossa said. "Sometimes they go away for a while, but they always come back."

The fish was waiting for them in the shed, next to the FEMbot and the old plywood sign it sat against. Pelayo claimed to have scavenged the sign from the Boardwalk, on one of his trips to the coast. Marta suspected he'd found it in the Trenches and hauled it back to the Delta. The faded peeling paint showed a smiling young woman in a blue dress. She had short black curls, black Mary Janes, and a generous red smile.

Isobol squealed. Pointed at the faded ad mask the FEMbot wore. "Her eyes are changing!"

It was true. They were going from blue to brown, turning a darker shade of honey. So was the FEMbot's dull, cloudy 'skin, dead for so many years.

Fabric materialized on the limbs and torso of the doll, a few threads at first. But in no time, it looked as if a dress had been fitted over the dry, splintered wood. Tufts of hair stirred to life under the tepid breeze that sifted through cracks in the foam-insulated sheet metal.

Isobol reached for Marta's hand. "I'm afraid, Mom."

Me, too, Marta thought. "Don't be." She squeezed the little hand clasping hers. "There's nothing to be afraid of. I promise."

"See," Nguyet said. "She's smiling at you. Nothing but good thoughts. Nothing but love for you."

And it did look as if the mask were smiling, nano-mated lips creaking to life.

Isobol's grip tightened in Marta's as an option d-splay, with a selection for Beach Boardwalk, opened over each of their eyefeeds. "Who is she?"

Nadice turned to the small voice. Marta forced her fingers to relax . . . her breath to slow. Blood hammered in her ears.

Pelayo squatted next to Isobol. "You didn't know? The fish never told you?"

Isobol shook her head. "Is that why you never took me fishing before? Because I already had one?"

"The most important thing about fishing," Pelayo said, "is patience."

Nadice shifted her attention from Isobol to Marta. "She's beautiful," the doll said over her earfeed. "Your baby."

Marta cleared her throat. *Our baby,* she thought. Easier to think the words than to speak them out loud.

Dry fingers touched the mask. "Does she know about me?"

Marta nodded. "I told her we used to be . . . friends. That you had to go away for a while, where you could live, and that someday you would come back and visit us."

Isobol pointed at the plywood sign, with its merry-go-round and roller coaster. "Is that where you live?" she asked.

Nadice turned toward Isobol. "Would you like me to take you there? Just for a while?"

Isobol bit her lower lip. She glanced up at Marta, seeking approval. "Can we?"

"If you want." Marta smiled as reassuringly as she could through her uncertainty. "It's up to you."

"It will only be for a while," Nadice said. "Then we'll come back and have some dinner. How does that sound?"

"Okay."

Nadice reached out a hand. Isobol hesitated, then stepped forward. Marta willed her fingers open.

What was it Pelayo had said? There are two kinds of cages. One others try to put you in, and the one you put yourself in.

Hold on too tight, she told herself, and all you'll create is a cage that she wants to escape.

The damselfish swam toward Isobol, wiggled into one hand. "I'll go with you," it said. "Show you the way home."

Seated beside the carnival scene, Isobol looked up to Marta. "Aren't you going to come with us?" she said.

"Not this time," Marta said. "We'll wait for you."

"How come?"

"We have to get dinner ready," Pelayo said.

"Have fun." Marta swallowed a sniff. "I love you." She touched a finger to her lips.

"I love you, too," Nadice and Isobol said.

A moment later two images appeared on the plywood, a young woman and a girl, accompanied by a flying fish, growing smaller as they walked away, one with the scene ghosted on the sign. Next to them, the girl's face went slack and her eyes dimmed as her thoughts drained out of her, into the mural and the simage that lay beyond.

Pelayo put at arm around Marta. "She'll be back," he said.

Marta resisted the hug, unable to relax into it. "I hope so."

"You came back," he said simply, matter-of-factly. And it hit her, the difference between her and Concetta.

The kiss cooled on her fingertip. Marta felt a part of herself evaporate with it into the tear-salty air. Not a release from the world, but a return to it.

SPECIAL THANKS

To Marina, again and always, with much love. Juliet Ulman—whose skillful navigation kept me from straying too far off course—Josh Pasternak, and everyone else at Bantam Spectra. Matt Bialer, for keeping things rolling. Tristan Davenport, Jim Gettins, Sandi Gettins, Bryn Kanar, Alexander Lamb, Christie Maurer, and Ed Weingold, whose honesty kept me honest. Tom Rogers, for unflagging moral support and suggestions. Navi Singh and Ashu Tewari, for technical advice. Lorraine Cahn, for social advice.

ABOUT THE AUTHOR

Mark Budz is the author of *Crache* and *Clade*. The latter won a Norton Award and was a finalist for the Philip K. Dick Memorial Award. He lives with his wife in the Santa Cruz Mountains of northern California.